SECOND
VISION

To Gladys Zitter with
appreciation for your warmth
and hospitality.

1996

RALPH VALLONE, JR.

SECOND VISION

A DUTTON BOOK

DUTTON
Published by the Penguin Group
Penguin Books USA Inc., 375 Hudson Street, New York, New York 10014, U.S.A.
Penguin Books Ltd, 27 Wrights Lane, London W8 5TZ, England
Penguin Books Australia Ltd, Ringwood, Victoria, Australia
Penguin Books Canada Ltd, 10 Alcorn Avenue, Toronto, Ontario, Canada M4V 3B2
Penguin Books (N.Z.) Ltd, 182–190 Wairau Road, Auckland 10, New Zealand

Penguin Books Ltd, Registered Offices:
Harmondsworth, Middlesex, England

First published by Dutton, an imprint of Dutton Signet,
a division of Penguin Books USA Inc.
Distributed in Canada by McClelland & Stewart Inc.

First Printing, August, 1994
1 3 5 7 9 10 8 6 4 2

 REGISTERED TRADEMARK—MARCA REGISTRADA

LIBRARY OF CONGRESS CATALOGING-IN-PUBLICATION DATA
Vallone, Ralph.
Second vision / Ralph Vallone, Jr.
p.   cm.
ISBN 0-525-93765-X
1. Eccentrics and eccentricities—United States—Fiction.
2. Millionaires—United States—Fiction.   3. Supernatural—Fiction.
4. Revenge—Fiction.   I. Title.
PS3572. A4132S4   1994
813'.54—dc20   93-45948
                                                         CIP

Printed in the United States of America
Set in Janson and Spire

Designed by Steven N. Stathakis

PUBLISHER'S NOTE: This is a work of fiction. Names, characters, places, and incidents either are the products of the author's imagination or are used fictitiously, and any resemblance to actual persons, living or dead, events, or locales is entirely coincidental.

To my mother and father

SECOND
VISION

ONE

Sayeth he who is in the tomb:

Graciously grant,

Oh weigher of righteousness,

the balance to establish it.

—inscription above the
head of Anubis,
Papyrus of Ani, from
the *Book of the Dead*

THIS MORNING I THOUGHT I AWOKE. AS THE FAMILIAR LONGING FOR movement crept into my limbs and the desire to open my eyelids took hold, a sense of helplessness invaded me. Panic. I experienced a sudden feeling of utter blindness. Grief. Like being in a wall-less, floorless room. I tried to cry. With ever present fear and apprehension, I thought, One can usually muster some level of activity in the morning. Even after a dozen martinis the night before. But try though I might, there was nothing to be done. Nothing to be moved. Not a finger, not a toe. I asked myself: Have I suffered a cerebral hemorrhage, am I to be a vegetable for life? Can this be the end of my abundant, exuberant existence? And then it dawned on me. I was dead.

I guess it's sort of a redundancy to speak about being very dead, or quite dead. Now I see there is only dead. No more, no less. I've recently realized I can perceive through my eyelids. Whether or not this is seeing is irrelevant. My arms refuse to move, and I feel strangely panicky that I might have to stay within this body which was mine. So as I lie here, I'm now aware of a number of things happening around me. At first the sensation was totally inward, meaning that I didn't notice anything in my surroundings. Little by little, I gained a greater understanding of my circumambience. The first thing I noticed was the light. Now I also hear the birds outside, and other ordinary noises. My previously blurry vision is clearing, and I can see sparrows outside fighting at a bird feeder. A little farther out, there are trees, and they don't have many leaves, so I suppose this is fall. Of course it is! What's wrong with my memory? Now it's returning in bits and pieces. In any event, it's a rather nice day, and I'm beginning to think I must be freshly dead.

There! One cannot be quite dead, but one can certainly be freshly dead. I always liked these little triumphs of the word. It's a beautiful day. The window is a bit open. I think I can smell the fall leaves beginning to mulch up the ground, which is singular, to say the least. Since my body seems to be the deadest part of me, I wouldn't think I could smell, but I am certainly perceiving things with a facility indistinguishable from my old olfactory sense.

With quiet perseverance, I'm attempting freedom. Like arms numbed by months of plaster casts, mine need exercise. Or at least the me inside of them does. I'm in bed. It's my own. God knows I've been in enough others. But this is definitely one of mine. The style is Empire. The real thing. Big, woody, angular, and full of superb sheets and cushy comforters. I'm lying on my back with one of the extra down pillows propped up under my head. This is in fact what I usually do in the early hours of the morning. So I must have died just a few hours ago. I wonder what time it is? As I looked over to the clock on my desk I felt a chill. As if there were something connected with this instrument that I should remember. But I will think about it later. There's a phone ringing softly beside me. Now that I won't be responding, I hope someone else will. The horn is very important to me, so I'm annoyed one of the servants, or my wife, Harriet, hasn't picked it up.

Hey, I just realized being dead legally separates me from my "extra rib." And to think I never thought of it as a way out before! Why, I could kick myself in the ass. Anyway, I don't like being imprisoned in my body. Come to think of it, though, I was always trapped in this body. So I guess the present situation is not much different. With the exception of my lack of movement and just a little rigor mortis here and there.

It would, however, be nice to be able to muster some motion. In addition to the physical need, I have this longing for some type of movement. Perhaps it's just something I'm supposed to do as part of the deal. You know, like baby kangaroos smelling their way to a far-off teat. Besides, if I could move, I might in some way be able to manifest myself. I might be able to materialize in order to ensure my memory in perpetuity. And with that done, if I had the time, I might manage to even up a few scores. But here I am projecting myself into the future when I'm nailed to this body and unable to move. I must forget these thoughts and focus my attention on trying to get out of here.

I'm becoming a bit frustrated. Hey, there's a little sensation of activity in my left big toe! Although I know the toe itself isn't moving, something inside of it is. I can actually see a sort of tenuous shadow stirring. I must attempt doing this with the rest of my spiritual body, but it's very, very tiring to try. So for a little while, I think I'll just lie here and think.

You know, this must be what babies do. What if instead of just goo-gooing and gaa-gaaing, they really do have a subconscious mind of sorts, and they're actually trying to get dumb limbs and things to work. In fact, I've heard of very intelligent children learning to speak before they attempt to walk. Causing all sorts of wonder in their parents, when they're induced to take a step and reply in perfect English, "No, I'll fall." Anyway, I now know what a baby experiences when it tries to move an arm or a leg, and has one hell of a time doing it.

Time to make the effort again. I think I'm going to be able to get the whole foot out of there. What do I mean, out of *there?* I mean, out of me. It would now appear that all those theologians were right, and the part that's exiting is the "real" me. That would make the body I live in "there" and ultimately meaningless. In any event, I guess *here* becomes *there* when it isn't your body anymore. Philosophical. Yes indeed, I liked philosophy. I spent a lot of time thinking about the whys and whens and hows of things. But getting back to the problem at hand, so to speak, this part of me that I'm extricating at first looks rather shadowy. It's now gaining a really nice intensity. As I become more dexterous in the use of myself I can better see and manage what, for lack of better language, I will refer to as my aura. I wonder if other people can see it? Considering there isn't anyone else around, I guess they haven't looked and assume I'm asleep.

I'm becoming better and better at this. If I really strain and persevere at it, I can now remove a whole leg up to the hip. Now the hands. Why are hands so difficult? I would have thought they would be the easiest thing. So we'll take it a finger at a time. Here goes. It's not a push and it's not a pull. In fact, it's almost like a letting go. As if the absence of exertion were a form of effort or a liberating force. Great, now I can withdraw a whole hand. And here goes the arm. Attaboy! Two hands, now two arms, and the rest of me is out too. But look at that: I see myself glowing in bright colors and I don't even make a reflection in a mirror. When I look down at my feet I view myself as sort of a gauzy, luminous spirit. I can hardly believe it, but that's what I am, all right. Well, now I can walk around this room. Slowly at first and then with more bravado. Before you know it, I'll be skipping about.

Yep. It's my bedroom, all right. Nice Oriental carpet on the floor. It's a Tabriz. But not one of the ratty commercial ones. This is a good tight carpet. You can hardly part the pile with your nail. Greens and browns and oranges and reds. Gee, I never realized the thing had so many different colors. That's the way it is. You can walk on something every day of your life and not notice it until you drop dead and start looking at objects as if you were seeing them for the first time. And to think this is what it takes. If all of that reincarnation razzmatazz is correct, maybe that's why children see things so precisely and objectively. After all, they're closer to the recollection with their recently buried unconscious memories. In any event, I could spend a whole week looking at the designs in this rug. Outer borders, middle borders, inner borders, flowers, rosettes, diddley-doos, and curlicues. Like a kaleidoscope of color bursting in my inner brain or mind, or whatever it is we spirits have.

There are other wonderful things in this room as well. There's a beautiful, restful Pissarro from the Pontoise period. And an excellent Empire desk. For some reason, I keep focusing on the large brass clock that sits upon it. Sort of gives me the chills, but I don't rightly understand why. It's a British clock with what they call a horizontal wheel escapement. It has a large shiny disk that relentlessly turns to and fro, making ever so slight a noise. It's actually a rather tranquil piece. Why then do I keep returning to it? And for what reason is it somewhat unnerving to me? I sort of think this may have been one of the last things to draw my attention. Why else would I be obsessed with this single item in my uniformly beautiful bedroom? But I must put this out of my mind, since I have a great deal to do at the moment.

Now I'm standing here completely beside myself. Cute. Incidentally, I forgot to say there really is something great about this business of being recently departed. To begin with, I feel incredibly light on my feet. Yes, I literally think I could skip all the way around this room without my tootsies ever touching the carpet. Actually, now that I can move about, there isn't any reason why I shouldn't try. Skipping is something out of my childhood. Mother used to watch me doing it when I was returning from class. I was a wisp of a kid, but I could skip up a storm. I'd skip up and down, back and forth, and all the way back from school with red lunch box in tow. Mommy, I miss you. Where are you now? I think I need you very badly. . . . You and Dad and my sister, Alicia, were the only truly tender people in my life. I had always thought one of the great things about being dead would entail being reunited again, but I seem to be quite alone here. Anyway, my mother used to love seeing me skip. It was sort of a trademark. And the time has come again, so here we go. Um-de-dum, up and down, and faster forward do I bound, till slightly giddy with sensation I approach the room's end, and then unable to stop on a dime as I might when I was a youngster, I discover *I can actually skip through the wall.* Now that's what I call a real thrill! Furthermore, I'm beginning to suspect I became a bit airborne when I got carried away with the motion. No doubt about it. I was actually floating around. Well I'll be damned. Oops, I didn't mean that. Especially not now. In any event, I have conquered the gentle art of flight. And what's more, I can put myself through things easy as pie. Like that wall to Harriet's bedroom. Bet I can walk right through it. Here goes.

One, two, cockledy-doo. Right step, left step. And here I am right through the thing. It's Harriet's room, all right. With the two

Monets I gave her as an anniversary present. And there she is lying in bed like an Oriental princess. I loved, hated, and desired her. Some would think it the perfect relationship. But I ultimately grew to despise everything at the same time, including Harriet.

She was the most beautiful flower available at the time. And I plucked. Not so gently at that. After all, she had the looks, and I had the bucks. I'm not sure I ever really loved her. Just the zeal to collect. I must later reflect on these feelings. Not now, though.

She's blond, and somewhat androgynous. With an almost Scandinavian set of very fine features, and beautiful gray-green eyes. Therefore, not big in the tit department. But what hips. And legs. . . . Those legs are her trademark. Long and lithe, they can wrap around your face and give you a real run for your money. Not to mention the rest of it. Thin bones. Tiny wrists. And size four and a half feet which look like they've been packed in rose petals every day of her life. Beautiful elbows and knees. Rare. And taut white thighs that resolve themselves into the prettiest little pout your eyes ever did see. When asses were passed around, they gave Harriet a humdinger. Round, and only slightly elongated, like the nicest Bartlett pear. Not entirely oval-shaped, though. More like a boy's ass. Like two firm melons. Years of ice skating and riding took care of that. She knows how to use it. I've often thought that in spite of herself, Harriet has a very educated ass.

Well, so much for the *derrière*. There she is sleeping under the ecru satin sheets. Like any other self-respecting odalisque. I personally never liked satin. Seems to me it's second only to a dead dog's tongue when wet. I'll take poplin anyday. But there she is under that shimmering sheet, in a slinky nightgown to boot! Crepe de chine. You can have it. Why, it's like sandpaper when wet. What's the good of a sexy fabric if you can't get it wet? Nevertheless, it's quite a picture. Madame No lying there in all her glory with a satin mask over her eyes. Used to call her that because in the latter years of our marriage, sex became a no-letter word.

I have mixed feelings regarding Harriet. And so does she, for that matter. You see, there are many contradictions within the woman. On the one hand she's rational, logical, and cold. On the other, she can be emotionally confused, beguilingly childlike, and inordinately superstitious. She can question a household expenditure of a pittance, and then turn around and give a beggar a twenty-dollar bill. Oh yes, she has this great fear of being deprived of it all, which translates into a feeling of guilt, keeping her from ever refusing a mendicant. I'm not kidding. Mean though she may be at times, I've seen her ask the driver to go around the block in order to catch some indigent she's missed. That's my Harriet, totally contradictory!

In any event, I must say there's a glow about her. It's the complexion. I'm not the only one who thought she had the most beautiful skin. Everyone else did too. It was always good, even if I did chide her constantly about the quantity of creams and things she'd smear on it to improve the tone. But no wonder I hated the creams! Most times I'd come in with a hard fandango wanting to slip it to her ever so rudely. And what would I find? A Chinese wall of cream smack between us.

I'm not so sure I should be thinking about such things. I must beware of framing my present opinions in the light of her angelically seductive figure lying there inert. Soon enough, she'll be up and about, and then that truly nasty personality will again begin to show itself. Why, I could just scream when I think of the times she turned me down in my need for some serious fandango intensive care. But that's not all she did. She ridiculed me, and complained about my work, and made me turn my pooch out to romp in the front park, just because he had a little doggie odor. I'll bet it turned her on. Why, when I met Harriet, and in spite of her cool and collected act, she could get turned on by a broomstick lying in a corner. It was only after ten million dollars' worth of jewelry that she began developing migraines. There's a lesson in it somewhere. It all has to do with what happens to women after they marry. The ones who don't turn matronly become fat. And the ones who don't become fat suddenly decide to drop sex. And then there's the greed that sets in. But unless you snag a truly virtuous one, you're definitely screwed. Unfortunately the goody-goodies are usually plain and uninteresting. Maybe I should console myself with the fact that I really gave my wife very little. When money's the cheapest thing you have to give, it doesn't represent a gift of very much. I kept the best jewels for my personal collection. She won't find them now either. They can tear Pyramid Hill apart, and they'll never get my toys. But we'll talk about that later.

This house, on the other hand, is actually Harriet's preferred residence. Let's take a walk out to the front and take a good, hard look. Gates. Twenty feet high. Bought them from European royalty. They make love to a wall that goes around the entire property. If you ever got to the top of it, you'd find it booby-trapped with very sharp spikes. Then there's the driveway, making a long, straight visual line up to the circle that lies half a mile up between it and the house. All of it flanked with now-mature red maples. Everyone said we should use oak or some other typical tree. Elms wouldn't work, since the disease makes them self-destruct. So I said I'd use good sturdy specimens. Maple, and red to boot.

This rather splendid country place reminds me of the very special edifice I built for myself closer into town. It's a genuine pyramid. No less. My present absence from it makes me think I must be visiting Harriet or something. I don't generally sleep out here in the country these days. You see, my wife and I have been estranged for some time. A lot of it actually had to do with my wonderful building. The whole thing was so imposing, people actually took to calling it Pyramid Hill. By constructing it, I really outdid myself, and at the same time, did Harriet's country grounds one better, so to speak.

But let me backtrack for a moment or two. I began my business life by virtue of a gush from the ground. Of the black, sticky variety. Later I branched out into all sorts of things, including an occasional brokering of weapons. Complete with fringe benefits. I once had a little arms deal with the Egyptian government and just happened to see a really spectacular obelisk. So I made them include it in the deal. Thutmosid. No less. Four thousand years old! Now standing in the front yard of my pyramid with all the glory of ancient knowledge and quarrying secrets long lost to time. Nothing there to envy the ones in Rome, London, and New York. Damned thing is just wonderful, soaring up in a straight line a good sixty-nine feet, and weighing in at about a hundred and eighty tons! It bears mysterious cartouches and the effigies of gods everywhere. Carved into the surface, you can see the Lord of Eternity with two jars of wine holding the attributes of his dominion over the realm of the dead. A man could certainly do worse.

The accompanying structure at Pyramid Hill is in the shape of a truncated Egyptian pyramid. But no sandstone there. Granite all the way. When I thought of it at first, I called two hotshot architects of our time and said, "This is what I want." Architects, you know, are like decorators, publicists, and the like. They bask in the reflected glory of their patrons' pocketbooks. And in this case, they proceeded with alacrity. Like hungry little mites, they sucked daily from my collected assets until even *I* screamed a little. But it was worth it. The first twelve feet or so of height were built without windows. The garages and basements, subbasements, and other miscellaneous rooms were all hidden down in that direction. And a few secrets as well.

The real house sits about fifteen feet above the terrain on a base of solid granite. Above that pedestal there is a wall of glass which circles the structure like a ribbon contiguous to the base of the pyramid. That section is another thirty feet high. Here, there are monumental windows flush with the granite. All electric. But no danger of losing power. My auxiliary plant is run by massive generators in the nether rooms, and they in turn hum to the strength of a brook which shows its countenance to the south of the house, and plunges with subterranean intent to a depth of one hundred and sixty feet below the structure, where it is then tapped. All the rest failing, there are even diesel tanks down there which could fuel it all for years. It has probably occurred to more than one onlooker that the better part of the thing is also a bomb shelter. But it's actually abundantly more. After all, you've got to know it must be special indeed when you take a look at your average semiparanoid, xenophobic, partially sociophobic, marginally agoraphobic creator like me. Then it must of necessity dawn on you I must have built some special goodies into this nifty edifice of mine. For instance, the foundation and superimposed base core wall of the house are composed of sixty feet of solid, reinforced, vibrated concrete. Beyond that, between it and the various rooms, is a high compaction of aggregate. If you were facing it you'd see a lot of granite and glass, but don't kid yourself. At the touch of a switch, all openings are shut tight with one-inch-thick surgical-steel panels capable of withstanding a direct hit. Also, wary of the diseases our government insinuates into the fluvial system, I equipped myself with full triple-reverse osmosis purification, as well as ultraviolet sterilization, true distillation, and sophisticated chemical monitoring devices. At the flick of a button a gas chromatographer and spectrograph automatically analyze the water. So the next time the government scientists playing with their genetic toys manufacture a bug in Atlanta, we have no intention of ingesting it at Pyramid Hill. The air-movement system is also state-of-the-art for bomb shelters. Why, it's better than the gas-purification system over in the bunker at Camp David. And just for safety, the whole park in front of the building and around it is mined with booby traps and explosives. My feeling was that if they were going to "get" me, they'd really have to put up a fight. Below, I outdid myself by creating a complex puzzle with the underground river. So if you break into one room, it immediately floods and keeps you from going on to the next. There are secret rooms down there as well. Eighteen of them, cut deeply into the bedrock. Carved like some ancient Middle Egyptian tomb, each one is hidden beyond or beneath another. And they're full of goodies. Freeze-dried food. And a whole horticultural room with seeds and lamps to grow vegetables. It sports full internal, self-contained eco-system engineering to guarantee survival.

But there are also other things there which Harriet has never dreamed of. Like weapons. And works of art, a whole operating room, and the Moguk Diamond, in addition to a few other goodies. I used to run my fingers through the gems late in the night when Harriet had shut me out. I would then repeat a very pleasant motto which has gotten me this far: *Mine, all mine.*

As I insistently think about my place near town, I am, to my great surprise, transported to a spot before the front facade of the pyramid, where there is an entrance. For a moment I pause, to catch my breath and compose myself from the otherworldly feeling of euphoria and levity inherent in this incredible phenomenon of teleportation. It's sort of what I used to feel when I'd been "flying" in a dream. But it's better, and lighter, as if for a moment that serenity were coupled with the exhilaration of having billions of champagne bubbles bursting within me. It's a sensation ultimately indescribable in words. But this pyramid isn't.

At first the architect and I quarreled on how one would enter the place. He suggested stationary stone bridges and such over the reflecting pool. But I didn't really like his ideas. So one night it occurred to me. To have the steps and bridge quarried out of one massive, megalithic, seven-hundred-ton piece of granite on a pivot which would incorporate itself completely into the structure when lifted, and therefore be flush with the surface, and invisible to the untrained eye when closed. I got a real chuckle out of the reporters on that one. Not to mention the federal judge who tried to have me served with a subpoena. The process servers and marshals had a real time trying to figure out how you get through that many tons of granite. As a matter of fact, they never did serve the writ. After eight weeks the matter had become moot by operation of time. Yes indeed, although money has been called the great reconciler, you've got to admit that time is also a very special temperer of both good and evil. I'm remembering an old Spanish saying: *There is no evil which can last a hundred years, nor a body that can resist it.*

My mother was Spanish. That's where I picked up all of these little Hispanic ditties and sayings. People used to think I was making them up. Like when I told the President: *The shrimp that falls asleep is carried away by the current.* He didn't understand then. But he sure did later.

Yes, I guess you could say I've been what they call a kingmaker. When I constructed my financial establishment, I didn't just build companies and factories. I also cemented relationships. One after another, I put together a chain of friendships and acquaintances which pretty much allowed me to do anything at all times. While no mafioso in the specific sense, I remained cordial with both the Mob and the Church. It was, however, more than a surprise to find that these two already enjoyed a rich history of cooperation and entanglement. After a while, I concluded that there really wasn't much of a difference between the two. They all want the little guy's money. And they don't want to give him much in exchange. I've always had the conviction that early on, I made a monumental mistake. I should have been in the clergy. By now I could have been a prince of the Church, like my old friend Cardinal Tucci, or maybe even Pope. Think of it. Me at the head of the greatest business enterprise in the world. Ministering to the most perfect gimmick ever invented: your money in this life, in exchange for glory in the next. Well, there will be no dearth of clergymen sniffing around now that I'm dead.

In the past, I could pick up the phone and press the Church, the mayor, or the governor into action, and even put a bugaboo in the President's hat if I really wanted something. Other times I'd use the Church to slam-bang people into action. But one way or another,

I got my way. And every year the President would call and say, "Henry, I was thinking of stopping by to pay my respects," and then the house would be full of advance parties of Secret Service men with walkie-talkies and sophisticated electronic links. Once the motorcade arrived, he'd find me at the front door of an impressive household. Polished, beribboned, and fully ready, my staff would have filled the house with fresh flowers from the ends of the earth. Usually I might ask him to stay for lunch, and invariably the invitation would be accepted. There was an exception. . . . That fellow was replaced shortly thereafter. And why not? After all, if steel was the topic, I controlled, and if wheat was on the agenda, I had more of it than anyone else. Of course, underlying all items was the matter of political support, and ultimately power. I learned early that it wasn't the possession of great wealth which created strength, but more likely, the proper control of it. So without the obvious expressions, the President knew I knew that he knew that I knew. And we knew they knew that we knew and vice versa. Of course, upon such understandings are the destinies of nations and the fortunes of men built. And all things considered, as the Spanish say, *to those who understand well, few words are necessary.* Yes, I accumulated political power slowly and deliberately, like *the chicken that fills her gullet a grain at a time.* To be sure, it involved many purchase and sale transactions, and some observation of honor. But when all was said and done, there wasn't much I couldn't command with this resource or that, through one person or another. As political parties succeeded one another, I witnessed no diminution in power. My hold was fundamental. And the successors were really very much like the predecessors. After all, it has been said that *the child of the bat has wings.*

All dalliances aside, I am again concerned with thoughts of my body, and immediately transported to my bedroom. Here's that incredibly stupid maid coming in with my breakfast tray. It actually looks pretty good today. Poached eggs, bacon, and a croissant. A little caviar to remind me of who I am. And keep me firm where it counts. There's a pot of espresso as well. She's knocking on the door, softly at first, and then with insistence. Faced with a total lack of response, she's cracking the door a bit, and peeking in. Muttering to herself in a thick German accent, she's saying something that sounds like "I have your breakfast" in pig German. She's coming closer with the tray. I really do look like I'm asleep. Now she's touching my shoulder to stir me a little. And all of a sudden the tray is flying, there's porcelain everywhere, and she's screaming something at the top of her lungs in German to the effect that I'm very, very dead indeed. A real commotion. For some reason, I feel unhappily compelled to look at that clock again. The houseman and the butler are running up the stairs. And Harriet, looking somewhat disturbed, is making her entrance in a long, flowery silk dressing gown. Someone is saying, "Call a doctor," but Harriet, cool as a cucumber, is quick to say, "It's just too late." Even *I* find it difficult to believe she managed to take my pulse without batting an eyelash. A couple of girls on the staff have entered, the maid included, and they're sobbing a little. I'm pleased at that. But you could comfortably grow cactus in Harriet's eye.

My wife is on the phone. She's calling our lawyer. Good old Tom Hooker. He's saying he'll be right over. I believe him, too. Rapacious and efficient. He's telling her he will call Mr. Onions, the funeral director to the famous and wealthy. After what seems like a brief interlude, I perceive a car coming up the driveway. It's a hearse. A big, black, shiny one. Through the door comes Mr. Onions, with physician in tow. I know him well. I had to deal with the fellow almost daily when I was erecting my memorial. I guess I'll get to see it from a different perspective now. Attendants in gray uniforms are pulling the covers away and gently placing me on a stretcher. They're collecting my arms beside me and neatly strapping my body to the contraption so I won't fall off. Out the bedroom door, over the diamond-patterned marble floor, into the elevator. Down to the first floor, through the pleasant foyer, and out the front door. The back of the hearse is now being opened. Always thought rear ends were sexy. The chauffeur is starting the engine. We're going around the circle, by the fountain, and onward to the entrance road. The electronic gates are opening, and off we go down a country lane through suburbia, into the morning city traffic.

I've been down these roads and streets thousands of times, but this is a new perspective. Fun. For the first time, I'm noticing things like people's feet. An anxious nurse is quick-stepping it to the hospital in her immaculate white shoes. A secretary on her way to work is wearing heels which are far too high for a comfortable day at the office. But she doesn't mind, because she's going to try to get the boss to take a swipe at her. The garbage men in thick gray soles look like they couldn't care less about the way they throw the cans around and tread on the pavement. A child is being walked to school and is stepping on the tips of his toes as if full of expectation. A street person is waking up with an empty bottle in hand and moves as if all hope had long been consigned to memory. His steps are shiftless and very heavy. The light is changing and we're off again. But I see ahead the sober facade of Trumble and Company, Morticians.

The hearse quietly drives through an opening into a subterranean garage. Here all sounds are hushed. I have now come into the entrails of the house of the dead. Four thousand years ago there would have been vats of nitre and the smell of precious unguents. Come to think of it, though, it's not much different. The uniformed attendants are wheeling me into something which looks like a surgical lab. I'm being placed on a stainless-steel table. In comes Mr. Onions, now beaming. I guess it isn't every day he acquires jurisdiction over a stiff of my renown. Some bastardly attendant is using the equivalent of a meat hook to pull out my brain. And they've stuck my arms with horse needles to wash out the blood and embalm me. The makeup person has just arrived. He's a slight, dour little guy with cosmetics kit in hand. He has an assistant, too, an attractive woman. She's sort of got me going down in the crotch. I really can't exactly feel my penis, and there's no erection. In this respect I've been cheated. I always told them I wanted to *go* in the Egyptian mode with an erect cock to act as my calling card in the underworld, even if they had to use a splint. After all, the Egyptians always said the gates of heaven were bolted with rivets shaped like the penises of baboons.

They're stuffing cotton in my cheeks. I guess it has to be done. He's made my eyebrows a little too big, but that's not much of a mistake. A little blush here and there with a touch of bronzer, and I acquire nice ruddy cheeks. I always looked that way after a few days in the sun. Not really a tan, but just enough to seem healthy. I used to like it that way. I have good teeth. My dentist always said they were nice. Actually, my wisdom teeth constitute somewhat of an anomaly. They are perfectly straight, and I have retained all four. The better to bite with!

Above a wide forehead she's combing my hair. It's an acceptable tone of dark brown, with a little bit of help from a bottle. My secretary always commented it matched the color of my eyes. I'm recalling, I liked her very much. Perhaps too much. Yes, I now realize she might have been the love of my life. But why did I let her go? Why didn't I follow through?

Down from the forehead, the undertakers labor with determination. Smoothing out my wrinkles is not a great deal of trouble. My big brown eyes are closed, but she's gently rubbing a little color on the lids. A little massage on the cheekbones to loosen things up. I guess I must be a little stiff by now. No need to touch my nose. It is, as noses go, a good one. But what's she doing now? She's putting lipstick on me. I guess I should be indignant, but on the other hand, purple lips won't do for the occasion. I always liked manicures. Sort of a fetish. Having my nails buffed here in the morning is no less of a thrill. Like getting spruced up for a party. Now they're rubbing my hands with cream and placing them on my chest. I think this girl is sort of nice. Professional, but nice. She's taking a little leather religious book and putting it in my hand. This gives me pause. I don't think I'm presently much of a believer. Yet my immediate state would lead me to surmise there is something else. Reincarnation would seem plausible and avoids the gobbledygook having to do with close encounters of the godlike sort. Perhaps I'm just in the antechamber, so to speak, of another existential plane. I guess I'll just have to wait and see.

All of this activity seems to have consumed a great part of the day. I'm surprised. I would have thought we were sometime near noon. Like casinos in gambling towns, this place doesn't have a lot of windows. So the evening has crept up on us. And these people are readying themselves to leave. This allows me the opportunity of walking around and examining the various halls of this incredibly opulent mortuary.

The lights have been turned off in most of the rooms. The last of the employees has left, leaving only the guard standing outside the impressive bronze entrance doors. I must say, this is a rather interesting place. In addition to the various laboratories and preparing rooms, there are also halls filled with spanking-new coffins awaiting their usually unwilling occupants. There's nothing cheap here, though. Lots of bronze and brass. And beautifully grained wood. There are props too. Couches and biers. And one room full of things that look like torches and lanterns. Well, to be sure, it's a very polished place. But I'm not at all happy to be here by myself. I think I'll scoot over to Mr. Onions's desk and take a peek at his appointment book. Yes, there's my name in anal-arrestive script. All set for viewing at ten a.m. with a subsequent transfer to church at one, and a burial at three. In all this haste, I perceive the hand of Harriet, who isn't wasting a lot of time. I'm tired. And now that I've seen the place, also a bit bored with this quiet atmosphere. There's a comfortable-looking Chippendale couch in the foyer. Maybe I'll just rest on it for a moment or two.

I must have dozed off or something. Since it's now morning, and there is renewed activity within this establishment. All sorts of people seem to be stepping up their routines here. Outside there's a procession of vehicles delivering floral arrangements, both small and large. Why, there must be several hundred of them. This is fun. I can pop through this room where I guess they're going to later place me and look into all the cards and ribbons on the flowers. There's the wreath from the Cardinal. Stargazer lilies. And there's a particularly beautiful one made in the shape of a cross with callas and roses. Must have cost a left nut. No wonder, it's from the Mob. There are flowers from people who worked for me, and from friends, acquaintances, and individuals who supplied me with linens and furnishings. There are flowers here from parties I don't even know. Blossoms from the President, and one enterprising cabinet member sent one with a little shovel. I guess he meant to say I was industrious. But the double meaning is not lost on me. There's one arrangement I'm missing, though. Perhaps it will arrive later.

So now that they've polished my nails and powdered my nose, and dressed me up in one of my sober British suits, they're going to "present" me, so to speak. A very cute Italian attendant in a white smock with boyish curly hair is wheeling me into this rather large room full of flowers. They have a table fully draped in velvet. On it is a very well camouflaged wooden casket. Contrary to practice, they've completely removed the lids so I actually look like I'm lying in bed. That rather pretty girl is now wheeling in an enormous blanket of white roses. Why, they're so thick you can't even see what they're adhered to. Four of the attendants under her supervision are now positioning the blanket so it begins just beneath my ribs and drapes down over my legs and feet like just another cloth. I must admit these preparations are in keeping with my instructions. But I've been looking at these flowers again and again and I just can't find what I'm seeking. Here comes another attendant with a whole cart-load of things. Maybe it's there. Let me take a much closer look. No, it's not that big round one, and it's not the one in the shape of a telephone. And whoever sent those chrysanthemums didn't know me very well at all. They're flowers for the dead! I wouldn't even think of sending them to anyone. Ugh! But what's that under there? Do I see a little white box? An attendant is opening it. He's surprised. Among all of the pseudo-magnificence of these sometimes not so well-intended floral tributes, he finds himself holding the simplest of nosegays. Violets. No more, no less. But beautiful and very fresh. The green leaves have been exquisitely positioned over a little piece of diaphanous old lace. Over the leaves are the little violets. No need to look at the card. I know. And I'm touched you remembered. Hey, wait, don't throw them away. This creep is making some comment about how that little nosegay isn't fitting for a funeral like mine, and he's throwing it into the wastebasket. I'm whistling and grimacing, but it's not doing any good. There it sits on top of the trash. That pretty girl is walking right by it. There, there. The little nosegay has been spied and she's going straight to the fetch. Now reading the card. Looks like a suspicion of a tear in that eye. She's looking to the side, like someone ready to steal something. Surreptitiously. And then in one deft gesture, she grabs the nosegay, lifts the blanket of roses, and pops it right in my crotch where no one will see it. Thank you, my dear. Thank you so very much!

The early morning has elapsed much more quickly than I would have expected. It's now approaching ten o'clock. There's music in the background. Bach cello suites. I'll never forget the first time I heard that sarabande from the fifth one. Stood my hairs on end. Sat me down, so to speak. So here it is again. Brief, eloquent, haunting. As I recall, I have an entire musical program planned for this event. If they do it right, they'll have the Pope's organist in from Rome to later play at the cathedral. But no need to think about that now. Attendants in livery are opening the two gigantic bronze doors which lead to this room from the foyer without. Visitors are beginning to stream in. My goodness! There are lots of people who've just come as curiosity-seekers. The members of government are here because they can't afford not to be seen. After all, politicians are very much like vampires. They don't do anything during the workday, while giving the impression of being industrious. But in the dark they suck your blood until you're dead. And merrily go on to the next body as soon as necessary. One of the great lessons in my life had to do with realizing such people must give the impression of being the handmaidens of change, while at the same time secretly resisting it. And all of this in order to perpetuate the status quo! I assure you they don't wish to abolish drugs any more than the drug companies want to abolish politicians or disease. And of course if we had truly efficient government, about ninety percent of these jokers wouldn't be necessary.

Harriet has just entered on the arm of Hooker, my lawyer. If you ask me, they look a bit too cozy. She's wearing a form-fitting black dress with a little black headpiece that carries a veil. At least the bitch has had the sense to look mournful. Wearing diamonds and pearls. Come to think of it, I could have done without the diamonds today.

A well-dressed crowd is now arriving. I should have known. It's the bankers. Here's a real group for the herpetology handbook. To begin with, bankers give new meaning to the word "ungrateful." They provide you with an umbrella when the sun is shining, and then promptly take it away when it begins to rain. Usually they're the fellows who weren't quite smart enough to become lawyers and didn't have the cold blood to be physicians. I will, however, say they have something in common with magicians. Bankers are charged with being the keepers of one of the great fictions of modern times. The way it works is simple. The government gives them the equivalent of a license to steal by allowing them to open a bank. When you have a bank you can borrow from the government at a rate far below what the public will pay. It's called the "discount rate." You then build a lofty edifice. Preferably the type of architecture which bespeaks solidity. With that building, its ultrasecure doors, its marble floors, and impressive vault, you will convince the poor, unsuspecting public its money is secure. In point of fact, though, the application of bankers' less than mediocre intelligence causes them to make endlessly imprudent investments in loans, bankruptcies, the market, commodities, and the Third World. Their miracle of existence is thus only verified by the rape job they perpetrate on the unwary and puny consumer, and the enormous spreads they make on their loans. True, occasionally the government closes them down. But the license to steal is, generally speaking, revoked only for gross incompetence, unquenchable larceny, or political enmity.

The head honcho of this banking group is approaching Harriet. She's doing her absolute best to exhibit a grief-stricken pose. But even with their marsupial intelligence, I don't believe they're taken in. He's muttering something to her about the capabilities of his institution for dealing with the complexities of a multinational estate. Deferring to Hooker, they're now walking arm in arm into the foyer, where, no doubt, a nice little deal is being concocted to bilk my estate out of a usurious percentage. All the other little bankers are just hovering like so many piranhas expectantly shimmering in the water.

My aunts are here too. Both of them. Aged. Beautifully composed. But genuinely grief-stricken. They almost look like little girls holding hands. This is what I call propriety. Pious women without makeup or jewelry. Ladies who bounced me on their knees and wiped my dickie-doo with baby oil. In their old age, they've consolidated their households. No need to worry about them, though. I set them up for life.

There must be five hundred people in this room now. In the foyer, the activity is assuming a cocktail-party atmosphere. No reverie now. They're no longer afraid. After all, *the rabies is gone when the dog is dead.* I can't believe the effrontery of some of them, who are actually sniggering about how ruthless and despotic I was. I think they should go home and clean their dirty houses.

Harriet seems to be leaning more heavily on Hooker's arm. In life, he and I had a relationship of convenience. Sheer symbiosis. People nicknamed him I.B.M. After all, he could skin the scales off a snake before the creature knew it. No doubt a relative of his. Master of the lightning reflex. Cerberus of the business world. Parasite to dying businesses. Symbiotic partner to the good ones. And now executor. Collector of his fee. Highway robber.

Mr. Onions, the funeral director, is thoroughly gussied up for my party. This funeral must be one of the crowning achievements of his necrophilic existence. Dressed as if for a wedding with deep gray cutaway and pleated trousers. After all, it is almost "correct" to wear the same clothing to weddings and funerals. A fresh rosebud shows itself on the lapel, and a pearl stickpin secures the foulard. He's perfect, right down to the patent-leather shoes, which are conservatively tied. I do, however, suspect I'm not the only gentleman wearing a little makeup here. Do I see a tad of rouge on Mr. Onions's cheeks? Now, assuming a directorial pose, he is indicating to the congregation that we are about to proceed to the cathedral. The music is stepping up a bit in volume, and the ushers are discreetly and efficiently organizing the family into its cars, and moving the flock toward the procession of vehicles now waiting. My aunts, bless their hearts, are weeping, and their old driver is attempting to usher them into their old and wonderful classic car. It's banana yellow with a black stripe. After all, these may be old ladies, but they are not without the elements of style.

I'm missing someone I've been hoping to see. Perhaps it's my own fault for harboring the expectation. It's been said that *he who lives with illusions dies of disenchantment.* Nevertheless, I'm pleased to note that this time I'm dead wrong. There's Susan Cleave rushing through the door. An usher is telling her we're on our way to church, but by the time he attempts to gently push her out, she's through the entrance and clicking over the marble in those exquisite tiny black ostrich pumps, until she stands smack in front of me. Those beautiful little shoes progress to aristocratic ankles and long, well-shaped calves. When Coco said that kneecaps should be hidden, she didn't mean these. As knees go, they are the zenith. Thighs too. Not too hard, and not too soft. Moving up to a waist that needs no exercise for accentuation. And a navel built for heavy tongue-lashing, and proportioned for museum-quality exhibition. The rib cage is delicate, but assertive, holding a dignified pair of luscious tits with small, hard nipples made for quenching the thirst of men-children of all ages. Those breasts curve up toward a perfect neck. Long and delicate like an Egyptian statue's. Above it, the chin is not too large, but big enough to be stubborn. And she has moist lips which give meaning to the word "petulance." The nose is long. Perhaps a bit too long, but Singer Sargent would have cleaved to it like the Red Sea before God. Eyes to match the emerald beads I gave you. How could one ever forget them. And auburn hair which makes you look a thousand different ways at your request and whim. You've got some more of those violets pinned to your lapel. No new suit for you. Classic. The kind you could wear for another twenty years. Don't cry. An exquisite finger pulls a hankie out of the tiny ostrich bag. There are a million things I want to say to you if only you'd stop weeping. But here comes the usher again, and now he means business. So we're both leaving by different doors. You know, it seems we always end up doing just that!

Six of my so-called friends and associates are carrying the casket and placing it in the hearse. Come to think of it, this isn't a bad box. Cypress. How appropriate I should be lying in a coffin made out of the wood of such tall, sad trees. Down into the city traffic we go, complete with police motorcycle escort compliments of His Honor the Mayor. Through intersections and past red lights. We've even made an occasional ambulance wait. After all, we have enough politicians in this cortege to altogether prejudice the national debt. The sun is shining brightly, but there are suspicions of a cloud or two up there. It's now about twelve-thirty. And it's beginning to feel like the weather may change, turning this one into a cool afternoon.

I seem to be suffering from some misapprehension regarding the nature of time. Late in life I realized old Albert had been right. Time is flexible and can be perceived as being lengthy or short, can progress, or be reversed, so to speak. As he put it, *When I hold a beautiful girl's hand, an hour seems like a minute, but when I sit on a hot stove, a minute seems like an hour.* In any event, it seems to me I must have lost track of some time here or there, because all of these people have managed to seat themselves in expectation of my arrival. I can see the organist made it across the Atlantic. No doubt my friend Cardinal Tucci had something to do with his presence. And as I enter with my six male nannies he whips up the phenomenal *Sonata on the 94th Psalm.* To be honest, and in retrospect, I would have preferred something simple and trite like the *Ave Maria*, but at the time I conceived the musical program, it seemed suitable enough. And quite frankly, the sonata is in keeping with the vaulted ceiling, stained-glass windows, and general sobriety of this surrounding. As we progress through the mass, I am struck with the fact that I, who was only nominally religious, do not now feel any closer to the Deity. Why am I so dispossessed of comfort and solace in the house of God? After all, I contributed a flying buttress or two to the success of this edifice. And those windows over there, the ones reminiscent of Chartres, also bear witness to my munificence. With their blues and reds, yellows and greens. Look closely and you'll see they bear my dedication. But none of it provides me with the reassurance or peace I would need today.

I'm amused to see Harriet didn't dare take communion. My aunts did, though. The light has changed, and is now beginning to stream in from the other side of the church. The mass now over, things are tensing up a bit as the sound of the Widor toccata bellows through the air, magnificently. Complete with twelve-vibration-per-second pipe.

I have often fantasized that this would be the music to accompany my triumphant entry into hell. In my reverie the dwarfs in their diamond, emerald, ruby, and sapphire vestments have diligently checked the massive diamond-studded platinum chains restraining the impatient albino elephants. The glimmering attendants have readied everything. I am seated on a golden throne, perched atop the largest of the jewel-covered pachyderms. At the cue from the bellowing organ, we begin making our majestic way down the fiery lane. The one paved with everybody's good intentions. Before us are beautiful and muscular white and black male slaves throwing nothing but the best gold coins and precious gems to the onlookers, cheering the sway of the mastodons and their jewel-encrusted howdahs. As we proceed down damnation's road, we can see seated in the distance, atop the highest mountain of hell, His Satanic Majesty himself, waiting to greet me personally. All of this to the cheers of those to be purged, the quasi and the totally damned, as well as the many souls totally devoid of hope. Yes, the adulterers are here, both male and female, *all* perpetually pregnant. The murderers are looking to the side, as they are assassinated by surprise each hour. The gluttons are all so fat they can hardly reach to clap. The slanderers have brightly colored serpents for tongues. The slothful are on permanent treadmills fanning the crowds, and the avaricious are all wearing large gold crowns encrusted with unbearably heavy burdens of gems. The liars have forgotten who they are. And the invidious are of course forced to see me pass. But as I snap back to that which I now call reality, I realize

I'm also being carried down the aisle in processional manner. So out we go and into the hearse for the long ride to the cemetery.

Having traversed the length of the city and climbed into the rolling hills of the suburbs, we begin driving by the river. It's a ribbon of water that meanders down from the mountains into the suburbs, running through the city, and widening as it flows into the ocean. It's crossed occasionally by little bridges. Down by the sea they're bigger and wider so as to allow boats beneath them. But near the cemetery the most you might fit under them would be a sleek rowboat or rower's skull. I've been thinking about that *Sonata on the 94th Psalm*, and of the letter of that song:

Lord, who thinks in death of thee, who thanks thee in Hades . . .

and I think:

Oh Lord God, to whom vengeance belongeth, show thyself. Arise, thou Judge of the world, and reward the proud after their deserving . . .

I guess those are the words to the music, but now that I think of it, I would have preferred the comfort of the 91st. The flowers on the hearse behind me are ebbing in the wind as the shiny cars roll along. The limos are climbing up a gentle grade now. I have always loved the sound of two hundred and umpteen horses humming beneath the hood.

As we approach the area of town where the cemetery lies, we proceed through the traffic lights with measured dignity. Some people behind me are weeping. Others are becoming a bit tense. I know that most of them are thinking, Let's get rid of this stiff. Let's get it over with. Give them a chance, maybe they're thinking, Poor Henry. But even if they are, nobody wants me with rigor mortis. We're approaching a massive brown sandstone Egyptian gate. It's of the carved variety. In the classic Middle Egyptian style, complete with pylons sporting open papyrus blossoms. I can't help noticing the monumental statement carved into the top of the gate. It reads, *The Dead Shall Be Risen*.

The lanes in this cemetery all have botanical names. So, we're now going down an avenue called Sycamore. Expensive plots with perpetual endowment and the smell of money all around us. The limos are slowing down. Somebody or other is whispering about my trust. All that money. Eternal care. Stained-glass windows with a touch of Art Nouveau here and there. They said the court wouldn't allow it. But I see it rising in the distance. Guess the neighbors haven't complained. Winding farther into the necropolis with a protracted hum. Engines straining up the hill. Past Posy Lane, and a little Greek Revival temple biding its time. We're by Petunia, then over Rose, and crisscrossing Marigold. Finally, we proceed to Brambletree Circle. Doors are opening, with women looking a bit pale. There are huffs and puffs from the pallbearers about my being on the level for at least one time. As a breeze makes itself evident, we proceed over the turf to a little lane that's called Camelia. The wind is whipping up, and whistling through the trees. A cold gust commandingly blows up wrinkled pant legs and see-through panties. Crevassed old women I only vaguely remember knowing are clutching their coats and jackets. People are saying things about me. A eulogy here and a eulogy there. It seems I've been a pillar of society. A person of sustenance to the Church, a dynamo of industry. And a lot of other hogwash and claptrap. Someone is saying I was a good guy in spite of it all. Sheer nerve. Nincompoopsical folderol! And now they file one by one beside me, as I lie in the entrance to this new habitation. And then as I'm being showered with flowers and sprigs of this and that, it dawns on me. They're going to leave me here. And I shall be alone.

The ceremony is finished, and they are now quietly walking away.

"Hey, all you people! Come back! Don't leave me so soon! No fair, no fair!" I want to scream and be heard. "I don't want to be dead anymore. Cut out the game! Hey, hey!" And I whistle and grimace, and scream in every known contortion, as I almost burst my nonexistent lungs. But even that explosion would be welcome in this world which is devoid of the satisfaction which physical limitations impose. Finding all other measures inadequate, I weep.

Back into the cars with haste now. The limos are really revving it up. They want to get away from me. Harriet always said she'd eventually be free. All of it is something of a bad joke on me. And for the first time, there's nothing to be done. There's no one I can call. There's no pressure I can apply. No mechanism of power to be wielded. All I can do is return to my newfound crib to cry bitterly for having been left behind.

From the positive angle, the sun is at least shining. Maybe this isn't so bad after all. I'll take a little walk and admire the edifice I had them build. Stone. Solid and perpetual. I'm proudly regarding the glass windows I brought from France. In the one a virgin weeps bitterly. Through another pane children sing a small, mute song. Impressive, to say the least. No stonecutters like my stonecutters. They hummed as they worked, their pockets replete with fresh banknotes I gave them. And you can tell. Just look at the building. A little line that begins as a wisp at the foot of the stiff bronze door curves narcissistically upon itself. Somewhere above a window, it blossoms into a full wisteria frozen in stone, and dwells upon itself, as a strangely supple butterfly poses on the bloom. Too bad the butterfly is stone.

The doors to this place are wonderful too. I held a contest like the one they had in Florence for the baptistery doors. Mind you, while they marginally pale to Ghiberti's effort, they have nothing to be ashamed of. There are scenes from my childhood on the panels of these doors. And they shine and glow in the light as if they were the gates to heaven itself. My temple sits on one of the largest plots in the whole place. It's beautifully planted in the English style, with a bench here and there under the willows and evergreens.

All excitement past, I roam. Over to Marigold Lane to look with marvel at the twin obelisks some resourceful soul had erected to his memory. Past the new, the old, the slightly weathered, to the massive gate. I wonder when I again read that *The Dead Shall Be Risen*, Is it true? Will I live another day reincarnated into the body of an Australian rugby player, or an Indian street urchin? Or perhaps a chicken or toad? I must admit to very little thought on such matters while I lived.

Back to interminable, cyclical paths. A beautiful city of death. Thistle bushes and boxwoods. Evergreens jutting into the sky, pinching a cloud or two in the rear. Hedges nicely trimmed. And holly. But there are no Christmas jingles here. No laughter. Just tough green bushes and a pale blue sky. I see a great big tower made of stone. It must be at least six or seven stories high. I guess they use it

as a guard's watch to secure the perimeter and make sure some vagrant brigand doesn't abscond with a trifle of stained glass, or priceless statuary. Why, they probably use machine guns in this place.
Reminds me of my childhood. I can almost see Rapunzel up there.
Golden hair shining in the light as the lover climbed her tress. But
no golden gleam of hair here. Just more stones.

I want to remove myself from this place where I can't even find
a dead person. I'll just have to tear myself out of this rut. Maybe it's
like when I woke up and wanted to move my arm. I mean, woke
down. I don't know what I mean. Anyway, I've got to do something
before it becomes dark and I get caught here with all these creepy
stiffs. I guess that wasn't nice, but I'm beginning to feel frightened.

As the light begins to wane, I first attempt to go through the
gate, and then to jump the walls, but find I can't. Some invisible,
mysterious force completely impedes my egress. Try though I may,
I am unable to leave the necropolis. I'm crying again. Maybe this will
help. . . . But it's not any good. It's very much like the bad feeling I
experienced as a child when I was homesick or remorseful. With a
funny metallic smell and feeling in my front teeth.

A moist velvety night is now falling rather quickly. There's a
blackish blueness to the sky. Nary a sound in this forgotten corner
of a larger world. Just solitude and quiet horror. I try to entertain
myself by walking to the limits of this little universe and watching
the headlights of cars zoom by. But I note with sadness that the
people in them aren't looking my way. On the contrary, they don't
even want to glance at this place. Unwanted, and unloved, the dead
weep silently in their tombs.

Somewhere in the nearby greenery something has stirred.
There's a rustling of dry ivy. A sound. Maybe it'll go away if I start
walking. No, it's still with me. I'm definitely being followed. Strange
that I should be afraid at this stage of affairs. So I promptly walk up
Brambletree and into Camelia to secure the solace of my tomb. I
crouch low and grab onto my bronze door. I wait, and as the rustling
increases, I hear a whimper. Someone is crying. My God, it's an
apparition!

No such thing. Just one hundred and seventy pounds of dogflesh.
Customarily docile. He saunters up. I shout, "Bozo." Nothing hap-

pens. I cry out again, this time more slowly. One gigantic ear perks up. I think he can hear me. I try once more, and then with one dexterous gesture Bozo curls his upper lip, and smiles. Before I bought him, I didn't really think dogs could smile. But quite early, Bozo developed that peculiar habit of curling his upper lip. The dog knows I'm here. He moves toward me and licks my nonexistent face. For the life of me, I can't quite figure out how he got here. The poor fellow must have walked all day. Thank you, Lord. Wherever you are.

Still wearing the stud collar I had engraved with his name, he is imposing. A small horse of a dog. Shaggy soft gray fur. Big enough to crack a coyote's skull in one pass. Gentle as a lamb, though. I know Bozo loves me. Not just because I took care of him when Harriet hated him, and not even because I saved him from the vet when he chewed on Harriet's alligator handbags. I kept him above and beyond marital dissent. But I never thought we would end up here together in the chill of the night.

Bozo is a leaner. That is to say, whenever danger insinuates itself, he is liable to come near and lean on you, interposing himself between you and the dangerous situation. This is what he's doing now, right beside me, dispelling the terror of the night. He's come to care. Anubislike, with ears erect at any sound, as wide-eyed hounds once did for Pharaoh kings.

The moon is now rising, and Bozo is distracted by the flight of an occasional bat. Clouds come and go over the brightness of the disk, and I can't help making faces and things out of them. On the horizon a bit of an electrical storm stirs and variegates. Since Bozo is afraid only of lightning, we huddle together under the canopy in front of my memorial. I wonder about the foundations of the universe. And think that perhaps now I'll have the chance to determine whether in fact the whole mess is holographic. By this I mean that everything we see might just be a reflection of a hologram with all its dots in a pattern which does not antecede the past to the present, or the present to the future. And where by gaining access to that matrix, one might gain access to All Time. But perhaps I should strike these thoughts from my mind, and take hold of myself. I can't rid myself of fear, but I can certainly marshal it. And at least for now, even though I know nothing is certain, and I'm frightened there may be no morn, I have this dog.

It's been a long and terrible night here waiting for the unknown. It must be six-thirty or so in the morning. Usually I was in bed at this time, but I must confess there are some very nifty things about the look of this hour. The few remaining fireflies have long died down. I guess the fall chill is killing them off. We're at that stage of the predawn in which the moon is still visible, but the light is beginning to insinuate itself on the horizon. Birds are beginning to chirp, and the mist over the graves seems less phantasmagoric and frightening than it was during the night. There are also little rustlings among the leaves as squirrels begin their daily task of putting things away for the winter. Pushy little fellows. I think they can see me. Bozo is lapping up some water which has accumulated in an empty font in front of a massive rococo tomb nearby. I can't help noticing the epitaphs on the various graves. Some of them give you a real chuckle: "Here lies Ida, nasty as hell and mean nonpareil. She said she'd take her husband with her, and she did."

When I chose mine, I was simple about it. Faithful to my Spanish heritage, I said, *La vida es un estado de mente*, which is to say *Life is a state of mind*. But in Spanish if you just play with those words a little they can also mean that life is demented. After all, what does "demented" mean but "out of mind"? I'm becoming a little worried about not being able to feed Bozo. I wish he'd return home. But my fuzzy behemoth doesn't seem to be going anywhere. He has a sorrowful look on his face, and yet, whenever he's really physically near me, he seems to glow with an intense happiness. No other way to cheer him up, though. In the old days, a couple of lamb chops would do the trick. I'm sure he's hungry, but I don't know what to do about it.

The increased activity of the morning includes the arrival of gardeners, who are scurrying around keeping it all neat. In the distance we hear a hum. Bozo crouches beside me protectively. For a while I watch a lawn mower going over the grass, which is beginning to assume fall tones. There's something about the smell of freshly cut blades coupled with the wetness of the morning dew that brings back many memories of my childhood. Actually, I've always thought our sense of smell was one of the most wondrous ways of transporting us back to key moments in our lives. Who could ever forget the aroma of Mother's fresh pancakes on Sunday morning? Or the scent of maple syrup boiling. How could one forget the fearsome odor of the freshly mopped halls at school on that first morning of the year? The comfort of one's own pillow . . . or the fragrance of peonies ebbing in the breeze. Not to mention the presence of fresh male sweat in a locker room. Or the perfume of a young, pink pudendum. Yes indeed, smell is a direct ticket to memory without any of the interference which is caused by standard mental processes. And that grass is reminding me of mornings as a child when I'd wake up to the whir of the lawn mower outside on schoolless summer days.

They're using the hedgecutters now. But no need to groom the Somerset memorial. Everything here is fresh. Manicured for the party. Carefully tended, boxwood and yew hedges testify to the solidity of perpetual trusts. I told them it would all go to my alma mater and the Hospice for Unwed Mothers if the will was challenged. As well as to the Society for the Prevention of Cruelty to Animals, Humans excepted. But even so, I'm quite sure I haven't heard the last from grasping relatives. Ugh. The sun has begun its daily journey, reminding me of the Hymn of Ra. Perhaps in another existence I was an Egyptian priest measuring the rising of the Nile and ministering to a world rich in gods and the expectation of eternal life. Come to think of it, though, nothing has happened yet to challenge or confirm my previous conviction of eternity. So it would seem I must now forcefully continue unraveling the thread of destiny until I reach my final place. As in life, however, I have no desire to hasten such otherworldly quietus. I might have some fun if I could only leave this lonely cemetery.

Bozo is becoming restless, and I note the perking of a gargantuan ear. There is a large black car winding its way up the little roads. Maybe someone is coming to visit me. With the anticipation of a child expecting Santa Claus, I center all attention on the vehicle, which is steadily moving toward us. It's a big, black mother of a conveyance. Impressive set of wheels. Imported. Expensive. Looks like it has all of the necessary toys and gadgets. After all, men never grow up, they just seek more expensive pastimes. It's stopping in front of a canopied area where a new tomb is being erected. The chauffeur is snapping out to open a heavy door. We witness the emergence of a figure. Tall, lean, straight. He's wearing a navy-blue suit. Italian, but nice. He's a dignified sort of a guy. Gloves, but no hat. Longish fringe of hair protruding. So he's walking up Willow Lane to the plot that is canvased off for building. I have to confess I took a peek yesterday. It's in rather good taste. Not as nice as mine, but nevertheless excellent. Sort of a pristine look. From the inscription on one of the two empty vaults, it would seem it will shortly be the repository of a woman who died some eight years ago. So, he's a widower. In Egyptian days, he would have been the burden of half a dozen slaves carrying him to supervise the workings of his tomb. But now it's only one man standing six feet tall. Erect with serious expression. Strikingly alone.

Bozo is stirring unusually. A little wind whips up, and the handkerchief the man had been using to clean the condensation off his dark glasses has been carried away to the limits of my plot. Bozo is out like a flash. Pouncing on it as the turf rips under his weight. He gently grabs the hankie, and returns it, barely slobbered, to the perplexed-looking man. At first, this fellow is taken aback by the sheer size of the dog. But it must have dawned on him that this is no pedestrian pooch. So with a bit of trepidation, he pats him on the head and wonders where he's from. Bozo quickly returns to me. He's leaning now. The man follows. Up the massive carved steps to the front of my edifice. Admiring glance. This guy's no yokel. Fingers running over my carving in a lustfully covetous manner. He's smiling, and placing his index finger against his nose in a coy way. A closer look reveals a man of about forty years of age. He's got a good angular face with a straight nose and salient cheekbones. Reliable chin. There's a good bit of gray around those temples. And a pair of wonderfully spaced eyes. Why, it's an interocular distance that would give new meaning to the ancient Egyptian depiction of the Sacred eyes. A "double udjat," no less. But these pupils, large and well spaced though they may be, are giving off in their very blue depth a feeling of the tragic sadness of life. The man is sitting on my steps while a discreet chauffeur looks the other way. There's a tear coming down there. Very gingerly, old Bozo sashays up and slaps a big, wet tongue across his face. And then does it again until he looks up and gives the superdog a suspicion of a smile. Now grabbing the collar as he pulls from his pocket an exquisite and tiny pair of folding glasses. He's reading from the twenty-two-karat-gold marker on the collar, and I think he's just noticed that the studs on it are also wondrously solid.

It reads, "My name is Bozo. If lost please call 799-3333." The fellow seems to have relaxed again and is smiling. Again resting his index finger against the side of his nose in that rather peculiar gesture. Then Bozo lifts his upper lip and gives him the hound smile, and he starts laughing as if he might split his sides. I'm sure they could be friends. He's going back to the car and retrieving a little brown bag. I guess he had planned on having a snack here while he oversaw the details of his memorial. But all four pieces of the sandwich are quickly finding their way into the mouth of my hungry creature.

The man has kept a bit of bread with which to coax the monster to the car, and Bozo begins to follow. For a moment, I almost catch myself screaming, "Hey, come back," but then I realize the extreme selfishness of the gesture. In spite of the fact that I don't wish to be left alone. Nevertheless, Bozo can't be coaxed into the car. Try though he may, this fellow can't get him into the limo. Bozo is just running back and forth between the car and me. Trying to convey a message or something. If I don't force him to leave with this guy, the dog is going to starve to death. So I start screaming, "Go, go . . . go away," but he won't. He comes and pulls at nonexistent me as if to enlist company. By now I'm bereft with tears and anguish, and feeling extremely confused. But the dog is just not giving up, and the man is looking at all these goings-on in a very questioning fashion.

As Bozo returns to me again and again, I have the distinct feeling his canine will is rapidly eroding my own. Last night's experience taught me that the land beyond the gates is barred. In spite of this, if I don't get into that car, the dog isn't leaving, and one new dead creature around here is enough. So I'll go along with the gag for now. Into the limo. Plush leather seats. Dog and I, and our man. As the hum of the car's engine reverberates in my mind I begin feeling terrified and tremendously disoriented. Mainly because I don't really wish to be left behind. We're going down a few short lanes which seemed quite long before. I haven't prayed yet in all this mess, but I'm inclined to do it right now. And I'm asking God to make these moments as long as possible before I'm shut into the cemetery again.

"Don't take it all away so quickly, please. Make the gate be far away." We roll rhythmically by laurel trees and boxwood hedges. Down lanes full of pines, beeches, oaks, and willows. We're approaching the foreboding gate. Those Egyptian columns are now strangely friendly. We roll through to the nod of an attendant in tight blue serge trousers, snapping to attention. Beneath the great inscription. Like just another camel going through the eye of another needle.

TWO

To say the least, I'm enthralled by this most recent develop-ment. For a while there, I was thinking I was going to be shut up within the cemetery walls for the rest of my immortal existence. As we approached the gate, I almost expected some wrathful hand like a jabberwocky out of hell to reach down and pull me back. But no such thing has happened. As the distance between the gate and the car increases, I begin to feel there may be a method to this exercise. I should, however, make clear that during my life, I did not manage to glean much of a meaning from anything. In fact, it was my thought that mankind is a failed experiment.

When you think of it in terms of geologic time, the advanced primates have been here in excess of forty million years. And that's just a drop in the bucket when you regard the myriad species that preceded them. Descended as we are from a tough little ratlike mam-mal, it's no wonder we spoil and damage everything we touch. Yes indeed, no redeeming value. And I further assert it's the insects, and not man, that will fully dominate the planet Earth. If the truth be known, the ants and bees deserve to inherit the prize. When you think about it, the Hymenoptera have been here since Cretaceous times, spanning at least a hundred million years. And through those millennia, they've comfortably lived an advanced existence with their nifty eusocial habits. Which means to say that two or more generations overlap, with the daddies and the mommies taking care of the young, and more important, that the adults are divided into reproductive and nonreproductive castes. Considering the way they work, I think they justly deserve to control the orb. But here we are approaching the city and all I can think about is social insects.

Our man has receded quietly into the leather seat. He's stroking Bozo's head. The dog really eats it up. This gives me a little time to think. I know that up to the time this fellow arrived on the scene, I wasn't able to transcend the cemetery walls. Some invisible power or disposition kept me within them. Since I haven't met any other dead people, I must assume I'm in a dimension all of my own, and I'm beginning to think some of the rules are distinctly personal. If this is the case, somewhere, there must be a timekeeper or board of directors deciding what will become of me.

In any event, there must be something very special about this fellow who's come to oversee his tomb, since my dog likes him so very much. I'm certain I've not met him before, but his face is vaguely familiar, so I might have seen him in pictures or something. He's an attractive sort, and I must confess I feel strangely drawn toward him. But what is the secret which brings all of this about and keeps me here? I can't help thinking it may be fraught with great difficulty or impossibility, like Kafka's message from the Emperor of China. Given to the lowliest of the low, whispered into his ear for him to take to the farthest corner of the empire, if only with his celerity he could ever finally traverse the infinite palace, or the interminable city. And all of this, in my case, with the added conundrum of not even knowing the secret, but merely suspecting it. In any event, this whole business of an afterlife is rather confusing. It is hardly what I'd imagined, and furthermore, not remotely like what I was promised. True to form, I was always skeptical about heaven, and I don't now see anything that remotely reminds me of my previous conception of it. There are no angels, harps, or puffy clouds here. No trials or stern elders to scold me for a life of self-indulgence. And definitely no other children to play with. All of these thoughts are interrupted by Bozo, who has decided to lick my face. Our host, who definitely cannot see me, must think the pooch is merely slurping up a gnat.

Here we are attacking the midmorn. Fleeting through town in a polished tank. I've always liked these cars. Big, hard, and armored. To put a barrier between us and the grimy crowd. People always said I was reclusive. They were right. But mine wasn't the desire for exclusivity based on money, position, or birth. Rather, I sought to separate myself from the disgusting without merit. From poverty of spirit without redeeming value, and the brainless antics of our chewing-gum, planned-obsolescence, media-loving, sensationalistic society.

Taking those traits one at a time, I've always hated people who chew gum. I sustained the impression it was a form of masturbation. In defense of them, I should note that such self-sex is highly personal and everyone should be entitled to do it in his or her own way. This should not, however, be taken to mean that I should be forced to tolerate the remnants of such masturbation on my antelope shoes.

Regarding obsolescence, my opinions were always kept private. After all, you can't manufacture spark plugs, plastic bags, and paper towels and tell people you despise a society where everything breaks, and in which everything is thrown away.

My opinions regarding the television were equally, and of necessity, hidden beyond the ears of the public, since I owned several transmitting stations. In point of fact, I always felt the television was an infernal, mind-absorbing device, designed to mire humanity in the cretinous mush of prepackaged situation comedies and polarized news.

As for the sensationalistic, it's one of my primary reasons for believing the human race is a totally failed effort. Why, you take your normal, civilized reader or listener, and he's totally bored by a nicety, or by an act of charity. But show him a face, preferably lovelier than his, torn apart by shrapnel, or a baby devoured by pigs, or the effects of your garden-variety thermonuclear device on children of twelve, and you then have the essence of a highly rated news program. Yes indeed, most people think the viewers watch boxing matches and hockey games for the thrill of seeing the team win. But there's another reality which exists at only a slightly more profound level. People are always hoping to see someone's brains spilled on the mat. Or a really ruthless fight between the hockey players. Similarly, when most people go to the circus, they're not hoping to see the trapeze artist successfully complete the exhibition. On the contrary, it's the element of danger which is attractive. Bullfights are the best for this. Almost everyone likes to see the matador receive a good goring in the intestine. When that happens, they usually cheer as if a goal had been scored at a football game. Movies themselves satisfy the natural and inescapable human desire for violence. We are a brutal, bellicose, and usually uncontrollable species. And we have a definite thirst for blood. People prefer death, blood, gore, pillage, disaster, famine, and torture to the imagined celestial virtues. So I learned early that "good" didn't sell, and proceeded to give them exactly what I thought they wanted.

Our man seems to be coming out of his quiescent mode. He looks secure. As if some gear has just been engaged within that brain. He picks up the telephone with one hand and grabs Bozo by the collar with the other. He's dialing my office number. Actually calling the company. *Die Firma.* He's notifying them he's got Bozo. Telling them he wants to return the pooch. I really don't like this idea at all.

"Hello, is this Mr. Somerset's office? . . . Please, yes, miss, I know he's not available. . . . But I seem to have come across his dog, and want to know where to return him."

They've asked him for his name, and he's identified himself as E. C. Douglas. They've put him on hold. I can imagine the little receptionist calling my secretary, who is probably trying to get through to Harriet right now. Well, they've come back on the line, and now it really is my secretary. The wonderful Susan Cleave. She's giving him instructions on how to return Bozo. Apparently indicating he's to bring him at four o'clock. But our man is telling them he can't wait that long. After some negotiation, they have agreed on two o'clock. "Click" goes the connection to my office. I'm extremely peeved at this business of telling him I'm "not available." What a way to put it. Bitches and bastards all of them. I was the ultimate provider, and now that I'm gone, that bit of claptrap is the best they can invent. They haven't even afforded me the dignity of remembrance in death. I know what it is. They're all afraid to say I'm dead because of the imagined financial consequences. Right now I feel like properly taking revenge. For every extra coffee break, proof error, lazy mistake, and act of petty theft. •

Back to the phone, it seems our man got something wrong in his instructions, so he's calling again. This time they put him directly through to Miss Cleave, and I've decided to eavesdrop. A beautiful deep voice. I could never forget the sound of it. He's going over his directions to the office. But Cleave is telling him now that she's glad he called because there's been a change of plans and Bozo is to be delivered at home to Harriet. She's also asking him how he ran across the dog, and he responds by reminding her that his name is E. C. Douglas, and "well, I was attending to some business at the cemetery this morning when, how should I say . . . I encountered Mr. Somerset's dog. Uh, I know how important Mr. Somerset was, and I thought someone might be relieved to know Bozo, I mean the dog, has been found."

She's telling him how pleased she is, and he's responding, "Well, that's very kind of you. I will return him at two, and incidentally, my telephone number is . . ." He provides her with a number and says, "Yes, thank you, I think it's a nice number too. Goodbye." Click.

There's a powdery look in those big blue eyes. This guy's a schemer. I can tell. I think when she heard his name she told him he was on one of my Rolodexes. Hah! If only he knew. I used to keep lists to hit people for charity, and for other more important reasons as well. I had catalogs of the powerful and the useful. Of kinship in wealth. This fellow is wealthy too. But not as rich as I was.

The car is stopping at a corner, and our man is lowering his window and motioning to an urchin selling a bit of newsprint. I truly despise the press. The window is rising again as the transaction is completed. Ignoring the news section, our man turns to finance. A quick look at the market quotes and his face begins to exhibit an almost imperceptible little smile. Yes, that index finger is again right up against his nose. He's pleased. Bozo takes the cue and slobbers all over that particular page of the paper. E.C. flips the page without a second's pause, and here is a headline to catch his eye, and mine as well:

H. W. SOMERSET IS DEAD AT 52

Noted personages of the financial world convened yesterday at Sleepy Heights Cemetery for the funeral of Henry Waldo Somerset, financier. Mr. Somerset was born in a small Pennsylvania mining town to an American father and a

Spanish mother in 1944. At the age of twelve, he is reported to have founded his own newsstand. In later years, he relocated himself and his family to the more affluent River section of this city. In the fall of 1960, his parents were victims of a fatal fire. In subsequent years, Mr. Somerset's reclusive and eccentric tendencies were partially attributed to this tragedy.

At the age of seventeen he was accepted to City University. Prior to his graduation, he inherited a property which gave him a fortuitous beginning in the oil industry. Upon graduating with honors, he became a trainee with International Consolidated Banks. His rise to success at Consolidated was swift. Subsequent to a proxy war, he became chairman of the board of the organization in 1973. He was chairman of the board of Somerset Consolidated Industries, which later obtained control of major European steel companies through Siderurgica Internazionale, S.p.a., the Liechtenstein holding company, after what was termed one of the most acrimonious battles in European financial history.

While Mr. Somerset owned controlling interests in forty-three other multinational companies and organizations, he was not an officer or member of the board of any of them. Mr. Somerset was noted for his idiosyncrasies and eccentricities. Rumor had it that a noteworthy one consisted of making large cash gifts to previously unknown parties. Mr. Somerset was also a respected musician, art collector, and connoisseur. His brief volume on the porcelains of the Sung Dynasty is said by many to be the most complete and finest work of its kind yet written.

On the lighter side, he would often attend art openings in unorthodox costume. Broad comment was elicited in public circles by his wearing of platinum roller skates to the opening of the Eastern Modern Art Association's newest building, which he is said to have endowed.

Mr. Somerset's private life was surrounded by rumor and cloaked in silence and reclusiveness. Important messages were often relayed by his assistants and other powerful members of his organization. At the time of his death, Mr.

Somerset had recently completed the construction of a residential edifice in which to house his vast art collection. The building, in the shape of a modified pyramid, and the surrounding botanical garden are said by knowledgeable parties to represent the most expensive construction per square foot ever undertaken in this country.

A spokesman for the family today confirmed rumors the pyramid will be sold to offset inheritance taxes. Speculation exists as to whether or not it will be auctioned to the city as a sole bidder, since it is believed a private purchaser might not be able to marshal the substantial price.

The Somerset fortune was conservatively estimated to be one of the nation's top two at the time of its owner's demise. Wide speculation exists regarding rumors pertaining to the ultimate disposition of the estate. Attorneys from Mr. Somerset's alma mater have indicated a substantial portion of the estate will benefit that institution. Reliable information would indicate this action may be contested by the family. Mr. Somerset was married to Harriet A. Weatherbee of Beacon Hill, Boston. He is also survived by the son of his deceased sister, Gustavo Somerset, from whom he is said to have been estranged.

I'm genuinely upset with this development.

"Down with the paper! Arghh . . . Bozo, rip that thing apart."

With a swift movement of his gigantic jaw, Bozo grabs furiously at the newsprint. Douglas saves it by quickly recoiling and petting the pooch.

"Selling my pyramid! Can you imagine that? Calling it expensive! Crass understatement of fact." I knew she'd do it. That's why I fixed it so the university would get a big share. Nothing for my nephew, though. He's a bigoted, perverted little prick. Literally and figuratively. But I'm sorry to say that bitch Harriet controls ten times more wealth today than she did yesterday.

Thoughts are racing through my mind. One thing is for sure— I'm going to have to take some action here.

Our man Douglas is pensive. I become more serene and start gearing down. I begin thinking an occasional and inconsequential thought. Like how this car must look like just another beetle crawling around from twenty stories up. That's what we are, all of us. Wingless bugs of the bottom of the air.

The car is slowing down and we're approaching a very fine-looking and expensive apartment house. Residence of E. C. Douglas. At the door, there is a smiling liveried attendant. Douglas is looking condescending. The chauffeur is gently grabbing Bozo's collar as only the best-appointed attendants can. After all, they can't ever risk bruising the family bow-wow. We're through the door into a foyer. It's a very pleasant room with a marvelously patterned marble floor which seems to be radiating from its central compass rose in tones of green, red, white, brown, and black. There are two very large Chinese urns in front of the entrance to the sitting room. One of the downstairs attendants is muttering something to our man about being in service twenty years today. Congratulations from E. C. Douglas. And a bank note for good measure. I perceive this was no ordinary gesture. There was practice in the way he peeled that note off the pile. Considerable roll and good form. I should know. Before I lost my body, I was awfully good at it. I even thought I became expert at making a sort of musically percussive sound, as one picture rubbed across another, and said a sad goodbye to his best friend. This building also has an elevator. The lift door opens into another little foyer with an unassuming entrance at the end of it. Good geometric Persian carpets. I always did like a fine Heriz. Fresh flowers. Shasta daisies. Nice, but I must introduce our man to orchids, peonies, and tiger lilies. I always preferred flowers that looked like they were ready to take a bite out of miscellaneous butterflies and incidental interlopers. Or nice philodendrons with strangulating tendrils alert in the night. In this respect, it was always my daydream to come home and find Harriet had been neatly ingested by the *Protea gigantea*.

This is actually a very comfortable room. E.C. has just interrupted Bozo's sniffing affair with a particularly seductive table leg. I do, however, agree with the dog. There are nice smells in this place. Good antiques and a touch of porcelain. But not the greatest stuff. He'll learn. There are, however, some proper carpets, and a few excellent paintings. Postimpressionists. Something will have to be done to introduce him to Dutch and Italian masters. From the upstairs parlor I follow him into the library. Today's mail is nicely set out on top of a large Victorian desk. Someone has placed the most shocking pieces at the bottom to save wear and tear on our man's nerves. His hand reaches out to a preknown spot and grabs for a decanter, which from the aroma is full of the real old stuff. First-rate whiskey. I once bought a Scottish castle just because I wanted the thirty thousand crocks in the basement. The glass is brought to his lips as if to be gulped down in one swallow, but the patience of the moment is interrupted by a calamitous scream about the end of the world in a nearby quarter. Ohmigod. Bozo squarely on top of a roundish, shouting woman in apron and cap. She's vigorously squealing that the end of the world has come, and that the spirits have finally been unleashed to repay us for our sins. There are exclamations about death by drowning as Bozo slaps a wet tongue across a wrinkled, panic-stricken face. The woman is saying *ay, ay, ay,* and going on about judgment and repentance in a Spanish accent as she opens her eyes to again find the doggie on her lap.

"What the hell . . ." says our man, slamming his glass on the desk.

Bad form, spilling all that whiskey. I actually thought he had more cool. E.C. is bounding through the door in the direction of the noise, as I demurely tiptoe through the wall. And here it is before us. Bozo playfully ripping off her thin cotton dress. Now E.C. is screaming, or at least raising his voice. With all these people screeching, it's just like the old days at the opera house.

E.C. is saying, "Consuelo, leave that poor dog alone."

And she's responding, "It is *un monstruo*, meester, it is *un monstruo*, meester. I queet. It is the anger of the Lord for all thees sin."

"Consuelo, stop babbling nonsense."

"But meester, please get him off."

"Consuelo, I demand that you immediately compose yourself."

"Sheet, meester, thees beast has me almost neked."

"Consuelo, put your dress on this very minute, and watch your language."

We hear "Meester, help," as she rolls into the reading lamp. Dog and housekeeper are now fully entangled. The maid is extricating herself from the grip. Running down the stairs to the kitchen. Returning as one, seminaked, splendor of revenge. A two-hundred-pound Diana emerges, breasts swaying, hips full, with the bang of a cast-iron frying pan in hand. The dog is bounding, with a last bit of not-so-great porcelain lost in the fracas. The beast has cowered into the corner to lick his little battle wounds, looking in awe at Consuelo. As if she were something good to eat. I agree, having on previous occasions partaken of a Rubenesque beauty or two. Somewhat intimidated by this rowdy scene, our man stomps out, leaving two hundred pounds of female to deal with the matter. I remain for a moment to watch.

I've always thought that *a house without a woman is not a house.* Consuelo constitutes a benign presence and has now returned to the kitchen, with dog in tow. She's honey-colored. About forty-five. Solid. Built for comfort. She sings as the pots go "gluk, gluk," and as a drop from the spigot goes "plink." Barrel-like waist with an apron neatly tied. Starched. Delicate, though. A touch of embroidery here and there. Big tough arms and hands. Powerful. She must be from somewhere in South America. With a slightly Indian face and the hair braided and tied up. Actually, the way her mouth turns up at the edges is rather jovial. She's strong as well. You get the impression she could handle a refrigerator with the flick of a wrist. I had a maid like that once. When I was a student. I remember she was imposing at two hundred and forty pounds of Nordic Splendor. I once tried to move an appliance, but was cast aside as she beat her chest and informed me she was much stronger than I. I'll never forget the day she took all my condoms and ordered them neatly in a row in one of my drawers. I crimsoned for a month. Till things got cozy. And I secured the solace of those very comfortable hips for the duration of that long, cold winter.

This present girl reminds me of her. In the kitchen, pans glitter, and silver gleams as if the elves have been at it all night. Polishing, shining, scrubbing. If anything, everything here is clean. Funny I notice all these things now. As I recall, my kitchen was full of expensive gadgets. All of that equipment from those mail-order houses and cookery shops. Most of it was stuff I bought on the spur of the moment. But in my case, impulse was not to be underrated. After all, it took a concerted effort to purchase that much junk. Into the shops I'd go, bank notes in hand, to buy a Malaysian diddlidoo, or an Australian thiggledibob. I was usually depressed when I went shopping that way. I remember on those days I'd come home from the office early. Usually after a great success or a great defeat. I'd be alone, and know it. Then I'd go out to blow a thousand or two, or ten. First there was the furniture. Several city houses full of it. And the farm, country estate, and beach house. There were corporate suites. Replete. Full of original whoozywhatsits, and signed whatchamacallits. Then there were the collections, including the coins I bought from those silver-hoarding brothers, and the rare books and maps. There were porcelains, and Fabergé, and lots of everything else.

Back to Consuelo. I again take note of the bun. There's something lovely and demure about a middle-aged woman's chignon. A nice, neat little bundle at the back of the head. A gentle touch. Gleaming black. She's singing something in Spanish about it "being better to sing than to cry." As the head of my monster materializes by pushing ajar the swinging door. For a second, woman and dog are nailed in one intent stare. All of a sudden a resolute hand finds its way to a stupendous bone of beef. No fair, my dear. That thing could conjure any mutt on the globe. Especially one as hungry as Bozo. And so, I leave the scene as woman and dog make friends. And the pooch is entrapped in the repetition of an age-old story.

I've been wandering around casing the silver. There's a good deal of Paul Storr here. And to be sure, that's good enough. But if I were in charge of his education he'd have a lot of Lamerie as well. He owns a particularly nice Monteith bowl, and the soup tureens are actually hot shit. Our man is sitting in a corner of the room in a rather pleasant needlepoint wing chair. There's music here. A Haydn quartet played by an Eastern European group. At last, civilization. Bozo tromps in, and dog and man stare at one another for a while. The man gets a tear in the corner of his eye. Inexplicably. And grabs for the gray, woolly mop firmly growing on top of Bozo's head. The dog plops down at our man's feet and closes his eyes. After a brief hiatus, I then notice that dog and man have fallen asleep. This little interlude is going to give me a chance to case the joint further. I should really say the apartment. I always liked to look into the houses of the rich. Makes me feel superior with my malachite bathrooms and occasional lapis lazuli bidets. As far as I'm concerned, my bidets were every bit as nice as the Maharani of Baroda's. True, rumors did seep in about Oriental nabobs having diamond-studded ones, and I even went so far as to commission a platinum commode. But found it cold on wintery nights.

He has a music room. It's enormous. I can float around in here unimpeded. Playing with the crystal chandelier. French. Valuable. The thing makes tinkly sounds if I go through swiftly. Hey . . . I'll try that again. I really did make a noise. This is truly remarkable. Here I thought I couldn't move things and now I'm finding I'm capable of making physical objects stir. It's a milestone in this new life. Besides, this is a lot of fun. Bang, boom, crash! As my effusive newfound power becomes evident, and the black marble floor is littered with broken glass. No matter. The mess was worth the effort. Later, I hope I will have ample use for such talents. Thank heaven Douglas didn't wake. Aha, there's also a piano here. Actually, two of them back to back. Fine German instruments, the ones with the extra keys. This fellow is obviously musical. I used to play "Chopsticks" on lonely nights, and learned to play "Für Elise" for Harriet. I'd also sneak a tune or two by ear. But look at this music. He really must be a virtuoso. Lots of notes here. Why, there are Mozart and Beethoven sonatas, and piano concertos. On the other side of the room he actually has an organ. A big, powerful-looking thing with a triple keyboard. I must be mixed up with a real music kook. Don't get me wrong. I believe in music. I've been known to listen to a string quartet or two in the evening hours. But Douglas has piles and piles of the stuff, hundreds of volumes, all neatly filed by authors. I mean composers. And all in rich bindings.

Back to this new and wonderful bit about being able to move physical objects. I'm like a child out of a cage. It's a real thrill. At first I couldn't even move myself, and now I can make all this glass tinkle. Maybe I can get this guy to even hear or feel me, without scaring him out of his wits. After all, I think I'm a presentable and friendly ghost. Except this fellow Douglas will probably think I'm some kind of ghoul. I could pull the supernatural bit and try to convince him I'm a spirit of light. A guardian angel, no less. Not a bad idea.

Through the wall like a pro, I resolutely approach E.C., who is now snoring a bit. What shall I try? What if I do something trite like hum a few bars of Beethoven's Fifth in his ear and see if I get a rise? Wow! He's jumped out of that piece of furniture like a bat out of hell. Back into the chair, he's shivering and shaking a bit. I think I'll do it again. But I'm not obtaining the same response. I wait for him to again fall asleep to repeat this little exercise, this time with a bit of Wagner. I was always fond of *Götterdämmerung*. Douglas rises and runs straight into the wall. Hair on end. And I just can't contain myself. I haven't had so much fun since my boys dynamited some meaningful railroad trestles, while I sipped wine from a cooler and watched it all go up in the distance. That was during my transportation craze. Douglas is dialing frantically for Dr. Curewhatever. Consuelo has just run in, rosary in hand, and is genuflecting wildly as she recites what sounds like a nervous prayer in Spanish with interspersed references to the chandelier. And now Bozo, who was always fond of Wagner, has decided to chip in with a long, sad howl. I'm still humming, but I have unfortunately confirmed that the trick only seems to work when he is asleep. This, however, indicates his greater receptivity at such times, which will be useful at a later date.

Consuelo's agitated state returns her with trepidation to the music room to clean up the mess. She's taken the phalanges of both hands and curled the heart and ring fingers, and is making a hex sign with the index and pinkie. I guess she thinks the house is possessed by some sort of devil. She's muttering something to herself about bringing in a spiritualist priest to exorcise me from the place. Every time she begins doing something she quickly turns around and gives the room that forked hex sign.

Our man has collected himself and has now decided to attribute the phenomenon to seismic tremor and sympathetic vibration. He and the pooch return to the chair, in which he again settles. This time with a book. I in turn am trying to go a step farther and verbalize, but alas, it would seem I am stuck with making only musical sounds for the sleeper. On a little table nearby there is a picture. A girl is looking out intently. She seems to be staring at me. Strong-willed, but beautiful. Just the type I used to like. Looks a little like my Harriet did when she was younger. Or that person who came to my wake that I would rather not think about at this moment. She also has a twinkle in her eye.

Either I'm transmitting, or we're beginning to think alike, because our man is now beginning to take the picture in hand. He's looking at it as Bozo decides to focus his entire canine attention on a loose shoelace, with which he begins to play. The man looks on into the portrait, deeply and pensively, while with obstinate perseverance, Bozo has almost obtained his spaghetti intact. E.C. dials a number on the telephone. It rings and rings without an answer. The receiver back on the cradle, he picks it up again to dial a second time. No answer. He's going to try it again and instead decides to grab for the lamp switch and flick it off. He looks really frustrated, like all obsessive lovers. Then he is deflated and says, "You know it's been over four months." He's pushed Bozo aside and is blankly contemplating his now thoroughly slobbered shoe. More collected and less vague, he places the book on its shelf, then walks out of the room and up the stairs. Bozo follows.

I'm wondering why he didn't keep his previous appointment, and hasn't yet done anything to return my dog. No doubt he has a plan in this respect. I also seem to have slipped through one of those time warps again, because just when I thought it was midafternoon, I've realized that night is approaching. I hadn't thought about it before, but I now know I am very tired. Perhaps I can catch a few winks. The cushy goose-down sofa in the library is beginning to seem quite inviting. I close my eyes, and try to pray. But this evening I'm not moved in that direction. After all, it's something I never really learned to do with conviction, and I feel a tad sheepish at the hypocrisy of this new gesture. I'm trying to remember that line about the "power and triumph of the coming forth of the soul." But things aren't making a great deal of sense right now. And I seem to be falling asleep. Into the arms of a welcome night.

THREE

IT'S MORNING AGAIN, AND I'VE JUST DISCOVERED A RATHER SINGULAR thing. I started thinking about that place again. I mean the cemetery. And all of a sudden I was back there at the portal. There's something magical about that entrance. A special quality I can't quite fathom. Anyway, to my surprise, there I was standing like a boy at the gate of the schoolyard on the first day of class. But there were no children playing. And it was very early, even for the gardeners. All of a sudden, I became panicky and started thinking I might be trapped within the walls again. Lest that be the case, and for safety's sake, I put myself in the same mood again, and wished myself back to E.C.'s apartment. Presto. There I was, right where I had been before. Watching over E.C. as he slept with Bozo nearby. It would seem I can transport myself at will.

   With new confidence, I've returned to the Egyptian gate. There's something very restful and serene about Egyptian architecture. It's a style that has not only mastered but integrated a multiplicity of lines and forms. Look at this structure! It has a squared-off top and slanting sides. All of them using a straight line. Yet within it all, there are papyrus columns with their voluptuous form and curved line. Above it all, with the magical inscription beneath, is the god Khepera, the winged scarab. When I went to the Middle East for the first time, I was able to see scarabs and beetles which were alive, rather than mummified or portrayed. The impact of what the Egyptians had done dawned on me when I first saw the insect assiduously rolling a ball of dung. I then realized the great god could roll the sun around just as the coleopteran rolled that little sphere. I've heard scarabs were put on the breastplates of the departed to keep their souls from lending false testimony against themselves. And to restrain the departed from doing obtuse things like drinking urine or forgetting their names. Back to the portal, though, the thing that most strikes me about Egyptian architecture is the timelessness of it. Monumental though the structures may often be, they are beautiful in their serenity, and compatible with almost every style of decoration. When I look at this gate I think of enormous undertakings, great occurrences, and priests four thousand years ago measuring the flooding of the Nile at Philae.

Once through the portal, I can't help thinking there's something very restful about the various evergreens and other trees here. I've just walked by a spruce tree with a gnarled trunk. Strong. Beneath it grows his daughter. And she is beautiful. And fully within the reach of his limbs. There's a bluish green to spruce which is visually comforting, like the celadon greens of the porcelains of China. Walk up to it and touch that corrugated skin. Hello, tree. And as he rustles, I almost begin to think he's responding to my touch. As his daughter approves and looks up admiringly. By this time, I'm beginning to believe anything is possible. So perhaps all creatures, large and small, are sentient to some extent.

I now feel getting away from it all is somewhat necessary. So I walk in the direction of the familiar structure. Up on Brambletree Circle a few late flowers are feebly in bloom. There are some beautiful creeping roses here attempting a last hurrah. I love the way they cradle that little concrete step before a granite marker. It reminds me of the collegiate tulips I planted under my window when I was in a quandary as to whether to finish the semester or commit suicide. It's funny how sometimes the smallest pastime can create the anticipation necessary for the preservation of existence. That's why old people should have plants and pets. It's a type of excitement you create for yourself. A future interest, so to speak.

Some romantic fixation made me select the plot on Camelia Lane for my tomb. I customarily had camelias flown in for Harriet, in an attempt at thoughtfulness. But in later years, all she did was laugh at me until she was red in the face, and I was black with anger. Had I lived, who knows? She probably would have had me committed for the platinum roller skates. Hah, the press first thought they were sterling silver. As if I'd have them made from anything which would tarnish. I guess I used to think I could take it with me where I was going. A great many items have suffered clarification since the other morning when I awoke again. And although I am decidedly different, I still have that old lustiness within me. I still want to fight. I can't let them do away with my memory and my edifice. I should really return to my memorial to think. Considering I can't be seen, I might as well go there under my own power. Except that I can't leave my dog at E.C.'s that long. Or, on second thought, perhaps I can.

This time I'm not afraid of the gates. Walking briskly, I can see a very comely male attendant pulling this morning's irreverent dose of pornography out of his hip pocket to jazz things up a bit. You know, while I preferred women, the barefaced truth is that my eye did stray to a beautiful male once in a while. Feeling a little perverse about it and figuring I might as well try my physical powers on the world of the living, I walk up behind him. To regard poetically the tightly stretched blue cloth over what no doubt is a creditable rear end. Regarding the buttocks squarely, I come forth with a stupendous pinch. A pinch right out of a midday peccadillo in an Italian piazza. Brutal howl. This guy really jumped. He's wondering what stung him. But there is no response. So he blames a friendly hornet. He's running up the hill now, leaving the gate totally unattended.

Having completed this little bit of mischief, I feel strangely refreshed. In front of me automobiles are being driven at considerable speed. Whoosh, whoosh. Swoosh, swoosh. Cars going this way and that. I have this tremendous fear of being caught under tire. Although the truth of the matter is that I don't suppose I can be flattened by anything like a car. A little girl with pigtails is walking slowly behind her mother, counting all the granite rocks along the cemetery wall. Her dolly is snugly quartered under her arm. I can't help thinking that doll, child, and mother all look very much loved. I shrink. For a moment I forget I can't be seen. Of all the ways I know to fear, this is the newest. I now fear frightening others. I'm approaching town now. The beautiful ginkgo trees on this irregularly shaped block that borders on a park are beginning to lose their leaves. I always thought *Ginkgo biloba* was the greatest botanical item. Oldest tree in the world! Self-contained. Uniquely shedding its leaves to fertilize itself. Hot shit indeed!

I must be careful with these two wonderful old ladies walking arm in arm in front of the Christian Science Church. That hair is bleached so bright it's almost blue. Stupendous hats. And longish fall coats. They've walked smack through me. But no matter. I've always liked the elderly. Even if they do sometimes babble on endlessly. I also spy a pair of teenage girls chatting excitedly. Their pussies all atwitter with thoughts of androgynous rock stars.

Across the avenue. Winding my way into the center of town. Here's a newsstand. And I walk up to a newsboy, who asks, "Paper, sir?" As I instinctively put my hand into my pocket to feel for money. Unfortunately, he puts his right through me, paper and all, as he hands it to a fellow who's crept up behind me. Wait a minute. Let me see that newspaper. Hey, that's a picture of my edifice right on the front cover. With a headline, no less! Gazeeks! I have to read this. So how am I going to get my hands on this newspaper? Feeling suddenly very cross, I make an explosive gesture that incorporates some real force. So in spite of my feelings for the newsboy, the papers go flying. And I get to read a copy now resting on the ground. The headline says SOMERSET PYRAMID TO BE AUCTIONED. I'm going to quickly read through this article, in spite of the commotion around. Having completed my examination of the newspaper, standing here in the middle of the square doesn't seem right. I want to think. I have to save my pyramid. Something must be done. I close my eyes tightly, and wish with all my heart. When I open them again, I'm standing in front of the twenty-foot-high wall I had them erect around the total perimeter of my thirty-acre lot. The enormous letters I had them carve into the wall become visible in all their gilded glory: *Love Thy Neighbor*. At the time, I thought the sentiment on the wall was pretty funny. Considering that no photographs of the interior were ever allowed. On clear days, the newspaper reporters and I used to play a coy game. They'd come out armed with cameras and telescopic lenses. And I'd emerge with a few look-alikes, as well as a crew of attendants with buckshot. Almost lost me a photographer one day when he stepped in front of the old double-barrel and insisted he be shot in the puss straightaway. He was some kook! But with genuine nerve. The lawyers hushed it up. Hooker greased his palm with maggot oil. Of the green variety, and in large denominations. So he took to sending us postcards from Tahiti or someplace.

I'm walking up to the gate with its great bronze plates. These make it totally impossible to peek in at all. Now I'm approaching the garden that was called magical by little Yoshimora, who was my gardener. Still looking manicured, tall trees start about fifty meters from the wall. Then there's the alligator moat, and safely beyond it, the fish pond. Set it up like a river, with enormous recirculating pumps, and purifying gizmos. Water clear as crystal. Previously full of goldfish. Calicos, Ryukins, Orandas, and Water-Bubble Eyes. Seeming to peer out with their noses and delicately sniff the morning air. They ate out of my hand. But no more. Some bastard from the township was unusually heavy with the insecticide and they died like limp feathers in the water. When they give up, they do it like children. Helplessly, they swim into your hand in a friendly gesture seeking protection. As if holding on to a mother's teat. And you cry and ask them not to die, please. And they perish there, jewellike, while you tremble on your knees with rage. That afternoon, Yoshimora and I went "hunting" and took the garden tools to the exterminators. We nearly drowned the head of the group, and left them with remnants of a rake embedded here and there. A finger or two broken, and an eye or two gone. As far as I'm concerned, a most uneven trade.

Later, Yoshi and I sat in the wine cellar, swigging Madeira, while betting on how much the affair would cost. As it happened, it cost a bundle. But I felt it was cheap. Hooker made the payment, and we found some way of subsequently deducting it from my taxes.

So now I walk up this hard, white driveway. With my celestial garden on both sides. Full of exotic trees and plants. All fully grown in what was called by a poet "one of the most beautiful botanical preserves in the world." He was probably right. But he still didn't know what he was talking about. Only Yoshi and I knew the toil that went into it. From the trees to the bushes to the flowers, to the tiny lichens growing on the rocks. All was preconceived. Rarity to dazzle the touch, and overwhelm the mind. Beauty to enchant even the eye of a jeweler. Here we created a dominion with free rein to our own little concept of perfection. Contained and controlled, it all grew. Protected of course by the brutality which is necessary to preserve the frail and delicate. You can't very well obtain an injunction when some character is annihilating your tulips. You've got to shoot the fellow. Or forget your flowers.

Botanical archaeologists delivered the seeds of that lotus growing in yonder pool, from a very distant place. It's the rarest of varieties. Four thousand years ago, its parent graced an Egyptian villa in the outskirts of Thebes. They found the seeds buried deep beneath a dry ancient site, and when I heard about it, I knew I must have them all to myself. We used the big jet that time to retrieve the pod. And even though some said I had tendered the price of rubies, they never knew I would have paid a hundred times more. Back in the garden, we nurtured, and placed them in the mud at the bottom of the pool. In time they grew. Luxuriantly. Basking in the sun with their deep green parasol leaves. They shook every time I went by. And each day they spit forth new leaves and pink flowers which exploded with yellow centers. Alone and in proximity to them, I would often delight in dousing water on the leaves. Only to see it trickle, quicksilverlike, off the impermeable surfaces. I think the plant knows I'm here. It's sort of whispering. And purring. Asking me where its goldfish are. Telling me it's not feeling well. Warning me it will soon die of neglect. For another spell.

I want to cry, but I'm going to contain myself. Better to go reconnoiter the rest of this preserve. Where some gloom has fallen since they so quickly sent Yoshi back to Japan. You wouldn't think such a thing would happen in a few days, but it has. Decay has set in. And I sense that everywhere the new seems to have temporarily lost the will to replace the old, and to renovate itself. It's as if the presage of the end of all that is green were upon us.

But this can't happen. I have things to do and triumphs to achieve. I sit down on a rock to think. Remembering how they used a Caterpillar dozer to lug it across the turf, where it accompanied the thousands of rhododendrons, violets, and roses. I also have fields of wildflowers. Spruce, juniper, maple, and yew trees. Ivy, which now seems to be upsetting the balance. Creeping stealthily like a lover on its way to an assignation.

There are thoughts now formulating themselves rapidly in my mind. I'm thinking about E.C. and Bozo again, and I know I must return to them. But I want to catch the day's last glimpse of my pyramid glistening like some sort of early Egyptian portent. Flat and white, tremendous in proportion, it sits here, seemingly doorless. Solid, perpetual, and defiant. I want very badly to enter, but then remember there is much work to be done. So I reluctantly conclude I must continue my little tour another day.

Back at E.C.'s house, things are beginning to wake. The dog greets me when I materialize on the premises. Curling that big, liver-colored upper lip. In spite of his phenomenal size, he's an incredibly graceful pooch. Even if it seems a bit strange to see that much dog fully spread on the Oriental carpet. Mind you, he's quite accustomed to the best. Consuelo is up. Singing a song in the kitchen. Full of life, that girl. In I go. Sniffing here and there in tandem with my pooch. The dog sashays up to a now-accustomed girl and adeptly shoves his snout between her haunches, obtaining a delighted squeal from this robust Latin filly.

I prod Bozo and we move out of the kitchen into the living room. Sitting here in the early morning while Douglas is slumbering is disquieting to me. He's sleeping too late for a weekday, and I've got to do something about this. It's eight o'clock already. Not my weekday custom at all. Granted, on weekends I slept late. But only then. Can't help remembering how I often used to wake at five on the dot. After a cold shower and a pot of espresso, I was routinely ready to cleave all their skulls. I'd catch the European crowd dumbfounded. They were accustomed to playing games with American money while its owners were in bed. By the time Saturday arrived I'd be exhausted and then sleep until ten or eleven.

I really do have to wake this guy. So up the stairs I go. Nice carpeted landing here. I really don't understand my new feeling mechanism, but I certainly do appreciate the padded stairs. I guess I'll snoop around in the upstairs gallery. Good juxtaposition of the wrought-iron banister, and all these dark-paneled French doors. Now I'm into a nice pink room. Obviously meant for a little girl. It's full of dollies and things. Another bedroom looks like it belongs to a lady of the house. This is an interesting and beautiful chamber. Spacious. And light in its feeling. Everything here is done in a beautiful pale pink silk fabric, with little embroidered flowers superimposed. There's a very large bed with a padded headboard. And two beautiful Louis XVI cabinets which double as night tables. The lamps on the tables are genuine famille rose. The carpet is not Persian, but nevertheless a genuine Savonnerie. On the matching bureau, there is a gorgeous tray of silver-and-enamel brushes and mirrors which look like they were just used yesterday. Next to them rests an embroidery hoop with a beautiful motif in progress. A closer look reveals that it's a gentlemen's handkerchief on which E.C.'s initials are being stitched. There are pictures too. In large silver frames. In one, E.C. and a dark-haired woman frolic on the deck of a boat. In the other, the lady sits formally dressed in lovely pearls with long dangly earrings. The woman isn't exactly beautiful, but very striking. She has lots of dark hair and very deep eyes. And yes, substantial breasts. I don't know why, but I'm beginning to feel like somewhat of an intruder in this particular room. To be sure, the bedroom suggests the ownership of a very gracious and beautiful mistress. Yet everything is so pristine and perfect that it gives me the impression no one presently inhabits it. So for the moment, I'm going to tiptoe out of this alcove.

I guess he's preserved these rooms just as they were before. There's a guest room too. Comfortable. I bounce on the bed just for fun. Not like all those houses where they dislike callers. This room is complete, right down to a little silver-capped jar full of cookies. Just in case you become hungry in the middle of the night. Considerate. Neat and well conceived. Just like everything else in this domain.

As I do a *grand jeté* into a warmly paneled room, I find a large four-poster maple bed. Big and heavy variety, complete with a mountain of covers. He's in there all right. Under all the quilts and blankets. I guess he feels cold easily. He's entirely covered, except for his face, and the knuckles of one hand, which are holding on to the very soft border of a white, white sheet. He's babbling about plugging himself into a wall or something. Ah . . . that's it . . . he's talking about a light socket, I mean receptacle. Something about getting all the power and the current. If you take my advice, kid, you'll secure the power by plugging yourself into me and your bank account.

What to do about this guy? From some of his further mumblings it might seem I'm stuck with a real case. A genuine obsessive-compulsive, neurotic, borderline-psychotic egomaniac. As I reach this somewhat sketchy conclusion, I seem to be working myself into my own private neurotic fit. Then I notice he's stirring. His arm is moving and grabbing for a nearby bell pull . . . no, it's a buzzer. I guess that's how he lets them know to have breakfast ready. He's sitting up in bed. As he pushes the covers away, I find he sleeps naked, except for a baggy pair of shorts. Ohmigod! This guy has an erection the likes of which I've only rarely seen. Definitely museum-quality. Enormous. It kind of knocks him off balance as he walks into the bathroom. He grabs for a toothbrush as his cock gently bobs to and fro. As he enters the shower stall, I can't help noticing he also has quite a body for a fellow of his age.

At this juncture, I must make a decision. I feel like some sort of pinko pervert looking in on his morning ablutions. And yet, I'm really curious. Sort of like when I was in school and you surreptitiously peeped at the other guy's cock in the gym. Just to make sure your own was big enough. I really want to look. Faced with the ultimate uncertainties of the day, I'm going to please myself. So I stay while the atmosphere becomes a bit steamy. And watch this guy masturbate the hell out of himself with the lather from a bar of soap. I would have thought he'd find a more fitting way to rid himself of such morning problems. Like sticking it up Consuelo's nice, round, fat one. Guess he doesn't do naughty where he eats. Out of the shower, and now rid of his problem, he moves into the dressing room. Surveys the rows of suits, and ties, and shirts. There is also a succession of shiny shoes. It would seem our man has mastered the art of the marginal detail. So he picks a navy-blue suit with a pink shirt, and a bright red tie. I'll say this for him, the people who make his shirts are using a good Egyptian cotton.

It's funny how every man has a different order of dressing. I always put my socks on first. And then my pants. And work things up to the tie. But this fellow is walking around with only socks, shirt, and tie. And not a trouser in sight.

After a look in the mirror, he moves into the pants. Then the jacket. This one has nice lapels. Just wide enough to be a tad oldish. And deep lateral slits. I definitely like side vents.

Just before walking down, he seems to remember something and returns to the bathroom. Oh yuck! I hate perfume. Always thought the smell of clean bodies was nice enough. But I guess each man has a style of his own, and this one includes wearing a scent. It's actually not too bad. It's a somewhat pleasing, spicy variety. With an after-scent which reminds me of baby powder. Back to the mirror for a last look. As he tucks a white hankie into his breast pocket. Then to the night table for a little green appointment book. A pen, billfold, and a wad of cash.

On this last point, we agree. Nothing substitutes for the real thing. Why, there isn't a credit card capable of what a little greenery will do. Just think of yourself stranded in the middle of nowhere trying to gain access to someplace. Or away from it. Attempting to buy some accommodating cop's integrity. Or for that matter, some nice noodkin's soul, or a hot piece of ass. I don't have to push my point to make it clear. It's the eloquence of cash that does the trick.

I remember many a time when it came in handy. Once Harriet had left, and I took to applying compresses of fresh thousands. Smelling that wonderful ink. Doctors told me money was dirty. Full of microbes. So I tried municipal bonds and the like. Yup. Right under my pillow. But it was no substitute for my good old cash. There was nothing like it to aid a wounded soul, assuage disillusion, or mend a broken heart.

He's now opening the door to the bedroom. And Bozo is happily greeting him on the other side. But instead of walking in the antic-ipated beeline to the staircase, he's quietly moving in the opposite direction, and entering the very beautiful bedroom with the silk fabric and the pictures of the striking dark woman. He's assumed a very quiet demeanor. And seems almost sad as he discreetly walks around the room, touching little things here and there. For a moment, he gently depresses the pillow on the left-hand side. And then runs his hand over the very smooth bedspread, as if wishing she were there. Now he's going over to the dresser and staring straight into the pic-tures of the person who is obviously his beloved. He's speaking as if she were present.

"You know, it's been eight years now, and every morning I come in here to visit you in disbelief that you are gone. I can't fully express how very much I miss you. If the opportunity arose, I might join you in a moment. I've been a coward for not doing it sooner. But now, my dear, I'm very tired. There's no one else in my life. You know that. Only failures. God knows I've tried, but there isn't anyone here remotely like you. How could there ever be? But until we're together, I'll be here every morning to say hello, and think of you."

My goodness, there's a tear in this guy's eye. He's really a totally obsessive romantic yokel. And quite obviously not recuperated from the death of his wife, though in fact he says it's been eight years. To be sure, he's a manic-depressive. Just as I was. But rejoice, old boy! Henry is here. And I intend to add serious spice to your life.

He's caught hold of himself, and is stiffening a bit as he leaves the bedroom and is proceeding down the staircase with Bozo. Into the dining room, where he says good morning to a smiling Consuelo.

We have eggs with steak. And lots of marmalade. There's coffee and newspapers. He opens one to the financials. And then to the obituary pages. I'm glad he finished with the money markets so quickly, because I was getting ready to do something to divert his attention to my favorite topic. "Hey, I want you to see this page. You ninny, listen to me!" This whole thing is an effort. But not one on which I'm willing to skimp energy. I try again. And yes . . . that's it . . . that's the page. Attaboy!

So here we are at the relevant text. Reading the headline about the auctioning of my pyramid:

SOMERSET PYRAMID TO BE SOLD AT PUBLIC AUCTION

It was announced today that the Somerset pyramid will be the object of public auction sometime next week. The city has expressed its desire to purchase the structure, which is located in the fashionable Medford district of town. It encompasses a plot bordering the river which is said by informed sources to be in excess of thirty acres.

Built by the late financier and philanthropist Henry W. Somerset, and decorated with materials from many foreign lands, "Pyramid Hill" is uniformly believed to be the most expensive building per square foot ever constructed on this continent. The surrounding botanical gardens have on many occasions been favorably compared with the work of historically famous landscape architects such as Capability Brown and André Lenôtre.

An attorney for the Somerset family has declared the cost involved in altering and maintaining the compound would place a strain on the now partially contested Somerset estate. He also said there is at present no logical use for the structure. When asked why the building and grounds were not being donated to the city, attorney Hooker said that under the very clear terms of the Somerset will, "if the structure is not to be inhabited by a member of the family, it must be sold at public auction." He went on to say, "Frankly, it's my feeling that the only capable bidder might be the city."

Informants in government circles stated today that in all probability, the compound will be turned into a home for the elderly or the mentally afflicted after being refurbished and stripped of its more expensive fixtures. Fobgate and Brumpkin, architects for the city, have repeatedly stated that the edifice would be suitable for such use after the addition of two postmodern wings. It is their feeling that "such would be in keeping with the eclecticism of these artistically advanced times."

Harriet Weatherbee Somerset, widow of the late H. W. Somerset, was unavailable for comment. She is said to be vacationing in the Azores. Speculation has it she will return for the auction.

As he reads, our man Douglas has dropped his piece of toast into the very large coffee cup in front of him. Being faced with this messiness has abruptly returned him to the world. He grabs for the phone behind the table. Calling his secretary. Rings and more rings, but no secretary. He's muttering to himself, "What the hell do I pay her for?" Now furious, he redials again and again. Finally he obtains an answer and asks:

"Where were you?"

"I was out powdering my nose."

"That was one time too many."

"Well, I do have to go to the bathroom, sir."

"From now on, you can do it on your own time."

"Do you mean I'm fired?"

"That is correct. I'll have your check drawn."

Click. Bang!

Our man looks horribly disturbed. I remember how difficult it was to dismiss people. Like the office boy who used to steal rubber bands to hold his contraceptives on tightly. When I caught him, he acted as if I owed him this extra support. True, it was sheer nerve, but I had to admire the originality.

So Douglas sits here in the morning now looking rather perplexed and disturbed. He's got a strange, glassy look in his eye. He grasps the phone again and grabs for Bozo's collar. He reads the number and dials:

"Good morning," says a sweet mindless voice. "Somerset Consolidated Industries."

"Good morning. Mr. Somerset's office, please."

"Thank you, sir."

Ringing.

"Good morning. The late Mr. Somerset's office."

"Yes, may I speak to Mr. Somerset's secretary, please?"

"This is she, Miss Cleave, speaking."

Our man is steeling himself up. Turning on the charm:

"Good morning, Miss Cleave. My name is Douglas. I called yesterday about Bozo, I mean the dog, Mr. Somerset's dog. I'm sorry I missed the appointment. This dog has very winning ways, and I have not been anxious to take him home."

"Oh yes, Mr. Douglas, I've been trying to reach you, and actually this all works out very well. You see, it would seem Mr. Somerset's widow doesn't want, I mean, is unable to care for Mr. Somerset's wolfhound, and would like to give him to someone who would provide a good home. She hasn't empowered me yet, but I feel certain that if you would like, you might be able to keep him."

"Thank you, you are very kind, but I don't generally accept gifts from strangers. Might I mail you a token check?"

"I'm sure that won't be necessary, although Mrs. Somerset would probably be very pleased."

"Do I detect a note of irony in that, Miss Cleave?"

"Oh, I'm sorry, sir, it's just that all of us at the office were all so fond of Mr. Somerset that we're a little on edge and say things we shouldn't. I sincerely hope you'll forget my tone."

"I won't do anything of the sort."

"You won't? Please, sir, I might lose my job."

"I still won't."

"Then forgive me for saying so, Mr. Douglas, but you are one rat of a bastard."

"Love your spirit. How much do you earn?"

"More than you can pay."

"Don't be too sure. Try me."

"You really mean that?"

"Yup. How about . . ."

"Gee, do you really mean that, Mr. Douglas? Like, could I come see you and make sure you aren't some kind of nut?"

"Sure. How about three this afternoon?"

"Forgive me for saying this, and I don't know why I'm being so frank with you, because we've never met. But I've been depressed since my boss's death, and this is the first good thing that's happened since."

"I know the feeling. Incidentally, what brokers are handling the sale of Mr. Somerset's pyramid?"

"The Garfield Agency."

"Thank you. See you at three."

"Yes, three."

"Thank you again."

"Goodbye."

"Goodbye."

Click.

If I know Susan, this little conversation has given her a new interest in life. You see, Miss Cleave is the type of woman who is not interested in wealth in the conventional sense. She is, however, enormously turned on by men who possess and know how to wield power. She lost her father when quite young, and has always tremendously admired gentlemen with a bit of gray at the temples and something substantial between the ears. Deep down inside she longs to be protected. And as we know, no one receives that type of care from a self-centered adolescent or young adult. So Susan can always be counted upon to elect the mature specimen over the young buck. No matter how muscular. No matter how hard. In a way, this possible union bespeaks the inheritance of our species in which women have traditionally been prized for their youth and ability to bear children as guarantees for the procreation of issue, while men have always been looked upon by females as necessarily possessing the qualities of more mature gatherer-hunters, and protectors of the hearth and home. Susan knows all of this. After all, she was a psychology major. But that doesn't mean she's been able, or even wishes, to alter these aspects of her behavior and predilection. I must say, she's a clever girl. A tad willful and individualistic, but extraordinary in every way. I had a very special relationship with her as well. And can even say I loved her. But that's neither here nor there at this point in time.

Getting back to E.C., I must say he's looking very satisfied with himself, and is now assuming that little curl at the edges of his mouth which I've come to recognize as a sign of self-approval. Of course, there is the ever-present index finger. Something is hatching inside that mind. The dog is right beside him, between the two of us. The man rises and goes to the mirror. Looks at himself with a fixed gaze. Bozo lazily nudges him in the ass. He smacks the pooch lightly, turns around, and resolutely grasps the phone.

"Harry, this is E.C. I want you to do a little numbers work and tell me just how much I'm worth today. I need to know how we can generate cash in the middle-to-low-eight-figures range. No, I have not gone out of my mind. And this is not another scheme or takeover. Yes, I know I pay you to be careful, but I also pay you to follow orders. Call me back in half an hour. Please, Harry. No shit. Just obtain the information and call me back."

"E.C., you know I love you dearly, but just for the record, you are bananas."

Click.

And all this time I'd been thinking being dead was such a bad scene. There's excitement in the air now. And this fellow Douglas is on the right track. I feel my canines sharpening, and the old power surging again. I may not understand it all, or always be able to push my point through, but I feel sure there's something in it for me. There's definitely a reason to this mess. It has been said *one never dies the day before.* So perhaps this was predestined and I'm being readied for something like a reincarnation, or helping to prepare someone else for one. Maybe both. Or possibly much more.

If I were alive, I might have my friend Cardinal Tucci allow me to take a peek at the future. It's really possible. I'm not kidding! You see, the Vatican has its secrets, and one of them has to do with delving into the paranormal. It seems that in the past it started receiving reports of incredible children, born blind, but with the very special gift of second sight, the ability to predict the future. Over the years, the Vatican collected and cared for them, and of course profited from their unique knowledge. Curiously enough, they lose the gift around the time of puberty. The ones from the first few generations are all priests now. But ever since they discovered these extraordinary phenomena, my friends in the Church have been engaging, so to speak, in the "futures" game. It's all very hush-hush, and they are terribly afraid to have the children fall into the wrong hands, so they won't even acknowledge their existence. I mentioned it to my friend the Cardinal once, and he blanched. Subsequently I had to gain my information from other sources. I can't, however, help dreaming about how useful such an access to the thread of destiny might be. Especially now. But even without the ability to predict events, at this juncture, any prospect is very exciting. After the initial stress and uncertainty, it would seem that *what didn't succeed as a will, might go through as a codicil.* There's definitely going to be something to this afterlife.

FOUR

IT'S THREE O'CLOCK SHARP. OUR MAN IS FIDGETING. AND PLAYING WITH some robin's-egg-blue chalcedony eggs which were on the coffee table. I can sense anxiety in the air, since he still hasn't received that call from Harry. He's right to worry about delays. It's often been said that *between the plate and the mouth, the soup becomes cold.*

The doorbell is ringing. Consuelo runs to open the door. I'm beginning to feel a tad uncomfortable. I sense that presence. Feel her coming near. Then it all happens at once and Consuelo shows her in. Miss Cleave. Beautiful, together, and smiling. She's wearing those exquisite tiny shoes. And a little blue suit I haven't seen. There's always something wonderful about the type of woman who knows how to put herself together. The first thing about this one is the quality of everything she's wearing. All of it is good, and beautifully sewn. I assure you it's that way right down to the panties and bra. The suit itself practices the fine art of understatement. It's not in the least prone to fashion or fad. Just timelessly beautiful. The quality of this very light woolen, the stitching, and the fit tell you it's expensive. But it doesn't scream out. And then there are handbags and shoes. Harriet always said you could tell where a woman came from by looking at the handbags and shoes. Miss Cleave has selected a beautifully stitched little black bag and pumps to go with her suit. Because she's long and lithe, the Chanel line sits well with her. In spite of the recent trend in skirts above the knee, hers is sitting firmly beneath that generally most unappetizing portion of the female anatomy. Women who are confident don't really need fashion because they have class. In the balance, you can always tell the true lady. She'll show fewer curves and wear less jewelry than she really has. The trollop will buttress her breasts and corset her curves. So you'll think you're getting grade A, when in fact the material doesn't meet standards.

She's walking across the carpet, hair gently moving to and fro as she approaches him. Now extending her hand. I can tell from the way she's eyeballing him that Susan's more than pleased with the looks of E.C.

"Mr. Douglas, my name is Susan Cleave, and I must say I'm delighted to discover you're not some kind of cuckoo."

"Ah . . . yes, Miss Cleave . . ."

"Call me Sue."

"Must I?"

"Well, you could call me Susan or Cleave."

"Susan would be nice."

"Okay, Mr. Douglas, no problem. But I'm sorry, I interrupted . . . you were going to say something."

"Well, I was only going to say we do have to be very careful nowadays about the crazies."

"Yes indeed . . . but you really didn't call me here to talk about eccentrics, did you?"

"You are a very direct young lady."

"And you, Mr. Douglas, if you'll pardon me, are not old enough to address me as if you were my grandfather."

"Oh!"

"Now you might tell me about the job offer. What would you expect me to do?"

"Well . . . uh . . . my business life isn't the normal, routine situation. Rather, I work at strange hours and require a certain amount of loyalty and understanding. Also, some people may consider me eccentric, although I'm by no means crazy. You seem to me like a lady of the world, if you'll pardon me for saying so. Therefore I would assume you'd have no trouble attending my business needs."

"Mr. Douglas, you're probably aware my previous employer was one hell of a unique fellow. Very few people knew him intimately, though many had the mistaken conception they did. So unless it's part of my work to buy suspenders and hang out the window by them, I assume we'll get along."

"I hear Mr. Somerset was sort of a gifted individual."

"He was, but I would hope my employment will not include revealing the intimacies of my previous boss. Nevertheless, I should mention a few things about him. In spite of the fact that Henry, I mean Mr. Somerset, had the most exquisite eye, and a most excellent taste in almost everything, he was also a male chauvinist. Something which always kept us slightly at odds, since I have been, and am, a feminist, and do not approve of such opinions. Personally, I don't bow to any man, which is not to say that in business I don't understand the nature of a boss-assistant relationship. I'm capable, and very efficient, and if you are not paranoid, and grant me entry into your states of mind, I'll soon be anticipating your feelings and needs."

"I understand. Incidentally, you have a very impressive résumé and fascinating background. I notice you have a college degree. Psychology, no less."

"Well, as you've probably surmised, I didn't really act as a secretary in the classic mode. I was an assistant in every sense of the word and handled many of the most sensitive details of Mr. Somerset's life."

"In any event, as I mentioned, I'm more than pleased with your credentials. Now . . . about your salary . . . what would you think of this. . . ."

Our man has taken a little gold pencil, wrought like a piece of bamboo, and written a juicy number on a little pad, which he is sliding in Miss Cleave's direction. She is regarding it, and has just done the equivalent of a panther or cheetah stretch. Without discombobulating one hair of her composure. Using body language, both firm and seductive, and with feline fluidity, she is extracting her own little writing instrument from the exquisite handbag. The way she's doing it can only be compared to the expertise of a limousine driver in opposition to the jerkiness of a New York cabbie. She's gently putting a line through the figure on the pad, and has now written another number beneath it. My God, this girl has spirit. I saw the amount he wrote, and it was a lot more than I was paying her. But she's holding her ground! E.C. is looking at the pad with a wry smile on his face. He's crossing out her digits, and has proceeded to write yet a third figure beneath the second. He is pushing it toward her, the way you gingerly push a diamond bracelet in the direction of a coy mistress.

My dentist once said he'd quote a client a price for bridgework, and the next person who spoke was drilled. As it's happened here, the tiger and the panther have toyed with one another, and it would seem both are winners, since a relaxed smile has now come across her lovely face. You can tell something very special has happened here. Psychologists call it imprinting. In layman's language, I would say that this whole little conversation has turned Susan on. In other words, she's hooked. After all, it was to be expected. This fellow exhibits a lot of the qualities and mannerisms she came to appreciate in me. In point of fact, she's a lucky girl to have found a second one. Anyway, I think she's totally smitten by the man. Now she's extending her hand once more.

"Congratulations, Mr. Douglas, you have a new assistant. When do I start?"

"How about now?"

"No, there are some matters I must put in order, but I would be able to start tomorrow bright and early. I do have some questions, which I assume will not distress you."

"Well, we'll see when you ask the questions, won't we."

"Sure."

"So ask me."

"Well, I must confess I looked you up in Henry's, I mean Mr. Somerset's, files, and found you listed under his nine-figure category, which is to say you've got a lot of what it takes. But you might give me a little idea of what area you're engaged in. To put it bluntly, where does the money come from?"

"I don't generally brief people on the more private details of my fortune. But if you are to be my assistant, I certainly see no reason why you should not have a bit of information. At the beginning it was real estate. And then shopping centers and office towers. Later, it was hotels and banks, but then I got out of those. The hotels were too much work, and the regulatory aspects of the banks became suffocating. Now I'm basically a speculator and an investor. We've done a couple of nonhostile takeovers, and dismembered the companies for the assets. I must say, I've never been into manufacturing or general sales. But that's not to say I couldn't be tempted. Mostly your duties will have to do with monitoring accounts, reminding me of commitments, and making sure we don't miss a beat in responding to the various details inherent in what is basically a substantial accumulation of cash, bonds of various governments, and both common and preferred stock in fifty or sixty companies. I sit on the boards of many companies."

"That's something my boss rarely did."

"I understand. I've heard your previous employer wasn't big on having himself related to the entities he controlled."

"That's right. A lot of people tried, but he was basically impervious to the delivery of a subpoena on anything."

"Except of course, that one subpoena."

"What do you mean?"

"Death. It's the one writ we can't refuse."

"Oh, you mustn't think about that. You're a young man. I'm sure there are lots of people to hold you here."

"Not as many as you would think."

"Well . . . we'll see. Anyway, getting back to business, do you speculate in the metals markets, or in commodities? I have some knowledge in these areas. You see, Henry, I mean my boss, liked the metals a lot."

"Did he do futures trading?"

"Yes. But he frequently also took delivery on the actual ingots and wafers."

"I should think that would have made things difficult at times. Metal bars are hard to transport."

"He didn't mind. For him they were soft and cushiony. And the material of dreams."

"Interesting. . . . I don't mean to be tiresome, but is there any reason why you can't start immediately?"

"Yes, there's something personal I wish to do."

"Oh."

"But Mr. Douglas, I want you to know, you won't be sorry you've hired me. Nor will you regret having taken me into your confidence on these business matters."

"I'm sure, and incidentally, you may call me E.C."

Our man is delighted with the woman before him. But he's a bit perplexed that she isn't beginning immediately, and a tad hurt in his ego. After that little repartee with the salary figures, he expected she would please him on this point. I must say I'm also a bit peeved. Why doesn't she stay? After all, look at the money he's paying her. She should be *as smooth and accommodating as a cat licking butter*. Maybe it was wrong of me to let him pay so much. Furthermore, she was bluffing. Yes indeed, I'm certain she was. She used to say I was awfully tight. And she was right. I could teach this guy a thing or two about preserving wealth.

I wonder if she has a new lover? That's probably it. They're all the same. Drop dead and where are you? Forgotten, that's where. And all alone. While women you loved are probably copulating with others like rabbits. I'll fix her, though. I'll follow her. That's the thing to do. I'll be hot on those tracks wherever she's going.

I witness two polite goodbyes, and one shake of hands. But not before Bozo bounds in and recognizes the presence of a friend, with a welcoming curl of the lip. Out she goes with me right behind her. As the mad Somerset rides again! In the past I privately referred to myself as Baron Münchausen when on demented rampage. Today I feel him gaining life again. Surging within. Growing out of his cage. There are possibilities around me, and I'm feeling alive again. Grasping at the air to convince myself I can actually act in the realm of the physical. Holding a little bug I caught tightly. It's a ladybug that was probably lunching on the aphids on a nearby houseplant. Probably the *Ansellia nilotica*. The little thing must be the size of Queen Mab's coach, which, legend has it, is wrought out of a single pearl. But strong enough to tow twenty thousand elephants behind.

Here I go. Out again. For another adventure in the sunlight. Whoops, I almost lost her. She's hailing a cab. Just in time, I jump in with her. As she begins to give the cabbie directions. This driver can't keep his eyes away from the rearview mirror. She tries to shift out of sight, but he's a real lecher. She's asking him to stop at the next corner and wait. Now going into a florist shop, where they seem to have something ready for her in a little white box. After a brief transaction, Cleave is back into the taxi. We proceed through the city. Wait a minute. I know this way. . . . There it is in the distance before us. We're at Sleepy Heights going through the massive portal where I am once again assured *The Dead Shall be Risen*.

Into the necropolis we wind, as I begin to feel very small indeed. Embarrassed. For all those mean-spirited little things I thought just a while ago. She's out of the cab and walking up to Camelia. But stops a moment and buttons the jacket of her little suit. As she approaches Camelia, she stops at a little grave, and introspectively reads a touching inscription to a dead child. I detect her paling a little as she reaches the area where the tall, long pines sway in the afternoon breeze. As my tomb becomes completely visible, Susan is now opening the little box. Bringing forth her violets. The nosegay dropping gently in tandem with the tears on my granite step. She's saying private little things under her breath, then sobers up a little and starts talking about having second thoughts regarding that new employment.

"Nonsense," I scream. But she can't hear me. In any event, she's just got to follow through with that job. So I try and try, until I perceive she begins to understand. I'm really not sure whether it's me. Or her own common sense. But we seem to have achieved a more optimistic mood.

She's running her hand over the carving. As if she really doesn't want to leave. Now speaking aloud:

"You know, Henry, I really miss you. I miss your ways . . . the power of your person . . . I even miss your little tantrums and jealousies . . . and especially the way you protected me. . . . But now I'm alone. And I've met this guy. He's got big hands. And I'm really attracted. You'd like him. He's a lot like what you were a few years ago. So I'm going to try. Even though I'll always love you."

There's a bit of a tear now. But she's composing herself. There's a moment of indecision. As if she were going to say more. All of a sudden, she turns around and walks away. Without hesitation, and without looking back. Briskly down the inclines, under the trees and past the bushes, beyond the slumbering lanes, with an occasional hard stone making noise under foot.

I'm taking advantage of the moment. Now that Susan has disappeared through the gates. It's quiet here. Just a little occasional rustle. Sort of like the whispering of a flock of children. Small, yet sharp and eloquent. Little noises which are clearly heard in the late afternoon and portend the coming of twilight. There's also a strong smell of freshly cut grass. And memories . . .

Enough. This atmosphere can get the best of you. I must recapitulate, and gain some sense of perspective about this whole experience. I've been so busy with what's been happening, I haven't had time to question this afterlife business. I continue to wonder where all the other people like me might be. Were they ever here? Have they been allowed to leave? Where are they now? These questions are driving me to a new height of distraction. Besides, *how did I die*? Whenever I think about this, that funny clock, the one with the relentless brass wheel, comes to mind. But try though I may, I can't seem to remember anything about that day with the exception of the turning of that wheel.

I'm also wondering about how much time I may, or may not, have. Is this status permanent? Or is it passing and illusory? Why am I bothering at all? Huh! I know the answer to that one. Just can't bring myself to separate from the things of this life. I desperately want to exist. One way or the other. So I clamor to Willie Shakespeare's deaf heaven that I don't want to go elsewhere. But there's no answer. It's just all very still. There are no devils to jeer at me, and no angels to push me forward. Just that little conscience inside, telling me no matter what I do, "none of it'll stick, none of it'll stick."

Then there's the matter of this Douglas fellow. Why did I meet him? Was it some sort of coincidence, or am I following the thread of destiny to the completion of some master plan? And my pooch. How come he took so well to this E.C. fellow? As I recall, he routinely chased the milk- and postmen. So why so chummy all of a sudden with a stranger?

Then there's Miss Cleave. Weird that I can still love in any way at all. I watched her cry here today while my heart melted away. I thought back to that evening when she first came to work for me. It was raining, and we were working late, as usual. I was a real tyrant in those days. I paced and she said something about how handsome I looked with my specs on. I was sensitive about my glasses. That evening I walked her home. It wasn't very far. I wanted to grab her as we stepped over the wet flagstones. Under the umbrella, my collar was becoming a little wet from the droplets. And she wasn't really saying very much. We reached her house. She said something about a pot of tea and brandy, and we walked up the steps to her loft. It had large, wide spaces. She lived under the stars, with potted plants under a great glass roof. And then there was that cello. And a monstrous black standard poodle named Tempest, who took after me like a phalanx of avenging angels till Sue said "No!" about a hundred times. That dog was weird. He was toeless on one foot where the piano movers had dropped their burden. And what airs! Almost as if he had been some sort of royalty in another life. But poodle-de-dum notwithstanding, no sissie-dog he. Nosiree, he delighted in uprooting the potted plants, and on later occasions delivered the homage of an *Arenga* palm or two intact when we became friends.

No pom-poms or sissie clips either. This was a hunting dog. Or so she said. At times I doubted it, though. Take his demeanor, for instance. In opposition to other dogs, he would never put his head on the floor. Sort of not good enough for him. And maybe he was right. After all, why put your head on the floor if you don't really have to. Cleave always said he was her guardian. She had some weird theory about dogs representing a superior state of development and coming to this existence to take care of humans. She contended they knew a lot about strange and occult things. In those days I doubted it.

But Tempest, where are you now? Are you still at the pet cemetery with the tabbies and pet-reptilians-supreme? Have you transmuted to another form or state? Is there anything else? Guess I'll never know. It all brings back memories of the day Tempest died. After all, it was the only day Susan ever missed work. I remember how peeved I was. All those untyped documents and letters of harassment. I didn't call until the night fell. But then I went to her. And just as on that first night with the tea and brandy, we did it under that old glass roof while the rain serenaded us peltingly. She bawled while I sucked on her nice, hard teat, which found its apex on one of those two most individual works of art.

Cleave was brassy, and coy too when necessary. She was very young when I first employed her and crimsoned the first time she saw it swaying. "Oh my God," she'd say, "it's eeeenormous." And she'd play with it for hours on end. Making it rise and then squeezing the blood out of it only to coax it to harden again. Sometimes I'd be ready to climax, and she'd rap it with the flick of a wrist to keep me going for hours. And all this while I kneaded those glorious breasts, and drew invisible curlicues over all her body. She'd rub her fingers on me too, as she noticed the stretch marks on my back from rowing. She'd ask me dumb questions like what it was like to row. And I'd explain, while she listened with great, wide eyes. And little shivers now and then.

Considering my offices in those days, it took her a long time to realize how rich I really was. That was before we moved. Those were the good old days of anonymity. With desk drawers snugly packed with bank books and municipal bonds. And closets full of silver and gold. But it was platinum which really held me fast. And out of it I had that artist model her breasts. What a quandary. I wanted them separate, and united as well. We finally opted for keeping them together in solid, compact platinum. Hard gray metal, sort of the color of ejaculate. They looked almost squeezable, but in the end, they were no more than a substitute. My psychiatrist said my fantasies required serious attention. So I got rid of him. After all, what would life be without a little kinky dream here and there? I used to fantasize about having one served for breakfast in vanilla syrup. Teat neatly standing up in a platinum chafing dish. Visions of taking a knife and fork to it, and there always being more. So in my fantasy, they were never less than round and plump. No matter how much I ate. When I found out she'd left her kidneys to a "bank," she joked and told me she'd leave the breasts to me in her will.

In any event, I'm happy to be near again. Joy for me in the aspiration of that perfume. The warm scent of violets. A remembrance which makes me feel better inside.

How could I forget that time a couple of months before I kicked off? We'd been doing a "quickie" before work. By then, there were also differences of opinion. . . . Maybe some premonition or something told me I should do something nice. Usually, she'd never let me buy her anything. But I must say, she had a hell of a lot of jewelry. I never inquired from where. Anyway, that day I asked the driver to let us off near work and we walked part of the way past expensive-looking windows with this and that. I'll admit I had that itch I'd feel when I wanted to buy something. Then a bauble caught our eye. It was a fantastic ring, but it was actually the stone that grabbed out at us. Umpteen carats of diamond. And pink to boot. Shaped like a modified triangle. No kidding. With a little culet at the bottom looking like a strangely delicate three-petaled daisy. Without protest I entered the shop. And bought it. Reset on a chain, it dangled like just another beach pebble between the ebb of those breasts. She loved that stone, and never took it off. I'll bet she's wearing it today under her suit.

These thoughts have served to bring me back to some semblance of reality. I remained here to think, not wishing to follow Sue. After all, she has a right to some privacy. What to do, though? It must be late. I should return to the house. I'm in this game for better or for worse, and I must become a serious player. After all, I'd like to win. I'd actually like to build things again. And create.

But I can't do it alone. Douglas could and will help me. And he won't be sorry, either. I like this guy. And think I can turn him into more than he's ever dreamed. Cloaked in my new resolve, I have decided to do it for both of us. Yes. I'll get to work on Douglas and turn him into the real thing. Someday he'll have to thank me for it. For having converted him into something more than your typical mogul. With what I know and what I've been through, he will have no equal. Anywhere.

FIVE

I'M BECOMING VERY GOOD AT THIS BUSINESS OF POPPING BACK AND forth between places and situations. I realize I must snap out of this mournful attitude so I can dedicate myself to the real stuff. So I'm blinking my eyes and wishing myself back to E.C.'s house.

He seems to have received his call while I was away and is still arguing heatedly on the wire. Just as I did. "Harry, there's absolutely no sense in trying to dissuade me. After all, the money is sitting around waiting another deal."

"E.C., I think it would be cheaper if you'd find a really good shrink. Or a whore, for that matter. The idea of spending eight figures on this thing really gives me the willies."

"But Harry, it's a work of art."

"So's the *Mona Lisa*, but I wouldn't think of buying it."

"You know what, Harry? You're a total Philistine."

"Yeah, E.C., but I'm a rich one, although not as rich as you are!"

"Harry, how about if we make a deal? I won't count your money, and you just tell me how much I have today."

"Okay, okay, I give up. I should know by now that when you get a bug up your ass, there's no convincing you. But bear in mind that stubbornness turns rich men into poor men, and happy men into unhappy men."

"Why Harry, I never knew you were a philosopher."

"You know what, E.C.? I'll bet you could convince them to put an extra angel on the head of a full pin."

"You might be right, but be that as it may, I'm going to need a lot of federal funds transferred into my operating account during the next few days."

"Okay, E.C., why don't you leave me alone so I can go do my job for you."

"Thanks, Harry."

"Don't mention it."

Click.

So E.C.'s hooked on that matter after all. He's got this wonderful glassy-eyed look. He's really going to give it a whirl. But he actually doesn't know what a stupendous deal he's making. It'll be my job to reward him.

I like the guy. He's just the way I was. Fixated, obsessive, and tough. I thought old Harry would persuade him to desist. But no such thing. He's fully baited for the quest. And now retiring back to his chair. Sensitively waiting like some sort of a caged animal which is also a hunter. So I sit here and abide with him. Ten minutes pass. Twenty. Forty. And then the phone rings again and it's Harry:

"E.C., I've got you cleared for anything from low to middle nine figures, and maybe a little more by Thursday."

"Harry, that's why I love you."

"Go stuff yourself. But on second thought, send me a case of Château Latour instead."

"You've got it."

"Good show."

Click.

So it's all set. And we're going forward into what nowadays is only a moderately expensive venture. Hold on to your socks, though, old boy, because unsubstantiated as I've become, I'm still full of surprises.

Bozo has just entered carrying the afternoon newspaper. It's been appropriately ennobled by the requisite amount of slobber. Canine saliva notwithstanding, our man grabs for the paper with excitement. Discarding the various sections on world events, souped-up sports, and deviant crime, he presses forward to the public notices section. And there it is:

NOTICE OF PUBLIC AUCTION

Pursuant to the order of the executors and administrators of the estate of Henry Waldo Somerset, the firm of Hooker and Goldfarb has been instructed to offer for sale at public auction the following property: thirty-two-acre estate located in Medford County, consisting of gardens, pools, garden sculpture, botanical garden of rare plants and trees. Located on the property is a main granite structure of truncated pyramidal shape of approximately two hundred thousand square feet, originally constructed to house a substantial collection of painting and sculpture. Also located on the property are six greenhouses, an orchidarium, stables, garages, and a large guest house. The property enjoys full electronic security and a moat, originally intended as an alligator enclosure. Incidentals are too numerous for listing. Considered unmovable, and included in the general auction price, is one Egyptian obelisk dated approximately 1680 B.C.

Auction to take place Friday, September 9, at 8:00 P.M. on the premises. The property will be open for viewing on Wednesday, Thursday, and Friday preceding the auction from 8:00 A.M. to 4:00 P.M. by appointment only to previously qualified bidders. Interested parties should contact the Garfield Agency at 777-3232 for an appointment.

Hooker and Goldfarb, for the Executors and Administrators.

Wow! I've got to move faster than I thought. E.C. has gone upstairs and is now bounding down the stairs with the pooch. Both stretching a little when they reach the bottom. Consuelo has apparently been ministering to wonderful things. In fact, the dinner table is fully set for one person in the dining room. In the kitchen, Consuelo's assistant is gently poaching the quenelles. Looks like pike and salmon, with a scrumptious white sauce. I think I'll take a peek at what they've prepared as a main course. Oh . . . very delicate. Calves' brains with capers. And black butter. Delicious, but fattening. They bake their own bread here too. And not that ratty French bread they sell in New York. This stuff is the kind that rises a full three times before it's finally popped into the oven. And what's for dessert? Ohhh . . . *Gâteau St. Honoré*. Not bad for a simple evening meal.

I note the table is set with good Paul Storr flatware. The knives are the real thing. Rare. I had this *nouveau riche* friend who put hers in the dishwasher. Where the shellac in the knife handles caused them to promptly explode. And the crystal isn't bad either. English. Engraved. We do, however, have to make this fellow buy some good eighteenth-century porcelain. He's using that new Hungarian junk, which just won't do. Even if it is hand-painted. He's sitting down, and the girls are bringing the first course to the table. This dimly lit dining room reminds me of something I did a long time ago when I was a student.

As it happened, I had been invited to spend the weekend at the New York apartment of my roommate's legendarily wealthy grandparents. Mind you, I was no yokel, and Mother had taught me how to dance a waltz and use a fish fork. But that late Friday afternoon when we arrived feeling natty in our Chesterfield coats, and the butler took my flowers for Madame, I was unprepared for the secret weapon of the very, very rich. As it happened, my jock nudnick of a roommate and I proceeded to take possession of our respective rooms, where shortly thereafter our bags were unpacked by anonymous and unobtrusive attendants. We were told by the butler that Mr. and Mrs. Traynor would receive us in the library at six for cocktails. The walk from my bedroom to the library was so long my new shoes nearly gave me a callus. But once I had arrived, I found that the Traynors were an exceedingly lovely couple. Gracious in their twilight years. Mr. Traynor shook my hand vigorously. He was wearing a velvet smoking jacket with silk lapels, and hand-embroidered slippers. The Missus was equally suitably attired for an evening at home. In a long, flowing cotton dress with silk peonies embroidered all over it. Her gray hair was pulled back into a discreet chignon. And on her finger, receding demurely, was one of the largest diamonds I had yet seen, set so low, it was almost embedded into that wrinkled but delicate old hand. Once she shook mine, I knew that age notwithstanding, she was truly the mistress of that great establishment. Mr. Traynor sat in a chair with a butler's table in front of him on which, I'll never forget, was the sum total collection of the bar. That is to say, scotch and gin, water and ice. I opted for scotch with a bit of water, which was poured out of a little silver pitcher with a curving lip. As it happened, Mr. Traynor was a bibliophile. And he delighted in showing me the wonders of his collection. I remember there was a Columbus letter, and Medina's *Arte de Navegar* as well. So after the show-and-tell, we walked what seemed another mile, Mrs. Traynor on my arm. Into a very dimly lit dining room. I'll never forget that room. Because it was almost the scene of my undoing.

My roommate was placed facing me at the long mahogany table set with priceless lace doilies and Dresden porcelain. Mrs. Traynor was to my left and the old gentleman to my right.

The prelude to the unsheathing of the secret weapon occurred just moments later when the soup was presented by what would ultimately reveal itself to be an instrument of absolute terror. I mean to say the Irish maid. There she was, silver soup tureen in hands, looking askance at what she supposed to be the riffraff brought home by the bovine grandchild. I caught the glance of disapproval at the outset and watched my step as we proceeded from the chowder to the lamb chops with mint jelly and parsley potatoes.

We all imbibed a substantial amount of claret. Only my hostess and I remained lucid. The old gentleman was now gaga with wine, and my roommate was more than a tad drunk. At that point, the dessert plates were presented with particularly lovely and diaphanous lace doilies on top of them, upon which ultimately rested the finger bowls and their plates. I had been taught how to handle a finger bowl, so I promptly placed it to my left, overseen by the approving glance of my hostess. What happened next was too quick and nasty for words. In came the Irish maid, like a Valkyrie out of hell, with that red hair glistening in the candlelight. As I turned to speak a word to

Mrs. Traynor, the pudding was unceremoniously dropped smack in the middle of my dessert plate, where I had neglected to remove that paper-thin lace doily.

Consternation was evident on Mrs. Traynor's face. But what to do? She couldn't very well acknowledge my "no-no," and she couldn't, by the same token, chastise the maid, who was now leaving with that look of ultimate triumph which is often generated by truly small minds. So here we were. Old fellow besotted. Grandson plain drunk. Hostess temporarily unnerved. And terrified guest. Not to mention pudding on doily.

It was then and there, at this crossroads of my life, that I made the first of the lightning decisions which would later characterize me in business. Dessert fork and spoon in hand, I decided the Irish maid would not receive the satisfaction of returning that soggy doily to the kitchen or of parading it beneath her mistress's nose. With quiet determination, I proceeded to carve and ingest it ever so adeptly to the accompaniment of the pudding. As the act of dismemberment progressed, I shall never forget the serene smile which came upon my hostess's face. It was that countenance you acquire when all security has been returned. After the rug has been yanked out from under you, and thankfully replaced.

So when the woman came in to retrieve the plate, there it was, with no lace in sight. At that point, Mrs. Traynor addressed her and said, "Mary, you didn't give Master Henry a doily for his finger bowl. Let it be the last time." After that, she winked at me as Mary huffed into the kitchen. To this day, I've always thought my friend and his grandfather never noticed a thing. But Mrs. T. and I became great friends and remained so until she passed away. I'll never forget the following morning. She was wearing a long housecoat and had the cereal box in hand. The old gentleman was in his pajamas and silk bathrobe. She questioned me with a wry smile as to how dinner had sat in my stomach. My response was to the effect that my digestion had been excellent. To which she beamed and exclaimed, "Oh to be young again!"

There was a valuable lesson in the whole incident. I've never forgotten how secret weapons of the human variety can unhinge the best-laid plans. Like the secretary who dislikes you because you wear a purple tie. And bars all access to her boss. Or the mechanic who throws the sabot into your machine, just in time to destroy it. And ruins all your careful preparations.

Enough of this, though. Our man is now having his dessert. And there isn't an Irish maid in sight. His napkin is still in hand. He's perusing that newspaper once more as Consuelo's characteristic hum is heard from the kitchen. Now reading my auction notice again. Muttering something about the Egyptian obelisk. Then he grabs for a nearby telephone which had been quietly sitting on the maple burl console. He's dialing for Harry again, who is apparently already in bed and is responding under duress:

"Harry."

"E.C., it's late. Do you know what time it is? Do you know how crazy you are?"

"Harry, I've got to talk to you again about this auction. I don't exactly understand why I've become so obsessed. Maybe it's this dog I've acquired, but one thing's for certain, I've got to have this house."

"Sweetheart, that's an expensive pooch. Can't this wait until tomorrow?"

"Harry, I'm not your sweetheart, and you are not my analyst, you are my investment counselor."

"All right, all right, but what the hell do you want this late?"

"I want you to sell all the airlines at the first hour tomorrow."

"What do you need so much money for? Besides, you could cause a run in those stocks by selling so much."

"Harry, I just want to have a lot of cash on hand."

"E.C., babes, if it's ransom money, or blackmail, I suggest the FBI. After all, you're no ordinary yokel. You're a taxpayer. You deserve America's best . . . so why don't we call the guys with the baby rattles in? Hah, hah, hah."

"Look, Harry, stop kidding about the FBI, they may be listening."

"Remind me to fart before I hang up."

"Well, old bean, can I count on you to get it done?"

"Old bean my ass . . . wait till you see the bill."

"Okay. Harry, I know you have a one-track mind . . . go back to bed."

"Sure, sure, you can say that, now that I'll end up staring at the ceiling, and you'll get to sleep."

"It's the price of empire, Harry."

"Get stuffed."

Click.

The days have become shorter and colder. There's a touch of frost on the windows. And there isn't an awful lot of heat in here yet. But our man is still walking around in a silk shirt without a jacket. I must say it's cheery here, though, and there are some nice touches to these interiors. Like that little porcelain lamp over there in the shape of an owl. Homey, but nice. I am, however, anxious for him to see the inside of my "little house."

It's dark now. Dog and man have had quite a day. Not to mention ghost. There. I said it. I've been wrestling with the whole issue of what to call myself. Actually, "ghost" is not my favorite word. Mainly because of the various connotations the concept has acquired. Most of them unmerited. But nevertheless ingrained in the popular mentality in unfortunate ways. This business, whether alive or dead, of referring to your person is the material of which psychoanalysis is composed. So I might as well face the issue and make a decision regarding what to call myself. I think I shall continue to opt for the word "spirit." The word has a lightness to it which I appreciate. Notwithstanding the fact that I've always liked *s*'s more than *g*'s. I'm also pleased with the loftiness of "spirit." As opposed to "ghost," which is something you think of as living under the floorboards, stealing your socks, and rattling chains through the night.

Our man had momentarily fallen asleep in his chair. But has now collected himself, and is walking up the stairs with dog in tow. To be sure, I feel a bit tired as well, so I think I'll explore the window seat in our man's bedroom, and settle down for a nice autumn sleep.

6
SIX

THIS MORNING I HAVE BEEN RUDELY DISTRACTED FROM MY REST BY THE
sounds of telephones, doorbells, and cars having their horns honked
in the distance. Douglas is in the bathroom. It's a commodious room.
Green marble. Lots of it. On one side it has a very spacious Roman
tub complete with rubber ducky. I always said no self-respecting man
should take a tub bath without his rubber ducky. Now that I remember, I think I even composed a poem to my squeezable friend when
once caught somewhat tight with a bit of quality juice in me. He's
wrapped in a towel. Good big feet pressing on that marble floor. Not
to mention calves, and reasonable glutes for his age. He's shaving
with one of those cheap disposable things. I like this bathroom. It's
got lots of mirrors, so it gives you the impression you're shaving with
another hundred men. As they endlessly reflect in parallel. He also
has a bidet in the other little room. A fancy one.

   Into the dressing room, where an attendant has set out some
clothes. He's selecting a very pale blue shirt. With a solid wool gab-

ardine suit, and good wing-tip shoes from those people in Paris who do such a nice job. The tie is French, as well, from that shop which began as a purveyor of equestrian garb.

He's moving over to a dresser with many little drawers. There's a contraption on top of it which is turning several self-winding watches. He's selecting one and putting it on. It's simple, yet elegant. It has a lizard strap, and the watch itself tells you the day of the week, month, date, phase of the moon, and, of course, time. As I recall, I had a similar one, but his has this little flower on the stem, while mine had a milled edge. Someone really must go blind making these timepieces.

Our man has acquired a certain bounciness this morning. He's coming down the stairs looking perfectly together. Someone is waiting below to take a brush to Bozo, who immediately accepts the exercise and enjoys it immensely. The breakfast table is set with a number of dishes. But E.C. pushes them aside in favor of a rather poisonous-looking cup of espresso. *Coffea arabica.* The real item! I always had a love-hate relationship with truly wonderful coffee. Rumor always had it the best stuff came from some island in the Caribbean where they grew it in the shade and dried it in the sun until the beans looked like wrinkled little scrotums of dwarves. Coffee was something I always anticipated in the early morn. Before I had it, the fragrance would be all-enticing. But afterward I would find the smell almost disgusting. Like popcorn. Or sex. I guess the old maxim still holds true, *Omnes homines post coitum tristes sunt.*

E.C. has drunk two of these cups of extremely strong espresso. He's rising after patting his lips with a napkin. Walking over to the window and occasionally glancing at his watch. Downstairs the freshly washed limo has been rolled under the porte cochere. Our man assumes a little look of satisfaction.

Into the kitchen for a word with Consuelo and then he walks through the rooms to the front door. I'm fast behind. So is the pooch. Outside, the chauffeur, who has a funny Balkan name, is holding the open door. As a now accustomed behemoth jumps in, and accommodates himself as if he thoroughly belongs. Our man follows, and lastly I slip in. Exchange of good mornings with the chauffeur, whose name is Szilagyi:

"We're going to Medford County, Szilagyi."

"Very good, sir. It's a nice day for a ride."

There's something comforting about good drivers. I've always found them very necessary. For one thing, they never accelerate too quickly, and never slow down suddenly without a reason. There's a sort of a genuine concentration to the way a skilled driver handles his machine. No hurry to speed or slow down. Just a pleasant, even type of affair. And so we judiciously wind through traffic into a throughway, and now placidly into the limits of Medford County.

The change of air is good for us all. A fresh little breeze is coming through the crack between the window and a rather secure vaultlike door. This reminds me of my own collection of such tanks. After a less cautious friend was given the once-over by unsavory business associates, I made my decision to prefer the bulletproof variety. I had another friend who was almost tarred and feathered when caught in a standard vehicle. It seems the rabble of some foreign country he was visiting was offended on account of some minor, but thrillingly perverse, sexual violation. They used the equivalent of a can opener on his car, thereby obtaining jurisdiction over the person, and in this way proceeded with their alleged act of social justice. I don't have to tell you there just wasn't very much left after they did that little job on him. He thought of suicide after realizing some of his most important physical assets had been lost in the tug, but opted instead for the time-honored solution of becoming a Holy Roller and the mahatma of a new religion.

I know this road we're on quite well. Medford is a rolling-hills sort of community. Still part of town. Expensive, exclusive, and restricted. We're going over little creeks and rivers. There are well-appointed stone bridges in this area. To our left appears the wall. That great, winding construction I had built to conserve and contain my little preserve. I could almost wax sentimental. But I can't allow myself to become gooey. The car is stopping at the gate. Here is my initial watch station, the little house with built-in machine guns. The security attendant is approaching the vehicle. Szilagyi is pushing a button to lower his window.

"Good morning. Going to view the property?"

"Yes. I have Mr. E. C. Douglas here."

"Do you have an appointment?"

"Yes indeed. Would you kindly check your list?"

"Oh yes, I have you here. Just ride up the driveway to the main house and ask for Mr. Fine. He should be waiting for you by the time you get up there."

"Thank you."

"Don't mention it."

We're winding up the road. The top of the pyramid is now visible, shining in the diffused morning light. I begin to feel impatient. Bozo is, however, showing his own variety of vitality, and has now become unbelievably lively. No sooner is the door open than he runs and romps over the turf in gleeful play. Back home. After the initial excitement, he approaches our man, who proceeds to firmly grab him by the collar. E.C. is really admiring this edifice. He can't seem to get enough of it. First he looks at the flagstone on the driveway, and then at the unpolished surface of the granite walk. The walls have caught his attention. Rough pearled granite. Eternal.

In the distance, a little man is walking toward us. Smiling. Pear-shaped is the only way to describe him. Blandly built. But there's something sharp about the features, which are sort of aquiline. There's a sting somewhere behind that Mephistophelic little chin and those beady, penetrating eyes.

"Good morning, sir, I'm John Fine. And you must be Mr. Douglas."

"You are correct. Nice to meet you, Mr. Fine."

"I'm very happy to know you, Mr. Douglas. Your secretary called and informed me you would be viewing the property this morning. As you know, my firm, the Garfield Agency, works in conjunction with Hooker and Goldfarb, and I am, of course, delighted to help you."

Brushing him somewhat aside, Douglas responds, "Shall we proceed with the tour?"

Mr. Fine is now informing our man that the dog will have to remain outside "due to the valuable nature of the objects within." I'd sure like to give him a piece of my mind. Bozo belongs here much more than he. While E.C. is visibly annoyed, he is a man with a purpose. So dog and Balkan chauffeur await further command.

"How do we enter?"

"Well, Mr. Douglas, that indeed is a very good question. I will admit there are, in fact, a great many things we still don't understand about the edifice. But we have managed to deal with the problem of access. As you may know, the late Mr. Somerset was . . . er . . . should we say, a wee bit eccentric, and the architects concealed the entrance rather masterfully. Now let's see . . ."

E.C. is looking somewhat cool as we approach the wall of the pyramid. Mr. Fine is just about overflowing with waves of honey and bullshit. Obsequiousness and condescension, unmasterfully mixed.

"Rumor has it the late Mr. Somerset was a grandiosely neurotic, manic-depressive, passive-aggressive, compulsive paranoiac. Now, mind you, I'm not saying that was true, but it would surely explain the dimension and magnificence of this property."

I'm beginning to become angry when just in the knick of time E.C. butts in and requests he be spared the particulars of my various alleged psychological illnesses and perversions.

"Uh . . . well, indeed I agree with you, Mr. Douglas. In any event, his various tendencies were not mentioned by me in an effort to defame the deceased. On the contrary, I thought it would enable you to particularly appreciate the uniqueness of this entrance and the succeeding building."

We're now at that spot where the empty alligator moat is at its slimmest. Up to the pavement in front of the rivulet, where two out of ten stones are depressed by a widely grinning Mr. Fine. As a faint rumble becomes audible, a gigantic rectangle of stone slowly separates itself from the facade of the building, exhibiting nine glistening stairs, above which are bronze-and-glass doors sporting traditional locks. The stairway must be a good fifteen feet wide. In point of fact, as I recall, it's actually sixteen feet wide.

Mr. Fine is looking as if he had just invented gunpowder unassisted. "I knew you would be pleased with this little detail. If I do say so myself, immense architectural skill was involved in the planning and execution of the structure. It's been said ten different architects were used in order that not one of them would completely comprehend the idiosyncrasies of the building. I don't know if you are aware the lead architect was quite aged when he conceived it and has now passed away. So we've had to refer to friends and relatives, who all have vague and conflicting notions regarding the house. Even the man's widow seems to know very little about it. I will, however, tell you we now feel a bit more comfortable with the topic, as you will see."

Hah. The nerve of this little guy. He thinks he knows my house. Why is it these little Chihuahuas always end up becoming real-estate brokers? I've always hated brokers. They have an ingrown conflict of interest. They must secure the highest price for the seller at the same time that they secure the lowest price for the buyer. Usually devoid of integrity, they end up screwing the seller to accommodate the buyer, and therefore generate a neat commission for themselves.

Douglas is like a man in a daze. I must admit the combination of this peculiar door I devised and the incredible entrance hall can knock a guy off his cool stance. But I really didn't expect an old pro like E.C. to be caught speechless. The room gives the impression of never ending. It is over eighty feet long, with black obsidian floors shined like mirrors. Flarelike lanterns give it a sort of holy look. At the far end a patinated set of green bronze doors is flanked by two ancient and majestic Egyptian statues of the seated goddess Sekhmet with her serene lioness head and voluptuous woman's body. Complete with sacred solar disks above their heads, and hands complacently poised by their laps. Just for an instant, I could have sworn one of them winked at me. . . .

This Fine character has just been bubbling and babbling all along. No respect at all. You'd think a little creep of a bug like this would have the good common sense to avoid description of what has been erected by his betters. It shouldn't surprise me, though—it's always the people who can't write or compose who become famous critics of Shakespeare and Bach. Through the bronze doors into a completely different atmosphere. Grand, but warm in its unabashed luxury. Persian rugs galore, like tissues. And more doors to the great hall that surrounds the rooms of the pyramid. Soft lighting. Statues. Modern, medieval, classical, Oriental, and pre-Columbian. It all has a place here. In the corner is the van der Weyden triptych I squeezed out of a Czechoslovakian princess. And nearby a brace of not-so-clean Renoirs I outbid a foundation for.

"As I was telling you, Mr. Douglas, the complete contents of the house will be auctioned off subsequent to the actual sale of the property. We, of course, feel it's unfortunate such a collection is to be fragmented. But these are the ways of the world, aren't they?"

As Mr. Fine begins to talk about how major museums will benefit, our man is coming forth with his delayed answer to that last rhetorical question about the ways of the world.

"Those are not necessarily the ways of the world, Mr. Fine."

"I beg your pardon, Mr. Douglas."

"Oh, not to worry, Mr. Fine, really nothing at all."

The little man insistently continues his tour of the house. There are parlors and sitting rooms. Bedrooms galore, and a kitchen big enough to feed an army with gleaming copper pans exposed. There's a library and a game room, as well as the interior swimming pool and palm court. From the look on his face, E.C. is already rearranging the furniture and thinking to himself that Consuelo would go wild in that kitchen.

You've got to understand I never really lived full-time in this house. By the time it was finished, I had begun smelling that Harriet was spending too much time with the lawyers. Besides, she was always in love with our country house, which is, in fact, the place where I found my way into this new mode of existence. Mr. Fine is going on and on about some of the interior moldings, some of which are made of padauk. And of course he's spending a lot of time waxing eloquent on the various semiprecious trims in the flooring. For instance, he's elaborating on the obvious when he tells our man the tiger's-eye border on the black granite floor is a "masterful touch." Getting back to Harriet, she never really liked the idea of being shut into this giant jewel box. So once it was completed I had full rein to come over here and spend the nights alone tinkering with my toys.

"They say Mr. Somerset's wife left him when he began construction of the house. I've actually seen the woman. Quite a looker. She told me she'd decided to stay at her country estate instead of moving here. So that's an opportunity for a man like you, Mr. Douglas."

Our man looks steely as he almost chokes on a couple of well-placed ahems and ahas.

"On the other hand, the representatives of the city were here yesterday, and I've got to tell you, they are emphatic in their desire to purchase the property. Of course, they don't have a use or a budget for the art objects, but we feel museums and institutions will disburse a tidy sum for some of these babies. I have to tell you, though, Mr.

Douglas, you shouldn't be surprised if you find the property some-what exceeds your budget."

Our man is looking a bit peeved as he responds, "My budget, Mr. Fine, is not a matter of public record, or even private conversation."

"Of course, of course, Mr. Douglas, just trying to be understanding here."

We now proceed into my more personal chambers. Mr. Fine is going into paroxysms of ecstasy over this detail of lighting or that curlicue of architecture. My rooms all overlook the interior court with its reflecting pool and small trees. It really constitutes an enormous expanse of rough granite. The glass roof overhead is regulated by a computer, which registers the temperature and air currents and accordingly opens or closes the panes or lowers or raises the shades.

So now we're into my comfy little parlor with the Louis XV chairs. And the rugs on rugs. To keep my tootsies warm in winter. But these aren't ordinary floor coverings. They're silk carpets from Heriz in Persia, and they encompass designs which are geometrical, but with a tinge of the floral in the borders. Beautiful rusts, reds, and roses. If you flapped the things upside down you'd find a thousand knots per square inch. Probably tied by the tiny little fingers of slave children without hope in those far and bleak environs of the old Persian empire.

The library is three regular stories high and sunk deeply into the ground. My beautiful glass-and-zebrawood shelves are now securely locked. Behind the shining panes you can find a Gutenberg Bible. Not the common type on paper, but a vellum copy. And a Constance Missal, and Kervers, and Pigochets galore. Not to mention the books I bought when old Mr. Traynor died, like the two John Smiths, the Oviedos, the Medinas, and the Nuremberg Chronicle. Late into the night, I would paw over them like a Nibelung hoarding his treasures. The room is roughly sixty by forty feet, but comfortable, with a fireplace you could walk into at the far end. Mr. Fine doesn't actually know very much about my house. His rather cursory treatment of the library is revealing. I'm not just speaking about his very middle-class paucity of taste and education. What is mainly galling is his plain lack of know-how concerning the premises. Mind you, I'm not talking about the real secrets. When my old architect kicked the bucket, he took some of those with him. I would just have expected they'd have obtained a more polished fellow to show this gem of a house. Regarding my mysteries, I have every intention of trying to figure some way in which I might transmit them to E.C. if he buys this place.

We're walking into my bedroom. It's large and protective. But also hushed and cozy. There's a fireplace with great gargoyle andirons. Poised. As if ready to chomp a piece out of interlopers. More great geometric rugs. Reds and deep blues, and an enormous Venetian bed. Certified to have slept a Doge. Posts. Good for getting a little momentum. Or gently tying a conquest down for a little sexual revelry. Manganese-blue velvet covers. There are bolsters, and pillows. As well as blue curtains. Dulled by the sunlight, coming through bulletproof panes.

I'm beginning to feel a little sentimental about the whole thing. I just saw the little Egyptian burial hippopotamus I bought for a bunch of thousands. Blue faience. Painted with lotus blossoms. I always thought he looked like he was smiling. Now he's been neatly catalogued with an auction tag underneath one of his pudgy hind legs. There's one thing I haven't told you. You see, I was somewhat superstitious. Whenever I was planning a business deal, I'd wake up and look at him. And if the thing seemed to smile, I'd know it was right. But if I didn't perceive that little smile, I'd never touch the deal.

My bedroom wall is faced with a series of long, rectangular panes. Every other one is made out of thousands of minute pieces of stained glass. They're medieval, and we had to smuggle them out of France under the guise of their being a modern rolled-up mosaic. Now they're snugly tucked between the safety glass, secure from the rabble.

Mr. Fine is gushing again. "Now, Mr. Douglas, I particularly want you to note the details in this bathroom. The walls are entirely covered with lapis lazuli. It's an opulent little touch, but not as rich as the spigots, which are solid eighteen-karat gold. You might have noticed, Mr. Douglas, that the bidet, toilet, washstand, and tub are entirely carved out of the same beautiful stone. If anything, it's more spectacular than the guest bathrooms, which are done in malachite, rose quartz, and tiger's-eye. While some people do not approve of the mural in the dressing room, it should be noted that the mosaic is of Pompeian origin. Hearsay has it the late Mr. Somerset was very fond of the scene with the erect phalluses, saying it dated from right before the eruption."

On the wall two lovely young creatures curve around one another. You could almost reach out and touch the bodies. Caught there in the ancient artist's mosaic. As he fitted in every last little bit of teat and cock, and breast and ass. The beautiful boy is giving it to her hot and heavy. And the attack is most insistent as he pops his fresh bow into her stern. Mr. Fine is actually embarrassed, and exhibiting a bit of nerve. As he intimates someone might not like my little bit of lenociny. Getting back to the little piece of art on the wall of what Harriet more vulgarly called my masturbatorium, you will find she has perennial flowers in her hair, while he has probing ivy around his head. Black locks and comely, hard haunches. Her head is thrust back in ecstasy as they meet in a passionate, contorted kiss. On lonely nights when the lighting was dim, I could swear they were moving. And now I happen again upon my lovers. Frozen in time . . . but always ready to please.

We're going downstairs. Out into the main dining room. High ceilings again. Seventeenth-century lamp cradled by a Spanish Renaissance ceiling above. I brought the carved panels on the walls from Italy, and dismantled a Spanish manor for the rest. One hundred chairs in all. Magnificent and stately. Also the scene of an occasional faux pas. I remember the night they served the quail on Mrs. Fitzpansie's lap. Or the time when deep in wine I got playful and dropped the pickled herring down Lady G.'s *décolletage*. Best of all was the evening we had the new butler. He was a crusty sort. Thought himself superior to his betters. I remember they had placed a soup bowl in front of everyone. Except me. As he wheeled the tureen around the table, ladling out oodles of fragrant bisque, all had proceeded swimmingly. Until he tried to serve me and realized I had not been given a bowl. I smiled, took the ladle in hand, and wishing not to admit this sort of forgetfulness went on in my house, proceeded to slop the steaming liquid onto the table, where it ran in naughty directions. He left that night, but not without a firm imprinting of the rules of serving. After all, when one has chosen to serve soup as a way of life, one must do it well.

So here we are again in the recesses of the inner hall. Climbing that great staircase to the absolute heights of the structure, but no pyramidion here. Apart from the movable glass-roofed center, it's quite flat, like a variation on early Egyptian pyramids, or pre-Columbian mounds. A roof you can pace on beneath the stars. I used to mark their placement on the granite with luminous chalk. The view from here is excellent. In the distance the river that becomes subterranean near the house winds its way through the outskirts of the city, where it ultimately will curve past a first cemetery where I once thought I'd like to be buried. Until I found they were admitting all sorts of riffraff. It moves onward, though, like the river of life, and ultimately borders the necropolis of Sleepy Heights. Now that I think of it, this ribbon of water is a means of staying in touch.

You know, I was talking about stars a while back. Douglas has stars in his eyes today too. I can tell no one has to do a great deal of convincing here. He wants this place. He hopes to walk the ramparts of this structure by night. Bozo and I might even be able to teach him how to howl at autumn moons. You know, I still don't know the reason for all of this, but I'm beginning to feel that old *gusto* flowing again within me. Almost like being alive. No, perhaps better.

SEVEN

It's Friday. Auction day. This morning they took Bozo and bathed him with care. Used some fancy shampoo, and then the equivalent of a bucket of creme rinse. His silver-gray hairs have become even softer and silkier. Particularly after all that brushing and combing. I note someone has been to the jeweler and purchased a glistening dog chain and new collar punctuated by a shiny stone here and there.

Szilagyi is wearing his best blue serge and bright black boots. Our man has been upstairs in the bedroom dressing. Black tie, no less. He's selected a beautiful Italian evening shirt made of Egyptian cotton. The hand stitching on the shirt is so tiny someone undoubtedly went blind putting it together. Then there's the suit itself. Simple and classic in midnight blue. I'm glad his evening clothes aren't made out of the standard black. Waiters use black, but gentlemen recur to midnight blue because it looks blacker than black at night. He's wearing a well-fitted vest and tied patent-leather shoes. I took a peek when he donned them and noted with pleasure that they're lined with bright crimson leather. You'd never know, though. He's going up to the mirror to tie an assertively proper silk butterfly bow. He knows what he's doing, but still has to try it a few times before it's perfect. The result, however, is rewarding, and the whole thing looks like nothing short of a swim in the lake could disrupt it. He's going into one of those thin drawers, from which he extracts a platinum pocket watch, complete with chain. The timepiece is very flat and unobtrusive. The cuff links are also platinum with blue star sapphires and studs to match. Altogether, it's a good show.

As he comes down the stairs the butler is handing him an ecrucolored silk scarf which sports ever so tiny embroidery. Also a cane with an ivory top carved into the shape of a lion.

"No, Thomas, I think I'll take the cane with the alligator on it tonight."

Thomas is going into the entrance closet, where neatly lined are malacca canes with every conceivable variety of carved animal top.

Into the car go dog and man. I note this evening they're using the large Mercedes. Mind you, this is a class vehicle, serviceable in every respect. But I personally prefer my old Duesenberg. Szilagyi is chatty tonight:

"Good evening, Mr. Douglas. Are we going to that crazy auction? I hear invitations to that thing are the hottest item in town. I should have known you'd have one."

"Yes, that's where we're going, but it's really not a crazy auction."

"Sorry, sir, I didn't mean to be offensive. It's just that I've been reading about that Somerset guy in the papers. It seems this place we're going to is some sort of a scary fun house. Boy, that guy must have had a ball. Imagine the women that go after a man like that."

Sensing his master is not exceedingly communicative tonight, the chauffeur has opted for greater discretion. Douglas has again receded into thought. As he lightly taps his patent-leather shoes on the carpet. It's a mute sound. Silent, yet insistent. The driver takes the cue and decides to keep his flaptrap shut for a while. He doesn't really mean any harm. All chauffeurs are the same. They all dream about being Lady Chatterley's lover. But usually, it's just a simonize and "yessir" job. I have, however, been told there are exceptions. I heard old Mrs.

Biglee up on the hill used to get it from her driver. Aged eighty-one and all. His name was Fritz. In her more alcoholic moments, she'd refer to it all very stiffly as being prescriptive for her health. They said he had an awfully big thing, to which she referred as her German injection. Alas, they took her off one day in a gleaming white ambulance. Apoplexy, they said. Screaming "wheeee" all the way.

Well, I must say, there's no mistake tonight about where we're going. As we approach the farthest perimeter of the wall, the sky is ablaze with what must be ten antiaircraft lamps. Gamboling over one another. Tripping over a star here or there. They lend a great sense of excitement and anticipation. The magnificence of the structure now fully reveals itself, heightened by the play of light. Something within me is stirring in fixated admiration and affection as I note that in the nocturnal illumination my house can almost be said to breathe and heave and sigh. The trees are rustling placidly, and yet there's a restless note as well. A feeling of great expectation in the atmosphere.

There are uniformed men parking cars. Impressive collection. That's right, put it there in between the Duesenberg and the Bugatti Royale. The staircase is down. Security guards everywhere. There's an attendant in livery taking names. A real old-fashioned affair. The guests are being processed effectively and expeditiously. After all, these are not people who appreciate waiting or delay.

As we approach, our man removes his scarf with one definitive gesture. Something remarkable has come over him. He's looking rather driven but serene. Powdery-eyed, but calm.

His name has been checked off the list, and we're now walking up the stairs. Complete with dog in tow. Saying hello to Mrs. Inchabout, wife of the oil tycoon. And the widow Wendover. Worth a hundred million if she's worth a cent. Chatting momentarily with Lady Fallop, in from the Marquesas, where she was taking the sun. And, of course, it couldn't fail. Mrs. Piggot withdrew her tiara from the vault for the occasion. It's got those five phenomenal emeralds on it that the Rani of Patiala used to wear as an anklet. But most people aren't aware of this, so her secret is safe. Even frail little Mrs. Jodes-Fandango, the Spanish taffy heiress, is wearing her best tonight. Her last husband is said to have died mysteriously after giving her a customary cane whipping. Rumor has it his hot toddy did him in. One can't help looking more closely at poor little Mrs. Jodes. She is a well-preserved sixty-five or seventy, with the true age lost somewhere in the tissue they removed during her last stretch. She's tiny, and can't weigh more than eighty or ninety pounds. Around her neck is an enormous rope of baroque South Sea pearls which practically reaches the hem of her black Fortuny dress. From the diminutive ears hang two gigantic pear-shaped diamonds at least the size of walnuts. She should have carried the hand in on a wheelbarrow. After all, the emerald cut must be at least sixty carats. And no South African junk here, they're all genuine Golcondas. She's also wearing a bracelet which is composed of stupendously large and heavy stones. Looking at her, one can't help thinking she's altogether like a feather dipped in lead. Nevertheless, magnificent. After tonight, of course, she'll retire to bed with one of her cases of allergic pneumonia. And afterward she'll be off to some Eastern European country where they'll inject her with extract of unborn embryo of this or that. But who cares? As we say, *the needle knows what it sews and the thimble what it pushes.* No one who is anyone would dare miss this affair. After all, this is a chance to take a peek into my lifestyle. I see the bankers and lawyers clucking in the corner. Half of them never got an invitation during my lifetime. So now they take advantage of the combination of my absence and their bankbooks to write themselves an entrance ticket.

Harriet has just arrived on the now never-failing arm of Tom Hooker. She's capitalizing on the widow image in a loosely fitting black silk velvet dress with an Empire line to it. It's not a bad look.

I remember all the grief she gave me over the construction of this place. She always said it was "all too much." And I tried to tell her about the journey of the soul and how destiny at its best only dealt with the options and not the selections. But she never even tried to understand anything. And just said she was thoroughly disgusted by it all.

Hooker is looking as rapacious as ever. He has one of those blotchy complexions that border on being freckly. But only to confirm themselves as constituting errors in one of nature's basic designs for pigmentation. That little curved nose can best be described as "beaky." And of course all of this is made further endearing to us by those weasely little eyes. I actually turned this fellow into a rich man, and didn't mind watching him get there. It reminded me constantly of who I shouldn't want to be. Lawyers are similar to vultures, but lower. I think Plato said one should get rid of the poets in the perfect state. Well, he was all wrong. It's these so called advocates who have to be blighted out. It's not hard to understand when you think about it. Most attorneys nowadays come from lowly or middle-class backgrounds. They usually study law for all the wrong reasons. It's socio-economic mobility which is paramount in their minds. So they grub their way through school and then compete with one another to be employed by the finest firms. These entities constitute very distinct powers in their own right. They have become glued to their major clients by a combination of ability and subtle blackmail. They frequently know where the bodies are buried, so to speak, as they hold on to their clients' testicles ever so gently. In spite of the fact most of them would contend that their job is instructing clients on the legalities of matters, the truth is they spend most of their time teaching them how to achieve illegal or immoral ends by technically correct means. They spend their lives coddled by the insensitive organizations they serve. Striving each day for a larger fee. Creating activity in order to warrant their intervention. And always feeding the great litigation cows which can be counted upon for "milk" through bleak and plentiful years alike. Into this atmosphere go the young and argumentative. At that stage, occasionally, even an ideal can be discerned in the bargain. I find that as attorneys learn that confrontation is the standard fare of the lawyer, and gladiatorial combat is the exercise of each day, they do only one of two or three things. They either crack up, get out, or become totally cynical and amoral.

I remember one nice associate at one of the firms that serviced my accounts. Poor kid just couldn't take the pressure and went crazy one day. So he climbed up to the top of the air-conditioning tower on the seventy-eighth floor, and proceeded to rip pages, one by one, out of the Supreme Court Reporter he had carried to the top. Giggling with discombobulated glee, he cheered each page as the wind took hold of it. And when the end of the volume was reached, he jumped. It was shortly thereafter upon visiting his firm to inquire as to the possible recipients of my condolences that I discovered his name had been magnetically adhered to the plate beside his door. And had been summarily removed without a trace, almost before he ever hit the ground.

A strikingly good-looking young man is helping us seat ourselves. He's smiling delightedly. But try though he may to seem a part of things, he's just *another cat at a dog show*. We have a nice second-row seat. Almost everyone is here now. Even that Middle Eastern fellow with more money than God has arrived on time. One seat is still empty, though. Well, we didn't have to wonder very long about who its owner might be. An off-the-rack-dressed public servant has just made his appearance and filled the empty chaise. You should have known he'd be the only one to arrive late. After all, it's been said that *punctuality is the courtesy of kings*. True to type, this guy is sweating profusely. He's going to need a bedsheet to dry it up before he's done tonight. And he hasn't disappointed us. He's pulling from his pockets a cheap little black book, a plastic felt-tipped pen, and a pocket calculator.

All of my little gilded chairs from the ballroom look rather impressive here in the great hall. In addition to the regular lighting, the candles in the wall sconces provide a rather comforting softness. The black floor with its tiger's-eye trim and the statues of Sekhmet lend a suitable degree of solemnity to the affair. My two lion goddesses are not smiling tonight either. They're just looking their dignified, otherworldly part. Up at the podium, which is set right in front of the great bronze doors, flanked by the statues, a thin little man in evening dress is calling the session to order. He beams as the lights are dimmed a bit and a hush overcomes this gleaming, varnished crowd. I'm feeling a little tense. The circus is about to begin. As if instinctively the auctioneer has tuned in to the fact that different parties will be using imperceptible gestures with which to bid. With measured calm, our man is pulling a handkerchief from his pocket and sniffing into it.

The auctioneer is extolling the virtues of the place, but no need to. At first, there are six or eight token bids. Then it becomes evident there are only three bidders in this room. The ready-made little government man is strong and tenacious. No one could doubt that this emissary of bad taste and smog-filled skies is from the city. For the moment, it's between the ready-made man and the Middle Eastern fellow, who is bidding with the flick of a solid-gold pencil. They're up farther than I thought. I'm looking at our man. "Hey, kiddo, where are you? Aren't you going to bid?" But E. C. Douglas retains that powdery look in his eyes. They've just reached a new plateau, and the bidding is going up five million at a time. I give Bozo a good hard pinch, and he pushes his large groomed head against our man's hand. Just when I'm feeling despair, as if by operation of magic E.C. snaps into action. With the flick of that handkerchief he rolls in clear and loud with a stupendous bid. There's a little moment of silence as the other two bidders size up the newcomer.

The auctioneer is smart to capitalize on the recent arrival. "Do I hear more? I have five million more from His Majesty."

The Middle Eastern fellow is nervously fingering his thirty-three amber worry beads, which end in a tassel, to ward off the evil eye.

"Do I hear more . . . yes, I have another five million from Mr. . . . Ummm . . . for the city. . . . Do I hear another five million?"

And up they go to what I think may be old Doug's limit. The sheik bows out first and bids no more with a genteel and deferential nod of the head to E.C. But that disgusting little weasel from the city is still going strong. Looks like he'll be damned if he'll let our man have it. But Douglas is fantastic and strong-willed. He bids onward with the self-possession of an El Greco grand inquisitor. With the flip of his white handkerchief. Up-tee-dum they go. Until you can hear a pin drop in the place. Douglas has made a final raise. The man from the city falters.

"Going once."

The man from the city is nervously fidgeting with his calculator. He looks like he's going to try to raise it once more. But hesitates. . . .

"Going twice."

More silence. The auctioneer is giving the city bidder a little look of encouragement. But no soap. He is sweating profusely and looking pale as with a defeated gesture he drops the little pocket ruler with which he was bidding. He has suddenly been brutally deflated as the auctioneer's gavel comes down firmly to the tune of the word "sold."

Everywhere there is rambunction. People are congratulating a now-dazed Douglas. The dog has snapped to attention and is leaning against him. E.C. is just sitting there with that smile on his face, and his index finger against his nose. I've learned to realize it's what he does when he's feeling pleased about something. Flashbulbs are going pop, and strobe lights are bouncing all over the blasted place. The press begins to crowd around our man, who has now resumed his glassy-eyed look. Attendants rush to his aid. As E. C. Douglas calmly seizes his cane and prepares to leave.

As he turns, Mrs. Fitzhugh is yelling something about how "marvelous the bidding was." Mrs. Pratt and Mrs. Peepodd are whispering about that bitch Harriet and Hooker, now holding hands brazenly. In the excitement, Mrs. Piggot's tiara is now crookedly awry. In a corner, little Mrs. Jodes-Fandango is beginning to gag a little, coughing pneumonitically under the weight of her diamond earrings. Our man has had a momentary lapse and, for a second, seems like he might collapse. But Bozo leans against him heavily, and Douglas stands erect. Now walking calmly out of the room. Down the granite stairs to the waiting vehicle. Szylagyi clicks to attention as he opens the door, and the dog bounds in. A hush rolls over the crowd when E.C. bows to enter. As the taillights of the vehicle are seen in the distance, there is much conversation about the memorable aspects of the occasion.

EIGHT

I CAN'T BELIEVE A COUPLE OF DAYS HAVE PASSED SO QUICKLY SINCE THAT night E.C. bought this place. There hasn't been a dearth of excitement, though. All morning they've been rearranging furniture and paintings. A Tiepolo finds a new place in the sitting room. Above the green silk velvet chairs, which are signed *Jacob*. A rather small Vlaminck is moved into an intimate niche. Next to a very precious Renoir of a child. The Riesener desk is back in the library, as are the Boulle cabinets, and the Greco. There's a lot of excitement here. So much that I almost can't keep up with it. Even though I've been the most avid witness at the last three nights of auction, I didn't fully believe the whole extravaganza was real until I saw it mirrored in this morning's paper.

BULK OF SOMERSET COLLECTION IS PURCHASED
BY E. C. DOUGLAS

With a flair reminiscent of the turn of the century and the pre-Depression Duveen auctions, E. C. Douglas has successfully bid on, and captured, some of the most precious objects in the world from the famed Somerset collection. The previously publicity-shy financier last night ended three sessions of sometimes relentless bidding against connoisseurs, collectors, speculators, institutions, and museums. Last night's sale of Old Masters at Pyramid Hill has successfully delivered to Mr. Douglas one of the finest collections still extant. In surpassing the estimates set by the auctioneers, Mr. Douglas has become the highest estate bidder in the history of the nation. His combined bid for the Pigochet and Kerver collection of French books of hours is one of the highest ever paid for an accumulation of books anywhere. Rumor has it that with the acquisition of the Somerset Caxtons, his collection of that early printer's productions now surpasses those of the Bibliothèque National and the British Museum.

The Impressionist paintings include works by all of the major artists of the period, including a large and late Van Gogh oil. But Mr. Douglas's interest has also extended itself strongly into Mr. Somerset's collections of carpets, furniture, decorative arts, silver, Russian enamel, classical antiquities, and nineteenth-century paintings.

Although no interviews have been granted by the somewhat reclusive financier, rumor has it the collection will be redistributed within its previous home, which has also been purchased by Mr. Douglas. Curious onlookers could not help noticing a certain flair reminiscent of the late Mr. Somerset in the Douglas purchases. This would seem to represent a departure from Mr. Douglas's previous personality.

Great disappointment has been generated in artistic and curatorial circles, where hope had existed regarding the reemergence of such treasures into museums and the public light.

Wow! All my things are here, minus a few odds and ends. In the library my little blue faience hippo smiles sardonically. As I go gamboling through the great hall, I take pleasure in patting these two now-giggly statues of Sekhmet smack on the breasts to remind them they're still home and Daddy is here again.

In the dining room, our man is supervising the hanging of the large Canaletto that I previously had in the sitting room. I must say it looks very good here. One can almost feel the majesty of the Grand Canal. With the gondolas ebbing in the swell. Back in the dining room my silver is being polished by attendants, as Bozo gnaws on a large bone of veal. Miss Cleave is doing inventory, checking out *this* marrow spoon and *that* Fabergé teapot. She's wearing a pale blue cashmere sweater, with boobies nicely stiff. There's a little note of familiarity here between our man and Sue. As he pats her on the shoulder, I have the distinct impression he wouldn't mind placing his hand a bit lower. Miss Cleave is complaining about the cheap sale tags the auctioneers stick on things. And she's right. I never could understand how they could take a piece of furniture which has survived the French Revolution and then put a gummy tag on it.

People are arriving with all sorts of odds and ends. From E.C.'s house. Clothes, shoes, pots and pans. No doubt about it now. He's really going to do it. Live here, I mean. Back to the dining room, where they're making an inventory of the china he's just bought. There are now more frequent glances between the two. Something seems to be happening here. Some sort of sneaky understanding. I don't mean to become trite about it all, but it does seem like boy meets girl all over again. It's as if they've known one another a lot longer than they really have. She mentions me. And he smiles. She says something about how he should wax jealous when she reminds him about us. But he merely looks placidly fascinated, as if he simply wants to take it all in. This fellow is really quite dazzled by my remembrance and everything I did in life. He wants to steal my spotlight. And I can't help thinking this can be perfectly arranged. Go ahead. Kiss her! That's right. Uh-huh. But what are you doing now?

Just when I thought there was going to be a little action here, he's walking out of the room. Oh . . . clever . . . he hasn't returned emptyhanded. Holding behind him, gently clenched, one perfectly beautiful red rose. Now walking up to her and gingerly placing it under her nose. I think that just clinched it. This is exactly the type of thoughtful gesture which is guaranteed to win Susan Cleave. The combination of the rose and that already-appreciated large hand is apt to send shivers up and down her lovely spine.

More conversation. He smiles while she looks on with a sad expression on her face. As if to say, "Will you never stop talking?" But he goes on and on about the house and how he would like to know more about it. I feel especially gratified at his comments about wishing to have met me. She's now giving him a very quizzical look. It's that countenance of disappointment women assume when all men can do is talk about themselves and their projects. But she knows what to do. She grabs his hand and breaks his train of thought. To-day, there will be no further talk about me. Silence for a while. One can actually feel the absence of sound bouncing off these walls.

Now they're off to the innards of the house. Over to my room. She sits on my bed and looks at him. Like any maiden looking at her lover. Bozo, bringer of the light note, saunters in and genteelly offers the tribute of one slightly used bone, plopped ever so nicely on the silk bedspread. Bone and dog are shown to the door, which closes with a sedate click. Leaving us outside.

I have mixed feelings about this whole affair. On the one hand, that guy is in there with my honey. And I know what's happening. No way like that way to rid her of my remembrance. Yes, *a new rivet always forces an old one out.* On the other hand, there's this bond that's been developing between E.C. and me. So in a way, I really don't know who to be jealous of. It's true he's taking her away from me, or at least from my memory, but on the other hand, it's very good to have her near. But I'll have to reach him somehow, and let him know she can also be disruptive. She could convince him that all this pomp isn't worth a damn and ruin my plans. As strange as it may sound, I'm also jealous she might make E.C. depart from my resolve.

It doesn't take me very long to collect my thoughts on the mat-ter. She can't see or hear me in spite of my love. And E.C. is very much the person of this undetermined present. I must therefore live through our man. I suppose I must also love her through him.

The door is unceremoniously opening, and Miss Cleave is emerging fully dressed and without damage. I guess nothing happened after all. E.C. looks like he wouldn't have minded. But I should have known. Sue is, above all things, a lady. And it will take a bit more than what she's seen to coax her into this guy's bed.

Now that they're returning to business in the study, I should mention something remarkable that has been happening to me. At night, I've been drifting off. Sort of falling asleep, if you can call it that. Anyway, I've been floating off into another dimension of sorts. And the most amazing part of it is I could swear I've been dreaming. At first, I didn't think I would dream again. But it's happening. In last night's little getaway, there was a shining table, and I was wearing a crown studded with beautiful stones of all sorts. The table was laden with halos. Among them was a wooden one, and a very beautiful one seemingly made out of nothing. I disremember what color. There was also one made out of very light and beautiful live butterflies. And lastly, there was one made out of platinum. I remember I took my crown off and selected the platinum one, which was very heavy indeed, and placed it on my head. Afterward, I wished for the butterflies, or for the halo made out of nothing. But when I made my first choice, all the others disappeared.

I sense there was more to that dream, but I can't remember it all. Anyway, something at that point made me stir. It was that damned clock again. And I became frightened and woke up, so to speak. In any event, I guess I shouldn't worry about the dream. It's sufficient to know everything is proceeding so well.

It's raining outside, and Miss Cleave has been dispatched home after a busy day. Outside the windows to the interior court, the steady droplets are coming down on the stone, forming resplendent, dark puddles which drain quietly and ceaselessly.

The phone is ringing. Our man grabs for it, only to hear one irascible investment adviser on the line.

"E.C., this is Harry."

"Harry, old bean."

"Don't old bean me, E.C., we're in serious trouble here."

"What's the problem?"

"You've overextended yourself with everything you've bought in the last four days, and the bottom has just dropped out of the commodities markets. Everything is down the limit, and tomorrow your margin call will be in excess of a hundred million. You see, E.C., I told you not to spend your surplus cash!"

"What can we do about it, Harry? How about selling some of the common stock?"

"You can't do that. Tomorrow morning this will spill over into the stock market, and you could turn into a piker overnight. What do you want to do?"

"Well, Harry, the market is closed and I have no intention of covering in London and raping myself. I guess for the moment I'll just do nothing."

"E.C., please bear in mind that before ten o'clock when the market opens tomorrow, something must be done or we're going to have a serious problem on our hands."

"Okay, Harry. I understand."

Click.

I can't believe E.C. has overspent. Pretty stupid. If he's anything like I was, he probably has a nice little wad put away for just such a day. I always compared myself to the Boy Scouts—always prepared. But he looks worried. And I'm thinking this fellow may not be as smart as I thought. Hours pass, as I sit here watching E.C. stare at the ceiling.

The phone is ringing again. It's Harry. He's hysterical. Screaming something about the market going lower in London. Expectations of a grim opening in the Orient. E.C. has very gently placed the phone on its cradle. He's looking genuinely worried. Moving now from the comfortable chair to the Riesener desk, where he's buried his face in his hands in a gesture of total impotence.

I myself am at somewhat of a loss. Even the white rabbit knew when it was too late. And it is indeed too late to be prudent. What to do? I can't let the vultures get their hands on this situation. I've got to find a way to insulate this guy from his financial problem. He's now looking blankly into the rain. In a state of quiet, contained desperation. Everything which had been gleeful this morning has now come down with a crash. I shall indeed go mad with him if I think about this matter any further. But I'm remembering that story about the king's horse. You've probably heard it. It's the one in which the cook had committed an act of *lèse-majesté* and was condemned to decapitation. It seems that at the moment at which the executioner's ax was about to swing down and the cook was asked if there was anything he wished to say, he exclaimed: "Your Majesty, if you grant me a year's stay of execution, I shall teach your horse how to speak." The king, who had nothing to lose, and no downside to sustain, thought to himself that this was a rather amusing proposal. So he acceded to the request. Back in the kitchen the cook's helper asked the cook why he had made such a terribly poor deal, to which the cook responded: "It's not a bad deal at all. During this year, many things could happen. I could die, or the horse could die, or the king could die. Or ultimately, the horse could speak."

With this in mind and noticing that our man is beginning to think of attempting what will undoubtedly be a fitful rest, I can't help thinking a little sleep might be good for me as well. So the three of us, man, ghost, and woolly behemoth, will collect ourselves for a bit of respite. On this desperate fall night.

NINE

I seem to have dozed quite soundly. Although it's still dark outside, I sense the morning light will soon be upon us. That clock there says ten after six. Which feels right. I think I fell into that dream state again last night. I'm beginning to remember some of it. Who would have thought you'd dream when you were dead! I recall it now. I was wandering endlessly through the halls of this pyramid. In the reverie, I had a large sack in my hand, and was gleefully enjoying my solitude. As I stealthily crept into the basement, I pressed some of the stones in the wall and the granite gave way to a staircase. It seems to me I went down that staircase and into a room which had no windows, but which sported a Bank of England chair and an English counting table. The atmosphere was overwhelmingly magical. In the dream, I was bathed in a lovely, intense yellow light. Out of my bag came bars of gold and a box full of diamonds. I ran my hands through them and then pressed some of the granite stones behind the wall of that room, and a large vault became visible behind the stone. I was about to put all those goodies away in the safe when I suddenly began thinking about that clock again, was somewhat shaken, and woke up. Wait a minute, though. . . . That whole scene was not something I made up! Now that I recall, that stuff is really there. Why, I could kick myself for having forgotten. What element of a dead man's subconscious would dredge up this bit of information at such a crucial moment? Seems to me E.C. could use those shekels. But even if I could remember what to push and how to do it, how could I transmit this information to our man?

I never cease to wonder at the limitless horizons of the mind. All those little gray cells. Neurons, and synapses. Billions of electrical impulses. All of it to service a unique creation. We always say the mind is like a computer, but of course, it's really the other way around. And all of the computers I've ever known have certainly been devoid of that reliability factor which unscrupulous salesmen are always trying to push on you. The mind and computer are really quite similar. We become tired, and the damn machines suffer electrical overload. We have amnesia and they suffer inexplicable loss of database. We're stubborn, and sometimes you have to press the key three times to make the machine work correctly. People in the twentieth century have been longing far too much for the supposed mechanical slaves of the twenty-first. But I have misgivings about the nature of the ultimate computers. Presumably they will not suffer from unreliability of the human variety. But I always say, beware. Because no machine by definition could really have an infinite ability to repair or protect itself, since such a capability would constitute the equivalent of creating itself. So instead of having the flu, and lover troubles, our machines will suffer from electrical imbalances and mechanical failure. This really doesn't vary much from certain lapses of electric impulses within the brain. Which gets us back to where I started: I was marveling at all the bits of information which we can store. I'm also now convinced the memory storage within the brain is holographic, meaning to say it isn't ordered like a card catalog, which would make it vulnerable to damage by sectors. But the holographic or dot matrix system would be consistent with the brain's ability to tap memory at random. And make great logical jumps. All in all, I'll pit it against the mechanical computer any day of the week.

I used to think the sleep process, in addition to resting me, served as a period in which my brain could unburden itself of all the bits of information which it had decided to discard. My present state of refreshment buttresses that theory. Also in that process, important or necessary information is obviously highlighted. Which is, I think, the reason why I had that dream last night.

I can now appreciate the first morning clarity, and the few birds still hanging around are chirping rather insistently in anticipation of the day. Bozo seems to have exited the bedroom, and is on his way down the staircase. Looking a bit languid. I think I'll cheer him up. So, I approach and scratch him on the head, speaking in quasi-baby-talk the way I often affectionately did in life. I'm getting a hell of a rise out of this pooch! He's curling that wonderful liver-colored upper lip as if to smile broadly. There's a ball he was playing with yesterday over there at the foot of the couch. "Bozo, get the ball. Fetch the ball." And to my surprise, he does exactly what I'm saying and mouths the ball, returning with it to place the thing smack in the middle of my lap. This is more fun than I've had in quite a while. It would seem they didn't take all my playmates away.

Actually, I'm having one of those epiphanies which begin in the most recondite regions of the mind, and blister forth as a slow boil into a very firm and relevant idea. If I could remember all the sequences in that mechanical play of rocks downstairs, I could probably teach Bozo how to help E.C. gain access to those goodies. In any event, it's certainly worth a try.

E.C. is up and around. So Bozo and I decide to bound into the bedroom. This guy actually slept in pajamas last night. Blue cotton. I guess he wanted to feel cozy in the face of the rain outside. He's not dressing yet, which is a bad sign. One of obvious depression. Bozo has gone downstairs and returned, slobbery tennis ball in mouth. He's dropping it ever so gingerly at E.C.'s feet. But our man is deep in thought, and just can't be bothered to play with the pooch this morning.

Ring, ring. It's that damn phone again. E. C. Douglas looks a little pale. Genuinely green under the gills. Harry apparently has a mouthful for him this morning.

"I tell you, E.C., things are bad here. The fellow downstairs went into the bathroom this morning after a brief conversation with his boss and left his rings, watch, and wallet on the washstand. The guy actually jumped out the twentieth-floor window. The markets are all down, and you're in the red this morning for about a hundred and thirty-two million. When the market opens in about an hour, we're going to need the cash, or it's curtains for you on Wall Street. So what are you going to do?"

"Harry, hold on to your britches, and busy yourself counting your balls. I'll be back to you within the hour."

Click.

He's just sitting there in his pajamas and bathrobe. Now he's grabbing the phone and calling some guy in London, who tells him it will take three days to liquidate those assets. So we're back to sulking in the chair and muttering ever so softly, "What to do?"

I've just got to manifest myself. It's time to mobilize this duo of man and dog. I tiptoe up to Bozo, who immediately acknowledges me, and whisper into his ear, "Bozo, bring the nice man. Bring the nice man!" The pooch is momentarily still. But then resolutely saunters up to E.C., grabs his bathrobe, and gives it a tug. E.C. thinks he's being playful and pats him on the head as he reaches for the ball and says, "Go play with the ball like a nice dog." The sphere is thrown, and Bozo looks torn between this diversion and his duty. Luckily, I have taught him the meaning of the word "no." So Bozo holds firm, bathrobe in jaw. Since our man has seemingly more important things on his mind this morning, he's beginning to seem a bit peeved. But I am steadfast and persistent in my command to Bozo. And no amount of E.C.'s vexation will deter us.

I'm now gently coaxing the pooch out of the bedroom. E.C. is beginning to realize that this hundred-and-seventy-pound behemoth has more than a passing fancy in mind. So now he's following as Bozo attaches himself more comfortably to the tassel on the end of the bathrobe belt. Down the stairs, into the great hall, where the lionesses are sitting with raised eyebrows and looks of wonder. Now through a side door, easy as pie. Down an elegant stairway into the basement. That's right, Bozo. Pull him into the cellar. Our man takes a slip of paper out of his pocket and is using the combination to open the massive vault door to the wine cellar.

"Hey, pooch, you didn't bring me down here to drown in Malmsey, did you?"

I note with pride that he can still chuckle within the quiet desperation of his situation.

The wine cellar is a room which is lovely in its rusticity. Gray Vermont granite floors of the rough variety and walls to match. With endless freestanding racks of fine wine, as well as those against the walls. One of the walls is, however, devoid of bottles, and sports the equivalent of a stone mosaic with scenes of the god Bacchus and the process of making wine. E.C. is affectionately patting the dog, and speaking to him.

"Well, poochie, you know, it may be a tad early, but my grandfather always said, 'When in doubt, drink Madeira.'"

He's going over to the wall and pulling out one of my best bottles of pre-phylloxera Sercial. It's 1892, no less. Of course, the wine's been recorked several times by a virtuoso of the art who can pull a soggy cork and replace it almost without a sound, in the vintner's equivalent of a nanosecond. The firm cork removed and the ambrosia poured, our man is now quietly sipping, after spilling a few drops on the floor for Bozo. The pooch knows what's good. He's slurping it up.

I'm speaking to him again. This time in my most beguiling tone. Prodding him over to the two-inch squares of mosaic, and giving him an order to press a little stone. Since our man is lost in space, I've got to make him realize something is going on here. So I talk to Bozo again and tell him, "Bring the nice man. Bring the nice man!" Bozo is all over E.C. with his pulling and tugging again, and E.C. has now snapped out of his little daydream. Over to the wall, Bozo is pressing that stone with his snout, "Attaboy. Now, go over to that other one and get up on your hind legs and try to press it." As E.C. sees the woolly beast up on his hind legs, he becomes intensely interested, which is just what I've wanted. Now he's helping Bozo push that stone, and of course has realized something is afoot here with this deceptively charming *pietra dura* mural. There are two more stones to be depressed. But Bozo is getting the hang of pointing them out, and our man seems to be picking up the cue with little delay. When the fourth stone is depressed, a tremor goes through the room. As the entire left section of the wall begins to recede into the wings, a narrow granite staircase pivots into sight. The passage has automatically become illuminated. Dog and man proceed down the thirty-three stairs to that room of which I dreamed last night.

It's all here. The Bank of England chair, upholstered in red leather. And the counting table. Our man is examining this vaultlike room with a look of disappointment on his face. I suspect he expected to find my treasures stacked up high where some cheap thief might escape with a trifle or two. Nosiree, Douglas, you're going to have to work at this one.

I'm discovering I don't have to speak to Bozo. I can practice a sort of telepathy, and thus influence him to do my bidding. So here I go to work on the four-by-four-inch blocks of granite running along the baseboard. That's it, Bozo. Take him to number three and number seven. Good, he's pushing them. And now show him number thirteen and number nine. He's pressing them one after another, but nothing is happening. Now he got the bright idea of bearing down on them together. There is an audible gasp as an entire slab on the wall recedes majestically and then slides away to reveal a not unsubstantial bit of old Henry's treasure. Gold bars. Lots of them. And boxes full of diamonds ranging from two to twenty carats. Wafers of platinum. In all, I'd say about five hundred and fifty million worth. Our man is becoming visibly excited. He's counting the bars and wafers, performing an astute mental calculation of value. By now he's determined he can resolve his problem without the diamonds. Bozo is looking bored and a bit tired after the pyrotechnics of all this mental activity. Our man is now looking renewed. He runs up the stairs. But just as he's leaving the wine cellar, he bolts back and drinks the remainder of that glass of Madeira.

Out of the cellar he goes. Into the great hall. Straight to the nearest telephone:

"Harry, everything is going to be all right."

"E.C., whatever you're going to do, you'd best do it quickly. We only have about forty-five minutes left. Where's the cash?"

"Harry, I don't have any cash."

"Oh, old boy, this is a very bad time to tell me something like that. What will we ever do?"

"I'll tell you what you'll do. You will alert the people at the exchange to post extra security, since I'll be meeting my margin calls by depositing bullion in my accounts."

"You've got to be kidding. Where would you get your hands on that much gold overnight?"

"Harry, remember I'm like the Boy Scouts. Always prepared. Why don't you stop babbling and make the arrangements?"

"I'm dumbfounded, you old fucker. All I can say is: Good show, E.C. Good show."

Click.

Our man is making an additional call, which has to do with armored transportation. His call completed, he runs upstairs, hops into the shower. Masturbates a boner. And emerges pink and refreshed into the dressing room, where he dresses in his best navy blue. The front bell is ringing, and the butler has been taken a bit aback at the sight of security armed with pump shotguns. But our man conveniently dismisses the help to the interior rooms, runs down the stairs, and shows the guards into the wine cellar, where a trusted retainer is now stacking the gold as another two carry it up from the little room. They are now slowly and methodically carting all this treasure into the truck. After a receipt is presented, the bullion is off to its new home.

I've often wondered why periods of intense activity are always followed by moments of quiescence and introspection. We are at such a juncture. All the excitement of the early morning past, E.C. is now quietly walking down those granite steps into my vault. Followed only by Bozo. He's been careful to lock the doors behind him. So he's completely alone in this almost noiseless world. My bullion is gone. But he's carefully directing his attention to the beautiful little polished steel chests which he is now removing from where he secured them while the gold was being carted and placing them on the table. There is a moment of trepidation before he again begins opening these boxes, each of them a good eight inches by six, and at least four inches deep. Nine receptacles in all, each containing different shapes and sizes of good commercial diamonds. One by one, with all reverence, the boxes are opened. Within them, my diamonds shine with the condensed light and energy of the ages. White and pure, they constitute my own little private galaxy of stars. With trembling fingers he caresses stones shaped like little pears. Brilliants, emerald cuts, hearts, marquise and cushion as well. He's making designs on the table with my gems. Like a kid playing with beach pebbles. Now he's spelling things with them. Uhuh. A true romantic, spelling LOVE with my cool diamonds. There is irony to this, since it has been said that they are linked to the passions of men, and the love of women.

I remember when I'd come here on emotionally cold nights. To visit with my babies. A heady consolation when I'd been rebuffed and forgotten. I'd sit here and derive comfort from their soul-warming light. I also played with them. I once stuck one in my navel for a costume party. And very occasionally, I'd give one or two away. But most of them remained *mine, all mine*. Coveted children brought out of the dark night by old Henry to bring comfort to a troubled soul.

There are tens of millions on that table. Finest water. Perfection. There may be more here than they kept on view in the cellar of the Bank Melli when the old Shah was in power. You know, I vividly remember my visit to that place. You see, I had a sort of surrogate aunt and uncle who had adopted me as an honorary nephew. They were well-to-do. And he was linked to government. Which gave me access to cheap transportation and official circles. Not to mention preferential receptions. I remember I had been invited to travel with them during a spring break. So I accepted and found myself in Iran in the days preceding my own empire. A private guide escorted us through the momentous collection after the room had been closed to the general public. That day I was stunned by the trunks full of pearls the size of marbles, and by the Peacock Throne glistening with emeralds, diamonds, sapphires, and rubies. A globe of the world shimmered in the corner, covered entirely in large and precious stones. On different solid-gold trays the empire displayed Burmese rubies, Indian emeralds, and diamonds from the old Golconda mines. In a case, a gem-studded ball was to be found. All in all, about the size of a player's softball. The curator indicated that while the ball had been in the collection for many hundreds of years, no one could figure out why it had been made. The only information or cue they had was in a painting. It had once been depicted lying informally at the feet of a reigning shah. My little gray cells immediately formulated a question: Did it make noise, did it rattle? And I'll never forget the curator then came forth with a sardonically quizzical smile. He responded, "Yes indeed, it does rattle, but it's too heavy for a baby." It was then I cleverly explained to him that the ball was meant for the sybaritic pleasure of a great royal ocelot or cat. I'll never forget how flabbergasted that old curator was when faced with the plausibility of my hypothesis. I must say, all in all, it was a great time. These days, I guess that treasure is gone, and so are those times in which my "aunt" and "uncle" and I breezed through Central Asia like *the butcher's family which had hit the lottery*, on the great Van Golu Express.

But these diamonds are here and very real indeed. And soon I may introduce him to the additional and unsuspected treasure below. To the colored stones and to the things I collected for sheer pleasure—as opposed to investment.

I have very mixed emotions about having given some of my goodies up so soon. On the one hand, I feel the instinct to keep it all for myself. But in a way, I'm gaining pleasure, happiness, and security from my association with Douglas. If he's smart, he can use these things for collateral. And so propel himself forward. He's sitting there, running his fingers through the gems. Don't look now, but I think he's as hooked as I was the day I made my fateful visit to the Bank Melli vault. He should have known someone would come to the rescue. After all, I was here, and I couldn't very well leave him to the vultures. Not to mention the fact that Somerset never started anything he didn't finish. After all my concerns, this would seem to be a beginning, rather than an end. Perhaps now I shall have the opportunity to even a few scores, and attend to some matters of honor which were interrupted by my demise.

My sweet Bozo is looking thoroughly exhausted. No wonder. All that cogitation was probably a bit much for his canine brain. But to be sure, he's again shown himself to be the most loyal and wonderful of pooches. As if to recognize my thoughts, I receive from him a good old-fashioned wet slurp.

Today has been a significant day. We're going places. Advancing. Moving along with what would seem to be a pattern. I was successful in masterminding this morning's affair. And it's working out. But I've got to hurry. I must introduce this fellow to my own brilliant magnitude of business.

TEN

After this morning's bit of tension and resolution, E.C. downed a very substantial breakfast. Bozo is none the worse for it, since he was the gleeful recipient of the juicy sausages which were left on the dish when our man finished his meal. Now they are on their way to the office, where no doubt a great deal of excitement will be afoot. It's a gray morning. The type of meteorological unraveling you would expect after a night of heavy rain.

We're approaching the Consolidated Corn Building. It's one of those remnants of that period in finance when the grains were king. As our hermetic black tank reaches the curb, a doorman in fall coat is ready to help Douglas and his dog out of the car. Through the lobby we go, into the elevator. Up to the thirty-third floor. E.C.'s offices are not at all bad. In spite of the excess of Barcelona chairs and Breuer furniture. I too had my Bauhaus period. But as time proceeded, I found myself cordially hating the stuff more and more each day. After all, it's pretty difficult to warm up to all that tubular junk.

The young like it because it makes them feel sophisticated and minimalistic. And because it's easy to understand in its unmenacing simplicity. Most of the time, they're all just hiding their own particular brands of rococo complexes, which ultimately blossom into efflorescences of Louis XVI furniture and marquetry commodes. In some cases, the involution takes weird turns, and they end up doing things like wearing women's panties or keeping pet sheep. But never fear. Behind each and every Bauhaus devotee, there is a closet case of this or that.

There's a bit of good art on these walls. Some of it is somewhat too modern for me, but nevertheless, I do recognize the Pollocks and the Kandinskys. Very soon I expect to see these walls covered with old masters, solid Impressionists, sporting pictures, and some good American luminists.

We're walking down a long corridor to our man's office. We've reached the outer room, where he's bidding an excited Miss Cleave good morning.

"Boy, E.C., you sure have created a stir in the commodities markets this morning. You're in all the major papers. They're on your desk. And I sure am happy you made it. It would have been hell for me to lose this job so soon after arriving."

Our man has a peculiar smile on his face. He's delivering Bozo's leash to her as she efficiently grabs a handful of dog biscuit out of a polished mahogany box. He thinks a moment and then parsimoniously retorts:

"I too would have been crushed to have lost you so soon, Miss Cleave."

He's through the door and into the inner office. I must say I'm surprised. This is a totally different atmosphere. There's an enormous palace Nain rug on the floor. The blues in it neatly match our man's eyes. The rest of the room is furnished with good-quality English antiques. This place makes me feel right at home. You know, I think I'll adopt that needlepoint wing chair as my place to sit. Our man is sitting at the equivalent of a very large banker's table with a burgundy-colored leather top. His desk is almost devoid of papers. It's always a tip-off. The really successful men process each day's paperwork with great efficiency. So there's rarely anything on their desks. The morning's papers are piled up neatly on the left-hand corner of E.C.'s desk. He's reaching for the noon edition of the *Times*. My goodness, we're on the front page of the financial section today:

E. C. DOUGLAS MEETS $135 MILLION MARGIN CALL

In the aftermath of yesterday's limit moves in the commodities markets, many speculators were summarily liquidated prior to the opening of business today. This morning's edition listed a number of substantial brokers and individuals who would be faced at today's opening with large cash requirements. One such mention was that of E. C. Douglas, of E. C. Douglas and Company. Extensive speculation had occurred regarding certain margin calls exceeding $135 million, which, it was expected in certain circles, would not be met. Mr. Douglas is a relatively new player in the commodities markets, and some concern existed regarding the size of his commitments. In a style reminiscent of Morgan and Gulbenkian, the Douglas margin call was met promptly with a deposit of gold bullion at today's opening of business. Mr. Douglas's very substantial positions have thus been preserved.

E. C. Douglas has recently been the object of publicity due to his large expenditures in connection with the purchase of real estate and art from the Somerset collection. A significant portion of the trepidation in today's pre-opening activity had to do with suspicion that he might be over-extended.

It is believed the meeting of such a substantial margin call will not only buttress the markets but may also very quickly inure to the benefit of the Douglas interests.

Hot dog! If I know anything about that market, it'll flip in the opposite direction and he'll make a mint. The phone is ringing in the outer office, and it's Miss Cleave on the intercom telling E.C. that Harry is on the line.

"E.C., you old bastard, you did it, you did it! You should see what's happening here. The markets are going wild. Up, up, up! I wouldn't be surprised if everything were up the limit by three o'clock. Shall I liquidate now?"

Our man is looking like he's teetering. If I were he, I would temporarily double up on these positions. But how in the world can I tell him what I have in mind? Miss Cleave is coming in while Douglas has Harry on hold. In saunters the superpooch. No doubt about it. I've got to get Bozo to do this for me.

"Okay, Bozo, lift those ears, boy, lift those ears, and stand up on your hind legs."

Bozo is looking a bit bored with all of this and doesn't seem to be acquiescing at all. Then I have an idea. I'll use the old whistle on Bozo and see if I get a rise. So while Douglas is looking at the wall and Cleave is patiently waiting for him to pop out of his introspection, I emit my most stupendous whistle. Up go those ears. Upper lip as well. E.C. catches it immediately, and takes it as a sign. He's on the phone in a second, and he's giving Harry instructions.

"Okay, Harry, now listen carefully. What I want you to do is to double up on all positions. Call me every half hour and let me know how we're doing."

"E.C., I know you're a brainy bastard, but this is money we're playing with, remember? So why don't you take it easy today?"

"Harry, do what I'm telling you and call me in thirty minutes."

"Okay, E.C., I'm just your diamond-studded slave."

Click.

Sensing the seriousness of the moment, Miss Cleave has again retreated to the outer office, where a cup of espresso coffee is being placed on a silver tray for our man. A few minutes later, she's again here, with the brew. Bozo is comfortably sprawled on the carpet. I, in my wing chair, am just sitting here, gleefully waiting for this afternoon's news.

It doesn't take long for the phone to start ringing furiously. Harry is on the line again and is practically apoplectic with joy.

"E.C., you're a wizard. I can't believe what's happening here. The grains are up-up-up! And that bullion you used as collateral to pay for the margin calls this morning has gone through the ceiling as well. Some of the people who were liquidated yesterday are pulling the hairs out of their heads with this sudden turn in the market. You know, E.C., I've never thought you were sane. And after the way you doubled up this morning, I'm reconfirming my opinion. But if there's anything that I admire more than sanity, it's balls. And baby, you've got 'em. You realize that if the grain markets go up the limit and the bullion does as well, you're going to be worth roughly an extra six hundred million in cold cash? Not bad for a guy who would have had to work for years to become a real billionaire."

"Good work, Harry. I'm excited. Do you pray?"

"No, but I'm going to do it now."

"You know, Harry, I might very well accompany you."

All of a sudden there's a racket at the other end of the line that, pardon my expression, would probably raise the dead. Something akin to the noise one hears on television on New Year's Eve when that obnoxious ball reaches its destination at the moment of the year's arrival. I have a very good idea of what is going on there. But rather than speculate, I might as well hear it from Harry, who is seemingly never at a loss for words.

"Wait a minute, E.C.. . . . it's sharply up again. There's such a racket here that I can hardly hear you on the phone. . . . E.C., you son of a bitch, everything's up the limit."

"Okay, Harry, what do you think we should do?"

"Well, E.C., it's liable to be up much higher tomorrow."

"But it could be down too. What would you do?"

"I'd wait."

E.C. is looking genuinely consternated. He's tired, and I can tell that this range of cash denominations still makes him feel nervous. I'm too smart a cookie to allow E.C. to stick further with that position. He could lose it all if something goes awry tomorrow morning. So I'm tuning in on Bozo's somnolent canine brain and disturbing the alpha rhythm of his complacent snooze. It's not an easy job. This dog sleeps with the angelic demeanor of a clean conscience. But love him though I do, he is not beyond my present necessity. I'm getting in there now. Bozo perks up, and is now repeatedly running toward the door at my bidding. E.C. is quick to catch the message as he returns to his conversation with Harry:

"Harry, I think we'd best not be greedy. If you liquidate the positions in London, we're liable to pick up an extra forty or fifty million because of the spreads those racketeers will obtain from the shorts who must desperately want to get out of the market before the morning."

"Okay, E.C., you've got it. Where's my Château Latour?"

"Very soon, Harry, and 1947 to boot!"

Click.

Our man is looking a bit drained after all this activity. Not to mention the dog. He fell asleep almost immediately after that little back-and-forth pantomime. One really shouldn't be surprised. I remember how I felt when I made that first billion in liquid cash. It was a very special mixed feeling. Primarily one of liberation from the daily concerns of pedestrian millionaires. But then came the horrendous obligations imposed by that magnitude of wealth. So I suppose E.C. is beginning to experience that panoply of feeling. He's moving away from the desk and sitting in the other needlepoint wing chair, which rests in the adjacent corner of this room. With dog nearby. Man and dog are soon sound asleep. I like watching the two of them when they're in the land of nod. There's a camaraderie in all of this which I deeply enjoy.

This is what male bonding is all about. It's something females will never really understand. Mind you, I have nothing against females. In fact, I've always contended they represent the stronger of the two sexes. If I had to think of a truly implacable force, I would definitely say it was motherhood. When the end of the world comes, and there's a man left, and a mother, the man will do well not to interfere with that maternal instinct. Which is, of course, why all women love their children more than they love their husbands. Getting back to the identification thing, it's precisely that motherly instinct which makes it impossible for women to bond. After all, their sons must compete against one another in the world. And each mother wants her son to beat the other woman's. Females in one way or another must also vie for the attention of men, so they're always rivals, beautifying their bodies to appeal to their male gatherer-hunters. True, women get together to talk about their babies. But you just wait until this lady's Jimmy smacks that lady's Sally. Then you learn just how ruthless mothers can be in the defense of their cubs.

If the truth be known, I was always torn between my love for the company of men and my relentless desire to captivate and screw beautiful women. Just as I'm thinking about that last nuance, I take a quick look at the clock on the bookshelf. It's one of those atmospheric jobbies. It captures minute variations in pressure through a little hair on the top. Which, in turn, magnifies the movement with frictionless bearings and causes a pendulum to turn. There's something important about this timepiece. It's telling me that between sleep and my thoughts on the sexes, some time has really passed.

It's dark outside and the phone is ringing again. It's Harry:

"E.C., I'm in touch with our people in London. They can unload everything at pre-opening prices. It'll cost us a little more, but I don't think you should care, since the profit is so phenomenal. I'm faxing you a handwritten list of approximate prices. It's coming through your machine now."

"Hold it, Harry . . ."

A very tired Miss Cleave is running in with the sheet in her hand.

"Thank you, Susan. . . . Harry, it's quite acceptable. Convert it all to cash, and put it into the overnight market tomorrow, since you won't be able to reach me during the day."

"Don't tell me you're going on a holiday, E.C. You owe me a fucking case of 1947 Château Latour."

"Don't worry, Harry, your wine is on the way. It has, however, occurred to me you should be sending *me* the wine with what you've made today."

"Don't be a cheapskate, E.C."

"Just kidding, Harry."

Click.

Our man has cheered up a bit, but has a remnant of that obsessive, blank, powdery look which is occasionally unsettling to me. He's pushing the button to recall Cleave.

"Sue, I'm going to need you a bit early tomorrow morning."

"Oh? How early? Seven o'clock?"

"No, that's way too late. How about if I pick you up at four-thirty?"

"Listen, boss, it's eleven o'clock now, and you want to pick me up at four-thirty!"

"Yes. Wear blue jeans, and something warm on top. No questions, please."

"Okay, boss, you sign the paycheck, and I follow instructions." Miss Cleave has now left the office and E.C. has returned to his desk. Where he's pressing a button on his dialer which is marked with a W. I think I'll eavesdrop. To my surprise, what I'm hearing on the other end of the line is nothing more than a weather report. It seems the rain will end by tomorrow and we are to have "bright skies with winds of fifteen to twenty miles per hour." So now we've gone meteorological. This fellow is beginning to astonish me. He's got the potential of being every bit as eccentric as I was. Which is refreshing and reassuring. But I'm wondering about tomorrow. I must admit to more than a routine measure of curiosity.

ELEVEN

IT'S THREE THIRTY-THREE IN THE MORNING. I'M HAVING A LOT OF trouble sleeping. So I might as well rise and roam around. Now firmly ensconced in this new mode of existence, I'm beginning to remember a series of matters to which I should really grant my attention. There's a lot of unfinished business which requires my ministration. In particular, I've been thinking about opening a few new pages in my little black book of revenge. As children, and from grade school on, we're fed a lot of claptrap. About how vengeance seriously damages the perpetrator. All of that moralizing was really invented by the "baddies." Who want us to turn the other cheek so they can blow it away. Once I learned the rules of the game, there were very few moments in which I didn't genuinely enjoy getting even. In addition, the pleasure increased markedly when I finally learned patience. It has been said that *patience is the reward of patience*, and I fully agree. When I began my business life, and some associate or government official gave me the old screw job, I'd react and explode. And was thus, on many occasions, manipulated. But as time went on, I learned the fine art of detachment. Of stepping away from the situation and looking in on it from afar. And thus determining the nature, time, and extent of the desired retribution. It's been said by the Arabs that *if you sit in the doorway of your tent long enough, you'll see the cadaver of your enemy pass by.* In this respect, timing is of the essence. And staying power as well. There's no need to rush in and catch an alerted enemy, who might do significant damage by taking a knowing slice out of you. Better to lie low and manipulate the circumstance. Or even wait for the hand of destiny, which in dealing out misfortune can then be helped along with zeal. Besides, *to a secret wrong, a stealthy revenge.*

As I grew older, I also became expert in what I call the double whammy, or two-in-one. I believe this is the ultimate distillation of the art of revenge. It consists of the fine technique of being able to flow with your own fortune while it directly or indirectly causes misfortune to your enemy. Sort of like brushing a fly off your elbow while with no further expenditure of energy you break somebody's rib.

As I sit here in the darkness, I can't help thinking I left a few accounts unattended. To begin with, there's Harriet. I haven't quite remembered what happened on the last day of my life, but whenever I give it thought, that clock immediately comes to mind, accompanied by a queer sort of fear. I have the distinct feeling there is something very important about that last day of my existence which I must remember. Perhaps the moment is not yet right, so it doesn't come through clearly, but there are glimpses of sadness. Of not resisting death. That's impossible, though. It seems to me I would have fought it tooth and claw. In any event, if I wait long enough I feel sure it will all be revealed. I must say I'm full of anger regarding everything Harriet did during the last few years of our relationship. Then there's my pathetic nephew, Gustavo Somerset. As I recall, I was getting ready to call the cops in on him. For stealing from his uncle in myriad, deviant ways. Ahh . . . how about Hooker? I have it on good authority he's been dipping his tallywhacker into Pharaoh's wife. A no-no to say the least. Then there are those miscellaneous parties in the steel trade and government who tried to screw me on the Siderurgica deal. Like the guys who took large commissions on the metal for the Franklin Bridge. Something's got to be done about them. So, as Gilbert and Sullivan would say, I have a little list, and they'll none of them be missed. The trick must consist of finding the necessary punishments. Hopefully imbued with a healthy element of poetic justice.

I've also been wondering what E.C.'s going to do today. I seem to be able to jump from place to place, but I certainly have not developed a talent for reading minds. He told Cleave to be ready at four-thirty in the morning. Which is hardly a time for anything. Except, perhaps, looking in on the markets at the other side of the world. I think I hear him stirring, so I'd best find out what's on the agenda. He's jumped right out of bed and is in the shower whistling something which vaguely sounds like *The Barber of Seville*. He's looking particularly gay and happy today. Nothing like an extra half a billion to put that glow on a man's cheeks. Talking about cheeks, this guy has a sort of sexy ass. You know, it's a rare fellow who doesn't occasionally think about men that way. Most people are constricted by faith and social custom. Religion, as we know, particularly the Judeo-Christian hogwash, is merely a business. Designed to generate and procreate power over the masses. And to advance its own particular brand of control. Which is why, in spite of the fact most religions frequently preach love and kindness, they all become hateful, spiteful, and aggressive when another religion gets in the way. The Catholics can't stand the idea of the Protestants controlling their people, even though the basic belief is ridiculously similar. Islam contends it tolerates. But we all know how Muslims feel about infidels. And so forth for all of them.

But getting back to the topic, a lot of men have looked at the next guy's cock longingly. They may never do anything about it. But the instinct is there. Left alone to ourselves without the phenomenal deterrent of guilt, we'd be like another bunch of chimps sniffing and smelling. Pawing and sucking. Fucking around.

In the upper classes, these things have always been taken with a grain of salt. As we all know, it's the truck drivers, farmers, and Bible-belters who uphold the traditions of restraint and prohibition. Among the wealthy, such things can be elegantly camouflaged, and palmed off as eccentricities. So I must admit E.C. is well built where it counts.

He's got the type of scrotum you end up with when you've had the mumps. And everything else matches nicely. I'm sure he's pleased the girls in town on many an occasion.

Out of the shower, he's vigorously drying off with that bright red towel. Some of the steaminess gone, he's proceeded to the basin, where he's lathering up for a very-early-morning shave. Into the dressing room to don a nice pair of gray corduroys, and a bright red plaid flannel shirt. Over the shirt goes a light black cable-stitch cashmere sweater. He's looking for some shoes to wear over those nice soft gray socks. Now centering in on a pair of desert boots. Elephant skin. Not bad at all. I remember the Sheik of Oman's brother had a pair like those, which he used when hunting on safari. Nice to know this fellow has some elements of style. He's pulling a number of things out of drawers now. Walkie-talkies, and three pairs of goggles. I really don't understand this at all. Lastly, he's selected a black ostrich-skin jacket with a bright red silk lining and a pair of matching skintight gloves.

The household has apparently been alerted for this early morning activity. There are two boiled eggs in a cup complete with egg scissors. I should applaud. All the most resolute men I know use egg scissors on their boiled eggs. There's a certain joy in snipping the top off an egg with one adept gesture, and then eating it. Sort of sexy, getting into something so neatly and surgically. It takes practice, too. I've seen many a novice make the gesture too slowly, and completely demolish the egg.

Our man is in a rush. He's eaten his two boiled eggs and half a piece of toast, and is now downing the inevitable cup of espresso. As we walk into the great hall, my two statues of Sekhmet seem to be smiling complacently. The butler, somewhat discomposed by the change in early-morning ritual, is standing there holding two large woven straw picnic hampers by the handles, which are being dispatched to a waiting vehicle. No driver today for our man. The red Ferrari is glistening under the shine of the morning dew.

Bozo has been invited. E.C. has just gone upstairs again and has appeared with a bright red cotton kerchief. Which he is proceeding to tie around Bozo's neck in a rather stylish fashion. Now this is really classic. He's actually putting a pair of goggles on poochie, who, far from seeming disturbed, is relishing the attention. Bozo and I have jumped into this missile. With the turn of the key, a respectable but somewhat muted roar comes from beneath the hood. So beast and man and I go forward in a burst of speed right down the lane and out the gate.

It really hasn't taken very long to drive into the city, thanks to the dearth of traffic at this hour. Bozo looks like something out of the movies with his head hanging over the side, goggles and all. I think that paper boy back there was ennobled by a dram or two of canine slobber rushing in the wind. Soon the silhouette of Miss Cleave's stylish building is upon us. It's still quite dark here, and once detained, E.C. has had to ring a bell to move the doorman into action. Yawning and stretching, he's calling Susan's apartment. We're informed she's on the way. You know, that's what I've always liked about Cleave. Most women will make you wait forever while they powder their noses or minister to their pudenda. But not Sue. She's a no-nonsense girl. To tell the truth, I feel a great deal of remorse where she's concerned. There was true love there. And having it within my grasp, I never took it as I might. Funny how we sometimes neglect the substantial things we have nearby to pursue less magnificent ones in the distance. Only because of momentary infatuation, or because they are more elusive or mysterious, or just not fully available.

The elevator door is opening and out comes Cleave. No blue jeans, though. Nice soft brown alpaca trousers. A silk blouse and a woolly green sweater to match the color of her eyes. Little unvarnished alligator loafers. Very chic. No shine. And a saddlebag, with belt to match. She's wearing a delightfully puckish cap which highlights the shape of her face. And those dimples. . . .

"Good morning, E.C."

"Good morning, Susan. You look beautiful."

"You're not so bad yourself. Hey, what's this all about? A girl could get wrinkles rising this early."

"If you got them, I think I would like them every bit as much as I like the rest of you."

"Flatterer. Kindly remember I'm your assistant."

"Well, I have no intention of telling you what we're doing this morning, or where we're going until we arrive there."

"Okay, you're the boss."

Miss Cleave is nodding with approval at the sight of E.C.'s red sports car, complete with goggled pooch. It's a bit tight, but we all fit. So we're off in a flash. And again moving in a rural direction. Driving through a sector which is mainly farmland. Cows are being milked and tractors are already in motion. Somewhere in those kitchens blueberry muffins and scones await hungry children on their way to school, and farmhands preparing for the day. We're driving up a country road and stopping in front of a large meadow. The hampers have arrived and a truck is here more or less at the same time, with a very large wicker basket on it, and some other large objects wrapped in canvas. It's not taking me long to put two and two together. Now I understand—E.C. is actually taking us all ballooning! This could be a lot of fun. You know, I've owned airplanes and helicopters, and I've even gone parachuting. But I've never been up in a hot-air balloon.

The three attendants are greeting E.C. and tipping their hats to Cleave. Pulling a large equivalent of a ceiling fan out from under one of those canvas covers. They're now producing a gigantic piece of plastic, which they're proceeding to unfold. Upon it all three of them are now unsheathing the silky material of the balloon. It looks like a brilliant, multicolored thing. They've pointed the fan at the opening and are filling it with air. The large wicker basket has been fitted with several tanks and a mechanism which will ignite their gas to heat the air in the balloon. A "burner" of sorts. It's now full. I'm delighted to say the thing neatly sports the effigies of two Jersey cows upon it. My opinion of our man's style continues to improve. Into the basket go the picnic hampers, Cleave, and pooch. E.C. and I are the last to jump in as we gently and noiselessly rise into the morning's luminescence.

I think the most striking factor about ballooning is the fact there isn't any ghastly noise to interfere with your appreciation of the elements around you. Not like helicoptering, in which you're forced to use earphones to communicate. We're now gliding just above the treetops. E.C. pulls the cord, and a larger burst of fire is elicited, which, in turn, heats the air in the balloon and causes us to rise more quickly. There's a mist over those meadows below as we glide ever so gracefully away from our point of departure. And many birds flying beneath us. Now that the sun is rising, there is increased activity. Over there to the left the cows are being released to pasture after the morning's milking. We cast a shadow over the meadow, and I think we're frightening them a bit. E.C. has also noticed this detail. So, with the additional whoosh of a burst of fire, we rise higher until we experience only the sound of the light morning wind and the occasional interruption of noise from the burner.

Cleave seems totally ecstatic, and transfigured by the tranquillity of the moment. E.C. is closely watching her reactions as if part of his delight were stemming from her enjoyment.

"You know, Susan, I'm a lonely person. I spend a lot of time thinking about business. But I really haven't recently been very successful in my personal life. It's not to say I haven't had my share of relationships. For a while before my wife died, I found true love. She was special and unique. The only person who ever made me feel like the Fourth of July. Since the accident, I seem to have developed a certain inability to communicate my feelings."

"I know. I understand. You've probably heard around town that I was a bit more than Mr. Somerset's secretary. Actually, at one point in time we became lovers. And he was a wonderful man. But he shared with you a diminished capacity to express feelings. It's funny. Here's a man who could flip ten billion dollars at the touch of a phone. And yet he had the hardest time making a decision to put his hectic existence behind him and give me the type of life I really would have wanted. In fact, I had begged him to divorce his wife and go off with me, and live on a storybook farm, or a Pacific island, for the rest of our lives. But it was impossible to tear him away from the life of buying and controlling. You see, E.C., he was really hooked. When he died, we were estranged. How could I think of living with a man, no matter how rich, who spent more time making love to the telephone than to me? He'd become accessible in moments of anguish or consternation. Like a child after he was all played out. That's not what I wanted. And it wouldn't have been good for my self-respect either. But tell me, what was your wife like?"

"Special. Like a southern Italian Renaissance Madonna. Fine, yet sturdy. But that wasn't all of it. She was extremely kind, and almost devoid of emotional hangups. A perfect woman. Sue . . . Susan . . . I know this will probably sound very strange. But I'm really quite taken by you. Your gentle kindness very much reminds me of her. I think I could easily fall in love."

"Have you thought you could end up hurting us both? I don't need to be hurt again."

"We can give matters a little time. . . ."

"Okay, but don't rush me."

Bozo is really enjoying this. His neck and head are protruding just a bit over the side of the basket. I've been watching him lately. And detecting qualities which, due to the haste in my previous life, I had never really appreciated. Bozo is reliable beyond reproach. He's sensitive, yet patient and very loving. Although acutely intelligent, he just doesn't use it in the conventional mode. And he's incredibly affectionate. I think one would have to be a very advanced type of soul to love so freely and without qualification. Look at him, so confident, so majestic in every way. I also have the uncanny feeling Bozo knows a great deal about what is going on. But it's not something I think is happening at the usual intellectual level. It runs deeper than that. I believe he is genuinely intuitive and empathetic. I think he feels as we feel. And perhaps by some mechanism of intuition or instinct which is more developed than the human variety, understands things in a far deeper way. He's looking at me with those big, pale blue eyes. A loving and very knowing look. It's the type of stare that undresses you completely and leaves you no place to hide. E.C. and Cleave are sitting in the basket close together. And I'm a little ashamed to be watching. Sort of an intrusion into their privacy. I continue to have very mixed emotions about E.C. touching my girl. But I also want him to go forward, since she can help him in very substantial ways. No other person knows more about my business affairs than she. After all, Susan was an officer of each and every company.

So, I'll look in the opposite direction for a while. There's a kid riding horseback down there. Funny how things look slower when you're up in the air looking down. I wonder if it all looks this way to God. I've been thinking about Him lately. I was nominally religious in life. And I must say, I occasionally prayed just to be sure I had covered all the bases. When I discovered I was dead, there was some resentment. But now, I have this ever so strong feeling. As I mentioned once before, I believe there may be a method to all this madness. Like the hand of God. But why aren't You showing yourself to me? If this is one rung on the ladder, why can't I see the next one? To be sure, I've spent a lifetime reading about the love that moves the sun and the other stars. I could sure do with a dose of it right now. Here we are cutting through the air ever so effortlessly. I would expect to be closer to Thee, my God . . . but all that's happening is that I'm stuck with seeing my new protégé fall in love with my sweetheart. And I'm not so sure it's the slam-bang type of love. It's more like he intellectually surmised he needs someone. I'm concerned. Susan could be seriously hurt in the balance.

As if to reproach me for my lack of faith and uncertainty about the future, a very strong ray of sunlight has just come down and flooded the exact spot where I now stand. It seemed to me there was something open up there at the end of it. But the light was so bright, and my eyes so stunned, I was unable to discern it, and now it's gone. What am I doing thinking about God and philosophy?

E.C. is allowing the balloon to descend gently into a very verdant hollow, now beginning to assume the fall coloration. Someone on the walkie-talkie is asking him if he wants help in securing the contraption. He's now telling them to hold still at their location about half a mile away. The balloon is down, and E.C. is quickly out of it, tying it to a nearby boulder. Sue and Bozo are now out of the basket. Which is temporarily on its side. E.C. is allowing the dirigible to collapse, and has held it pending the proximate arrival of attendants to return it home.

The picnic hampers are none the worse for wear. A needlepoint cloth is extracted from one, together with two bottles of champagne, and a simple breakfast. Cold quiche, caviar, and deviled eggs. There's china in those hampers, and nice goblets as well. E.C. is popping a bottle of bubbly without making a noise. The only way to do it. It's the kind in the clear bottle. Good stuff.

Bozo hasn't been forgotten either. A trifle of chopped beef with some dog biscuit neatly finds its way into a gleaming silver dog dish. So everyone is happy. Except me. Here they are looking at one another like they're going to make love. And there's work to be done, money to be made, and revenge to be reaped. I'm trying to get Bozo to interrupt whatever is happening between them. But he just gave me that very complacent and loving look which you often get from cows.

Maybe if I muster my strength, I'll be able to move things around a bit. The way I did with the chandelier. I'll turn myself into a veritable horror. And then we'll see if we don't return to work. First I'll whip myself into one with the wind, and blow everything about. That's good. The caviar is flying. And the other bottle of champagne just popped with a loud noise. Wetting everything. There are napkins everywhere. I am a success!

I've actually managed to dissipate the mood here. He's grabbing for the walkie-talkie. Which should put us back on the road to town in the twinkling of an eye. Miss Cleave is looking disturbed. I know that look. It's the one she assumed that day when I told her I couldn't leave my exhilarating life behind. With its thrills and splendid exaltations. So the truck is coming nearer. The attendants are at the balloon, and are proceeding to wrap everything up as the limousine appears, to return our picnickers to town.

The doors to the car are now open, and Miss Cleave has entered with a rather defeated look on her face. Bozo is sitting next to her looking reciprocally mournful. But I've been whispering things into E.C.'s ears. And even though he may not hear the words, I have a feeling I'm reaching him. He's on the phone:

"Good morning, Mrs. Andrews. Miss Cleave and I should be in the office within the hour. Will you have them retrieve the Ferrari from South Black Hollow Road. Also, have the staff obtain all of the information it can on H. W. Somerset's last big deal."

"I think, Mr. Douglas, that you're talking about the Siderurgica deal he did in Europe. I'll have the research analysts put together a complete binder for you."

"Thank you, Mrs. Andrews. We'll see you a little later."
Click.

Susan has become even quieter. She's pulled that big pink diamond out from between her bosoms, and is stroking it in a pensive fashion. Try though I may, however, I can't read thoughts. And to be sure, I don't think I'd like to involve myself in these even if I could. For a moment, I thought I saw a suspicion of a tear in her eye. But she's composed herself in her own inimitable fashion. I'm sure she'll get over it. They always do. I, in turn, have begun smelling the chase again. He actually wants information on the Siderurgica deal! Let him become familiar with it. Then we'll supplement his knowledge, and feed his appetite. This will be fun. Destiny is with me, and I must admit some anticipation of that old ecstasy. There is blood in the air.

TWELVE

We've been back in the saddle for a few days now. So far, I'm happy to report, it's been strictly business as usual. None of that romantic hogwash. When the binders having to do with the Siderurgica deal were placed on the conference-room table, they mesmerized our man. He's been spending most of his time in there going through all the information the staff accumulated in accordance with his request.

The Siderurgica deal was to have been the crown jewel in my collection of businesses, and certainly the largest single transaction in my life. It originally hatched when I realized American steel was losing ground to the much more efficiently manufactured European product. One day while I was having my usual Wednesday luncheon at the Forum, the whole thing dawned on me. The Forum, as everyone knows, is the type of restaurant where the rich and powerful go to feed and water themselves. While the food is exquisite and flawless, the real reasons for which the lofty flock there have to do with reliability and sociability. You see, it's impossible to have a poor meal, or even a mediocre meal, at the Forum. And there aren't any riffraff there. The first thing which strikes you about the place is the floral arrangements. A gifted lackey labors on these after a four-thirty-in-the-morning visit to the wholesale flower market. They are always fresh, vibrant, and pristine in every way. The linens are a crisp white. And starched so stiffly you could almost cut yourself with their edges. The atmosphere is very Continental, with a touch of Art Deco here and there. As is the silverware with its square handles and fluted grooves.

Then, of course, there is Antoine. This man is an institution among restaurateurs. He would have to be, in order to avoid the potential social difficulties of running such a place. You see, he must know, first of all, whom to receive. And whom not to. He is always careful to be sure you are not, unless it was specifically requested, next to your most assiduous enemy, this year's palimony suit, or last year's mistress. So Antoine, sometimes without direct knowledge, must be very sure to avoid sitting the pretty young man who is en-gaged to the billionaire's daughter across from the equally attractive rival who just happened to screw him last night.

That fateful Wednesday I was in fact at one of the preferred tables against the wall when the whole thing crystallized in my mind. Such realizations always occur at moments of leisure. Which is to say that Archimedes was correct. I remember I had just ingested a small but very tasty pie of pheasant and baby carrots. The confection when presented sat in the middle of the luncheon plate in a small puddle of Port sauce. A sauce of that type always puts me in a phenomenal mood. Particularly if, as on that day, it is washed down with a gen-erous amount of La Tâche. As it happened, I had an extra bunch of billions lying around, just itching to be used. And access to more through my European connections. Most of it was sitting in the bank accounts of those Caribbean corporations which by some felicitous quirk of the Internal Revenue Code were forever generating income which was not subject to taxation. So when the endive and sun-ripened tomato salad was presented, gently blanketed under a dress-ing of tarragon and Parmesan cheese, the whole thing came to me. I would gain control of the major manufacturers of European steel through a new corporation which I would call Siderurgica Internazionale. At the same time, I would begin to accumulate an enormous "short" position in all of the American steel stocks. Since my monopoly would be in Europe, where the cartel is a way of life, I would be totally beyond the reach of our stupid and ultimately inoperable American law.

Americans, you see, are the only people who habitually regulate against human nature. Take the civil rights laws, for instance. People in this country really harbor the foolish thought that they can force the races to mingle by busing them to other districts or driving them to school together. Mind you, I believe in basic humanitarianism. But discrimination is a way of life among mankind, and if you regulate these issues, people just find more subtle ways in which to discriminate.

In business, Americans are equally *contra natura*. On the one hand, there is the great American tradition of cornering the markets and gaining the upper hand through inside information. Enter the twentieth century with regulation that makes it illegal to even "whisper" a bit of private knowledge. When you get down to brass tacks, it's all a smoke screen to give the little guy the impression he's going to be treated fairly, when in fact the government couldn't care less about him and dedicates itself in more subtle ways to making the rich richer and the poor poorer. Also, there are the ultrasecret government agencies that steal from the public by speculating in the markets on the basis of their superior knowledge of events. But of course no one speaks of such things, since they are effectively beyond the law. As I've said on occasion about politicians, the whole trick lies in convincing the people that they're the freest in the world when on a daily basis, through economic constriction and the limitation of opportunity, the python of government has compelled them into involuntary servitude. As one son-of-a-bitch friend of mine once said: "My slaves are all very happy. They all think they're free."

But getting back to the deal, the whole arrangement was coupled with a very special trump card. Professor Von Richter's process. You see, I had recently purchased an international patent for a steel formula which would revolutionize the industry. The patent made it a lot cheaper to produce the stuff. At a later date a substantial and negative catch became evident, but I kept it to myself, and took the secret flaw of the invention with me to my grave.

By going short in the American companies and restricting the use of my process to the Siderurgica companies, I would get the American position to very quickly pay for my European purchase, thus obtaining the whole ball of wax for free.

Everyone knows that when you go short, you're really selling shares of stock you don't own. If the stock goes down, you make a lot of money, because when you buy the stock back to cover your position, you buy it at a much cheaper price. Of course, if the stock goes up, you must replace the shares at a loss or deposit more money to cover its increased value.

So I proceeded with enormous stealth to plan this greatest of deals, over dessert, which that day just happened to be my favorite. Floating island. Antoine's meringue is a work of art. I will never fully understand how they manage to poach the beaten egg whites in milk so each spoonful is exactly the same size as the next. But they invariably achieve this wonder of culinary execution without a flaw. On that day, as I scooped up that last bit of cold beaten egg white and vanilla syrup, and felt the crackle of candied sugar over that very sensitive left third molar, I hatched the scheme to go short on about sixty million shares of prime American steels. It was gargantuan. The whole thing was so brilliant, I trembled as that last bit of ambrosia eased itself down my throat.

The next day we were on our way to Milan, complete with private jet, Cleave, Thomas Hooker, and my then-tolerable nephew, Gustavo Somerset. Once in Milan, we met with our local factotum, Flavio, and with the lawyers, who had flown in from Geneva and Zurich to put the whole thing together. We actually had the ones in Geneva use the ones in Zurich as nominees. Who in turn used a Liechtenstein corporation owned by a British West Indies company. The fact no one ever intends to have anything to do with Liechtenstein or the British West Indies always makes these deals all the more delightful.

So we immediately entered negotiations to purchase the basic companies in Italy, Germany, France, and Japan. I deposited my billions with the hope of very quickly picking them up again, when the existence of Von Richter's process was disclosed and my plans for the European cartel became evident. As a safety net, my friends in the Vatican and their partners provided additional financing in the way of a very large letter of credit. I also traded Siderurgica shares for controlling interests in vested European steel companies held by my friends in the Church and the Mob. After all, they helped me a bit, and the least I could do was let them in on the deal. So they became major holders of Siderurgica stock as well. All we had to do was sit and wait for the American steels to plummet in the face of the great European production economies which would be felt with the advent of Von Richter's process. Everything was going swimmingly until for reasons unknown to me, the American steel markets failed to respond and instead assumed a firm upward trend. I recall the scenario as if it were today. It was a Friday. We were already dangerously near the point where I would have to liquidate the American positions if the market did not take a turn downward. My broker, a guy not unlike E.C.'s Harry, was apoplectic. As he put it, he had never seen a market so contrary to logic in all his years of expert wheeling and dealing. So we held on, never realizing that the rats in the comedy were gnawing at us from within.

It was actually my fault for applying logic, and confiding in others. I held on a bit too long, and the next morning's margin call was predictably large. Of course, I met it. And continued selling short and losing money as the issues steadfastly refused to plunge. As I later corroborated, my enemies were buying shares cheaply each time I dropped the price by selling. And then forcing it to rise with their very large purchases. As a result, even though I was able to pay each time, I was ultimately forced to license Von Richter's process to the American steel industry in order to put it at comparative parity, which turned the entire business deal into a relatively pedestrian and normal one instead of the rape job I had originally planned. Mind you, we made a little money, and my partners were actually pleased and impressed. But it was nothing at all like what I had planned or expected.

Late that Monday evening, after what my broker and I came to call "Black Friday," we sat in the basement of my pyramid drinking ice-cold vodka. He kept on saying, "It doesn't make any sense, it doesn't make any sense. You should be the richest man in the world by now, and it's all gone sour." And I kept pouring that private-label Polish stuff, which is what self-respecting fellows drink when they wish to become barefacedly inebriated.

After a while, the combination of vodka and our two very sus-

picious minds brought us to the inescapable conclusion that somewhere there had to be a rat. Or two. Or three. With care and in the
greatest secrecy, I engaged the type of sleuths which only billionaires
can afford. Men who smell a fart in New York when someone lays it
in Zurich. Slowly, over the next few weeks, they came forward with
copies of documents evidencing secret Swiss accounts which had held
large amounts of American steel stocks. More alarmingly, the entire
set of documents pointed without a doubt to three parties. Thomas
Hooker, Gustavo Somerset, and Harriet.

At first, I couldn't understand how Tom Hooker and Gustavo
had been able to put their hands on enough cash to artificially raise
the price of the steel stocks. But it later became evident one of my
enemies in government had facilitated very large loans at the discount
rate to a dozen or so smaller banks of which Gustavo and Hooker
were trustees on my behalf. So the fuckers used the discount window
at the Fed and my own banks to outbid me in the Siderurgica deal,
therefore lining their own pockets with the money I lost. Each time
I sold, Gustavo, Harriet, and Hooker bought. Since I was artificially
depressing the market, I ended up paying the bill. As I met my margin
calls, they enriched themselves by a billion or more through their
purchases.

You see, in the market, for every winner there is a loser. Since
they had the firm inside knowledge that I was selling short, all they
had to do was continue buying and wait me out. They also knew my
limits. It was the equivalent of knowing when to raise a poker player
by virtue of having had a peek at his hand and pocketbook. They
merely made a raise that I just couldn't meet, and by operation of
fact, sliced off my balls.

But the day of reckoning is coming quite soon. And perhaps I
was, in retrospect, quite right to insist on the 94th Psalm at my funeral. Now I shall have the pleasure of seeing the proud rewarded
after their deserving. You see, I just remembered where I stashed all
those incriminating documents on the Von Richter process before I
passed away. . . .

E.C. is sitting at this table today with a perplexed look on his face.
He just stared Bozo straight in the eye and said, "I don't understand
it, I don't understand it. Why didn't he make more money on this

deal?" Bozo has merely looked back and slurped up an accommodating gnat which has made a test flight from the adjacent potted plant. After staring at the pooch for a while and noting the premature demise of the minute flying friend, E.C.'s looking a bit tired, and has momentarily nodded off. I am anxious to answer his question. But first I want him to really get a feel for the beauty of the deal, and perhaps he will concoct his own to match. I wish to teach this fellow. And to help him develop style. I want him to be like me.

THIRTEEN

I MUST ADMIT A RECENT BIT OF CURIOSITY REGARDING MY PREVIOUS life-style and wife. Since I'm now quite expert at this business of changing locations at the twitch of my will, I think I'll maneuver myself to Harriet's old country place while E.C. naps, and take a peek at the bitch herself.

Easy as pie, I am relocated. It doesn't seem like much has changed at the country house. The maids are quietly walking around performing their duties. I don't see Harriet, though. I think I'll take a peek into her bedroom. No, she's not in sight here. But wait a minute. I hear that familiar hum coming from farther within.

Harriet's bathroom is a pink marble affair. A bit trite. With swans for waterspouts. And gold-plated washbasins and faucets. The area is divided into four rooms. The first of these is a gigantic dressing room paneled and painted a pale apple green. Following the dressing room, there is sort of a powder-your-nose area with mirrors and a makeup table, all brightly illuminated. Beyond that is the bathroom with a large pink marble Roman tub sitting smack in the middle of it. The last room is the actual privy. As I go through the dressing room, I can't help noticing the stylish black silk dress with printed colored flowers which Harriet is apparently going to wear to dinner tonight. Into the next room, and I'm confronted by the goddess herself, lying in full state under the bubbles. Yes indeed, Harriet does like her bubble bath. But not too hot. She's suffered from high blood pressure for the longest time, and has it rightly in her head that it isn't good for her if it becomes too steamy. She's excitedly lathering herself up in all the nicest places as she hums some little melody which I am not readily recognizing. I've always admired small shoulders in women. Harriet's are exquisite, and very much like Renaissance Italian alabaster. She's just raised her right leg and immodestly watched the suds slide off that exquisite little foot. The phone is ringing, and she's reached for it.

"Hello. Oh, Thomas, darling, it's you. How are things going . . . not so good? . . . Why? . . . Oh, he's probably just got a cursory interest. Listen, sweetheart, every time someone becomes interested in reexamining the Siderurgica deal, it doesn't mean they're going to unearth all the truffles, now does it? . . . I really think you're jumping to all sorts of conclusions here. Henry didn't have the foggiest idea of what was going on. In fact, that last day of his life he spent most of the time sulking and playing with his postage stamps. So I really don't think there's anything to worry about. . . . Gustavo? Oh, I spoke with him yesterday. I was thinking of sending him to Zurich to do an errand or two for me. . . . What do you mean, don't touch the cash? . . . Now that Henry's gone, I shouldn't think there'd be any problem in spending a little money. . . . Yes, I will be careful. You know, we shouldn't be talking about this on the telephone. I'll see you at seven-thirty. Don't worry, everything's going to be fine."

Click.

She's humming now, as she lathers the other foot. This conversation has given me a substantial amount of insight into everything which has happened. And also whetted my curiosity as to that last day of my life. But one thing is now totally confirmed. Hooker and my wife were in on the Siderurgica deal. And they've got the cash stashed away in Zurich. Gustavo is the bagman, and will be very conveniently making a trip to retrieve some of the goodies. Or probably to dispose of them in Europe for purposes connected with milady's pleasure.

Of course, there was no need for this except pure greed. Harriet had all the money she could spend. Except you have to understand this woman's psychology. As a child, she came from an upper-middle-class family. They had a little money, but this was far exceeded by her mother's aspirations for her three daughters. If you think Harriet is bad, you should have met her mother. Here was a woman who had achieved practically everything she had wanted, and squarely intended to obtain the rest. The old bat had married somewhat well. Harriet's father was a physician in a socially prestigious suburban town. Her mother had always hoped Harriet would marry for money. From the very earliest time, her entire emphasis was on properly schooling her daughters in the graces which would be necessary to entice and ensnare rich husbands. I'll never forget. I met Harriet at a mixer. Such were the stiff and ridiculous dances which occurred when boys' and girls' schools were not coeducational. It all seems pretty silly and outmoded now, but when I went to school, there was some myth which made them think boys and girls would screw less if they were separated into their respective sexist schools. So the boys masturbated a lot, and so did the girls. And occasionally, the boys fucked around with their comrades. And the girls bumped pussies at pajama parties. Self and same sex notwithstanding, the cheese was usually rather ripe by the time a mingling affair was scheduled. The desperate social dances at which boys would meet girls were therefore called mixers.

The hand of destiny scheduled the affair at which I would meet Harriet at a particularly vulnerable point of my last year in college. I had been depressed and nervous about getting my fangs into the business world. The sluggishness of the educational process had disturbed me, and I was suffering from junior-year blues. Nevertheless, I was a pretty good-looking bastard, so she came up to me and started chatting. I gave her some punch. And we danced. I was immediately besotted by her figure and charm. The joke was on her, though. She thought I was one of the legendarily rich Somersets from Boston. And I must admit, I did very little to dispel this bit of myth. So we started dating. Until that fateful weekend when I was invited to Saturday dinner at her parents'. The old woman had for some time been "on" to me. Sensing a humiliated beau would do more to discourage her daughter than anything she could say, she invited me to dinner for the sole purpose of making me look bad. It seems she had discovered I had no money in my background, and so she assumed I would also have no class.

Saturday dinner was a glittering middle-class affair with lots of food. The artichoke was designed to give me a hassle. But alas, my mother had come from Spain, where *alcachofa* was a household word. It was into the roast beef and potatoes when the old bat popped the question and asked me where my family was from. I certainly had no compunctions about telling her I came from a small mining town in Pennsylvania. She then proceeded to tell me how very nice it was that Harriet had a friend. And no doubt I could be helpful in counseling her on how to marry the right man. In the nicest way possible, she let me know that I was totally unacceptable and out of her plans. Inconceivable as a possible husband. But she was wrong. I was eminently conceivable.

That night, I proposed to Harriet. She told me she'd have to ask her mother and father. I explained such a move would constitute a terrible mistake, and suggested we should elope. But she wouldn't do it. So I went home feeling rejected and unloved, but nevertheless, still in lust.

What subsequently happened was just too funny for words. I had this maiden aunt who was the black sheep of the family. She had escaped from her rather staid religious upbringing and become a famous ballerina of her day. In her old age, when she could no longer do the thirty-two *fouettés* from the second act of *Swan Lake*, she came back to our region, where she bought a rather sizable farm. I was her favorite, since I too was somewhat dark in the wool.

Auntie passed away just before graduation. I was totally crushed, since she and I had spent many a pleasant afternoon sipping tea and reminiscing about her dancing career. She was in every way my favorite relative. I used to run little errands for her, which were excuses for rewarding me with fresh fifty-dollar bills. She really loved me, and responded accordingly. No wonder I was terribly saddened when she died.

I was, however, totally unprepared for what happened several months after dinner at Harriet's. I'll never forget the day I received a call from my aunt's attorney. She had left me her acreage and house.

But the communication came coupled with a kicker which really put stars in my eyes. It seems a very large oil company had been bidding for the exploration rights to her farm before she passed away. And now they wanted to do business with me. The rest is history. They hit oil with the ease with which a child puts a straw into a soft drink. And there was lots and lots of it. One well after another, the oil gushed forth. And my percentage of each one of those barrels brought me a little closer to having that very special portion of Harriet for dinner. Of course, I always fed the newspapers that story about selling newspapers as a child. It was, after all, in keeping with what people wanted to hear. And with the maintenance of the American Dream.

As a matter of fact, the old bat suddenly became convinced I was an acceptable candidate. Very. And a wedding was carefully planned. It was scheduled for the following spring. We had six bridesmaids, and a corresponding number of ushers. With each new well, I was quickly coming closer to the realm of the superrich. So Harriet's parents spent their life's savings and really did a number on our wedding. I guess Harriet was at her most beautiful that day, with the orange blossoms and lustrous white silk ribbons in her hair.

Our wedding night was the first in an initial series of calamitous sexual encounters. You see, having been brought up with money and things as objects of desire, rather than people, Harriet found it very difficult to cozy up to a good hard cock. She decked herself out that night in the traditional peignoir as I hastily ripped my clothes off in the bathroom. I proceeded to practically run into the darkened room and pounce on her. I will admit, I was a tad brutish. And that's exactly what she didn't like. Wishing to seem somewhat demure, and ashamed of her pleasure, Harriet found it very difficult to go to bed with a man possessed with the libido of a truck driver. Ultimately, though, I developed style and tenderness. And actually think Harriet came to appreciate our sexual encounters. At least during those early years. I guess we had a good ten years during which she was really rather good company and tolerable sex.

Later, Harriet became the most expensive lay I ever had. Since women are the passive entities in sex, they really hold the keys to the kingdom. Sort of like sadomasochistic relationships where the masochists invariably set the parameters. Harriet learned early that she could contain and control me through sex. And that she could also punish me by withholding it. In our later years, she found she could trade it for a new diamond necklace or a country house.

Once, I thought she might like it rough and just wanted to be taken. Oh boy, was that a mistake! She wept for days after I gave her the Rhett Butler treatment and then said she'd been raped.

So as time went on, Harriet and I became more and more estranged, with only an occasionally sublime moment or two when she either inexplicably softened or wanted something. Usually she'd catch me when I'd had a drink or two and my reserve was low. Then I'd fuck and pay, so to speak. No miracle I began to stray, and look in other directions for my pleasure. Although I had always wanted to have children, the entire issue became untouchable as Harriet became increasingly paranoid about losing her looks and figure. This was a matter which became unnegotiable, and which to this day has always made me feel depressed and unhappy.

She's out of the water now. And is patting herself dry with one of those rather soft towels. Looking almost pre-Christian with that demure gesture. She didn't get her hair wet, so she won't have to primp much in order to look stunning. There she goes, sitting at that little makeup table. Engaging in a ritual which is as old as time itself. If you think about it, an Egyptian woman would have probably gone through all of the same steps. Which reminds me of the little makeup jars of Princess Sit Hathor Yunet, who was a daughter of Sesostris III. Really no different from our modern dragon lady. She's carefully made that line which enhances her eyes and makes them look even bigger and greener. Eye shadow, blush, and lipstick all find their way to that angelically cold face. She's slipping on that black flowery dress. Now into little black pumps and a quick turn for a look in the mirror. Not bad at all. I have a feeling this evening might not be all romance. Harriet doesn't waste this much time unless there's a little something in it for her on the acquisitive side.

Over to her jewelry case. She's selecting an emerald bracelet. Good stones from the Muzo mine. I should know. I paid a tidy sum for that thing when trying to cozy up to her after a blatant infidelity. I guess the whole slip was really a cry for help. Otherwise, I would never have allowed myself to be discovered doing no-no. I always liked emeralds on Harriet, though. They match the color of those deep, cold eyes.

I think I should follow her around tonight. And maybe catch up with everything that's been happening since I dropped dead. I saw them wiping the black sedan out there, so she must be meeting him at the restaurant. If I want to go, there isn't much time to lose. Because she's now completed dressing and is looking at herself for the last time in the mirror, now ready with handbag. She's going over to the dresser, and pulling a little lace hankie out of the drawer. Coyly stuffing it into the purse. Very dainty, yes indeed. One last look in the mirror. And she's off!

Her old chauffeur has opened the door to the car, and she's bowed ever so slightly to enter. I'm fast behind.

"Good evening again, Mrs. Somerset. Where shall it be tonight?"

"We're going to the Forum. And actually, Fred, I'm running a little late, so please spare me the scenic route."

That's just like Harriet. When she's not sucking up to someone for something, she just speaks her mind. She's nervously twirling her square-cut diamond engagement ring. In fact, it's not the first one I gave her. As the years went by, I traded her rings for ones with bigger stones. This one is what they call an Asscher cut. Which is to say it's a bit deeper and has a few more facets, making it glisten nicely in the evening light.

The restaurant is upon us. The door is open, and Harriet proceeds to the foyer, where she's shedding the elegant broadtail fall coat she's wearing.

Antoine is greeting her, and quietly gushing.

"Madame . . . how nice to see you here tonight. I have your very special table all prepared."

"Has Mr. Hooker arrived yet?"

"Yes, he's waiting for you at the table. You might like to know the Worthingtons are dining with the Cabots and will be across from you."

"Antoine . . . is there anyone here who I should know about?"

"No, madame, we would have immediately advised you!"

Harriet makes her grand entrance into the room, which is dimly lit. Just enough to create the necessary shadows on those extraordinary arrangements of flowers. Heads nod, and there's an occasional interruption while she accepts a condolence or says hello to a friend on the way to her table. Tom Hooker snaps to attention as soon as he sees her enter. And is now standing, with that artificial smile reminiscent of Pacific sharks. I must say Antoine did well by them tonight. They have a corner table from which they're able to survey the entire establishment. Hooker, as usual, has the first word.

"Sweetheart, I thought you would never arrive."

"Am I late?"

"No, you're perfectly on time. It's just that since we now don't have to hide in pool houses and conservatories, I've become a bit more anxious."

"Thomas, I do love the sex, but spare me what Henry would have called 'the claptrap.' "

"Oh, did you really have to mention the H word? You can't forget him, even after that overdone funeral, and all the money you've come into."

"As far as I'm concerned, it's not nearly enough. And that's your fault for not rigging the will or doing one of those things you lawyers do."

"Honey, there were ten attorneys in on that will, and you know Henry was sharp as a tack."

"Well, I will say, the one thing he had the decency to do was die in time. You know something, though—I've actually been up nights trying to figure out what happened in his mind after we decided to delay our little plan."

"Oh, you are one to talk about things I don't want to hear. Don't you think it's unchristian of you to be so pleased Henry has died?"

"Of course not, darling. You know I'm thoroughly delighted."

"It's just like you, Harriet. I keep trying to forget you don't believe in God, and you keep reminding me."

"Don't give me that holier-than-thou attitude. You were in on the whole thing with me. You just keep the pretense of belief because it assuages your guilty conscience."

"Stop it, Harriet. Speak more quietly. Antoine is on his way."

Just as I suspected, they were at it before I died, and they're probably screwing like rabbits now. But what was this business about "our little plan"? I really do need to hear more about this.

They've decided to have the fresh goose liver from France as an appetizer. Followed by the breast of duck, with purée of chestnut. There's a little watercress salad after the main course. With an apple Charlotte for dessert. Not bad. I could have done better, but this will certainly do. Hooker cheaped out on the wine, though. I think it's a throwback to those lean years before he met me. Now that Antoine is gone, they're at it again. She's harassing him about a business matter.

"You know, sweetheart, Flavio called me from Lugano . . . it seems we still have an awful lot of those American stocks stashed away in nominee accounts. He wanted to know if we might sell. I'm sending Gustavo to Europe to wire a little cash to Hong Kong for some purchases I'm making. He could get rid of those steel stocks for us while he's there."

"I'm not sure, Harriet. I don't think we should ditch the steels just yet. This morning I heard a rumor someone is exhibiting a lot of interest in the Siderurgica deal. I think I mentioned it to you on the telephone. Once I got through being frightened, it occurred to me that as trustees for the estate, we could ditch Siderurgica and enhance our American position."

"I don't understand. The Europeans have whosiwhatsit's process, don't they?"

"You mean Von Richter's process, darling. And yes, they do have it, but I'm just wondering if we could find a buyer who would purchase Siderurgica without the process rights."

"A neat trick if you can pull it."

"Actually, Harriet, I was a bit frightened this morning when I heard this fellow Douglas was interested in Siderurgica. But if his interest is legitimate, we might very well pawn it off on him, and line our pockets on both sides."

"Well, let's drink to that."

I'm thinking of doing something in the way of a manifestation here. But on second thought, I think I'll just carefully file away all of this valuable knowledge. And later use it on a rainy day. Now that she's had a glass of wine she's loosening up a bit. And giggling. Old Hooker's probably going to get it tonight. She'll end up totally controlling him as well. She's just laughed at something again.

"Gustavo . . . oh, Tom, don't worry about him. You know he gambles, which keeps him on my own personal string. Besides, we can probably rid ourselves of the little worm with ten or fifteen million any day of the week. Henry was soft on him. All that nephew business, you know. But I saw through him from the beginning. He's a perfect little Latin shit."

"You do know how to put things, sweetheart. And talking about putting things, that white asparagus they're serving at the next table has reminded me of something I'd like to give you tonight."

"Oh, Tom, a diamond-studded letter opener . . ."

"Don't get cute with me, Harriet. It's been a few days now, and I need it."

"Thomas, I don't want the servants to see you at odd hours. It just isn't right. Remember, I'm supposed to be in mourning. Besides, I have an early meeting with Gustavo tomorrow. So why don't we do it after that, or the next day."

"Okay, Harriet, what can I say. . . ."

Hooker is now dejectedly gulping down that glass of wine rather quickly. He'll eventually realize sex is a programmed activity for good old Harriet. This is just another one of her very clever tricks. When she's not truly interested in a man for his body, which is almost never, she finds these not so subtle ways of diminishing his importance by letting him know the sexual act can be postponed without damage or stress to her feelings. It's a way of apprising the other person that she can take it or leave it. But I think old Tom just cooled off and engaged his business mind again. After all, the watchword for this dinner is definitely greed.

"You know, Harriet, I can't stop thinking about taking that extra billion we have stashed away and maybe turning it into some serious money."

"Well, as long as I have enough to go shopping in London, Paris, and Hong Kong in the style to which I'm accustomed, I'll be happy."

"I know you are an expensive package."

"Very much so."

"Show me."

"Oh Tom, you can be vexatious!"

So we're back to the sex business again. And for a second time, she's brushing him off. They've finished the main course and the apple Charlotte has just been presented.

"You know, Tom, I think it just all went very smoothly. I mean the funeral, the reading of the will, the sale of Pyramid Hill, just everything. Sometimes I become a little frightened at night. Thinking it's all been too easy. It wasn't at all like Henry to go so quietly. Some days I almost expect a great hand to come back from the dead and strangle me."

"I think you're letting the wine affect you. Henry is dead. Extremely dead. And there's nothing he can do now. We're in the driver's seat. It's what you've wanted all along, isn't it? So enjoy it. You're entirely safe from him now."

This last bit of garbage has really incensed me. I need more information, particularly about that last day of my life, which I can't yet seem to remember. I'm hopeful it will come to me eventually. I wonder. . . . Is it that I can't recall because of the influence of external forces controlling me, or have I blocked this day out because of something I don't want to face up to? I'm beginning to think it might be the latter. In the meantime, I think I may spend a little energy proving them wrong. They haven't seen or heard the last of me yet. I'm starting to feel a bit feisty and playful again. I actually think I can probably tip that wineglass on Hooker. I'm making a phenomenal effort now. And as he turns to say goodnight to a departing comrade, I tip the glass. It went all over his crotch. Good show. Harriet is ganging up on him now.

"Oh, Tom, you're always so clumsy."

"Listen, Harriet, this isn't funny. I really didn't touch the thing."

"Of course you did, darling. I think you've had too much to drink. We should go."

"You know, you could offer to take me home and clean it up yourself. Like with your tongue."

"Oh, Tom, don't be vulgar. Besides, I don't like tacky things."

"You like sticky money."

"That's an exception."

They're both standing now. Tom is looking a bit embarrassed. But Harriet is proceeding majestically through the room, saying good night to the evening's assembly of racketeers. Yes indeed, they're all criminals here, but the kind who usually don't get caught. Once in a while the government makes an example of one or two, who for other independent reasons have fallen out of grace. But it's all a show for the little fellows. To convince them of the impossible. To make them think there's justice. If we added the crimes up, there are probably more years here than in the whole state penitentiary. Anyway, they've successfully maneuvered through the remainder of the room. Harriet's coat is back on her shoulders, and they're now out at curbside.

"Harriet, I've got to see you soon."

"Why don't you center your attention on that business deal you mentioned at dinner. Find a buyer for Siderurgica, and I'll give you a night you won't forget."

She's getting into the car, opening the window, and blowing him a kiss. As he stands there looking consternated. Complete with wet crotch. She always did drive a rather hard bargain. But nothing as tough as what I have in store for them.

FOURTEEN

WHEN MY SISTER, ALICIA, LAY DYING IN THE HOSPITAL, WITH A CASE of pancreatic cancer, she made me promise I'd take care of her little boy, Gustavo. At the time, I did not suspect the child could grow up to be the archetype of my most negative misgivings regarding the Latin culture. Alicia had also been a black sheep, and had run off to find what she deemed her Latin roots. Down in some execrable Caribbean country, she married a man by the name of Fernández. He was in many respects the epitome of what one would expect from a Latin. He was handsome, suave, and extremely charming. He had dark hair and eyes, and a lot of animal magnetism. His psychology was also prototypically Spanish. To begin with, he had extremely strong family ties. Mind you, there's nothing wrong with loving your family. But Latins frequently suffer from monumental Oedipal complexes. It actually has to do with the way society and the sexes are organized in those steamy places.

Traditionally, women have not been held in the highest esteem down there. They may tell you they love their daughters. But there's a big difference in celebration if a boy is born. Males are unquestionably preferred. Females are terribly underrated during their formative years. And generally, the attention, expense, and interest all go in the direction of pampering the males. The whole psychological con job is so effectively marketed that the women themselves ultimately become the handmaidens of their own undoing. In the lower classes, girls do housework. And in the upper classes, they do needlework, play the piano, or take dance lessons. But the boys are only rarely put to work. The standards to be applied to men are also quite different. When a son is fifteen, he's expected by Daddy to copulate with the maid. In fact, if he should make a real mistake and get the housekeeper pregnant, mother will cry, but father will secretly boast to his clubmates about the prowess reflected in the issue of Junior's penis. Women are brought up in many respects to be seen and not heard. And thus, the phenomenon which characterized the late Roman Empire is rekindled on a daily basis.

There are definite stages to a Latin female's life. The first, of course, is childhood, which compared to the heavenly infancy of a male is disadvantaged, to say the least. The second is young womanhood, in which after the initial flow of blood it is whispered that your sister is already a señorita. Now females will be carefully guarded by their parents. Because while honor is possessed and enforced by men, it can be lost with the flicker of the labia. During these years, females will be demure and quiet. They will seem to admire men and will be especially subservient to the wishes of their parents and future husbands. At this stage daughters are seen as pawns. They will be used to form unions and as instruments in the creation of alliances. Above all, they must be married. For the greatest sin among Latin women is to be a spinster. Which in their language is referred to as being a female ham. Which is to say an old, tough, salted piece of meat!

The next act in this comedy can be referred to as early marriage. Upon marrying, girls cease to be under the control of their fathers and will now respond to the orders of their husbands. While a recently married girl may receive a household of her own, she really doesn't control very much at all. In fact, in young marriages, the husband will routinely restrict expenses, and fiscalize all matters. During this period, the paramount desire on all sides is pregnancy. Legitimization occurs the minute a young bride becomes gravid. Her parents will be delighted, as will his. And the husband will be boastful in the hope the distended womb holds, not a child, but a male. That is to say, a *macho*.

Once the child is born, women's opinions become more important. They become matronly, and start to tell their husbands what to do, just as their mothers and their grandmothers did before them. They now have committed to their care that most precious of all resources, the male heirs. As a result, they can spend money on their households, and on themselves. Their husbands may routinely stray, but these Agrippinas and Clytemnestras will not endanger their new-found power by making a fuss unless it is clear they are to be replaced. In fact, most Latin women have been brought up in the Catholic religion, and trained in their teenage years to believe sex is perverted and evil. They are therefore frequently relieved when their hubbies find new wells in which to bury their tallywhackers.

In the final stage of development, the husbands are shrinking and shriveling with age. And frequently dropping dead. At this point, the women blossom and become glutted with power. Potency which is wielded through a network of other similar females, who now have substantial control over their young sons. The matriarchy then enters full bloom. As a result, all Latin men, *machos* though they may be, are pansies where Mother is concerned.

Gustavo Somerset is just such a Latin. I should explain his full name is Gustavo Fernández Somerset. When he was born there was great celebration. In a way his arrival brought me together with my sister again. Then when Gustavo became a teenager, Alicia, whom I had always adored and who was my only link with Mother, became terminally ill. After my sister died, I mourned and wept without consolation. I attempted to obtain custody of Gustavo after his father blew their fortune on gambling and women. At that time I failed. But after the child grew up a bit, it became evident to him that an association with the Somerset surname would be profoundly advantageous. So with my approval he came into our family and began calling himself Gustavo Somerset. Unfortunately, by that time, the harm had been done.

Whenever I visited him as a child, I found he was a mean little bastard. Totally selfish. Self-centered and very much apt to tell you to take it or leave it. Which is, of course, a passive way of forcing you to make the decision, without an alternative, since making a decision to take it would be to forgo all alternatives anyway! Early on, I realized he had all the makings of a perfect little shit. Nevertheless, he was my sister's son, so I expended a considerable effort in both his formal and social education. Besides, he was a physically attractive child who brought to the surface all of my longing for a boy of my own. Everything was all for naught. He was a horrible little boy, and grew up to be an even ghastlier teenager.

While he was in college, I was forever repairing the results of his indiscretions. Later he embarrassed me on more than one occasion by imprudently using my name in business circles. Finally, and in desperation, I employed him in an effort to keep him under my hand. For a while, he applied his intelligence to the task of learning finance, and I was pleased. After all, I had no son of my own, and longed for someone to follow in my footsteps. Perhaps because of this, I began idealizing him a bit as he progressed in his training. It is a sad lesson that whenever we idealize our loved ones, we predispose our relationships to failure. As it happened, I had begun recouping a bit of confidence when the Siderurgica situation crystallized. In fact, it was my mistake. I delegated to him an essential aspect of the deal, with which he promptly turned around and screwed me. Unfortunately, I placed Gustavo in charge of monitoring my short position in the American steels, and entrusted him with exact information on my possible sale or liquidation points if the going got rough. So he knew at all times where my limits were hidden, and when and where I would be forced to abandon ship.

Yes, a few days before I died, I held in my hands the irrefutable evidence of Gustavo's larceny and perfidy. The little bastard had teamed up with Tom Hooker and Harriet to peel off my socks. I never understood it, though. He would have enjoyed great wealth had he exercised a modicum of loyalty. But he was too impatient. And there were those gambling debts. And the *macho* ego. He thought I didn't know. But the ripples from the high-stakes rooms in Nevada and Monte Carlo reached my ears almost immediately. In that respect, he is very much like his father.

Then, of course, there is the business of wishing to do your creator one better, so to speak. Yes, all lovers, children, nephews, and the like who have benefited from the care and ministration of a superior mentor possess a secret desire to best their idol. It's one of mankind's fundamental complexes. Not content to be the beloved of God, the Dark Angel has to challenge Him, and not willing to follow the rules, Adam and Eve must taste the forbidden fruit. Yes, all of the people in second place wish to be in first, even if they are not apt for the position. Not knowing that this may ultimately bring them great unhappiness and pain.

So here is Gustavo Somerset. It's eight o'clock in the morning, and I'm standing in front of Harriet's country house. He's just driven up in a steel-gray Maserati. He's not bad looking. About five feet nine inches tall. He's inherited the delicate Latin bones from his father's side of the family. But there's definitely something a little sleazy about him. Perhaps it's the tiny mustache.

To be sure, I sent him to the best boarding schools. Where he presumably learned manners. But he still occasionally grabs his crotch as if to adjust himself. Very much as his father used to do. It's almost as if these guys have to reassure themselves their penises are still there. Gustavo likes women. But he also screws around with boys. He's ashamed of it, which is unfortunate. It's one of the problems Latins have. The original programming is so strong, they can never come to accept themselves as they are. They might long for a cock up their asses, but they'll never admit it. So in Latin countries, the gay bars will be filled with a procession of married men cheating on their wives. Or of younger men who have deposited their girlfriends safe within the tentacles of parental supervision and have later in the night proceeded to procure themselves a slice of man.

Latin men are also often vain beyond measure. They actually spend a great part of their day primping and combing themselves. Yes, hair is extremely important. If they have it, they flaunt it. And if they don't they're forever camouflaging the fact. These fellows are best described as peacocks. They must always be the center of attention. No wonder, since their mothers made such a fuss over them as children. My sister, Alicia, was a prime example of this. And it got worse as she became ill. The children therefore become self-centered and egotistical. They frequently grow up thinking themselves the belly buttons of the world. In spite of the myth, it has been said by many that they are universally bad sex. Of course, their wives may never come to know this, since many are virgins when they marry, and they may never gain access to another man.

Gustavo is just such a Latin. He's wearing a navy-blue chalk-stripe suit, which he probably got at my tailor, and for which I probably paid. He's also carrying a very lightweight blue cashmere coat. And sporting a rather brightly colored tie. The kid likes gaudy cuff-links, and of course he has a solid-gold Rolex watch. The maid is admitting him, and he's proceeding into the conservatory, where Harriet is having her breakfast among the potted palms. Yes, I remember them well. *Allagoptera* and *Arenga. Chamaedorea* and *Nephrosperma. Pigafetta* and *Rhapis.* They're all here. I must say, she looks rather fresh with that backdrop of bamboo palms. And today she sits here in deceptively quasi-maternal fashion with the silver coffeepot before her. Complete with the croissants, the jams, and the jellies. As she sees Gustavo entering, briefcase in hand, she smiles and leans over ever so slightly to be kissed.

"Gustavo, darling, how are you today?"

"Fine, Harriet, I'm all ready to go, but I must admit those pastries look awfully tempting, so I'll have one with a little coffee. We still have some time before my flight."

Gustavo is pouring himself a generous cup and flavoring it with four teaspoons of sugar.

"Gustavo, I'll never understand how you can taste your coffee with all that sugar."

"It's something I picked up from my father's side of the family."

"Just add it to the catalog of bad habits you managed on your own, dear."

"Oh, Harriet, I'm not all that bad. After all, I did help you become an extremely wealthy widow. If you'd relied exclusively on Uncle Henry you'd be out in the cold right now with a mere trifle while his old college got most of the money."

"You're right, Gustavo. You do have your virtues, even though we both know what a little horror you can be. The next time you decide to rattle skeletons, remember, dear, that I know about all your bad habits, including the nasty things you do to those girls and boys. Frankly, my dear, I couldn't care less. But be careful. Don't cross your Aunt Harriet."

The two really do get along famously. Gustavo has avoided commentary on his aunt's little observations, but is smiling broadly now and helping himself to an ample amount of orange marmalade.

"Well, Harriet, I agree, I can on occasion be somewhat of a shit. But I'm your little turd. And right now that makes you and Tom Hooker about a billion richer."

"We won't talk about that anymore. But there is something I want you to do for me while you're in Europe. I've decided I want to have the funds which are not committed to steel stocks reinvested in American steels. I also need to have two million transferred to my Hong Kong account."

"I'm going to need a little money too, Harriet."

"Gambling a bit?"

"Just a tad, but it's none of your business."

"It's my business if I have to pay for it."

"You know, you owe me a great deal. . . ."

"How much do you need?"

"A million or so now. Maybe a little more later."

"You have my authorization to draw that amount on your own behalf, but you'd better not play around with any of the other funds, or as I said, you'll regret it."

"I understand. Shall we go?"

"Let me find my handbag and tell the staff we're leaving."

Harriet is pulling a pair of sunglasses off the commode in the foyer and is now proceeding, Gustavo in tow, to enter her black limo. She's babbling on about some dresses she wants him to bring back from the Paris apartment. This is girl talk, and I'm not about to waste my time on it. I've confirmed what I needed to know this morning. I no longer feel a responsibility of any sort toward Gustavo. He's not only cheated and stolen, he's violated my sacred trust. That should take him down to the ninth circle, where such transgressions are rewarded with the severest of punishments. While that place is not readily in sight, it's presently my fondest desire to make him wish he were there. But not wanting to continue with the self-deception that brought me to this juncture, I must face up to my own lack of judgement and assume some responsibility for my actions and selections. After all, *one does not send a dwarf to measure the depth of a river.*

FIFTEEN

THE SPANISH ALWAYS SAY *THE TREE RESTS WHILE THE AX GOES BACK and forth*. E.C. has had his little respite. And I'm now back at Pyramid Hill with him at this early-morning hour, where he has decided to work for the day. Miss Cleave and he are sitting in the library before stacks of binders containing documents and facts on the Siderurgica deal.

I've done my best to use all available powers of suggestion, and I really have him totally fired up for the deal. Now I must turn a neat trick, and provide him with a slight advantage. After all, where would we be in life without a little push here and there? It has been said that *he who does not have a godfather cannot be baptized!*

I'm pleased to report I recently remembered where I put those very special documents which fully incriminate Gustavo, Hooker, Harriet, and their cohorts. Also, I'm ashamed to say there's a bit of additional information on Von Richter's formula which came to me after I had committed to the Siderurgica transaction. As everyone knows, steel is an alloy of iron and carbon, in which the carbon doesn't usually exceed two percent of the mixture. There have been a number of advancements in the process over the years, including the Bessemer method and the various improvements introduced by Siemens. In the 1950s, basic oxygen steel emerged, and it revolutionized the industry. What Von Richter did was take the process one step further by inventing a more substantial and easily cooled rotating oxygen nozzle. His inventive genius also included the use of an additive of sorts which is burned off as part of the process, and is therefore subsequently undetectable. At first, we all thought the thing would again revamp the industry. Unfortunately, before Von Richter kicked the bucket, he came to me one day with an alarming discovery. It seems the new process negatively affected the electron affinities involved, and in the long run, produced a metal which exhibited fatigue at an alarming rate about two years after its initial use. It was only through a series of unique tests which Von Richter devised to accelerate the rate of fatigue that this information became available to me. Naturally, I was quite alarmed, since I was waist-deep in European steel companies and up to my chin in commitments. So I bought off the scientist's scruples and made quite sure that when he lay dying, his chances of a return would be slim.

I should explain. I'm not proud of having snuffed out a life or two. In fact, I spent many nights wrestling with the concept and then convinced myself it was all expedient and meritorious if not of forgiveness, of justification. Perhaps today I might agree it was wrong to mess with anyone's spiritual pathway. But at the time I saw myself as a man guiding the destiny of the world, as a champion of my own financial ideals. I rationalized and told myself it was all for the common good. In truth, I never took action against a "little guy" or anyone who had not committed himself to the risks of the game. I went after the big players. In this respect I was sporting. But in spite of that reasoning, and after properly analyzing my actions, I must conclude there was no proper reason for the taking of lives, since it was all for my own selfish gain.

To be sure, I'm ashamed of this. But in my middle maturity I learned one of the great lessons of living. Many people spend their lives consumed by guilt for the various deeds and misdeeds they've fostered. Guilt in a civilized society can certainly serve as a deterrent.

But among moguls and men of genius, it's definitely an impediment. And certainly among members of the ruling class. So I learned quite early to forgive myself for my unforgivable acts. You'd be surprised —it isn't as bad as it sounds. When you learn to pardon yourself for the unpardonable, you actually become more humanized. And therefore when you wish to, capable of forgiving others. Or so they say.

Although not without some initial difficulty, I then proceeded to promptly forgive myself for the steel which went into all those bridges, buildings, government installations, orphanages, and asylums. In spite of it all. I also thought I had forgiven myself for giving Von Richter that extra little push. But I must confess, I've recently found I'm still ashamed of that last one.

God only knows when that steel will begin to flake at the core. Now that Von Richter is gone, I'm the only one with any evidence of these alarming facts. Which, of course, may be useful at the appropriate time.

E.C. and Cleave really work quite well together. She's looking as scrumptious as ever in a black-and-white houndstooth suit. He, in turn, is a bit more casual today. Wool pants and a tweed jacket. He handles the informal look a lot better than I ever did. I always marveled at the way my Wasp friends could throw anything on their backs and manage to make it look stylish and unstudied. Why, I remember rich friends at college who had patches sewn over the holes in their elbows. Just to avoid throwing a fine, soft garment away. They not only mastered the trick but turned it into all the rage.

I've managed to work Bozo into a hyperactive mood today. There's a particular binder there which has a penciled note. Cleave must have surreptitiously obtained the volume and supplied it to E.C. It's basically my notebook of the transaction. If I could draw his attention to the penciled notation, he'd be aware I stashed some extra documents away here in the house. So Bozo will be my messenger again. I'm telepathically moving him as best I can. He's going over to the stack of books and toppling them off that little table. No. Not the green one. Not the blue one. Grab the tan one. Yes, yes . . . he's taking it over to E.C., who by this time has learned to notice his cues. Now I have to manage a more substantial trick. Bozo is a bit clumsy at this type of thing, so I can't very well induce him to turn pages. I'm going to have to insinuate myself physically into the situation, and flip those leaves. I'm making my maximum effort, and nothing seems to be happening. I feel as if I'm going to explode from the stress, and the pages are not budging. I really don't understand it. I certainly moved that chandelier some time ago. All right, I'll become serene, and won't even try hard. I'll just will it to occur.

Presto! We have a result. I'm turning a page. It actually seems as if it's being moved by the draft from the air-movement system. Which is fine with me. A few more to go, and here we are at my little penciled note, which says, "Secured the documents." Now I have to get E.C. to pay some attention to this thing. Well, it may be the waste of a good teapot and china, but I think it's time to make something happen here.

Bozo is wired right into me. So with one gesture, the tea tray is now all over the floor. The dictation is promptly interrupted. And Miss Cleave is off to enlist help. E.C. seems to be musing about the effect of the tea on the carpet. And now he's looking to the side and glancing at my open page. That's right, take a good hard look at that note. Cleave is back with a maid as our man plunges into the topic. Headfirst.

"Susan, do you have any idea of what your boss meant when he made this note here which says, '*Secured the documents*'?"

"I don't have the foggiest idea what that could mean. But I'll tell you this much—Henry never wrote an extra word or expended a meaningless gesture. He was the type of guy who would plot his daily errands on a map so he could avoid unneeded expenditures of time and energy."

"Then there must be documents somewhere which have to do with things that happened after the deal."

"Are there any numbers under the note?"

"Yes, Susan. There are some numbers here, but I don't fully understand them."

"Just read them backward, and it's probably a date. You know, he was paranoid, so he put the dates on things backward."

"Well, this is very interesting, then, because the note was written just a few days before his death."

"Boss, I just wish I could figure it out, but I never saw any other documents having to do with these matters."

Well, at least I've managed to transmit some of the information.

Now I'm going to have to figure out how to tell him where the papers are. You know, it's one of the drawbacks of having been so secretive during my mortal life. I customarily hid things in books, in jars in the kitchen, down in the wine cellar, and practically everywhere you could think of. I'm still trying to remember where I hid a certain ruby which I was afraid might otherwise be lost. Oh yes, I had bank boxes and vaults at home. And there are secret vaults down there in addition to the one I showed to E.C.

I guess a psychiatrist would say I was incredibly paranoid. Of course, he'd be right. But I also think the whole thing was coupled with my knowledge of the beautiful and my understanding of the rare. In reality, there are only two ways of protecting beauty and rarity. The first is the one I've mentioned before. Which is to be unremittingly brutal. Thou shalt not obtain an injunction to keep thy neighbor from mowing thy prize flowers. Rather, you shoot him in the head. The second alternative is more passive, but equally effective. And that is to hide things. To sequester them away where they can't be touched and handled by the greasy, grimy, undeserving nincompoops who surround us.

I originally hid those documents behind a piece of removable granite baseboard in my bathroom. The thing was properly rigged with clips when the house was built. So you could take it off with any small intrusive object. Later, I became doubly paranoid and removed them to one of the cabinets in the secret filing rooms beneath the pyramid. Now the question that's gnawing at me is, how to do it? How to put those documents in E.C.'s hands? I have definite ideas, but they must be refined. And I will need Bozo's assistance. Which will take some training.

The light is beginning to wane. There are still some birds chirping as if to reassure themselves in the now cooling exterior scene. I've drifted out into my garden, where I'm looking at the recently cleaned fish pond. There aren't any fish here yet. That will wait until spring. But I have a feeling E.C. is going to do well by this entire establishment. I know all sorts of people have been working to bring the gardens back up to snuff again. Now with the light practically gone, the pyramid looks almost magical, sitting serenely in the park. Reflected in its pool it possesses an extraordinary dreamlike quality.

Whenever one thinks of dreams, one just can't help ruminating over Hamlet's dilemma. And his thought that it is better to have a known evil than the unknown possibility of something better. Yes, the prince of Denmark contemplated Yorick's skull, and I in a manner of speaking must contemplate my own. But here I am, and there are still dreams. Of course, when I was a student, I read lots of things about the world of dreams. There was even a Spanish play which contended *life was a dream*. Now that I'm thinking about this business of dreams, I'm wondering if I might not be able to enter a live person's dream world. If I could, I might insinuate ideas into E.C.'s mind. It's actually a rather clever thought. And it's certainly worth a try. I've decided I will definitely try to pass into our man's slumber life tonight. In the meantime, I might do a little test run on Bozo. My only problem is I don't know where to start. It's not as if I could go through an ear or something. Or up a nostril. When I moved those pages the other day, I was able to achieve the momentum by negating it. Perhaps what I should do is try to enter a meditative state and see if I can achieve a merging process.

Bozo is compliantly fast asleep on the Heriz carpet in the library. I'm going to lie right next to him and see what can be done. I must say, this is very frustrating, and I feel very foolish lying here attempting to enter a dog's mind. I'm thinking, perhaps something like a mantra might help here. Let's try the Lord's prayer. "Our Father . . ." Hey, this is working! I'm beginning to feel free, and even lighter. As if I were a spectator at the movies or something. But I'm also a participant. I'm now entering the vast and boundless world of Bozo's mind. It's actually charmingly and brightly colored in here. With pulsating flashes of red and green and yellow. Wonderful fragrances and lovely strong smells. Bozo is dreaming about that enormous bone of beef he ate some time ago. Now he's leaning against E.C., protecting him from something. I don't know quite how to explain it, because my perception of all of these things is most unconventional. But it's delightfully beautiful in here. And puerile. Yes, that's it, this is a childlike world. Secure, and devoid of evil. Bozo is running through a field of wildflowers now. He's chasing something. There are wonderful feelings of touch and pleasure in the proximity with all these flowers. Oh God, it's a bee. I've got to stop him. Bozo, don't chase that thing, it will hurt you. "Stop it, stop it." Too late, this bee is zooming in on Bozo's snout. And he's waking up with a start. With the impact of a howitzer cannon, I'm ejected from the canine dream state and into the world of man.

I have to admit, I'm somewhat ashamed at having mucked around in Bozo's beautifully dreamy mind. It was very interesting to find myself ejected the minute he woke up. It would seem I'm unable to penetrate conscious states. I wonder if this will also apply to humans? Appropriately enough, Bozo's world was totally unverbal. Nonlinguistic but full of wonderful smells. Fresh pancakes, roast beef, and lily of the valley. Will it be that way with men and women? Well, I'm going to know soon enough. I've decided to try my little experiment on E.C. tonight. He and Cleave are now in there having dinner, and she will soon be leaving. The combination of good food and wine should make him an ideal subject for tonight's exercise in suggestion.

SIXTEEN

Gustavo Somerset arrived in Europe a couple of hours ago on a smart supersonic flight. It's now about two o'clock in the morning in Paris. I've decided to look in on him. Which is not very difficult, since I've developed these new locative skills. It seems I'm now able to place myself in the company of any person known to me by merely willing myself into his or her presence. Gustavo is sitting at the hotel bar having a bit of Armagnac. He's with that creep Flavio Pertinore, who is one of our attorneys in Lugano. I guess he flew in to meet Gustavo.

Flavio has acted as bagman for some of the wealthiest people in the world. Me included. His commission always sticks nicely to those perfectly manicured nails. He's tall, and carries well those features one usually associates with northern Italians. Long bones, and long fingers. And a cock which likes to find its way into very young little girls. I've always been disgusted by pederasts of various varieties. He's actually gotten himself into an occasional bit of trouble over this business of little girls. I always assumed there were also little boys, since at that age there really isn't much of a difference.

Flavio is a greedy fellow, and not beyond larceny. I will, however, admit I was very much surprised to find he'd participated with Hooker and Gustavo in bilking me out of what should have been my just prize in the Siderurgica deal. They seem to be having a rather animated conversation. Flavio's heavily accented English is excitedly coming through.

"Gustavo, I theenk what you are proposing is extremely dangerous. We have invested about nine hundred meellion in American steel stocks presently. If you are right about this possible new buyer for Siderurgica, you will be very, very reeech indeed!"

"Flavio, I didn't bring you here to discuss conventional business. You know as well as I that my aunt and Tom Hooker will give us the crumbs out of the deal and keep the cake for themselves. I'm just suggesting we help ourselves to a sure thing by going on margin and doubling our position."

"But Gustavo, this margeen theeng is very dangerous. If the stock goes down, you will need very large amounts of cash . . ."

"Flavio, I just want you to take a Valium or two and let me call the shots. Incidentally, I'm cutting you in on twenty percent of the profit."

"How about thirty-threee?"

"Twenty-five."

"Thirtee."

"Twenty-five."

"Okay, okay, you've convinced me to do this theeng. All I hope is that La Santa Madre helps us."

The bagman is making the sign of the cross as he mentions the Holy Virgin. It's a pretty sight. Religion and crime. Not unusual bedpartners. But in this case, we're just dealing with petty thieves and hustlers. Not the real guys at all.

In life, when cavorting through five continents of financial entanglement, I dealt with the genuine fellows. The heavies. In proper order, the Vatican and the Mob. Originally, when I started out in business, I thought the one would be celestial and the other would be plain mean. As I ascended into the world of high cash denominations, it became clear these were merely two vast and great corporate entities, intimately linked to the fiber of world economy. Both necessary, each dependent on the other. I remember one particularly amusing evening when I was invited to dine at Cardinal Tucci's in Rome. His apartments in the Vatican were unabashedly magnificent. As were the antiquities and antiques within. The paintings on the walls were borrowed from the Vatican Museum, so to speak. The servants were all beautiful youths. Like the angels in a Fra Filippo Lippi.

Congregated there were luminaries from the world of art, literature, music, and finance. I shall never forget the dinner table. Instead of a tablecloth, it was set with a tenuously worn silk Persian carpet. On which rested priceless porcelain and solid-gold goblets. In the background, the soft music of Benedetto di Marcello could be heard as the ancient Barolo Riserva was poured, followed later by the Lacrima Christi. The most surprising part of the evening was, of course, the dinner guest who sat to the right of His Eminence, and therefore to my left. Don Salvatore Orsini, no less. Supreme leader of the Cosa Nostra. I had never met the man. And it was evident the Vatican thought it expedient to make the presentation. He was charming and polished. Worldly, without being crass. Obviously interested in very many of the same things the other guests were. Had I not been discreetly briefed, I never would have suspected. That evening, we cemented a relationship of trust and friendship, which I assume would have lasted a lifetime. All under the aegis of Our Mother the Church. When I subsequently met with the Cardinal, I had a very curious conversation which I can practically recall verbatim.

"Your Eminence, I hardly have words to express my gratitude for last night's invitation. Dinner was absolutely wonderful in every way."

"Did you enjoy my dinner guests?"

"Yes. I thought they were all very interesting and very kind to grant me such a warm reception. And of course Madame Rosa was very gracious to sing for us after dinner. Such a beautiful voice . . ."

"And the gentleman to your left . . ."

"Your Eminence, I found him particularly interesting, and, of course, fascinating. But I must say, without offense, I was rather surprised to find him at your table."

"My son, I should caution you that Don Orsini has been a guest in the finest Vatican apartments for three decades, and is received by the Pope himself. When you know more of the true workings of our world, you will understand that God cannot exist independent of darkness. Had the darkness not existed, He would have created it to complement the light. It is like life and death. They are not good and evil, they are merely sisters in time. Each with her own mission, each with her own pain."

I shall never forget those last few lines.

Perhaps the safest thing which can be said of all of us refers to our missions and the existence of our pain. I've tried to find happiness in things throughout my life. And I guess there were times when I was, in fact, legitimately happy for an instant or two like all those craggy Wasp couples who found true felicity while their favorite stock was rising. But all kidding aside, when I think backward into time, I also remember the unique pain associated with every instance and situation. In a very real way there must be suffering in order to achieve growth and happiness. I've been wondering about some of the things old Cardinal Tucci taught me. And the business about having a mission has particularly stuck in my mind. I never expected an afterlife so similar in its feelings to my former existence. I often wonder why it's all happening. Just as I was curious before when I had a body. I've also been wondering whether there are things here which must be done, and assuming that such is the case.

Gustavo and Flavio are now standing. Flavio has paid the bill. Gustavo avoids touching such things. He's trying to dissuade my nephew from his scheme to pyramid that very dirty nine hundred million into a larger amount by going on margin. But Gustavo will have none of it. So they part cordially, and the little creep is on his way upstairs for a night of sleep.

As usual, he has secured a very expensive suite for himself. This is one of the better rooms in the front part of the hotel, which, being located as it is in a very old building at Place Vendôme, is subject to the vagaries of having two elevators which lead to different parts of the hotel. This room actually looks out on the main street and that wonderful column. I personally always preferred the slightly smaller rooms which surround a quiet courtyard on the Rue Cambon side, and which are reached through the rear elevator. They come complete with a courtyard view, ivy by the window, and birds chirping in the morning. But there's nothing wrong with this room, which, in fact, has very nice high ceilings.

Gustavo is already in bed and fast asleep. It's a combination of travel, stress, and alcohol. By this time I had hoped to beam back to E.C.'s and intrude on his dream. But the opportunity of using Gustavo as a guinea pig is all too tempting. I shall catch our man Douglas at a later time. I'm wondering if I might not be able to intrude within this sleeping mind, and suggest a thing or two. As I'm thinking this, I'm also prematurely becoming self-congratulatory about the idea. I think I'll wait a few moments until he's truly fast asleep. Since that will make it substantially easier for me to penetrate. Yes, penetration. A wonderful word, if I do say so myself. Somewhat akin to rape. I think I'll sit in this nice, cushy Louis XV chair and meditate my way into his dream world.

Very, very softly. Like a spider tiptoeing in ballet shoes. I shall enter under cloak of sleep like the bleakest, blackest ballerina. Here I go. . . . Oh! . . . I don't like what I'm seeing here. Very much in the same way that Bozo's mind was like a field full of sunflowers, Gustavo's is like the municipal dump. There are all sorts of awkwardly palpitating colors and noises here. And the smell of apprehension is everywhere. Not to mention the foul odors of chemicals, stale cigarette smoke, and old sweat. I always said these tormented minds were actually responding to fear. And from what I see, Gustavo is very much afraid. Why, there must be two thousand and one self-centered, frustrated sexual encounters on file here. Only pleasure for Gustavo. Not for anyone else. And there are waves of selfishness and self-interest. And lies. I have to keep a very stiff upper lip to deal with the anger and hatred that's oozing around everywhere. The lust. The gluttony. And especially the greed. Here all things are shades of black and gray, and brown. And there is a stench everywhere. It's a claustrophobic sort of smell. A space in which the air is clammy, and spent. Gustavo is dreaming about our business deal. He's thinking there's a lot of money here. But he hasn't yet centered on the magnitude of what is available. So I shall help him by appearing in his reverie as his loving, appreciative uncle:

"How's my nephew doing today?"

"Uncle Henry! . . . but you're dead!"

"Of course I am, Gustavo. Now don't be afraid. After all, you know, you've always been my favorite nephew."

"Ah . . . uh, this is a really weird dream, Uncle Henry. Is there anything you're after me for?"

"Of course not, Gustavo. Don't be paranoid. I'm just a part of you that thinks it's Uncle Henry. I'm the inner and grandiose Gustavo dressed as your uncle, and I've come to put you in touch with your destiny. You see, Old Bean, you're going to be very, very rich."

"Richer than Harriet and Hooker?"

"Oh, lots richer."

"How am I going to do that, Uncle Henry? I already think I have a pretty good idea about putting all the money on the margin, and doubling the position."

"Gustavo, that's child's play. What you should really do is get your hands on another eight or nine hundred million by pledging the presently existing amount."

"Hah hah, Uncle Henry. You really are a crazy figment of my imagination. You know no respectable banker would take that sort of risk."

"Gustavo, you have to remember there are people linked to us by codes of honor who will lend us the money."

"Like who, Uncle Henry?"

"I suggest you go see our old friend Cardinal Tucci."

"Uncle Henry, I could make an extra two billion dollars."

"That's right, Gustavo. And you could have it all for yourself."

The various shades of black and gray in here are palpitating like hyperactive pimples trying to explode. There's a lot of excitement going on in this mind, in which the premonition of stirring is all too strong. Lest I be rudely ejected when he wakes in a few moments, I think I'll gently leave and watch the action from outside.

Gustavo is moving restlessly under the white starched sheet. All of a sudden, his eyes open with a start, as he jerks up into a seated position. Now he's sweating profusely and muttering, "What a dream, what a dream." He's acquiring a smile on his face, which is converting to a broad grin, as he turns on the night-table lamp, and writes two words on the pad which rests there. *Cardinal Tucci.*

Our little shit is again tucking himself under the sheets. And will probably involve himself in another dream quite soon. But I don't think I want to again visit that place inside him, if it can possibly be avoided. Mind you, I'm not easily frightened or disquieted. Nor have I shunned the unpleasant when truly necessary. But there is something about the ambience of that unhappy psyche that makes me shiver with revulsion. It's also exhausted me to the extent that I am unwilling to attempt my foray into E.C.'s dreams at this time. So for the present, I'll stay right here, cuddling into the down cushions on this chair, to rest quietly for the remainder of the night.

SEVENTEEN

GUSTAVO OVERSLEPT AS USUAL, AND CONTRARY TO CUSTOM, HAD BREAK-fast in his room. He had to change his shirt, since he spilled coffee all over the first one he tried. He's on the telephone to Rome now, and has identified himself to Cardinal Tucci's secretary, who, in view of the Somerset mystique, has granted him an appointment for three o'clock tomorrow. Of course, there are people who wait weeks or even months for such a reception. But Gustavo is riding on my coat-tails. And this will allow him to fly high. At least for a while.

In the meantime, he's decided to call his favorite Parisian bookie, and he's placed all sorts of bets on the races. Now he's speaking to the concierge and setting up his flight to Rome for the earliest hour tomorrow morning. The concierge at this hotel is like a great power in his own right. He knows everyone in the world of travel, food, and accommodations. And there are a few other things of which he is aware as well. He knows all the other important concierges in the greatest hotels in the world. And also, the various sins and indiscretions and proclivities of his guests. No doubt the driver and limo have already been requested, as has priority seating on the morning flight.

Gustavo has just indicated he's going shopping for the rest of the day. And he'll probably be stopping by my Paris apartment on Avenue Foch to retrieve Harriet's dresses. I assume he didn't stay there to avoid being spied on by the servants while he screwed some businesslike harlot. Which is probably what he has lined up for tonight. Having myself partaken on occasion of the world of pimps and prostitutes, I must admit to ultimately having become inordinately bored by the whole scenario.

Don't get me wrong. There's absolutely nothing which could make me object to prostitution. It's an age-old institution which merits full respect, and also fills an important need. On occasion, I've purchased the prettiest girls and boys money ever could buy. A lot of people go to prostitutes. And for various reasons. Some of them are terribly obese, or horribly ugly, or just very old. Others are perfectly acceptable, but have the type of sexual hang-ups or self-images which make it impossible to procure traditional sex in the usual places. Still others are terribly jaded, and are totally uninterested in love, so they seek only immediate pleasure. Of course, when you're extremely wealthy, you never know the difference between the true lover and the call girl. You give the harlot five hundred dollars. But your sweetheart hustles you for a diamond bracelet. Ultimately, the good thing about your encounter with prostitution is that the professional makes a deal and keeps it. She promises you hot sex in exchange for your cool hundreds. Giving you no more, no less. If you cherish the idea of a blow job and it's part of the bargain, you will receive it. With your wife or lover, you may wait weeks for that fellatio, if it ever comes at all, and possibly suffer the anguish of rejection or lies.

Unfortunately, it's the very certainty of such contractual arrangements which ultimately makes you tire of them. Each call girl or boy-toy is pretty much like the next. Bigger, smaller, cuter, prettier, they're all the same. I guess it's a matter of free will. The contractor is bound by agreement to provide the thrill. So within the confines of that arrangement, you've robbed it of free will in exchange for money. Yes, they will perform, and sometimes even with virtuosity. But your self-esteem will never be stroked with the intensity of the casual encounter, in which you presume you are attractive for reasons other than your bankroll. It's that very absence of freedom which always makes prostitution so boring to me.

There is, however, a twist here. Why do we feel demeaned when we pay money, but think nothing of using the enticements of intelligence, looks, a nice life-style, or a hot car? Has money become so totally discredited in our minds that its exchange for sex has become synonymous with infamy? It seems to me that somewhere in this bargain, money has been dealt a rude blow, or poor hand. Bad press, so to speak! Is it that in our hearts we feel that there is no control greater than financial power? And that therefore its use is unsporting? In that case, the commentary would be on us, and not on poor maligned *pecunia*.

I started realizing these things during the midyears of my life. I'll never forget the time my first mistress left me. I was crushed in every possible way. And I wanted to get even. By that time, I was worth a few hundred million or so. Not a great deal by my standards today, but enough to wield a modicum of control. I visited my psychiatrist, wearing my bruised ego like a misplaced diplomatic decoration. I ranted and raved. And told him about all her weaknesses, and how I would play on them to get her back. He just looked at me for the longest time through those big thick glasses. And then asked only one question: "Can a person whom you fully control ever really love you?" I remember I heard it, and refused to really listen. But I knew it was important. So I asked him for a piece of paper, and wrote it down. That evening, I looked at those words, again and again, knowing quite clearly that sooner or later I would have to allow them to find a place within me. A little past midnight and a bottle of Calvados from Peuchet, my ego capitulated, and I realized the wisdom of his words. If we're smart, we can not feel loved by robots or people whose free will we have hindered, compromised, or stolen in any way. Which is exactly why I will always hazard the dangers of the chase. No matter the price, no matter the peril. It's the real thing that counts, and no substitute or facsimile will do. But in spite of this, once the prize is won, I must admit, there are still times at which I revert to my old patterns of control.

I think there's a knock at the door. Gustavo, now fully dressed, is opening it. Only to find a very pretty and rather exquisitely small bellboy, holding the requested American newspapers. This is a pleasant development, since I really do want to catch up on everything that's been happening at home. Of course, I could just will myself there, but I also don't want Gustavo to get out of hand in any way.

My nephew has decided to leave the papers on the bed and forgo taking a swipe at the bellboy. He's now off to his shopping spree. With old Henry in close proximity, there isn't much mischief he can get into this afternoon. In the meantime, I shall busy myself reading the business sections. Oh, here's something about how megacorporations keep on telling the public they're losing money. Hah! If the poor public only knew. The working classes are the ones who really get it smack in the teeth. The poor devils never stand a chance. They work for salary, then the government takes a great big chunk out of it for taxes. Not to mention the additional thievery of social security. After all, under the usual actuarial tables, by the time most people reach the age at which they will collect it, they are far too old to enjoy very much. And the money itself won't buy a great deal. In the meantime, the government takes your tax money and spends it on fifty-thousand-dollar hammers, ten-thousand-dollar wrenches, and million-dollar screws, so to speak. It's not the illegal graft which sucks up all the money. It's the perfectly legal variety. Like when an airplane that should cost a billion costs five. The other four billion finds its way into all those corporate expense accounts and salaries. Private jets, hotel rooms, meetings in Monte Carlo, and corporate yachts. Yes indeed, the poor yokel earning thirty thousand a year can't even deduct a necessary sanitary tissue. But to the chairman of Consolidated This or That, the horizon is virtually without limit. The company buys the things he needs and he just uses them. The distinction is one which forces the poor into involuntary servitude and forced labor. Unless, of course, they wish to completely relinquish every semblance of control. In which event they collect welfare. And this payment separates them from yet another slice of their free will. And here they have the nerve to say slavery doesn't exist anymore!

Now I'm going through the financial section again. And this time, I'm detained by a real eye-catcher:

NEW RUMORS SHROUD SIDERURGICA DEAL

Amid rumors from both sides of the Atlantic, yesterday's close of the London and New York stock exchanges found Siderurgica common stock up almost two and one-half points. The significant buildup in volume during the preceding two days would indicate concerted buying on behalf of a rumored American purchaser.

Siderurgica has previously been the object of a successful takeover bid by Henry W. Somerset, of Somerset Consolidated Industries. At that time, over a year ago, Somerset purchased approximately 39 percent of the common stock of Siderurgica, giving him what then became the equivalent of control. It is rumored another 30 percent is held by European banks for unnamed parties. Analysts have speculated as to the intentions of the presently anonymous buyer in the market. Also with the recent demise of Henry W. Somerset, it is entirely possible the 39 percent owned by his estate may also come into play. It is expected there may be continued activity in this issue. No American filings have been made. Some sources have traced the buying to a highly discreet firm of brokers, which services, among others, the accounts of E. C. Douglas, who has recently been in the public eye in connection with other aspects of the Somerset estate.

Aha! So the cat's out of the bag. And E.C. has decided to go for it. I happen to know where that other thirty percent is, and as far as I can recall, they won't have any intention of selling. Although, of course, everything has a price. So, if E.C. wants the company, he's going to have to buy it from the estate. And Harriet and Hooker are not exactly barefoot Carmelite nuns. So he'd better be expecting to pay a rather hefty price. I'm becoming rather anxious about this whole matter. And since Gustavo is probably somewhere between here and the farthest confines of Rue St. Honoré, chin-deep in silk shirts and new junk, I might as well momentarily will myself back to the presence of E.C. and Miss Cleave.

Presto. I've really acquired expertise at moving through great distances with the flick of my will. I even seem to be able to bend time in the process and cheat the clock in both directions. Here I am back in the library of the megastructure where E.C. and Miss Cleave are again hard at work. It's morning here, and there's a certain amount of excitement in the air. Our man is on the phone to Harry, with whom he is apparently engaging in a heated repartee:

"Listen, E.C., we bought practically everything we could sweep up from the curbsides. But that only gets you to eleven percent. Unless we make a private deal for the estate stock, you're not going very far in purchasing this company."

"What about your inquiries regarding the thirty percent held by European interests?"

"We approached three of the Swiss banks involved, and the response was more watertight than a frog's ass. They simply don't want to sell. They were actually a bit huffy about it and didn't invite further inquiries. So I had my partner Ralph contact this Hooker guy, who is one of the executors of the Somerset estate. They were typically noncommittal, but I'm happy to say they didn't discourage further conversations. So you have a meeting with Thomas Hooker Esquire tomorrow afternoon at three. Don't be surprised if the Somerset widow is there. Ralph charmed one of the lawyer's secretaries over a drink the other night and found out they're pretty thick these days. You know, like pit vipers in heat. I've got to tell you something, E.C. Of all the fucking companies in the world, you have to choose the one that's in the hands of some of the meanest-spirited people in this whole country. I'd count my fingers and toes when I left that room if I were you."

"Harry, old boy, I appreciate the effort. And I promise to count those digits."

Click.

E.C. has a triumphant smile on his face, and is looking like he's ready for a brisk volley of tennis. He's responding to a quizzical look on Susan's face:

"Well, Susan, it seems like the initial moment of truth is at hand. I'm to meet Tom Hooker, and possibly the widow Somerset, tomorrow at three. Any tips?"

"Well, it had to happen sooner or later. I'd be very careful in that sort of company. Tom Hooker is an extremely sharp little guy, and also very greedy. My boss used him because he's the type of fellow who delivers. But he always told me Hooker could only be trusted to meet the peripheral limits of his contract. I don't think he'll come out into the open and play a dishonest game, but I do believe he'll wipe you out within the law if that's at all possible. Now, Mrs. Somerset is another thing. She's a very intelligent woman. Beautiful, but very cold. And if you allow yourself to be taken in for one second by what my boss described as her 'beguiling smile,' you'll be sunk. She's turned on by wealth, and especially power, but she wants to run the show. So having money around her isn't enough. She has to own it, lock, stock, and barrel. Henry always said her insecurities could turn her into a dangerous woman, whatever that meant. All in all, they make an extremely unpleasant pair. I think the only weak spot is actually their greed. When blinded by it, they might occasionally lose sight of a detail or two."

"Thank you, Susan, for a brilliant description. I'll just have to wear my best suit of body armor."

As I watch the two of them, I'm beginning to fill with glee and anticipation of tomorrow's meeting. If E.C. plays his cards right, he'll have a chance at purchasing the European Siderurgica interests. Yessiree, everything is on its way back to Daddy!

My needlepoint wing chair is looking very enticing. It's funny, my spiritual body doesn't tire, insubstantial as it is, but my mind sometimes becomes weary. So I'm going to need a rest, since I must hop across the ocean tomorrow to witness Gustavo's meeting with old Tucci. Actually, I don't have all that much time, since he will be boarding a plane at seven in the morning. Which is to say one in the morning here. Well, I can nap until midnight or so, while occasionally eavesdropping on the action, and then whisk myself to Paris for the brief ride to Rome with Gustavo. That sounds good, so I'll catch a few winks, before the action begins. Of course, I could always be on time by bending it, so to speak, but I'd rather ride with him and oversee his activities.

The little noises concomitant to closing things down for the night have made me stir. It's a good thing too, since it's five minutes to midnight. And I should be blinking myself over to Paris. Before I go, though, I think it would be expedient to do a quick reconnaissance of this terrain. They've left the library, and I assume Cleave has gone home. The old butler is clearing up the debris of coffee cups and brandy snifters here among the books. With a quick blink, I'm in the bedroom, where Douglas has shed his clothing and is now fast asleep in that very large bed. Bozo has also progressed into slumberland, no doubt dreaming again about the bone of beef, or maybe chasing a chicken. They constitute a pleasant picture of domesticity. Dog and man, fast asleep at midnight.

I'd really like to allow the pooch and his new friend to slumber unimpeded, but this is a great opportunity for me to finally pop into E.C.'s mind and reinforce his new desire. I'm becoming rather skilled at inducing the meditative state now, and I must confess I have a great level of curiosity about what I'll find inside. I'm letting myself go, and now drifting into his dream world. I'm pleased to say this is a rather delightful place. Not as pretty and childlike as Bozo's, but definitely very summery. Which is not half bad. It actually compares favorably with Bozo's springlike mind. There aren't as many bright colors or naive tones. But there are some very interesting geometric shapes. And good smells. Like the aroma of freshly bathed bodies. Of talcum powder, soap, and lavender. Here there are clearly defined pathways put together with the confidence and aplomb of a good New England garden. At the end of it all, Douglas is sitting on a dune at a beach watching the gentle surf come lolling back and forth. There's a wonderful fragrance of fresh salt sea air. I think I'll pop into a bathing suit and sit beside him. Of course, everything is possible for me here. All I have to do is will myself to change. He's seen me, and is smiling.

"You know, I've been expecting you sooner or later."

"Well, the time is now right. And I wouldn't have disappointed you for the world."

"This is really funny, meeting you in a dream this way. You see, I know I'm dreaming, but I also know I've felt your presence about me rather strongly in recent days. Are you here to be helpful? Or are you going to torment me?"

"Oh, come on, I think by now you must have a strong feeling I'm going to be your buddy. I like you. You're a lot as I was before

I became hard and tough. After all, you didn't really think running into my dog was an accident, did you?"

"I sort of wondered about that. It was too uncanny to be a coincidence."

"How did you like my memorial?"

"You mean the one at the cemetery?"

"Of course."

"Well, I thought it was fabulous. But maybe a tad overdone. Now, your pyramid is something else. I really like the place."

"You know, you're profiting from all my good taste. But I don't mind."

"That's nice of you, though I can't think you'd be able to use good taste now."

"Don't get fresh, buster. After all, you know nothing of my present state."

"That's right. But tell me, are you here to help me count these grains of sand?"

"No, Douglas, while I do discern some very pretty metaphysical corridors in this mind of yours, I am not here to help you count grains of sand."

"Too bad. We might have achieved it together."

"Now now, don't turn sentimental on me. We have work to do."

"What sort of work?"

"You know . . . the Siderurgica deal."

"I have second thoughts. It involves so much money I'm a bit frightened."

"Don't be. I will sustain you."

"How do I know this isn't some crazy dream?"

"You're forgetting. I got you out of your little jam with my gold bullion."

"Oh . . . so that was you. I feel a bit sheepish. Like I stole that money from your estate."

"Well, old bean, you don't think Bozo does integral calculus, do you?"

"I should have known."

"You're damn right you should've. And regarding that sheepish feeling, think nothing of it. The money would have gone to Harriet and Hooker, and they are thieves. My mother always said that *a thief who steals from a thief has a thousand years of forgiveness.* The only thing you have to do is maintain silence about the source. If you start babbling to people about my presence, they'll only think you're crazy. But we're wasting time. Forget about this business of counting grains of sand."

"Why?"

"Because it just isn't good for you, and furthermore I have plans to propel you into the business world with gale force!"

"But Henry, other things are happening . . . and I think I love Susan."

"My dear boy, I loved her too. But there's always time for love. And the time for business frequently runs out."

"I don't know, I'm not sure . . . these grains of sand . . ."

"Leave them alone. I have more treasure for you. And a brilliant future. Let me be your magician, your magus, and I shall paint your horizon in diamantine tones of gold and platinum."

"But I *have* riches."

"You will have *more*."

"Whatever for? It's these grains of sand I've got to count."

"You will have control over others. The power to make them do your bidding."

"But I love Susan."

"She will love you more if you follow my footsteps."

"I don't think so. I'm confused."

"Don't worry. Just take your cues from me. I'll be your mentor."

"Will you be back in my dreams?"

"Perhaps, when you need me."

"I love your dog."

"Of course you do. He's special. But now I must leave, so go to sleep. You needn't remember our meeting too clearly. Good night."

"Good night."

Imagine him in there counting grains of sand! That, and pulling petals, is what lovers do. I think I have him on the right track now. For which I heartily congratulate myself. Now he'll go to that meeting with a single purpose in mind. And he'll buy that damn company, and I shall dance my little quickstep of revenge.

I'm again willing myself into Gustavo's presence. With the speed of light, I'm back at his hotel room, where he's now fully dressed and ready to leave. It would seem I've arrived in just the knick of time. My nephew has apparently decided to keep this suite, and will merely be traveling to Rome for the day. After all, the flight lasts less than a couple of hours. So I guess he can be comfortably back to his favorite Parisian whore late tonight. He's dressed in a navy-blue chalk-stripe suit. Which is actually somewhat becoming. He's grabbing his dark brown morocco briefcase. It's the type I taught him to use, if you're going to carry a briefcase at all. I personally always thought only assistants carry briefcases. And it should be noted, the Queen of England doesn't carry money. We're down in the lobby, where Gustavo is having an early-morning chat with the assistant concierge on duty to see him off. Yes, indeed, he's being handed his tickets, complete with seat selection. And we're now off into the Citroën crouching at the curb.

This ride to Charles de Gaulle Airport is one I have always found very pleasing. Paris is still asleep, and seems almost magical under the anticipation of the first morning light. It's not a city which wakes too early. In a while, they'll start washing the sidewalks down. And the smell of fresh bread, pastries, and coffee will be abundant everywhere. We've wound through various streets of the city to a throughway on which we're now speeding toward our morning flight. We're making very good time. Gustavo is looking a bit fidgety. His French was always atrocious, so there isn't much communication with the driver, who is pleasant enough, but quiet.

An airline attendant is waiting for us at the terminal curbside. Having opened the door, we're now on our way through customs. The typically colorless agent has taken one look at Gustavo and whisked him through. We're going into a small private lounge for VIP passengers, where a very attractive girl has handed him a weak cup of coffee. It's what I call "airline java." Now I note our flight is being called. So we're off to our waiting airplane without further ado. Once on board, I'm happy to note the absence of anyone seated next to my nephew. I guess I'll make myself comfortable here and settle down for this very pleasant flight south. I won't get much rest, though. Gustavo is fidgeting as usual. He's now going through a series of sheets which are quite interesting to me. Aha! Here are the secret numbers of the accounts in which all those American steel stocks are being amassed. I guess he'll give the final order to double up on everything when he returns to Paris. But it's nice to know he's carrying that type of documentation. This could be useful at a later date.

A very charming stewardess with blond hair has served a nice little breakfast which includes cheese and fruit. I always like the way Europeans handle their dining. Even on airplanes. If one must take a commercial flight, it's always best to use a European carrier. I haven't taken such a flight in years, but this is actually fun. You also get to watch the people. Which you can't do on your private jet. Like the older woman with her grandchild a few seats back. The little boy is adorable. About six years old. Full of questions about this and that, and obviously very excited about flying. His grandmother is delighted with the detachment of surrogate parents who know they can deliver Junior back to mother and father when the fun is over. Those two very handsome young men seated next to one another aren't fooling anyone. They're either lovers or they'd like to be. Of course, the Europeans are so much more understanding about these matters. After all, *when less is swept under the rug, there aren't as many bumps underfoot.*

All this thought has taken a little longer than I expected. The dry Italian countryside is now evident as the plane's wings are shadowed on the ground. Yes, we'll shortly be arriving at Leonardo da Vinci Airport. They're asking us to fasten our seat belts, and Gustavo is dutifully taking care of his. The pilot is obviously experienced. Not a cowboy at all. Those flaps are in perfect position as we touch the ground *as gently as the kiss of a maiden on a spring morning.* Mind you, I've had landings which were actually *uglier than a toothache at midnight.* But not this one. This is a lovely, smooth touchdown, and a proper preamble to our uneventful taxi to the terminal gate.

Gustavo and I are the first off the airplane. Almost immediately, I note the Church has managed, as usual, to circumvent all rules and has passed through the customs and security barriers without incident. There at the gate, dressed in full regalia, is a suitably obsequious monsignor.

"Mr. Somerset?"

"Yes . . ."

"I am Monsignor Albani. His Eminence Cardinal Tucci sent me to greet you and be sure you arrive without incident at the Vatican."

"That was very kind of His Eminence. I'm very pleased to meet you."

"The pleasure is mine. . . . Shall we make our way to the car? Do you have luggage?"

"No. Actually, I'm just here for my meeting with the Cardinal."

"That is too bad. The fall has been particularly gracious to us this year, and the city is in ferment with delightful activity. You really should stay."

"That won't be possible, this time, but I'm most grateful for the offer of hospitality."

With the flick of monsignor's wrist, the customs official at the approaching box has whisked us onward. I keep forgetting the Church owns everything here. And of course what it doesn't own, it controls indirectly. If you drink water, perish the thought, it's liable to be the Church's. And if you use electricity, it also owns that. No wonder the Church had a bit to do with steel as well. We are now out of the building where a flawlessly polished grand Mercedes awaits us, complete with yellow-and-white diplomatic flags. The car is driven by a young priest, who I must say looks a bit wet behind the ears. Monsignor, Gustavo, and I are in the backseat, comfortably rolling into the city of Rome with its ancient buildings and streets.

St. Peter's is now overwhelmingly upon us. To the left of the Bernini Colonnade there's a watch station with the usual brightly attired Swiss guards. We are through it without fanfare or ceremony. After all, this is a cardinal's conveyance. We drive into a little courtyard and come to a stop. Monsignor is indicating we have arrived. I know the place well. It has the definite charm of a couple thousand years about it. There are old imperial cobblestones underfoot. Gustavo and I are following the monsignor down a very short lane, through an unprepossessing door. Up a wide marble staircase, to an impressive landing with Renaissance flavor. There's a priest at a desk who is smiling at the monsignor and providing him with a smooth nod of the head. No doubt a signal indicating he may proceed to the antechamber of the Cardinal's offices. Once through the double doors, we are greeted by His Eminence's secretary. A tall, good-looking man in his forties with circles under his eyes. Indicative of concupiscence or guilt, or both. And full of suspicion. He has the determined aquiline nose of men who organize, guard, and protect.

"Good morning, Mr. Somerset. I am Monsignor Altieri, secretary to His Eminence. Cardinal Tucci is attending a trifle of urgent business, but will receive you shortly. Please be seated."

So we sit. And we wait. Old Cardinal Tucci wouldn't have done it to me, but I'm glad he's making Gustavo squirm a little. After all, I assume he's trying to ascertain whether *the* supposed *splinter is of the same material as the tree.* The Cardinal's secretary is approaching us again. Indicating His Eminence is now ready to receive. Gustavo is looking a bit nervous and stiff. The doors to the inner chamber have been opened to reveal the commanding presence of my old friend Cardinal Tucci, who is smiling benevolently, and, as always, unabashedly looking like the beneficiary of ten thousand gourmet dinners. He's rising from his Renaissance desk chair to greet Gustavo with hands outstretched.

"My son, it gives me great pleasure to welcome you here at the Vatican."

"I'm very grateful you've received me on such short notice."

Gustavo has had enough common sense to kiss the ring, which was only halfheartedly in his way to provide him the opportunity. At the same time, he's taken a quick little look around the room. And is naturally awed by the frescoed ceiling and art-infested walls. On the Cardinal's desk before him sits a rock-crystal-and-gold rhinoceros with diamond eyes, on a blue chalcedony base. Gustavo's glance wanders toward it as the Cardinal catches his eye and explains.

"It is somewhat of a joke, you see. To remind us we all turn into hideous beasts sometimes. Even if we are laden with gold and diamonds. You see, my son, *you can dress the monkey in silk, but it will still be a monkey.*"

"In spite of your commentary, Your Eminence, I believe it's still quite beautiful."

"Very frequently the most hideous and tempting things are . . . *la bestia . . . la bestia.* But you did not come this far to chat about my bibelots, did you?"

"Actually not. I'm here to see you on an inspiration in connection with my uncle."

"Ah, yes. Your recently departed uncle was a friend of the

Church, and a personal friend of mine. A man of ambition and exquisite taste. Sometimes a troubled soul, but always a friend. I am told the Nuncio attended the funeral on our behalf."

"Yes, indeed, and we were very grateful. In fact, Mrs. Somerset asked me to convey her deepest gratitude."

Now the atmosphere is beginning to tense up a little. Gustavo is fidgeting a bit, and thus giving himself away. Of course, nothing is lost on that angelically benign face.

Tucci is a man in his late seventies. He's an aesthete. But also a statesman and capable businessman. Wily in the ways of the world, he has additionally been through the pain of over seven decades. And the decay of the body. There is, however, a look of complacency, knowledge, and equanimity on that face that one may or may not mistake for inner peace. After all, it has been said that *the devil is more knowledgeable because of his age and experience than because he is the devil.* This would apply to Tucci. He's a man who occasionally worries, as can be seen by the two little dark circles under his eyes. Yet when he smiles, his two dimples make him look younger and more relaxed, clearly indicating the fact that this is a person who has learned to forgive himself for his sins.

He's also a man cut with the ancient scissors of camaraderie and friendship. Here is a fellow who will always keep his promise, but will not make one lightly. A dedicated servant who can be counted upon on all occasions to further first the interests of the Church and then his conception of honor. He is also learned and diligent. No doubt three or four handsome youths worked overnight to assess the various possibilities and probabilities of what this meeting might entail. There are no accidents here. There is homework.

"My son, what was that you said about an inspiration?"

"Well, Your Eminence, you are probably aware that when my uncle passed away, he left a vast empire with positions in many industries."

"Yes, I have a vague knowledge. . . ."

"Well, from very private conversations with him, I was led to believe the Vatican had more than a cursory understanding of his affairs. I can't reveal all of the absolute details due to propriety, but my uncle left somewhat of a mess in certain sectors. And while the estate is extremely solid, there is some business I would do on its behalf which would require some very substantial additional funding which I do not immediately have at my disposition."

Just when Gustavo has worked himself up to this little climax, there is a knock at the door, and a comely young priest is entering with a tray and coffee. The scene is actually quite striking. The young priest has a shock of black, curly hair. And deep, dark eyes. A Botticelli gaze. He is quietly assessing the situation with the eyes of one who is trained to adeptly scrutinize in the service of his master. Beneath the free-flowing folds of his cassock, there is a suspicion of muscular bulge. Biceps, and pectorals. From the look, I wouldn't be surprised if he doubles as a bodyguard. Or indeed, even as something else. The hands are manicured. Not the type consigned to menial tasks. But there's strength there, and they firmly grip the baroque curves of that gold tray. Upon it rests an exquisite lace doily, and a pair of napkins with a Russian enamel coffeepot and sugar bowl, glistening like jewels. Two little espresso cups are daintily sitting on the needlework in expectation of the powerful brew. The coffee is being handed to Gustavo and His Eminence with the lithe and silky movement of the young acolyte's hand. The priest has now looked into old Tucci's eyes, and has received an almost imperceptible nod indicating he may leave. Gustavo is back at his mission with renewed vigor:

"I was sitting in Paris at my hotel trying to figure out how our family might weather this little storm, and it occurred to me to pray. During this prayer, I am certain I received an inspiration. It was the thought of seeing you, Your Eminence. And the profound feeling that perhaps you might be able to help."

"My son, I am of course flattered you thought of coming to us . . . but I must know the extent of your need if I am to be of any help. What is the amount?"

"Well, it's sort of a sticky situation . . . we need about nine hundred million dollars."

Nothing is moving in this room. It's as if everything had momentarily been frozen in epoxy at the mention of that gargantuan figure. Unwilling to seem or be surprised by anything, Tucci has not moved a hair. He is staring intently into Gustavo's eyes. Attempting to ascertain the extent of this need, the sincerity of the petition, and the price Gustavo might be willing to pay. Oh yes, even among friends there is always a price. As might be expected *when sparrows presume to shoot at hunters*, Gustavo is the next man to open his improvident mouth.

"Actually, we could probably do with eight hundred million, but nine hundred would be comfortable. And although I know friendship is involved, we would be willing to pay a rather unconventional rate of interest."

Tucci's eyes have now become hard and beady. He is regarding Gustavo with that look which can only be compared to the one female mantises give their husbands before they devour them bit by bit. There is further silence. And now he's looking blankly out the window. Which by the chirping of birds reveals the presence of a garden below. All of a sudden he snaps back.

"My son, to be sure, I would wish to help. But as you may know, the Vatican's resources have recently been depleted by unfavorable banking situations, and associations which have been disappointing to us. Your uncle, of course, had an impeccable history with the Church. And the legacy of that interaction extends to his family. But in this case, I believe you may need other help."

Gustavo is looking deflated. And like all amateurs, is making ready to leave before the final cards are played. Just as he's beginning to rise, His Eminence points an imperiously jeweled index finger at him, indicating he should stay. That same digit finds its way up to his lips in a symbolic gesture of silence, as he gives the impression of hatching a thought. Viewing the scene, I, of course, am sure there is no such unscheduled event.

"Actually, my son, I too have just suffered an inspiration. No doubt born of the Holy Spirit. . . . There is someone who might be able to help you. An old friend of your uncle's. These days he is a reclusive gentleman . . . but he is in Rome this week, and if you were to stay for dinner this evening, I might also invite him. And this, in turn, might, just might, bring forth some good."

"Actually, I had planned on returning to Paris tonight. But I'm sure I can alter my plans in order to accept your most gracious invitation."

"Then I will see you at eight. My secretary will instruct you as to the location of my apartments."

The Cardinal is rising, and Gustavo jumps to attention and is now leaving with the necessary reverence. As the doors quietly meet in closure, there's a brief moment of introspection in which the prelate stands, paces, and then makes an obvious decision. I can tell what's going through his mind. More because I know him than because I can read it. It's entirely too big a risk for the Church by itself. They'd have to do it in partnership. Traditionally they've had many associations. But in recent times, it's always been the same one. After all, the first business entity in Europe can hardly avoid doing business with the second. It's a connection which is enriched by family ties and the bond of honor. In this case, they came from the same town and went to school together as well. So I am not surprised to hear His Eminence on the phone as he judiciously exclaims three words: *Caro amico Orsini . . .*

EIGHTEEN

THE OFFICES OF SOMERSET CONSOLIDATED INDUSTRIES ARE LOCATED in a building owned by the company. At various times, it's been referred to by a series of appellatives and nicknames. Of which the most affectionate are Hardrock and Blackrock. The building is actually somewhat ominous, rising eighty stories in a column of polished black granite. Within the tower, high-speed elevators whisk businessmen and lackeys alike to the various floors in the virtual twinkling of an eye.

Now I'm back across the Atlantic to witness E.C.'s meeting with Hooker and Harriet. It's five minutes to three in the afternoon, and E.C. and I are at the curbside, ready to sally forth into the building. I must say our man is looking splendid today. He's wearing a gray gabardine suit—a little light for the season, but very becoming in its natural line. Over his arm, he's carrying a limp baby llama coat, which is a darker shade of gray. Soft and luxurious, just what I would expect. No briefcase or portfolio, just the man. And quite on time at that.

We're into the lobby, where with the customary *ping* the elevator door has opened. A few people are also entering. E.C. pushes the button marked 80, the floor on which my old offices are located.

I've always thought elevator rides have their own character. People always seem very awkward in an elevator. It's too short a ride to really strike up a conversation. And yet, human beings are thrust into the proximity which would normally breed communication. The interval is also long enough to create the presumption of chatter, so there is always an unsettling feeling about riding in an elevator with others. People will try to seem detached while sneaking a look at a miscellaneous breast or crotch. The secretary type in this elevator is attempting to seem aloof by chewing gum. The uniformed messenger is happy to again be in an air-conditioned space, and is nervously looking at his watch in anticipation of quitting time. The well-dressed lady in a suit just stole an admiring glance at our man, but didn't have the guts to do anything else about it. So she's departing with an "excuse me" born of longing and frustration. They've all exited now, and our man has fully regained his territorial imperative. Seventy-eight, seventy-nine, and here we are at eighty. As the doors open, we emerge into the very large foyer of Somerset Consolidated Industries, with its immense Oriental carpet, and pretty receptionist seated at the end of the room. There's a scent of leather here, as well as furniture polish of the lemony variety.

This is not a high-traffic environment. It's sedate and cushy. Our man is calmly walking up to the desk and announcing himself:

"Good afternoon. I'm here to see Mr. Hooker. My name is Douglas."

"Oh yes, Mr. Douglas. Mr. Hooker and Mrs. Somerset are expecting you. Someone will be out to accompany you, in just a second. May I take your coat?"

"Yes, thank you, you're very kind."

E.C. is quite naturally looking around. It's a beautiful room full of English antiques. With good sporting pictures, as well. There are horses, and dogs, and hunt scenes, and even some foxes. Mostly good British pictures from the eighteenth century. Pleasantly unmenacing things you can live with, without feeling psychologically crowded.

A young lady is coming through the double mahogany doors. I

don't know her. She must be new. "Mr. Douglas, my name is Pauline Reza. I'm Mrs. Somerset's secretary. Mr. Hooker and she are waiting for you in her office. Would you please follow me."

We're going through the double doors now. Into the corridor with the extremely long runner. All along the way, our man's eye is drawn to the various sporting pictures on the wall, which are now being superseded by a similar complement of nautical paintings. The Fernsleys and Herricks are giving way to nautical scenes by Robert Salmon and Domenic Serres. At the far end of this corridor, there's another set of double doors. With a discreet knock, we're entering the sanctum sanctorum of my office, now Harriet's.

I'm a bit peeved to find Hooker seated at my desk. Harriet has placed herself on the couch nearby, smiling her reception best. Hooker is rising, and walking toward our man with that beady-eyed grin. He's extending his hand, and is now proceeding to the necessary introductions. "Mr. Douglas, I'm so happy you were able to come. Have you met Mrs. Somerset?"

"No, I haven't had the pleasure, but I'm very happy to meet you. I was sorry to hear about your husband."

"Yes . . . thank you. It's very nice to see you, Mr. Douglas. You seem to have linked yourself to us in more ways than one. If you don't mind my asking, what on earth do you expect to do with that incredible structure my husband built?"

Our man is now carefully assessing the pair. As usual, Harriet is not shy, sitting there in her little black suit, with the large South Sea pearl brooch on her lapel. Similarly, our man is no fool, and he's decided to measure his words. But he's not going to give the impression he can be intimidated in any way. Also, I note with pleasure, he's engaging in that lustful body language which frequently makes him look like a big cat, taking a stretch prior to the fuck. Now he's also assumed that little-boy look, which is both charming and disarming. "Actually, Mrs. Somerset, I'm already living in the place. I must say, I like it a lot."

"Well, I'm glad someone likes it. And you did do us somewhat of a service by taking it off our hands. Although I never would have let you know before the auction. You see, if you'll forgive me, I do think you overpaid."

Harriet is smiling broadly. Hooker is looking nervous, and not altogether pleased at the sight of these two athletes of the subliminal sexual message cozying up to one another.

"Now, now, Harriet. I'm sure Mr. Douglas is a very busy fellow and hasn't come here to make small talk about Henry's pyramid. In fact, Mr. Douglas, why don't you give us an idea of your reasons for requesting this meeting. I must say we do have more than an inkling . . . but I think we'd like to hear it from you."

Our man is now at the apex of his charm and intensity. I'm projecting myself into him in different ways to provide that extra aura of strength. Also, I'm trying to transmit my idea about sticking them with Von Richter's process. He's pausing like a Shakespearean actor detaining himself for a second to assess the expectation level of the public. Once assured, and totally convinced he is seized of himself and the occasion, he proceeds.

"Well, to be sure, I'd like to spend the afternoon making small talk. But I have a feeling you're as busy as I, so I'll get right to the point. According to the public filings I've read, your late husband's estate owns about thirty-nine percent of Siderurgica stock, which, as we all know, controls various steel companies in the United States as well. It's unlikely in the present financial climate that you would be able to unload your Siderurgica stock without causing a sharp drop in the price. I propose to negotiate a purchase price with you for that interest. What do you say, Mr. Hooker?"

"Well, Mr. Douglas, we're perfectly happy with our American steel companies. Which, given the new preeminence of the Von Richter process, are doing very nicely indeed. So I don't think we'd like to sell our Siderurgica stock."

"The Siderurgica interests control the four American steel companies. I propose a transaction in which I would purchase Siderurgica, and then sell the American steel companies back to you."

"Why would we want to have you competing with us in the marketplace? The European companies were always able to deliver the product more cheaply than their American counterparts."

"Actually, I'm going to act on impulse and tell you I'd be willing to make the deal very sweet for you by turning the original license to Von Richter's process over to the American companies as part of the sale. Of course, the pricing would have to reflect that very special consideration."

Harriet and Hooker are looking at each other as if they've been struck by lightning. They're trying to refrain from smiling. After all, this is the material of which their fondest dreams are made. Hooker is going to play hardball. I can see it clearly as he zeros in with those rimless glasses and squeaky little eyes.

"Mr. Douglas, it would seem yours is a very interesting proposal, which I'm not going to disqualify at the outset. But Siderurgica is a company functioning outside of American regulatory bounds, and is therefore very valuable to us. We are, however, in some need of substantial cash flow with which to pay inheritance taxes. So I'm going to suggest you provide us with a letter of proposal."

"I don't mean to be offensive in any way, but if I provide such a letter, it must contain a deadline, and may not be shown to anyone under penalty of substantial damages."

"Mr. Douglas, I'm a lawyer. I fully understand your purpose."

Now Harriet is jumping into the act. Women, of course, have an advantage men lack in business. That is to say, the combination of inordinate suspicion, coupled with intuition.

"But Mr. Douglas, I'm very curious. What made you become interested in Siderurgica, of all companies?"

"Believe it or not, Mrs. Somerset, I've been asking myself that question. I guess it's sort of a whim. I'd really tell you if I could manage a full reply."

"Well, I'll be delighted to hear from you when you come up with the answer."

They're exchanging pleasantries now, and our man is out the door. I can catch him on the way home. In the meantime, I'm anxious to overhear the inevitable conversation between these two, who are now squarely staring one another in the face and have just burst into laughter.

"Tom, stop laughing. He may hear you."

"Don't be silly. He's down the corridor by now. And besides, those mahogany doors are two inches thick."

"Don't you think it's wonderful? It's a blessing in disguise."

"Well, the simple thing would be to think him very stupid. But he doesn't strike me as being rich and dumb. That's not a combination one usually sees. Unless it's inherited. And in this case, I assure you he's self-made."

"So tell me, Tom, what's the angle? Where's he coming from?"

"I don't fully know. Maybe he's all caught up in some romantic reenactment of Henry's career. After all, he did buy the pyramid, and almost all of the art. There was a rumor he'd run out of money. But he must have funding for the deal if he's here to see us."

"Sweetheart, don't overanalyze the issue. There can't be much about this deal we're not aware of. So I suggest we get it over with and sell him Siderurgica before he changes his mind. Can you imagine offering to sell us all the rights to Von Richter's process? We'll close him down in six months. Honey, don't take any paper in the deal."

"You know, Harriet, that's what I like about you. You're such a greedy little dear. How about letting me have it tonight?"

"You may have it when the deal is done."

"You drive a very hard bargain."

"I shall let you drive a hard one into me when it's done. In the meantime, I'm late to an appointment. So I'll see you tomorrow."

Harriet has whisked out with the demeanor and confidence of a breaking wave on a sunlit day. Hooker is, however, the more intrigued of the two. And is sitting at my desk wondering where the angle in the deal might be. He's being interrupted by phone calls, and I certainly see no reason to stay here looking at his miserable carcass. It's actually time to peek in on my nephew. I guess I'll have to catch up with E.C. a little later.

NINETEEN

GUSTAVO HAS ACCOMMODATED HIMSELF FOR THE NIGHT AT ONE OF MY favorite little hotels above the Spanish steps. Don't kid yourself. This hotel is small, but inordinately luxurious, and discreet too. He's taken one of the suites on the top floor which have terraces overlooking Rome. How well I remember wiggling my toes in the early morning while regarding the bright and hazy Roman sky. Breathing in the musky smells and heady fragrances of the timeless city. And the sound of church bells everywhere.

He has cleverly managed to involve our Roman correspondents in properly attiring him for the evening at Cardinal Tucci's. Such evenings are formal. And Gustavo is splendid in his new shirt front and dinner suit. They got him patent-leather pumps. The kind with silk bows, which I've always despised. But they do fit well with his look. Harriet always wanted me to wear such things, but I never capitulated. My formal shoes were always tied.

As I sit here on the terrace watching Rome lose itself in the haze to the peal of the Angelus bells, I can't help musing on the recent history of mankind. Around me are the visible remnants of a great civilization. We are all aware the Romans, as inheritors and enhancers of the Greek tradition, conquered the known world. But that was easy. Lots of people have prevailed over others before. The real trick was in the maintenance and administration of the empire, which was in every way masterful. Sort of like the difficulties billionaires experience after the money has been made. At this hour of the day, one can almost project oneself back to the time of the Julio Claudians with their loves, lusts, and intrigues. But also with their discipline. And virtue. Those very substantial components of their collective psyche. Guilt as we know it did not exist here. To be sure, there were prohibitions. But their religion was devoid of Old Testament harshness. One can't help thinking the purity and the beauty of this city have somehow been corrupted by the Judeo-Christian concepts of culpability. I used to have dreams of being a Roman general and riding triumphantly through my own arch into the Forum. Up to the Capitoline steps, to receive the tribute of the empire.

What one sees here is strikingly beautiful decay. Of course, the question is not why Roman civilization fell. I suppose everything has to be undone. The real puzzle is why it took so long. Which brings me to my inner thoughts about everything that's going on. A few days ago, when I was sitting in the portal of my tomb with Bozo, you could never have convinced me I'd be here in Rome on my way to Cardinal Tucci's for dinner. I'd like to stop and think about why all of this is happening, but there is an inner force and compulsion within me to go forward with my revenge. Why, though, do I feel so vengeful? What is it I'm seeking retribution for? What do I expect to achieve with all of this? Is it my ego merely wanting to feel satiated? Or are these things which I really must do because they will also impact the lives of others? Maybe it's a little of each. Sometimes I think my head will explode. But then I think of the challenges at hand and proceed full-forward.

Gustavo has been sitting nervously on the little love seat in his bedroom. He's looked at himself in the mirror more times than I'd like to count. Yes indeed, in spite of the borrowed duds, he's rather handsome. Too bad it's all mush inside. The clock is striking seven-thirty. He's standing. And now collecting himself to leave. Out the door and into this rather small elevator. Through the lobby, receiving the nod of a knowing concierge, to the street, where one of Tucci's cars again waits. We're approaching the Vatican, and as usual, we are through that gate without difficulty. We're going to a different place. Up a tiny street to a building with carriage lanterns. The car door is opened for Gustavo, and he departs with a terse thank-you. A brief knock at the door finds it opening almost immediately into a very large downstairs foyer with a magnificent checkerboard marble floor. The young priest who unbolted the door is the same one who served the coffee in the Cardinal's office. He has carefully avoided looking Gustavo in the eye. I don't know if this is studied or if, like many in Italy, he's afraid of the evil eye. He's motioning my nephew up the staircase to an atmosphere that is decidedly very Venetian. Through a pair of double doors, into a truly magnificent drawing room. To the opposite side of the entrance, tall bronze-framed glass French doors lead to a terrace from which the Vatican gardens can be seen. The room itself is a work of art with its gesso and moldings. Upon these walls I spy a Raphael and a Botticelli. Not to mention the Tintoretto and the Caravaggio. It's the Caravaggio I'm drawn to. With its lights and shadows. And its flesh. . . . As I enter the room I'm overtaken by the swish of silk taffeta, as Cardinal Tucci enters to greet Gustavo in full princely robe, complete with gleaming diamond-and-ruby pectoral cross.

"Your Eminence . . ."

"Mr. Somerset . . . how good to see you here tonight."

"I don't think I would have missed your invitation. You see, my uncle frequently spoke very highly of his evenings here with you."

"I'm sure Mr. Somerset was too kind, and exaggerated."

"Oh no . . . we both know my uncle was not prone to exaggeration."

"Be that as it may, we are very happy to see you here. Allow me to introduce you to some of my guests at the other side of the room."

We're walking across beautiful silk Kashan carpets faded by the sun and worn bare by the pitter-patter of many nuns and priests. A lot of the furniture here is Venetian. Which I always personally felt was a bit much for my sedate character. But it all fits in very well with Cardinal Tucci.

"Allow me, Mr. Somerset, to introduce La Contessa d'Este."

"I'm very happy to meet you. I've heard a great deal about you and your work with fashion."

"La Contessa is also very much involved with our Vatican charities, specifically with orphans. And this is Margherita da Benci, our famous writer."

My nephew is bowing and behaving obsequiously with the two rather formidable ladies to whom he's just been presented. The Countess is wise and older. She has the fine and transparent beauty which is best achieved by centuries of breeding aided by the fine hand of providence. She's actually giving Gustavo a very hard look. As if to inquire why he's here at all.

"And allow me to present Signorina del Piombo, who is a noted harpist. And whom we may just cajole into playing a bit for us after dinner."

This is a very large room. And I had almost overlooked the two high-backed chairs facing the now waning light coming through the French doors. There hunched in his exquisitely tailored evening suit is my old comrade Don Orsini. He seems just a tad older and grayer than when I last saw him. And I'm afraid those sloping shoulders bespeak the weight of many unconfessed sins. He's off in a reverie of his own. And has not noticed Gustavo's entrance. His Eminence is now approaching those large chairs with Gustavo in tow. My nephew is a good medium height, and Don Orsini is not tall at all. But between the two of them, irrespective of physical height, the Don is the striking and towering figure.

"Mr. Somerset, allow me to introduce my dear and very old friend Don Orsini, who was also a friend of your uncle's."

Don Orsini is rising while carefully examining every inch of Gustavo's presentation. His are indeed eyes which were made to see beyond the folds of cloth and sustaining skin. These are the instruments of penetration into the motivations of men. Into their desires, dreams, necessities, and sins.

"I am pleased to meet you, Mr. Somerset. Cardinal Tucci has told me much about you."

"I do hope he told you the good things."

"Well, we are here, aren't we?"

That very comely priest is upon us again with a tray. He's carrying exquisitely etched champagne goblets about half full, of what looks from here like very good champagne. Gustavo is grasping one. But Don Orsini has waved the young man away with a thankful gesture.

"Do you like Rome this time of the year, Mr. Somerset?"

"Why, yes. I've always been fond of it when it cools a little."

"But it's been particularly fine this season. You know, Mr. Somerset, I met with your uncle many times. Often to drink excellent wine and eat good food. Yet he rarely mentioned you in his conversation."

Gustavo is looking consternated in the light of so direct and immediate a salvo. He's somewhat at a loss for words, since he didn't expect Don Orsini to so quickly question the basis of his existence as a Somerset. But he's collecting himself and coming around full swing. "Actually, my uncle was a very discreet man, and found it quite difficult to exhibit emotion. I'm not surprised he didn't mention me much, in spite of the fact I know he was extremely fond of me. Huh . . . I don't know how we got into this conversation, but we're being called to other important matters, namely, dinner."

A liveried attendant has just hit a profusely decorated bronze bell with a metal hammer, indicating the imminence of the awaited meal. The Cardinal is proceeding with the Contessa, and the others are following, into the small dining room. I recall having been here once, although usually I was a guest at much larger affairs in which the state dining room was used. This is, however, a striking atmosphere with its frescoed walls and ceiling. There are candles everywhere. Yes, it is unmistakably a place in which you could divorce yourself from the cares of the world.

His Eminence is at the head of the table, and the attendants are seating us accordingly. Gustavo has been placed at his host's right, which is a great honor. Don Orsini is to the left, facing Gustavo, where he can regard my nephew with a stern and discerning eye. This being fall, it's not surprising to find quail with apricot glaze as an appetizer. Afterward, there are *gnocci ala Piemontese*, and then little rolls of very thinly beaten veal stuffed with sweetbreads. In Madeira sauce, no less.

There's a lot of small talk going on. And not a business conversation in sight. Gustavo is somewhat as a cuckoo in a robin's nest, in this rarefied atmosphere of culture. But he's doing his best to hold his tongue and speak when spoken to.

The Contessa is wearing a necklace almost completely composed of large star sapphires, with occasional diamonds. They match the color of her very blue eyes and properly set off her stately gray hair, which is unpretentiously gathered into a well-groomed little ponytail. She's engaging Gustavo in conversation now with a warm smile.

"Tell me, Mr. Somerset, are you related to a very interesting man I once met here by the name of Henry Somerset?"

"Actually, he was my uncle. I'm unhappy to say he's passed away."

"Yes, I heard. Many of us in Rome were very much saddened. But tell me of yourself. Are you here on business or pleasure? I do hope it's pleasure."

"I'm afraid I'm here mostly on business."

"Ah, but you must leave time for enjoyment as well. We have a wonderful season of opera this year. And La Corsini is singing. Last night they say she hit two high F's. You know, she is a great sensation. No one had heard of her a year ago, and all of a sudden we found ourselves with this incredible talent upon us. It is the find of the century. The type of voice you encounter once in a lifetime. If you are lucky!"

"Oh, she sounds very exciting. I'd love to attend, but I'm afraid I must return to Paris, and then to New York."

"I suggest you take a few days and enjoy Rome."

His Eminence is now interjecting, and is speaking with her about lending a famous cello player one of his Amatis. The young lady who plays the harp is chatting with Don Orsini, who is observing her as one might regard a fresh flower or butterfly. Through the corner of his eye, he's been watching Gustavo. Carefully scrutinizing each movement of the hand and each nervous twitch. I wouldn't be surprised if the old bird already has a full picture, even though it's not much of a match. After all, *the eagle doesn't usually hunt flies.*

Dessert makes its triumphant entrance. Two attendants carry a large tray on which rests a baked Alaska. Complete with little doves made out of meringue. After dessert, we are ushered into the music room, where two concert grand pianos placed back to back make love to one another, and where a golden harp awaits the nimble fingers of Signorina dal Piombo. The never-absent espresso coffee is also making its rounds, as well as a box full of fine cigars. Signorina is playing Bach and Scarlatti. And then some Granados. After she's through, and we finish with the necessary congratulations, Don Orsini wanders off to the adjoining terrace with his cigar, to contemplate the Roman night. Gustavo and His Eminence are together. The Cardinal has adeptly decided to follow the Don's steps. And all three find themselves on the terrace.

"Don Orsini, our young friend came to see me quite recently with a matter of the utmost importance. We, of course, were unable to help, due to the magnitude of the problem. But since you were friendly with Mr. Somerset's uncle, I thought you might be helpful in some way. Ah . . . ah . . . I note my secretary is motioning to me on some matter. Please excuse me for a moment."

With this rather unclever gesture, His Eminence has left my nephew and Don Orsini face to face. Gustavo is being regarded directly now by the obsidian obduracy of those very strong eyes. He's about to open his mouth when Don Orsini takes control of the conversation:

"You are of course aware—"

"Yes, I know who you are."

"Since your uncle had great credibility and credit with us, I will permit myself to inquire as to the nature of your need."

"To put it bluntly, Don Orsini, we need an extra nine hundred million dollars. The nature of my uncle's business was such that he accumulated very large indebtedness. Also, we are faced with phenomenal inheritance taxes. So the extra cash would be of necessity to us."

"And what would you have in mind as collateral for this debt?"

"We have a certain Swiss brokerage account with about nine hundred million dollars' worth of steel stocks. The entire account could be pledged. You should, however, be aware that the position includes some heavy margin trading, so in spite of the fact that the value is there, it is presently committed to certain American issues of stock."

"What you are really telling me is that the available borrowing margin has already been occupied by a substantial risk. So you would not be able to obtain this money from a bank or brokerage house."

"That is correct."

"And if I were to obtain this money and lend it to you as a consideration, what would the time frame be?"

"No longer than six months."

"My young Mr. Somerset, are you fully aware of the penalties for a default in payment?"

"Well . . . I, ah . . . assumed . . ."

"You assume quite correctly. You are honored in friendship by His Eminence, and possibly you will be trusted by me regarding this amount. But you must understand that in this world there can be no mistakes or misunderstandings."

"The interest?"

"Twenty percent for the period. Payable with the principal."

"That's very steep."

"This money is an accommodation. Perhaps we should not speak of it."

"No, no. That will be fine. How shall we proceed?"

"It is very simple. You will personally provide His Eminence's secretary with a slip of paper indicating the account to which you wish these funds transferred. Day after tomorrow the deposit will be made. Tomorrow morning you will appear at the notary's office to sign a note and pledge the account. I of course assume you have the necessary powers. One last item. I require a hair from your mustache."

"Ah . . . I don't understand. Why would you want a hair from my mustache?"

"It is a personal custom, among other things, indicative in our mind of the capacity to contract. I shall return the courtesy by providing you with one of mine."

With one adept gesture, Don Orsini has pulled a thick gray hair from his mustache. And has placed it on his white handkerchief and offered it to Gustavo. Somewhat perplexed, and still fidgeting, Gustavo has managed to pull one of his own. And is now uncomprehendingly delivering it to Don Orsini on his own handkerchief, in which it is carefully wrapped and pocketed.

"Don Orsini, I have to tell you, I still don't understand."

"Mr. Somerset, these are matters of honor. Not to be toyed with lightly by children or women. Once sullied, you are undoubtedly aware *honor can only be washed with blood.*"

With these words, and an almost otherworldly stare, and a good night, Don Orsini has turned around and placed his brandy snifter on an adjoining table, and is now making his way to the Cardinal to bid him *grazie* and *buona notte.*

My nephew has taken the cue, and suppressing the smile of triumph on his face, is now also approaching Cardinal Tucci.

"Ah, my son. I trust your conversation was profitable."

"Indeed, Your Eminence. I am profoundly grateful for your help."

"You are very welcome, but with true friends, one need not express excessive gratitude. With enemies, of course, there is usually little to be grateful for. I do not know what has happened between you and Don Orsini, nor do I care to. But if I were you, I would minister to this relationship as one cradles quail eggs in a silk velvet bag. Did you enjoy the evening?"

"Very much, Your Eminence."

"Perhaps then you will return when it is possible. In the meantime, I give you my blessing and good night."

His Eminence's assistant is seeing Gustavo to the door as the other guests are dispatched home without ever suspecting they have witnessed a great transaction.

I have lingered and left Gustavo alone for the short ride back to the hotel. The guests now gone, these candlelit apartments have taken on an almost eerie and romantic look. I'm following the swish of that red taffeta robe into the library. He's pensive. Somewhere his wrinkled hand finds its way to the 1513 edition of Ptolemy with the Waldseemüller map. I know it. It's a phenomenal book. In fact, it contains one of the first maps of the New World. He's turned to the Tabula Terra Nove, a map specifically devoted to America. He's gently passing his hand over it while he whispers under his breath the words *America, giovane America.* Not without effort the heavy book is returned to its shelf.

Now I'm following him into the bedroom, which incidentally I've never seen before. It's actually very serene. Done in a deep royal blue. Sort of like the blue you'd expect in the Virgin's robe. He's reclining now, and praying. While he prays, I'm struck by the enormous simplicity of this chamber. A small bed, a single chair, and a table on which that pectoral cross rests, shimmering with the forboding of conflict. He's troubled. And I think I know why. The man has seen through Gustavo. But he must not judge before the arrow is shot. So he will do what holy men will. Pray and hope.

I've whisked myself back to the hotel in time to catch Gustavo gleefully opening a bottle of champagne. True to type, my nephew is not alone. He's picked up a very pretty Italian girl, who's inquiring as to why he's so incredibly happy. He's not telling her, just drinking. Soon he'll become violent, and want to whip or beat her. You see, he really doesn't like women very much. Like many men, he just uses them. She'll acquiesce, though. After all, Gustavo is today a very rich man.

Normally, I'd be just as inclined as the next fellow to witness an X-rated movie. But there's something about him which constitutes a definite turnoff for me. The girl is pretty enough. But I'm disliking the man more and more. I think it's my sense of disappointment. This was a child who sat on my knee. Someone to whom I tried to teach class and manners. And what did he do? He threw it all away, and opted for greed. But there are times when the greedy are ensnared in their own traps. As I observed tonight, Gustavo performed on cue. I did not expect him to do it with such alacrity. And so speedily devour the treacherous bait. Now I'm wondering if he really understands what he's done and with whom.

From the terrace, Rome is quiet in the darkness, and presently blanketed in sleep. I'm sitting here while Gustavo fucks his last, and leaves another welt on her bare behind. I'm lonely. I feel desperately the need to speak with someone. Or to have an interaction in which I'm the visible party. There must be other spirits like me. Why can't I see or hear them? Could this be hell? I always feared that place would be very lonely. Sometimes I think my incomprehension of this state will make my head burst. When that happens I've learned to attempt sleep. Perhaps I need a rest. I'll sit here on the veranda and try a welcome bit of slumber.

This is really extraordinarily strange. I'm asleep. And I'm dreaming. But I have a consciousness of everything around me as if I were awake. I am, however, certain I'm not. In this reverie, a portal at the end of a long corridor is bathed in extremely white, bright light. It's a beautiful brilliance. One of serenity and peace. I am experiencing a great deal of happiness and goodness pervading everything. Someone is coming through the gateway in my direction. But I'm not afraid. Why should I be? It's my mother. Untouched by time with her beautiful dark hair. She's walking toward me with outstretched arms. Now she's hugging and kissing me. And encouraging me to go with her through that portal at the end of the corridor. She's also telling me Daddy and Alicia are beyond that door, waiting. There's something in me which would go with her in an instant. And yet I can't. She's gently pulling me by the hand. But now I'm recoiling. And telling her I must stay. I'm mentioning the things I must do here. Speaking about my revenge. And now she's weeping. "Mami, don't cry, don't cry, just hug me. Don't leave. . . ."

And all of a sudden, I'm awake again. With nothing except the damp Roman night to console me in my loss.

I haven't experienced this previously. I mean . . . having a dream about someone else that's so vivid. I'm wondering what might have happened if I had gone through that door. I can't think about these things, or I shall become even more of a fruitcake. I am nevertheless unnerved. In any event, that poor harlot has left, and Gustavo is fast asleep looking totally satiated in every way.

That reverie I had has been enormously disquieting. What if there are other layers or zones of comprehension? Other parallel realities? What if for each spirit every situation is personal and unsubstitutable? I've got to formulate a theory about this in order to quell my troubled mind.

My nephew is sleeping like a pig. Why is it the evil always sleep so well, while the good are frequently troubled? I guess the answer is actually a simple one. The truly amoral have no consciences to assuage. They needn't be concerned about anything, since they either never had basic programming in morality, or somehow managed to discard it along the way. The abjectly wicked who are not fully amoral may, in fact, possess basic programming, but it's either in itself of the wrong kind and therefore malevolent, or has just been overridden by evil. It's the good who don't sleep. They toss and turn in bed with a nightly resurgence of every possible moral dilemma and choice. I guess there are some fine people who are devoid of problems, and who have not felt the necessity to deal with moral contradictions. But I haven't met too many. I need very urgently to contemplate matters. And these rooms, with their smell of mendacity and evil, are not conducive to the proper frame of mind. I know what I'll do. I'll rest for a while. Then I'll blink myself back to the cemetery, where everything is peaceful and secure. To a place where I can properly think.

TWENTY

It's six o'clock in the morning here at Sleepy Heights. We're now well into the fall. And there are leaves rustling about everywhere in the wind. It is, however, nice to know these lanes, Brambletree and Posy, Petunia and Holly, are still here, and the same. And then, of course, there's Camelia, with my memorial. Always salient. I think I'll walk down through the winding roads to the river and just sit for a while. It was very dark when I arrived. But now there's a diaphanous morning reflection coming upon us. Here by the river they've lined the quay with good New England fieldstone. So there are lots of rocks on which to sit and meditate. I've found a particularly round one which accommodates me nicely. The last insects of the season are beginning to stir and hum along the river's edge. And there are birds flying. Making noises. In the distance, the mirrorlike finish of the river is interrupted by the sleek cutting edge of a rower's shell. It's a light single, I can tell. And he's pretty good at it, stroking faithfully and rhythmically, following the meanders of this old river. I've always thought the rower's perspective the mirror image of mine. He's stroking with his face to the past. But cannot see where he's going for the life of him.

I'm now certain I'm here for a reason. It's not likely I've been placed here to achieve revenge. No doubt there are additional ends for my present mode of existence. I'm not fully sure what they are, though. I'm alone, but I know there must be other people like me. So I assume we each exist in our own private and parallel realities. Unable to touch one another, or to interact. I'm certainly here to deal, not with the world of my present state, but with the theater of the living. And there are probably thousands and thousands like me. I'm hoping there's something after this. That dream I had recently has given me an inkling into what might exist. Mother wanted to take me down that corridor, through the door. Toward the brilliant light. What if there really is a portal with something very beautiful behind it? Perhaps the key is through our dream states, which allow us to intersect with different planes of reality and others who are also departed. Maybe it's meant to be this way in order to allow a measure of choice. But if it's so extraordinary, why didn't I want to go forward in the dream? Why am I holding on to the things of the living? Why not just forget about E.C. and Miss Cleave, Gustavo, Harriet, Hooker, and the rest of them?

I don't even know how much time I have. When I died, time became a relative thing. Possibly it had always been, and I was merely unaware. Now I can sit and meditate, and the day can pass almost without notice. I can transport myself with great speed from one place to another. And look back to previous moments in my life. Traveling back in time is not something I do a lot of. It requires an effort, and I'm very much interested in this present. It is, however, comforting to know I have such a mechanism in my inventory, for use on a truly rainy day. It has been said that all travels are travels in time. And I definitely am a time voyager. Look, I blinked my eyes, and here I am back at the cemetery in the early morning. You know, when I was alive, I noticed how every successive year seemed to grow shorter. When one was a child, the years were awfully long periods. The span between one's birthdays was akin to an eternity. And from October to Christmas was just downright interminable. But as I grew older, this changed. Birthdays began to succeed themselves mercilessly. And so with the period between holidays. It would seem I'd be through this year's gift list, and all of a sudden the oncoming one would be upon me. All things began to accelerate without regard to desire. I now see the possible reasons for this. When you're a child of seven, a year is, in fact, a great big chunk of your existence. One seventh, no more, no less. And if we were to judge it by experience, at that stage, each year is quite unique, and therefore noteworthy. But when you're fifty, a year is a mere two percent of your elapsed life span, and not really a very big deal. It's been said people who jump from buildings experience feelings similar to a span of years during the brief seconds of the fall. And yet, I've heard that for others who are dying, and desperately holding on to life, a year can go very quickly. It's all within us. I don't believe time exists as such. Or in the conventional mode. At least not as we conceive it. And yet, it obsesses us. We try to create watches and clocks which are accurate, knowing such total efficiency can never be achieved. And if it were, it would merely be the handmaiden to the fiction of time's existence.

A teenager has walked his way down the lane. What's that he's carrying? It's awkward. My goodness, it's a musical instrument. A cello, no less. He's approaching that rather new-looking gravesite with the two marble urns and bench. Hey, this kid is actually weeping. I assume he's lost someone recently. Now pulling his instrument out of its case. He's taken a curious little square thing that looks like a piece of flooring and has placed it on the turf. I guess it's to keep the end pin from going down too far into the mud. He's not an attractive kid, but the little fellow's not ugly either. Here one can perceive the studious look of children who grow up too soon, and don't fully enjoy those middle years between their childhood and adult phases. He's tuning the instrument. And now playing. What is that melody? I've undoubtedly heard it before. Beautiful, but sad, and troubled. . . . I know what it is, it's the Fauré Elegy. He's not doing badly, in spite of the fact that it's a difficult piece of music. I know a little about this. I once took some string lessons, but gave it up later in favor of just slightly better skill at the piano. Look at him. Instead of playing that particular B natural on the D string, as he did a second ago, he's catching it on the A string. Without a glitch and without a hitch. Now the tune is moving into a middle section where it constitutes an accompaniment. But I note with pleasure he's achieving a creditable vibrato on these notes as well. By this point, I'm totally engrossed in the piece. Going into scales. Six notes to a bow. Faster, until at the climax he hits that high A clearly, and without hesitation. Now the notes are resounding plaintively and with confidence. Until those last few phrases where the piece seems to recede farther and farther within itself in total and absolute resignation and retreat. That final note is fading away until you are not quite sure just where you thought you heard the music end. . . .

In many respects, life is very much like this young man's piece of music. We are reluctantly thrown into the sadness of it all, and we fight, sometimes leading, other times accompanying, until we reach a climax. And then all mountains scaled or abandoned, and all hurdles jumped or declined, *we fade*. The young man is sitting on his bench, firmly grasping his cello with his left hand. He's put the bow down, and is using a handkerchief on that tear-stained face. He's asking heaven for help. Good luck! For the first time, I think my heart will burst with his. I really wasn't a great one for delivering myself to the grief of others when I was in my previous state. I guess I disqualified their suffering by either making light of it or ridiculing. In these brief instants, I have felt a change of viewpoint. I'm weeping with him. I feel his grief. I would wish to help.

There's a perfect and beautiful leaf on the tree above. It has turned a particularly lustrous tone of golden yellow. I'll just bet I can pop it off the limb and gently drop it right on that soggy hankie. To indicate someone cares. To show him his suffering is perceived by someone or something else. I'll do it. Let me reach up there with one jump, and gently pluck it. There! It's really a gem among leaves. And it's all for you, my little man. I've surprised him. He's now regarding that leaf as I'd hoped he would, as a sign. And he's been comforted. He's putting his cello back into the case. And now, more serenely, leaving the site. With leaf firmly in hand. I never knew providing comfort to others could be so enormously satisfying. I actually feel much better. I shall try it again very soon.

My mind returns to the chess game I seem to have started, which now requires all my attention. I occasionally have these second thoughts. And to be sure, I have a feeling I'll be returning to my rock by the river to cogitate more about matters. But now, I think things are probably beginning to stir back at E.C.'s. So I'll separate myself from this introspective state and scrutinize today's action.

There's a lot of hustle and bustle here. E.C. is up and about, and has apparently already enjoyed a hearty breakfast, although the cup of espresso is still in evidence. He's placed himself in front of the television in the sitting room. Our man seems quite attentive to the beginning of the financial news. Hey, that's E.C.'s picture on the screen! With big bold words which say TAKEOVER BID. The rather pretty, but typical, commentator is now proceeding to disclose the awaited bit of information:

"Well, there's news in the world of high finance today. A takeover bid has been made for fifty-one percent of the stock of Siderurgica Internazionale by E. C. Douglas at thirty-six dollars a share.

"The news is out that Douglas has quietly acquired approximately nine point nine percent of Siderurgica stock and has announced a European tender offer for the remaining shares. As a result of the takeover bid, the stock was up sharply to thirty-five from yesterday's close at twenty-nine and a half.

"Our viewers will recall Siderurgica was previously the object of takeover battles in the U.S. and European steel industries by the late Henry W. Somerset. It would now appear the game is again afoot. Wall Street is asking itself whether Mr. Douglas will attempt to purchase a large block of stock from the Somerset estate, or whether he will resort to private transactions in Europe for the remainder.

"E. C. Douglas has recently been in the public eye in connection with a buying spree in which he purchased the now famous structure built by Henry Somerset to house his art collection, as well as the greater part of the collection itself. The going is bound to become a bit rough with such a big player in the marketplace. So we recommend keeping tuned to the business channel for further information."

E.C. is looking a bit peeved at all the publicity. We all know he actually has thirteen percent, but the public won't know that for a while. It has to do with dumb laws and public filings. There's a knock on the door, and Cleave is entering wearing bright red leather shoes with a matching purse and belt.

"You look like a candy cane."

"Well, don't get any ideas this early in the morning. It definitely is not Christmas."

"I know how unyielding you are, my dear. But at least I can think about it."

"If you'll wipe that smile off your face, we can go over your schedule for today. Let me get my book, and I'll read your appointments. At eleven, which is in just fifteen minutes or so, Archbishop Fromaggio, the Papal Nuncio, is coming to pay a call. They really didn't say what they had in mind. At three, you have your second appointment with Mr. Hooker and Harriet Somerset. Then tonight you dine at the Faulkners'."

"Can't you cancel the dinner?"

"You canceled last week. Besides, they own a little Siderurgica stock. And I'll bet you want them to tender."

"Okay, okay, I'll go. Say no more. Do you have any idea at all why the Church has decided to pay a call today?"

"None whatsoever, but I think what you did for that orphanage last Christmas has put you on their 'nice' list. Remember, I haven't been around you long enough to know about such things. You should probably have your checkbook ready in any event."

"You know, that leaves luncheon open. Why don't we go out and have ourselves a bite together."

"My dear boss, I'm very wary of your bites, and besides, we have a very athletic luncheon planned for you here in anticipation of your safari into piranha-infested waters at three."

"Too much duty."

"Listen, this takeover thing was your idea."

"Sometimes I wonder about that. . . . Haven't you felt the presence of your previous employer all around us? Has it ever occurred to you that perhaps he could be motivating us to move the pieces on the chessboard?"

"Well, he may be suggesting things to you from beyond the grave, but he's certainly not doing it with me, nor would I welcome the encroachment on my free spirit. . . . Oh, I think the clergy has arrived. Brace yourself."

The butler has just announced Archbishop Fromaggio, who is elegantly walking through the door with a flash of purple sash. He is, in every sense of the word, a diplomat. Trained in the Vatican Department of State to listen carefully, and to speak with measured words. Like most princelings of the Church, he is exquisitely groomed. You could see yourself in the shine on those nails. There's a tad of gray at the temples where they meet a fragile pair of gold-rimmed eyeglasses. He's a man of medium height with good posture. And soft-spoken in every way.

"Archbishop, how good to have you here. I'm sure you've met my assistant, Miss Cleave."

"It is not my first time in this house, but certainly my first time with its new and esteemed owner. A strange and wonderful place. Built by a man we at the Vatican held in very high regard. And of course I am happy to see Miss Cleave again."

"To what do I owe the honor of your visit? Not that there has to be a purpose, since my home is open to you for calls at all times. . . ."

"Well, Mr. Douglas, I was actually visiting the orphanage of the Sisters of Charity, and they told me a heartwarming story about how you had donated bicycles for each and every child, and are a continuing benefactor of the home. This and your other works seem quite noteworthy. And I just thought I would stop by and tell you how very pleased we are. His Holiness is very much interested in expanding our American work with orphans, and would wish to count on your continued interest in perhaps somewhat larger ways."

"Well, you certainly have my support, and I'm quite flattered to have a person of your rank visiting me on such a subject. Would you take coffee?"

"Yes, thank you very much."

A very large silver tray is being presented with cups, saucers, steaming coffee, and a plate full of petits fours. Cleave is pouring, and making small talk with our guest. There's a certain amount of calm expectation in the atmosphere. Hah! The Papal Nuncio doesn't come to pay a courtesy call to talk about charities and orphans. Something much more important is afoot here. I know old Fromaggio quite well. He's sharp as a straight razor. Honest, though, and a totally devoted servant of the Vatican. He's got to be on an official mission of one sort or another. I like to watch him calmly taking the cup of coffee and munching on a little cake as if he had all the time in the world. He's a first-class operator, yes indeed! E.C. and Miss Cleave are not as practiced in the art of waiting, so they're fidgeting a little. But if I know our visitor, something will be forthcoming after the next sip of coffee.

"Every time I come to this house, I'm overwhelmed by the gardens as I approach it. And then when I'm inside, by the magnificence of the artwork."

"Well, Your Excellency, I did my best to buy as many of Mr. Somerset's fine things as I could afford."

"And I see you could afford a great deal. Incidentally, I note you're in the morning news today. Not that I pay much attention to such things, but I could not help noticing your name was mentioned with . . . in connection with an entity called . . . ah yes, Siderurgica."

"Yes, we're trying to buy the company. Actually, now that you're here, Your Excellency, we've heard there is a large block of stock in Europe held by nominees, but we've been unable to ascertain the true ownership. Do you think the Church could initiate an inquiry or two?"

"Well, I'm not very good at these things myself, but perhaps I could call my friend Cardinal Tucci, who is knowledgeable in such affairs. This is rather providential, since I was at his table in Rome just a few days ago, and he was mentioning he expected to have Henry Somerset's nephew to dinner. I suppose it's happened already."

"Oh, how interesting. I don't know Cardinal Tucci. Do you think the proper introductions could be made?"

"Oh, I'm certain. Please call my office whenever you are next planning to be in Rome. *Perhaps you will travel soon.* I'm sure the Cardinal would be very pleased to receive you. . . . Ah, but it is getting late, and I have another appointment. It was very nice coming here and chatting with you about the orphans. Miss Cleave, I am very happy to have seen you again."

E.C. and Cleave have kissed the ring. And with a gracious turn, the Archbishop is on his way out the door as quickly and effortlessly as he arrived. E.C. and Cleave are now looking at one another with smiles on their faces. And questioning looks.

"Tell me, Susan, you've seen this man before. Why did he come?"

"Well, it wasn't to discuss the orphans. It's funny, though. I don't think he came to obtain any information. I think it was the opposite. There's something they want you to know. Considering the only other piece of information which changed hands had to do with Gustavo Somerset's going to dinner at Cardinal Tucci's, I would say that avenue requires serious inquiry."

"We'll do it. Follow up on this meeting with a fifty-thousand-dollar donation to the orphanage for a new roof . . . no, make it seventy-five thousand. And then call His Excellency's office and suggest we have weekend business in Rome and might like to make a courtesy call on Cardinal Tucci. I have a feeling as well about our visitor's comments."

"You know, E.C., it's a little disquieting. What do you think that sleaze Gustavo Somerset is doing in Rome?"

"I don't know, but I have a feeling it may be intimately linked to Hooker and Mrs. Somerset. What is Gustavo Somerset all about?"

"I told you there were better people to do business with. To reply to your question, Gustavo is the son of Henry's deceased sister. My boss adored her, and therefore, lavished a great deal of care on his nephew's upbringing. But none of it stuck. Gustavo is sort of a cad. Not extremely intelligent, but enough to do damage. Toward the end, Henry developed a phobia for him. I never learned what Gustavo had done to merit such distaste, but in spite of Henry's other bad habits, I can't say I previously saw him be arbitrary or unjust, so Gustavo must have dealt him some sort of real blow. Even so, I don't think his lethal potential is even a fraction of Harriet's and Hooker's. And you're the lucky one. You get to see them again at three o'clock today. Incidentally, what's your plan?"

"My intention is to buy their stock."

As Susan and E.C. continue their chat, I am drawn to some necessary analysis. I find it fascinating that the Vatican's long arm has reached this place today. And ever so lightly planted a meaningful piece of information in a strategic place. That's the way they work. Smoothly and without barriers of any type. I'm now wondering whether old Tucci hasn't had second thoughts about Gustavo. Or perhaps he has information from one of his very secret sources. Like the ever-prescient children. . . . And may consequently be attempting to strengthen his Siderurgica position through E.C. Not a dumb thing to do. But I shouldn't marvel they move so swiftly and quietly. After all, they've had almost two thousand years of practice.

Cleave and E.C. are now going down to lunch. In the meantime, I think I'll pop back to Rome and monitor Gustavo. I just can't get over how a mere blink of the eye moves me across great distances.

Here I am in my nephew's hotel room again, where he's sitting at the desk making a call to Zurich. I presently enjoy eavesdropping even more than I did before. He's asking his Swiss contact whether the deposit has been made. That smile on his face is definitely a nine-hundred-million-dollar grin. Now he's giving an order to purchase an extra billion and a half dollars' worth of American steels on margin. It would seem they balked a little on the other side, but the Somerset name goes quite far even in Zurich. So they're going to do it. But they've cautioned him in no uncertain terms: If there should be any serious drop in the market, they will liquidate.

It's the usual treatment from the Swiss. No wonder they're absolutely the most hated people in all of Europe. Swiss attorneys and bankers are basically in many respects the same thing. If you have the dollars, they are willing to provide the services. They'll buy stock, bullion, or bonds. They'll broker your diamonds, or buy you a bank in France. They'll purchase a castle on the Rhine for you or supervise the outfitting of a new private jet. All of it for a commission; all of it for a fee. Generally speaking, they don't care who you are or how you acquired the wealth. You just have to have a lot of it. Then in a very businesslike way, they fawn over you, and are willing to do things like deliver boxes of chocolates to your mistress in London.

The gnomes want your money, but they definitely don't want too much of your presence in their country. If you want to become a citizen, it will take you a good twelve years. And until quite recently, they wouldn't even allow foreigners to own property. All of it is designed to keep Switzerland for the Swiss. So when you arrive at the bottom line, it boils down to the fact that the greedy little bastards will rent you their asses, but they won't sell them.

Today Gustavo is on the right side of the transaction. He has an extra nine hundred million dollars to play with. And the fellow in Zurich will dance to his tune. This, however, can be quite different.

When the customer is in trouble, the Swiss cease dancing. And as if it had been thoroughly expected and understood, they turn their backs on you completely. Which returns us to where we started. They are for their lack of morals, greed, and exclusivity despised by all their neighbors. Used, but not abused, they are like high-class whores. Available only to the gentlemen of means, and only while the money lasts.

Gustavo's business completed, he's now bouncing around the room singing something between his teeth. He's reaching for the phone again.

"Concierge?"

"Yes, Mr. Somerset?"

"Do you think you could get me a seat on a flight to the United States very quickly?"

"Yes, Mr. Somerset, I think I might."

"Oh, you'd have to call my hotel in Paris and have them forward the things I left in my room, since I anticipated returning there on my way back."

"That is not a problem, Mr. Somerset, let me check on it. . . . Yes, I confirm I can have you on the evening flight. I can send someone to help you tidy up and we can have you driven to the airport within the hour."

"That's great. Of course, I'll see you on my way down."

Click.

So Gustavo has decided to hightail it back to America without again going through Paris. He must be very anxious to make sure his little deal is going to work. Well, he can't do very much harm on an airplane, and I do recall E.C. is going to be meeting with Hooker and Harriet at three, Eastern Standard Time. So I might as well pop back home, take a brief rest, and wait for the action. I must say that this business of being able to beat the clock and time zones at will constitutes a dandy bit of help.

I'm back at Pyramid Hill without a bit of hesitation. I've tried to sleep. But for the life of me, or whatever it is I have within, I'm finding it impossible. Bozo just sauntered in, and has been complacently sitting there, staring me in the eye. When I think about it, he really is a wonderful fellow. Much more than a dog. After all, if you knew a deaf-mute human who just happened to look like Bozo, you'd decide he was a triumph of the soul. Kind, generous, loving to a fault. He's actually quite childlike. Amused by things that move. Like birds, and postmen. Once in a while he catches one, but he just slobbers it up. Generally speaking, if someone is hurt, it's merely because Bozo's such a big fellow and really doesn't know his strength. I assume, though, that if he or a loved one were deliberately mistreated, he might react with speed and strength. Even a dog knows the difference between being stumbled over and receiving an intentional kick.

E.C. is now ready to proceed, and I shall accompany him for the short ride into town on this dark afternoon. You know, there's something about gray afternoons which I've always found depressing. I guess in some respects I was a true creature of sunlight. Whenever it became dark or rained, I'd immediately become moody, and upset. Almost a hormonal type of thing. I do think the elements have a great deal to do with our demeanor. Now that I think of it, a full moon does that type of thing to people as well. Physicians and the like have constantly tried to convince us that this just isn't so. But talk to any self-respecting Southerner, and he'll tell you, "The nigra get rowdy at the time of the full moon." It's not a racist comment, just a fact. Besides, it happens to all of us. This type of thing is gleaned from centuries of good old-fashioned observation. People involved in holistic medicine will tell you that if you want to have a successful operation, you'll do it when the moon is waning, because then you bleed less. Of course, if folks really put faith in this sort of thing, the hospitals would all be empty when the moon was waxing. And consequently out of business. So the populace is kept ignorant as the enlightened continue to profit from their knowledge. I really do think the elements have great involvement with our moods and humor. More than we dare suspect. Possibly this is why our man is looking a bit taciturn and very quiet today. His eyes are actually very special. They are a tone of gray-blue. On cloudy days they're much grayer and on sunny days they are decidedly blue. What is curious, though, is that his mood also influences their look. For example, today they seem glazed over and hazy. Which is what happens when he's given to great introspection. They also become this way when he's plotting something. Today I suspect it's a little of each. When he speaks of love, they are sharp and crisp. Sparkling, as if you could plunge into them and be consumed by the vividness of the phenomenon.

Blackrock is looming large in the distance. In a second we've arrived. And now we're waiting in the lobby for the familiar ping of the lift which will take us once more to the eightieth floor.

A rather delightful little shoeshine urchin has just entered the elevator with face partially smeared with a familiar peanut-and-chocolate candy bar. He's carrying a parcel for the seventy-eighth floor. The cab has stopped on eleven. Where a fat middle-aged woman has entered with a profound look of preoccupation on her face. Oh God, I think I've figured it out. This lady is presently having trouble with a bit of flatulence. I'm wondering whether she's going to hold. Somewhere between the fifty-sixth and fifty-seventh floors, she rips forth with a truly silent and deadly one. Of all the farts in the world, I've concluded the deadliest is the quiet gas that is born in the elevator. Granted, a close second is the fart under the winter sheets. But at least you can escape from that one. Even if you do freeze as a result. When you're riding to the eightieth floor, you're caught without recourse in that inescapable blanket. The urchin has grasped the fact that he's going to be blamed for this bit of brigandry. Not a bad assumption, considering the woman's demeanor, which is masterful in its chicanery. She has absolutely assumed the it-must-have-been-someone-else look. But the kid isn't going to let her get away with it. He blurts forth, "Hey, lady, you're the one who farted, not me!" The woman is now beet-red, and the normal reserve of the elevator riders has been interrupted by peals of laughter. Our man is laughing as well. Heartily. On the seventy-second floor, the fat lady gets out. I don't even think it was her destination. But that gush of air from the open doors is allowing us to go forward without the benefit of gas masks. The kid departs when we reach his floor. A triumphant exit. Our man is still laughing when he arrives at the eightieth floor and approaches the receptionist.

"Good afternoon, I'm . . ."

"Yes, I know, Mr. Douglas. They're expecting you in the boardroom. Miss Reza will be out in a moment to show you in. May I take your coat?"

"Yes, thank you. I think I'll look out the window for a moment while she comes."

E.C. is rather calmly regarding the cloud formations around the tower. On dark rainy days, Hardrock or Blackrock, as you may care to call it, is like a great mountain perpetually surrounded by clouds and mist. In a way, it's quite otherworldly. And E.C. has grasped this and seems to be enjoying it. Miss Reza is upon us with her business-like gait. When you look at this type of woman, who is purposely attempting to hide her curves and promontories, you can't help thinking something went wrong with Western civilization. After all, we should be running around chasing one another bare-assed. Screwing whenever delightful or expedient. Instead we invent clothing and bustles and corsets. And even chastity belts. As if purity were entirely a thing of the body. While I watch her ass wiggle back and forth on the way to the inner sanctum, I can't help thinking she would provide a rather comfortable ride. And from the look on his face, E.C. seems to agree, cruise control notwithstanding.

Here we are at Olympus! The boardroom of Somerset Consolidated Industries. With its postmodern cathedral ceiling and interminable dark mahogany table. I used to sit right there at the head of it, and quietly spit forth orders. From that vantage point I controlled my companies. And especially a lot of people. I'm hoping today I'll be able to again make it all happen. That kid in the elevator was somewhat providential, since he put E.C. into a much more positive frame of mind. Hooker is here in a dull-gray glen plaid suit. And Harriet is looking smashing in a woven black-and-white houndstooth outfit. She's wearing those fifteen-millimeter black pearls I picked up in Rome one year. Pinctada margaritifera, no less. Which is to say the real thing, as far as black pearls are concerned. You can stare through the holes of these little suckers, and all you'll find is black luminescence upon black transparency. The true and unabashed pain of that very special oyster. Come to think of it, it's a pretty good look. Severe, but very together. Of course, if the maid wore those babies, everyone would think they were fakes. But when the widow Somerset wears them, they snap to attention. Because they know those marbles have got to be the real thing.

"Mr. Douglas! Mrs. Somerset and I are quite pleased to see you again."

"Thank you very much."

"Perhaps you might give us an idea of what you have in mind today?"

"Well, you did receive our tender offer, didn't you?"

"Yes . . . actually, we did receive it, and we've read it with great care, haven't we, Harriet?"

"Why yes, Mr. Douglas, Thomas and I gave it our greatest consideration last night, but I'm afraid we haven't yet reached a decision. Thomas, why don't you explain it to him."

"Actually, Mr. Douglas, I might as well get to the point. We really don't think thirty-six dollars a share is enough to justify our tendering the Somerset stock."

"What would merit your tender?"

"Well . . . we were thinking of something like, let us say, forty-two."

"How about thirty-seven?"

"Forty-one."

"Mr. Hooker, before I abandon the project completely, I'm going to make one last nonnegotiable offer, which is to say, thirty-nine dollars a share. Would you tender at that price? You realize I'll have to raise the entire tender."

"Yes, but there is also one more little detail, Mr. Douglas. You will recall we had some conversation among us regarding an exclusive license for the use of Von Richter's process. Should we understand this will be part of the deal?"

"You push an extremely hard bargain, Mr. Hooker."

"That's the only type of bargain one should push."

"Well, apart from the fact I do not require the philosophy lesson, I'm willing to meet your demands and sell you the license to Von Richter's process for five hundred million dollars, all of it wrapped up in the same deal."

"That's a very large amount of money for what is basically a new process. We were thinking more in the vicinity of four hundred million."

"Mr. Hooker, I really hate this haggling. You know, we're not at the bazaar in Istanbul or something. I trust you've been."

"Yes, Mr. Douglas, we've all been, but we're still talking about four hundred million."

"No, four-fifty, not a penny less. And I'll pay you thirty-nine dollars a share for the stock."

There's a moment of tension here. Hooker is looking at Harriet, trying to suppress a smile. And Harriet is staring back with a face harder and tougher than the granite facade of this building. She's actually trying to impart the message that he should try for more. But Hooker is a polished negotiator. In one hearty, and now smiling, gesture, he's putting out his hand with the words "Mr. Douglas, you have a deal."

Finally there is some talk about little formalities and attorneys, and how in the balance our man is going to owe them a number of hundreds of millions. There's an offer of champagne to celebrate. And in view of the impending transaction, Harriet is actually suggesting he come to dinner. Hands are being shaken again, and our man is again on his way down the corridor and into the elevator with that glassy-eyed look.

As he emerges from the building, Szilagyi provides the shelter of a needed umbrella. The chauffeur, who had been rather quiet during the ride to Blackrock, has now become inappropriately talkative. Our man is attempting to field his conversation with a combination of monosyllables and closeout responses:

"It looks like you've had a rough day today, Mr. Douglas."

"Yes, perhaps a bit."

"It's nice to know the end of it has come, right?"

"Yes, I agree."

"And after all, this is Thursday, and tomorrow's Friday, so you'll have the weekend to rest up."

"Actually not."

"How come? You're not going off on us again, are you?"

"I was actually going to tell you to be up a bit earlier tomorrow. We have takeoff reserved for five a.m."

"Where to this time, Mr. Douglas? You know, you're always flying off to these exotic places like Tahiti, and India, and Holland, and people like me who work for you have fantasies about what it must be like."

"Believe me, Szilagyi, it's not nearly as exciting as you think."

"Aw, come on, Mr. D. Don't shatter my dream. You know, we

look up to you, and there isn't one of us who doesn't think it's exciting."

"Sometimes it's just hard work to travel. And rough on the body too."

"But your new plane even has places to sleep, doesn't it?"

"Yes, you're right, but they're not very soft beds—I mean berths—and of course there's no bed like one's own."

"Well, you're right there, Mr. Douglas. I guess it's good to sleep at home, but I'd trade places with you for just a little while. Are you off to some exotic place tomorrow?"

I'm actually surprised E.C. hasn't become impatient with this very chatty chauffeur. I would have had them tape his mouth. Preparatory to sewing it up. But he seems to have a pleasant rapport with his employees which allows this sort of occasional conversation. Actually now that I think about it, I could have done a little better in this respect. I was often prone to disregarding too easily the vicarious pleasure employees obtain from the achievements of their masters. In a sense, I think I frequently cheated them out of their legitimate right. But in contrast, E.C. is pleasant. And instead of being upset at having the question of his destination posed twice, he is merely smiling a bit and responding:

"No, it's not really an exotic destination. We're just going to Rome."

TWENTY-ONE

I ACTUALLY MANAGED TO CATCH A FEW WINKS LAST NIGHT. E.C. AND the staff must have been up since two or three in the morning. Even before I was. His whole mood has changed, and he's rather electric. The fellow is sort of bouncing around. He has this rather strange way of walking on the front parts of his feet. Which almost makes him look like he's tiptoeing about. Most people come down on their heels first. But when he's happy, or in some way stirred up about something that's on his mind, he walks in this very peculiar fashion. Bozo is in the kitchen looking a bit mournful, suspecting he's to be left behind for a couple of days.

Susan Cleave has just arrived looking absolutely smashing in a golden-brown suede suit. Umm, I can smell the skins. Very, very soft indeed. And most appropriate for travel aboard E.C's private plane. The staff has already placed her bright red leather suitcase in the trunk, next to E.C.'s smart black bags from that famous Parisian maker. She's carrying a small case which I assume contains items of toiletry and jewelry. Judging from the way she looks at him, I can tell she's very taken, having fallen totally in love. It has happened altogether too quickly, and this concerns me. It might ultimately interfere with things. I guess I'll have to wait and see.

"Good morning, Susan. How are we doing today?"

"Well, apart from the fact I think you spent too much money yesterday, we're doing all right. We're in line for the five a.m. takeoff. I just spoke to Captain John, and we have a very direct route over the Atlantic."

"Good. We don't want to be late, do we?"

"No, I don't think so. You know, after I called Archbishop Fromaggio's office for the appointment with Cardinal Tucci, we not only received the invitation to the opera and dinner afterward, but there were later two calls from the Archdiocese, making sure it had all been confirmed and reconfirmed."

"Yes, there seems to be somewhat of a strange insistence."

"You bet. I think the Vatican is hot for you, boss. That's it. In any event, I'm glad I can still make you smile."

"Well, we might as well be on our way. Wait a minute. . . . Bozo—?"

At the mention of his name, Bozo has leaped up and come tearing through a number of rooms to say goodbye. In a moment, he's up on his hind legs licking our man's face.

"We'll be back, old boy, don't worry. You be a good dog and hold the fort."

With these last words, E.C. grabs his briefcase, and we're off to a Roman adventure. This is actually going to be a lot more fun than my recent foray with Gustavo. After all, these are nice people, and I can relax a bit. I am, however, wondering what old Tucci has up his ecclesiastical sleeve. It's very rare to have him tender a first invitation of such unusually social proportions. A night at the opera, no less. And I'll bet that woman who's been in the papers is going to be singing tonight. The one who hits all the high notes.

There isn't much traffic at this hour of the morning. As we speed down the pike to the same suburban airport which occasionally serviced my own needs. Szilagyi is now turning off the thruway and onto the road approaching the strip. I've always been fascinated by the concept of flying. As far back as I can remember, I've been convinced flight is the precursor of time travel. After all, if you were able to walk into a chamber and be in Rome one second, as opposed to seven hours, later, you'd say you had been magically moved. Or transported in time, so to speak. I'm wondering if you could really ever go so fast that you were standing still. Perhaps at that moment it would actually become time travel.

We're now approaching E.C's very good looking state-of-the-art jet. I'm glad to see he didn't cheap out and buy one of the little ones. They're just terrible for long flights, because you can't even stand up in them. Not to mention you're always banging your elbows in those tiny heads. This is a comfortable plane. Captain John and the copilot are now greeting E.C. and Cleave. He also has a very cute young steward named Tommy, who is dealing with the luggage, and tried to take Miss Cleave's little case before she protectively declined. Szilagyi is now being dispatched back home, and we seem to be ready to depart. Captain John and his copilot have accommodated themselves in the cockpit, and Tommy is securing the door. Miss Cleave is taking a last look in her handbag, efficiently checking the passports, currency, and other items in her charge. E.C. is having a bit of fresh grapefruit juice. Minutes later, we're bolting down the strip and into the thin morning wind. Moments of takeoff have always provided me with the greatest feeling of exhilaration. If there were ever a school for megalomaniacs, there would have to be a class entitled Takeoffs 101. Very much in the same manner as there would have to be one called 1812 Overture and another denominated Götterdämmerung. So as the view of the city is quickly left behind, we find ourselves over the dark Atlantic, headed for Rome.

E.C. and Cleave are actually a bit chatty in spite of the early hour. He's smiling as he interrogates her regarding preparations for the evening.

"So tell me, did you pack something appropriate for the opera tonight?"

"Modesty aside, I don't think you'll object in the least."

"I'm quite sure I won't, but I do hope modesty isn't aside, and you're not going to give His Eminence a touch of heart failure."

"Boss, when I dress for the opera, it's every man for himself."

"In that event, I will carry my nitroglycerin pills. Incidentally, I note you've been holding on to that little case of yours. You know, it can't go anywhere between here and Rome. May I inquire as to the reason?"

"Oh, I have a few bits of glitter to wear tonight. And I wouldn't wish to misplace them."

"I understand."

"You know, I'm still amazed at how easily it went for you with Hooker and Harriet yesterday. They've really agreed to sell you Siderurgica. With that block of stock the company is basically yours."

"Actually, it was a bit too easy. I'm concerned. Although they did receive their piece of flesh with Von Richter's process."

"I don't understand how you're going to make the situation profitable with the license for the process in American hands as well."

"I thoroughly believe we can be competitive. But it certainly won't make us wildly profitable."

"Then why did you do it? Why have you gone through this painstaking process to acquire a company which is not going to be very lucrative?"

"You know, I've asked myself that question. In many respects it's as if everything to do with your former boss has bewitched me a little."

"I'd be careful with that if I were you. Henry Somerset was a great guy. I should know . . . I loved him. But he was also a very unhappy man, with an inability to give himself to others completely."

"What do you mean?"

"I really don't think this is the time to discuss it. Besides, we should try to sleep. It's going to be a very long day for us."

"Susan, your suggestion is my command."

The doubtful lovers are now accommodating themselves on the couch-berths on the sides of the plane. I, however, am left here awake thinking about everything she just said. So she loved me. Well, I thought so, but you know, I wasn't ever sure. And this was one of my shortcomings. I never could fully believe anyone loved me. Always suspicious and perpetually paranoid. I inquired, and queried, and tested until every relationship I ever had fell apart under the strain. When that wasn't enough, I bugged them, which is to say I eavesdropped electronically. And had detectives apprise me of my love's every move. But I'm not ashamed of it. If the truth be known, the only one who didn't cheat was Susan. And now I'm gone, and have to sit here listening to her inform another man she loved me. But I'll tell you one thing. That business about my incapacities regarding giving of myself isn't accurate. In my own way, I really did love, and deeply. It was just more difficult to realize because of all the excess baggage and paranoia.

In a way it wasn't my fault. I grew up in a hard world, and later, as a business person, had to face a lot of severe realities. After dealing daily in the snake pits of international con artists and financial markets, it's no wonder I found it impossible to develop confidence in my amorous attachments. Then there were the actual incidents of my love affairs. Why, look at Harriet! She was cheating on me with Hooker during the last few months of my life. And God only knows how many more she screwed along the way. So you lose your faith. And with it much of your resilience. Then a good one comes along, and since you can't tell the difference anymore, you handle her just as you've treated the rest. And, of course, since she's seized of the last bit of integrity in the world, when you doubt her, she tells you to stuff it up your teddy bear's ass.

The two of them are now fast asleep. I'm looking around, rather excited to be up in a private airplane again. The pilot and copilot are making a remark about Miss Cleave's curves. I guess she does this to men. There's some talk about giving a lot of money to trade places with E.C. The steward is in the small but well-appointed galley putting together a little lunch, and maintaining a perpetual shine on everything. He's a member of that class of extremely decorative gay young men not singularly endowed in the intellectual department. If they're serious, as this one is, they end up with good jobs and some exposure. This frequently allows them, if they're alert and know how to keep a bargain, to go forward, bartering their looks, charm, and companionship for an extra rung or two on the ladder. This kid is perfectly in character. Lots of dark hair. A twenty-two-year-old complexion, and bright blue eyes. It looks like he works out a bit. So his medium-height frame is athletic without being chunky. Small hips and a nice tight ass. For the present, until it fades, that latitude of his anatomy, frontward or backward, as the case may be, will provide substantial pleasure to its accessees. Mind you, these pretty boys and girls are not the materials of which fantasy and dreams are made. To be sure, they're human, and consequently suffer motor failure at the damnedest times. After all, they're made in the U.S.A., and not in heaven. But at that age, and at their peak, their function is without mechanical concern. And if you know just how to drive, and don't expose yourself to a broken heart, you can end up having a nifty ride up and down and roundabout their racy curves and splendid bumps.

I've never liked traveling east. It gets dark very quickly as you go through the various time zones. And before you know it, you're rocketeering in the darkness of the night as if suspended in that time chamber I previously mentioned. Thank goodness we left early, so we're just blanketed in perpetual grayness. We've taken a route which has brought us over Spain, and we're now approaching Italy. Very soon we shall be at Rome's airport, where arrangements have been made to service the aircraft overnight. In the twilight of the fall sky, Rome seems a bit sleepy. Not at all like seeing Paris or New York. In part, it's the haze, and the fact that at this hour the city is not yet fully illuminated. We've made excellent time, and will be able to stop at E.C's hotel, dress, and proceed to a promising and exciting evening. Our pilot came down very smoothly. It's the type of landing one grows to expect from the private fellows who are not allowed the cowboy behavior which you suffer in the armed forces.

Once on the strip, E.C. and Cleave are noting with pleasure the presence of the official Vatican conveyance. Monsignor Albani is here, hat in hand, anxiously awaiting the arrival of His Eminence's guests. As the door opens, the prelate and his chauffeur-priest are approaching.

"Mr. Douglas, I am Monsignor Albani. And this is Father Bruno. His Eminence has sent us to make sure you reach your hotel on time. And to greet you upon your arrival in Rome."

"Thank you, Monsignor. This is Miss Cleave, my assistant. I believe His Eminence's office has been in touch with her regarding the arrangements."

"Yes, yes. Father Bruno will carry your luggage. We should be at your hotel in twenty minutes."

A second vehicle quietly awaits the pilots and steward. With a few last instructions, E.C. and Cleave are now bowing into the grand Mercedes, and without further ado, they're off to the city.

"Mr. Douglas, did you have a good flight?"

"Yes, quite excellent. Thank you. We're here a bit early. I was pleased to see you were already waiting, in spite of our early arrival."

"Well, that is only as it should be. Miss Cleave, have you been to Rome before?"

"Several times, but it always makes me feel like a schoolgirl."

"Yes, even though we live here, we also think Rome is a magical city. But allow me to brief you on this evening's activities. As you probably know, His Eminence is Secretary of State of the Vatican, and as such is frequently in charge of receiving honored visitors. He was extremely pleased with the recommendations he received from Archbishop Fromaggio. He has insisted on having you as his guests to the opera tonight, which is apt to be a very special performance, since Signorina Amalita Corsini will be singing. Afterward, he has a light supper planned at his apartments in the Vatican in your honor."

"Well, Monsignor, we're very flattered with all this attention. I do hope we're not putting His Eminence out in any way."

"*Prego*, I do not understand this putting out."

"I mean, I hope we're not inconveniencing him in any way."

"Oh, oh, I understand. . . . No, His Eminence has very much been looking forward to your arrival and to the evening of activities."

Everyone in this car is smiling broadly, so I assume we're in for one hell of an occasion. We're approaching the same luxurious but unassuming hotel at which Gustavo recently stayed. As E.C. and Miss Cleave come forth at curbside, the manager, who has been quickly alerted, is present to greet them in the inimitable Roman style.

"Miss Cleave, Mr. Douglas. I am Giulio Sebastiani, the executive manager of the hotel, and I am very pleased to welcome you. Allow me, madame, to take your case."

"No, that's all right, it isn't heavy."

"Mr. Douglas, we have a very nice two-bedroom suite on the top floor for you. It has a lovely terrace, which I'm sure you will enjoy for breakfast. I will be pleased to personally present it for your approval."

"Thank you very much."

With this, they are disappearing into a rather small elevator, and reemerging on the sedate top floor of this establishment. The suite is obsequiously presented and found acceptable. Then the manager is off to further duties, leaving E.C. and Cleave to some quick preparations for the evening ahead. They are now proceeding to their respective bathrooms, he for a shower, and she for a tub bath. He's emerged from the steamy stall, looking pink and a bit younger than his years. Now donning a silk shirt with little star-ruby cufflinks and studs set in platinum. He's also wearing that pocket watch, with chain ready to be strung over the front of that very stiff vest. Yes indeed, it's white tie tonight. No tuxedos or dinner jackets, please. I always think people look like waiters in those short jackets anyway. E.C.'s tails emerge magnificently pressed, with trousers holding their crease. He'll be wearing the works tonight. Suspenders, garters, and a midnight-blue cape to match his evening suit. But fully lined in red. He's dressed except for his bow tie, which is now the object of some contortion in front of the mirror. Hah, if that thing had been mine, it would be tied already. I guess he's a bit nervous. And this white grainy fabric doesn't help. But soon enough it's fully executed. He's walking into the sitting room, and now eyeing a bottle of Cristal, fresh from the management's larder. He opens it ever so stealthily, so as to remove the cork without making it pop. This, of course, is the proper way to uncork a bottle of champagne, without vulgar displays of noise or unseemly flying objects.

Just as he bows to partially fill two glasses, Susan comes through the door. E.C. and I are both gasping. She's wearing an evening gown in a 1930s Chanel cut. It's a smashing garment made out of a very rich burgundy-colored crushed silk velvet. Contrary to her normal style, this dress does not sport a substantial *décolletage*. It does, however, have a rather plunging back. A clever dress which achieves the purpose of safely being in the presence of the clergy, while incorporating an element of the *risqué*. E.C. is looking dumbfounded. Her hair is conservatively pulled back, showing off her features. Around the neck is that pink diamond I gave her, framed by a very long strand of opera-length South Sea pearls. Their creamy pink sheen is most complimentary to her skin tone. There is also a substantial ruby ring with earrings to match. The general effect is altogether smashing.

"You look incredibly beautiful."

"Thank you very much, kind sir."

"I assume the beads and baubles were the object of your zealous guard with the jewel case."

"Correct."

"Well, your efforts have been totally justified. Let's have a glass of champagne and then proceed before we're late."

"Very good."

"Incidentally, Susan, it completely slipped my mind to ask you what we'll be hearing tonight."

"The opera is *Faust*, and the soprano, as was mentioned by the monsignor, is Signorina Corsini, whose voice, I understand, is only exceeded by the attractions of her legendary bust."

They're both smiling now as the phone rings, indicating the readiness of the Vatican car below. Miss Cleave is accommodating a wrap made out of the same deep silk velvet, and E.C. is grabbing for his cape. They make a splendid couple tonight. Both have that avid look which is most usually associated with experienced adventurers and discoverers.

As we speed through the now-darkened night toward the Rome Opera, I can't help feeling a substantial degree of excitement. It's actually been years since I've been to the opera. At a time, it was something I really enjoyed. I had my own parterre box and frequently went to every performance in the season. Harriet, however, was forever weary of the genre, and never failed to find excuses either to avoid it or to depart at mid-performance. What I particularly loved was the grandiose conception involved. For me, it was very much as the Greek tragedy must have been to the Athenians. A vehicle of catharsis, designed to purge and cleanse. And possibly a handmaiden to those occasional epiphanies of the soul. Not to mention the sheer pleasure of hearing great singers engage in dazzling vocal pyrotechnics. Well, we're going to hear it all tonight. And *Faust*, to boot. It's the type of cozy story that always gets me right in the gut. After all, there is Faust, sitting with all worldly knowledge, but it's not enough. He wants more. I don't have to tell you what this little caprice of dissatisfaction ultimately costs.

It would seem my daydreaming has allowed me the feeling of traversing Rome very quickly. Here we are at the theater. E.C. and Miss Cleave are being accompanied by a young priest who was sent to direct them to the Cardinal's presence. Old Tucci is hosting a pre-opera cocktail in a little room within the house. They are now mounting the stairs and entering the grand hall. Up another staircase, and through a pair of little doors, there is a magical, candlelit atmosphere with His Eminence in attendance. The Cardinal has rushed to the door at the entry of E.C. and Cleave. It's actually refreshing to note he isn't standing on ceremony as might be expected from a senior prince of the Church.

"Mr. Douglas, Miss Cleave, I am very happy to meet you, and especially pleased to be able to offer a bit of Roman hospitality."

"Your Eminence, you are just too kind. Miss Cleave and I are overwhelmed with this invitation to the opera."

"I trust your journey was a good one. Have you heard La Corsini sing?"

"Why no, we haven't."

"Then you have an incredible treat in store for you. Actually, a double treat, as she will also be a dinner guest at my apartments after the opera."

"I would think she'd be exhausted, wouldn't you, Susan?"

"Why yes, Your Eminence, I'd assume she'd want to go straight home to bed."

"Well, my friends, perhaps this would be the case with a normal singer. But Amalita Corsini is an extraordinary woman who sings as if without effort. A driven soul. She is also possessed of a very interesting and engaging personality."

"We very much look forward to meeting her."

"Miss Cleave, I would like to introduce you to my good friend the Contessa d'Este. The Contessa is very much involved with our work. But I think she would be pleased, in spite of her busy schedule, to take you shopping in Rome tomorrow. . . ."

Cardinal Tucci has artfully steered Susan into the presence of the Contessa, and is now taking E.C. by the arm into another corner of the room, where he's engaging him in conversation.

"I have been reading a great deal about you in the American and European press, Mr. Douglas."

"Oh, really . . . you must understand the press. They always exaggerate everything."

"Well, it is not an exaggeration to say you are on your way to purchasing Siderurgica."

"Yes, that is correct. I wasn't aware you were interested in such things."

"Actually, we at the Vatican are acutely interested in steel. As you know, we are on the side of the angels, and are always watchful that the balance of business power does not place such things under the tutelage of enemies, or in the hands of ruin. You see, when major businesses which minister to the interests of goodness fail, it can only in the balance allow the evil ones to proliferate."

"I must say, Your Eminence, you are dealing with a wider picture than I."

"But Mr. Douglas, you are part of that picture. A very important element indeed. . . . Ah, but we are being called to our box. The curtain will shortly rise, and I am sure you do not wish to miss a moment of the opera."

As the doors to the little room are opened, a different demeanor takes hold of His Eminence. Now, ready to go into the public eye of music lovers and gathered luminaries, he has assumed, as if by operation of fact, the pomp and majesty of a full prince of the Church. The look is courtly, but also powerful. And somewhere down there, as he strides at the head of his little procession, one can sense there might also be a capacity for strength verging on ruthlessness. In the box the ladies have been placed in the first row with His Eminence. The gentlemen are behind. The otherwise chatty public cannot help noticing this little assembly, and we are the object of more than one stare through black and pearled opera glasses alike. His Eminence is smiling and conversing pleasantly with his guests as the lights are dimmed and the conductor makes his appearance to substantial applause. As the curtain rises, there is an Italian hush. Which is to say, more genteel and measured than the ones in Australia or the U.S.A., yet not as military or defined as the ones in Germany and Austria.

In spite of the fact we have now proceeded to the music, there are still eyes upon us. The women are appraising Miss Cleave. After all, it's unusual to have a new and unknown beauty sitting in the golden horseshoe. The Contessa d'Este is seated next to Susan in a pale blue embroidered silk dress. And splendid blue sapphires that nicely match the color of her eyes. She's one of those women obviously born to the aristocracy. Her gestures are natural and self-assured.

As I watch Faust reflecting bitterly on his life, I can't help musing on the parallels. I too spent some time trying to discover the meaning of existence. I must say, I never invoked the powers of darkness. At least not directly, in the manner of this protagonist. But perhaps in a sense I did. There are things I've been ashamed of. Topics I don't like to think about. Like the time one of my best friends asked me for some money years ago when I was beginning my career. I'll never forget that period. It was right after the first oil well. I had amassed my first two hundred thousand dollars. Which to me, at the time, represented a very respectable amount of money. My friend had undergone terrible difficulties. First of a legal nature, and then, as a result, in his finances. We had been bosom buddies at school, and had shared a very intimate relationship. In point of fact, we had frequently worn the same trousers, tennis shoes, and underwear in those early, reckless days. I admired my friend because, in many respects, he was possessed of a keen intelligence, frequently more comprehensive than my own. The year before, he had dropped out of school. I had not seen him for a number of months, but knew he was undergoing difficulties. Nevertheless, I stuck to my shekels like the narrator of *Moby-Dick* clinging to that wooden coffin floating in the sea.

One day he called and asked me for a loan of just the amount I had put away. While I had known of his necessity and said nothing, being put on the spot made me angry and upset. I didn't bother to ask him how he might repay me. Nor did I even assess the risk in traditional terms. Denying him my friendship and all courtesies, I merely refused the request. Since I found it unacceptable to face the reality that I was not a charitable and giving person, I picked a fight. And told him he should not have put me on the spot, and that I was not a lending institution. In doing so, I of course conveniently forgot the many ways in which he had helped me to become the person I was, and the fact that he had been to me not only a lender, but a restaurant, a hotel, a surrogate parent, and ultimately a giving institution.

After I said no, I found it impossible to be his friend, in spite of his making it clear my denial would not affect his opinion of me. But I couldn't face it, and requested an apology. Which of course was not forthcoming, since none was warranted and my friend was a very proud person. The matter was compounded by the fact I'd indicated he was to be one of my heirs in the event of my accidental or premature death. His viewpoint was that he was perfectly warranted to ask me, in a moment of need, for something I'd indicated would be his at some point in time. Mine, on the other hand, was a confused smoke screen of excuses, designed to protect my psyche and ego. The problem was not in his asking, but in my not being able to accept my own refusal.

To be sure, we all have our miserly tendencies. And somewhere, a beggar may starve to death, unbeknownst to the fellow who didn't give him the requested dollar. That's fine with the fellow, as long as he isn't told the beggar died. If he is, he has several real choices. The first, of course, is to attempt to mend the situation if he genuinely wishes to turn over a new leaf. The second is to hide behind some other issue, argument, or justification, while secretly cherishing the nasty behavior and deceiving himself in order to feel good on all fronts. The third alternative is to suffer guilt and pain over the refusal, while not changing, because the part of him which wishes to change and suffers the remorse is not strong enough to prevail over the darker instinct. The fourth, and last, possibility is to accept himself and the consequences of his nasty act. Also if the act is unforgivable, to forgive himself for it anyway.

My personal beliefs always tended toward accepting myself, and forgiving myself the unforgivable. Until, of course, that became impossible, since there was a fly in the ointment. My friend had not indicated that in addition to everything else, he had terminal cancer. Would I have given him the money had I known this? I'd like to think so, but searching within myself, I'm now sure my answer would have remained in the negative. Unfortunately, I was never able to pardon myself for this unforgivable act. And now a bit too late, I'm thinking I would have done best by trying to mend the situation, as opposed to merely accepting myself as an evil entity.

That's why they've always said it's important to know yourself. But I still have questions. Are the best relationships the ones where everything is out in the open and people are not deceived by their respective idealizations of others? Or is it the other way around? Are the strongest bonds the ones which we base on incredible neurotic needs and deceptions bordering on psychosis? I now realize many of our distortions of reality are purposefully designed to obtain benefits we actually don't deserve. Like the woman who really doesn't love a man, but maintains the illusion in order to accept the diamond bracelet which he provides because he thinks himself loved. In this sense, when I told my friend I had made him my heir, I was accumulating merit points which were not based on the absolute truth. It was, in fact, a way of getting something for nothing. Or stealing.

To be sure, it was his decision to decide whether or not to be my friend after I denied him my shekels. But once he indicated a willingness to continue, then I was put in the situation of having to confront my own denial. I could no longer be a miser and enjoy the image of generosity. This was intolerable, so I terminated the friendship by forcing him into an apology I knew in my heart he would never provide. I was unable to go forward with the knowledge of my own unfortunate actions between us. Then I married. Became wealthy, and attempted to bury many of the unpleasantnesses of my past life. But none of that really helped. On many nights after his death, I've felt myself confronted by this dilemma.

Quite clearly, I've practiced self-deception with this bit of sophistry. In spite of what I've said and thought before, by definition, one cannot forgive oneself the unforgivable. When one forgives oneself, it is only because one has been able to turn the unpardonable into the pardonable. And there are many instances in which I have still been unable to achieve this.

It would have been easier if Mephistopheles had blatantly appeared in the same fashion in which he's standing on the stage. Offering all earthly kingdoms and universal riches. Offering love. . . . But my selections were unaided by the unabashed presence of the devil. My decisions all responded to conscience, or lack of it. But who would really know? Perhaps he was always quietly there, suggesting things to me from the periphery.

As I'm sitting here thinking about the past, the great Signorina Corsini has just made her entrance to an incredible round of applause. This woman looks familiar. I'm wondering where I've seen her before, and all of a sudden, I am struck as if by lightning. As I live and breathe, the star is the spitting image of E.C.'s dead wife! If I thought I was dumbstruck, you should see E.C.! He's looking totally unnerved. And pale. He's seized Susan's opera glasses, and is staring so intently at the star that even old Tucci is wondering whether something might be seriously amiss. Susan is tapping him on the thigh now, and regaining control of her little binoculars. E.C. has caught the Cardinal's stare, and is composing himself, now pulling a hand-kerchief from his pocket to wipe the sweat from brow and neck.

The first act has ended, and the members of our party are now chatting about the performance. Susan is approaching E.C. with an obviously concerned demeanor:

"Boss, are you okay? You look like you've seen a ghost!"

"No, don't worry. Everything is fine. I just have a little stomach-ache."

"For a moment there I thought you were losing it, the way you were staring at Amalita Corsini."

"Oh, it could have been anyone. I really wasn't looking at her. Just gazing into the distance."

"Oh . . ."

The music lovers are called back to the second act, during which E.C. proceeds to further scrutinize Amalita Corsini. I could swear the woman onstage is an exact look-alike to the one I saw in the pictures at E.C.'s house. It's the same European face. The same eyes. The same mouth. And what's more, it's the same body. It's almost as if his wife has been raised from the dead. I'm just waiting for Cleave to notice the resemblance.

The opera has run its course while I've mused over all of this. We're now almost at the end. The beloved Marguerite lies in prison awaiting execution for the murder of her baby. Her mind wanders, and His Satanic Majesty urges them to escape. That trio at this point of the opera always stands my hairs on end. It's the music of ultimate heroism. Of goodness conquering over evil. Now she makes her se-lection and opts for redemption. The angels are crying, "She is saved." And Mephistopheles cries, "She is condemned." But he has lost. And her now-rescued soul rises to heaven.

I'd like to understand my mood, though. Why am I thinking about moral issues? I was never a goody-goody in life. And I very conveniently avoided such thoughts so as not to trouble myself. Or stray from my appointed goals. I've pushed E.C. this far, and now have to see him through to the end. There's going to be a lot of satisfaction in this. Faust was a fool. He could have had everything. It was just a matter of growth and vision.

The opera has ended. People are oohing and aahing at the ex-cellence of La Corsini's voice. The trio, I must say, was sublime. Her voice rose above the others effortlessly. I agree with the critics. There is nothing with which to compare it. They're crying *brava! brava!* and asking her to repeat the trio. This never happens in America. Another curtain call. A bouquet of roses is delivered. She graciously curtsies as that breast of soprano quivers to the beat of the excitement. My goodness, she's going to do it again! I think when His Eminence stood and clapped and looked her straight in the eye, she decided to grant this very gracious encore. I feel sorry for the tenor and the basso, though. To be sure, they're excellent. But with La Corsini on the stage, even the best would pale by comparison. The woman is singing as if possessed by Satan himself. Or by the angels, as the case may be. There's a wealth of quality and intensity to this voice. For the first time in many years, I am stunned and dumbfounded. But of course I have other thoughts as well. I am curious regarding the reasons for the emergence at this time of an exact look-alike of E.C.'s wife.

Now that the encore is over, His Eminence is glancing at the guests, who are all showing signs of approval. In a very polite fashion, a portion of the corridor has been cleared by the two priests, who are quite adept at moving him in and out of tight places. In a moment the little party is down the grand staircase and out the door to the waiting cars and motorcycle escort. This is a brilliant evening. I remember such occasions in Rome before I passed away. To be sure, there were some wonderful soirées. But we are not yet finished with this one. And it already compares very favorably with the best.

Our little motorcade is winding its way through the city in a bumblebee line to the Vatican. In the evening light, St. Peter's dome shines prepossessingly like a giant jeweled miter. Miss Cleave is looking very confident now that half of Rome has gazed approvingly at her rather smashing gown. But I can tell she's a bit preoccupied with E.C.'s lapse during the performance.

As we arrive at the Cardinal's apartments in file with old Tucci and the other guests, I'm struck by the beauty of this ancient part of town. And the glow of the buildings in the moonlight. In a moment, we're up in the Cardinal's apartments. The entire suite of rooms has been beautifully decked out for the occasion. There are candles alight everywhere, and enormous arrangements of rubrium lilies from Holland. I note with pleasure the pistils have been removed from each and every open blossom. On the practical side, these little male organs are messy buggers, since they stain everything they touch. We used to have them removed with tweezers. Sometimes in the dead of the night, I'd compulsively do it myself. I must admit, I derived an obtuse and secret bit of pleasure from removing and discarding all those male organs, and leaving the pretty flowers safe and unsullied. I grant you my psychiatrist could have done much with this little act. But after all, what would life be without a little perversion here and there?

In a corner of the sitting room a string quartet, with very well matched and balanced instruments, is playing music by Haydn. It's a polished and subtle performance. Which as we enter serves as a background for the tinkle of tall crystal champagne glasses being carried with immediacy by supple young priests. To the now exhilarated and chatty guests. Miss Cleave and E.C. are the object of great attention from this little crowd. Tucci is walking toward them with a buoyant smile.

"My good friends, what did you think of the opera?"

"Miss Cleave and I think it was absolutely wonderful. Amalita Corsini is a breathtaking woman in every way."

"What Mr. Douglas means, Your Eminence, is that he enormously admires her voice. That is what you meant, isn't it?"

"Actually, I think the voice is better than anything I've ever heard. But I have to stand on my initial comment and say I find the woman striking, enigmatic, and interesting."

It would seem Miss Cleave has been a bit rattled by E.C.'s attention to La Corsini. Sage old fellow that he is, His Eminence has picked up on the little dispute brewing and is now attempting to skirt the issue.

"We have many fine singers in Italy, as you know. Perhaps you will stay and hear some of our other performers. Incidentally, the quartet is playing my own matched Guarneris."

"Mr. Douglas and I were commenting on the beauty of their tone."

"Ah, but we were talking about La Corsini. And here she is."

His Eminence is sauntering toward the door to greet the star. Like an aging tiger, but still with teeth. She is suitably attired in a black lace gown which plunges toward the bodice, showing a bit more cleavage than one might think can exist. The dress is tailored at the waist, and then blossoms forward into a wide skirt with tiers of very thin and gauzy black lace. Her hair is set with diamonds, and the panache of the woman is given away by the black feathers of a diamond-set aigrette. On her bosom rests a necklace composed entirely of brilliants which are roughly the size of nickel coins. As she enters, some are clapping and others are making a tinkling sound with their champagne glasses. Very dramatically, she is curtsying to His Eminence and kissing his ring. This is a woman who quite evidently knows how to take hold of a room with the firm grasp of a strangler. The look in her eyes is incredibly strong, with a touch of the gypsy-wild. It's curious. One couldn't say she's anywhere near as beautiful as Cleave. Susan is classically proportioned and has the body of a thoroughbred. Yet there's something untamed and mysterious, and terribly attractive, about this raven-haired artist. Especially since, in a manner of speaking, we've seen her before. Now old Tucci, obviously delighted with the presence, is parading her among the guests and making the necessary introductions. He's approaching E.C. and Susan. I must say, Douglas has that look men acquire when they're incubating a little excitement in the crotch.

"Allow me to present Signorina Amalita Corsini."

"Miss Corsini, we're honored to meet you. Both Miss Cleave and I were overwhelmed with the beauty of your voice. But I must tell you, you are also a great dramatic actress."

"*Prego*, thank you. I am very flattered by your comments. And how beautiful Mrs. Douglas looks!"

"Oh no, Miss Corsini, I'm not Mr. Douglas's wife, I'm his assistant."

"Oh, please forgive me. I never understand such things. You know, I am so involved with my own little world that I frequently make such mistakes."

"Not to worry, Miss Corsini. I'm always flattered whenever Miss Cleave is mistakenly referred to as my wife, but you too are a very beautiful woman. I feel I've known you all my life."

"Ah, I see. . . ."

As she turns to speak to the Cardinal, I can't help thinking she's actually speaking for our ears when she says, ". . . such a handsome man, and unmarried as well." Miss Cleave has picked up on the fact, and is also beginning to make comparisons and establish parallels. She has instinctively done what women do when their captive penis looks like it may be getting ready to suffer its own Waterloo. She's now firmly holding on to him by the arm, as a bright-eyed young priest with black curly hair brings them two fresh glasses of champagne. Almost simultaneously the bronze bell is struck once, indicating the commencement of dinner. Cardinal Tucci is proceeding first with La Corsini, and E.C. and Susan are right behind. The last of the guests to arrive has just come through the door. It's Don Orsini. He looks composed and alert, as well as impeccably attired. His Eminence has interrupted the little procession to motion him to the front. So now the second trio of the night proceeds headfirst into the state dining room.

We parade through the double doors. Now fully within the dining room, I'm overwhelmed by the beauty of this table. The cloth is Brussels lace. Down the middle of the setting, about every four feet or so, are very tall candelabra, which by virtue of their height do not in any way inhibit the view from one side to the other. Between them are low, round silver vessels, each containing dozens of very closely arranged multicolored roses. As the Montrachet is poured, tiny Mediterranean crayfish are presented, swimming in basil sauce. The contrast of colors on the pink-blossomed Sèvres plates is made doubly beautiful by the flickering of countless candles, both at the table and around us. The diva is sitting at His Eminence's right. At his left is Miss Cleave. E.C. is next to La Corsini, facing the Don. I fully intend to nestle up to this little grouping at the head of the table, since I know our presence is no accident. E.C. is looking admiringly toward La Corsini, as Susan decides to carry the conversation.

"Miss Corsini, I can't keep my eyes off your diamond necklace. It really is breathtaking."

"Thank you. Actually, I think they are Russian. I love diamonds. But I never buy them for myself. I must say, though, Miss Cleave, I might almost trade mine for your single triangle—of course, I mean your magnificent pink diamond. So large. . . . A gift from Mr. Douglas? Forgive me, I do not mean to be indiscreet."

"Oh no, you needn't worry. Mine was a gift from a gentleman who has unfortunately passed away."

"Yes, men . . . they are all so fragile. I am always accused of hurting them. They tell me, 'Amalita, you are a black widow.' But it really is not my fault. It is the men who cannot take, how would you say in English . . . ah yes . . . the wear and tear."

E.C. has a rather smitten look on his face. Don Orsini is merely observing, without participating in the conversation. Susan is looking a bit irritated. And Amalita's bosom is heaving, as if she's getting ready to pounce on E.C. Noticing a slight strain, His Eminence is quick to enter the conversation.

"Luckily for me, I am exempt by profession, and immune by operation of age, from the charms of beautiful flowers like Miss Cleave and Amalita here. God has been good to not put such temptation before me at an earlier time. Don't you think, Don Orsini?"

"Indeed, Your Eminence. But you and I have been here long enough to know there are other temptations as well. For instance, greed."

The Cardinal has stiffened a bit at Don Orsini's cue. But almost without a shift in gears is proceeding with the smoothness of a dolphin slicing through water.

"A very adroit statement, Don Orsini. We are actually very curious as to Mr. Douglas's business activities, since he has become interested in a very substantial European holding company, Siderurgica. Perhaps, Mr. Douglas, you will tell us about it. Why did you decide to purchase?"

"Your Eminence, I'm not skirting the issue when I tell you I really don't know. As it happened, this whole thing started with a dog. A very big one. No, no. Don't laugh. I really do mean a dog. You see, recently I ran into this extraordinary creature that belonged to the late Henry W. Somerset, and with him began a series of situations which led to my purchase of Mr. Somerset's home, his art, and now Siderurgica."

"This is very interesting. We at the Vatican have some knowledge and belief concerning destiny. But we are also experts on free will. I understand you have negotiated to purchase the Somerset block of stock."

"Why yes. How do you know?"

"I think Archbishop Fromaggio let it slip in a casual conversation."

"Does the Vatican have any interest in Siderurgica? I know there's a large block of European stock."

At this point, Don Orsini's eyes are shining brightly. And he's decided to enter the conversation.

"You know, Signore Douglas, a lot of people are betting Siderurgica will fail, or at least suffer great losses if it is separated from the American steel companies. Mr. Somerset was my respected friend and a frequent guest at my dinner table. As a matter of fact, he originally put Siderurgica together with the American steel interests in an effort to avoid competition, and created great earnings. I do not know if you are aware, but his nephew, Gustavo Somerset, was here just last week. I believe his trip has some connection with the Siderurgica matter. But we must be boring these beautiful ladies. I must say I am torn between speaking of their beauty and their talent."

Exquisitely and totally boned pheasant breasts have now been placed before the guests. There is a dab of carrot purée, and a dark plum sauce. The tiny dish is punctuated by the presence of a superlative Bonnes Mares. A tiny endive salad follows. Then some very simple peeled peach slices, with a Château d'Yquem. You see, the peaches are actually the accompaniment to the final wine, the "liquid gold," which very cleverly has become the actual dessert.

The guests are rising and are on their way to the library, where coffee is being served with chocolates. His Eminence has attracted the presence of the ladies, as Don Orsini takes our man by the arm and walks quietly with him into a dim corner, where the incunables sleep.

"Mr. Douglas, I don't know if you are aware, but I was a very close friend of Henry Somerset."

"Why no. I was unaware, but he's someone I've come to admire. You know I've purchased his pyramid. Have you seen it?"

"Alas, no. Regretfully I do not often travel to the United States due to . . . shall we say, political reasons. Mind you, when the United States government has had no other alternative, and has been forced to call upon me for help, I have journeyed there, but under a special type of diplomatic immunity."

"Yes, I understand. Did you have business with Mr. Somerset? Or perhaps this is prying too much."

"Mr. Douglas, there is no need to avoid frankness and honesty.

I am a businessman. In a manner of speaking, while I do not represent a country, I am in fact a head of state. As such, I enjoy the fruits and bear the burdens and duties inherent to leaders of men. In assuming our responsibilities, we are no longer judged by the standards of regular individuals. As you know, we can never be murderers, only generals of war. Our goal is not even necessarily to seek improvement, since we know all finance, industry, and government are never less or more than their sum total. We are fundamentally interested only in stability. The prize is, of course, riches and power beyond measure. Which means anything which can be bought is available. The ultimate price paid is the loss of many standard or perfunctory desires and longings. In any case, we are charged with keeping balance. And I am concerned for myself and my friends at the Vatican, who I know have a great interest in this matter. Specifically regarding a possible upheaval in the steel market, which might put the American companies in the position of strangling us here in Europe. I have recently learned some disquieting facts which force me to take you into my confidence. You see, this Gustavo Somerset came to see us. And on the basis of his dead uncle's credibility, obtained a substantial credit facility. Supposedly, this money was to be used for the purpose of defraying death taxes. But instead, my informants in Zurich indicate the funds were used to pyramid a very large position in the American steel markets. We are therefore in the extremely embarrassing situation of having to act protectively and decide which side to support. Since we have been lied to, we have only one road open. And that is to look to you for the cultivation of a new relationship of trust and confidence. You should also be aware that we legally hold substantial collateral related to the matter."

"What sort of collateral?"

"We have acquired a first lien on the entire account in Zurich in which the pyramiding or purchase on margin is being made."

"And what are the terms of your security agreement? I don't mean to pry, but if I'm to be helpful in any way, I must understand the situation."

"The account was certified originally as having a value of nine hundred million dollars. It is, in fact, an account owned by the Somerset widow. Which was, of course, an added source of confidence to us. While we knew the inventory was composed of about a billion and a half dollars' worth of steel stocks on the margin, this did not give us pause, due to an agreement drafted by the attorneys, whereby we have the ability to liquidate if the net value of the entire portfolio falls beneath eight hundred million. Of course, in a very speedy market, such an amount could be lost quickly. Since the money was to be used for supposed payment of death taxes, we assumed there was a need, and in honor of old friendship decided to abide with the normal business risk. But instead, our funds have been used to purchase an additional billion and a half dollars' worth of steel stocks. A substantial change in the market could completely destroy the value of that account. We will deal with the lie in our own fashion. But attention must be given to the financial matter. And it would seem to be coming to a head with your rumored purchase. As a matter of trust and confidence, I require that you describe your intentions in the Siderurgica matter."

"I have no difficulty doing this. My plan is to purchase the Somerset stock, since I have been unable to obtain it elsewhere, and to then simultaneously sell the American steels, granting the Somerset estate control over them, as well as a license to use Von Richter's process."

"You understand competition will be difficult if the American steels are able to manufacture with the exclusive benefit of this process."

"Yes, I do. But there's something which keeps telling me I should do this deal."

"What is this something? Would you explain it to me?"

"Don Orsini, if I understood it, I'd tell you. But ever since I ran into Henry Somerset's dog, I've been doing some very odd things, and almost feeling influenced by Somerset's remembrance. The funny thing is that I never met the man. You might think this is all very absurd, but it's the truth I'm telling you."

"Mr. Douglas, we Sicilians learned many centuries ago that a situation is not less real because it is absurd. We believe in many things which would be laughed at by persons of less experience. And this, of course, would not be a bad time for me to make you the gift of a charm with a little clenched black fist. I do, however, have an idea. Very soon, when it is revealed to him that I know what has been done with the money, Gustavo Somerset is going to be feeling like what we would call the proverbial *cockroach at the chicken dance*. When that happens, he will have to give us something very, very quickly, or suffer the consequences. Do you know if he has control over the Siderurgica stock in the Somerset estate?"

"No, I don't. All I can tell you is that the estate has agreed to sell me its stock, and we're about to complete the legalities of the deal."

"It is my intention to demand this Siderurgica stock in the estate as additional collateral for my investment."

"Oh . . . but if they can't sell me the Somerset stock, I will fail in my tender offer to gain control of Siderurgica."

"There is a detail I have not apprised you of, but which is now timely. Between the Vatican and my organization, we hold the European percentage of Siderurgica in various nominee accounts. We will tender these to you at a token dollar below the price you negotiated with the Somerset estate. This will provide you with your controlling block. You, in turn, will attempt at all times to act in concordance with our interests. I can arrange for the tender of the stock early tomorrow morning."

"I understand, and that's excellent. But what will happen to the other thirty percent if it's posted as additional collateral?"

"It could conceivably fall into our hands and thus replace what we had tendered. If that were to occur, you would have us as partners. We are trustworthy in such respects."

"I'm sort of overwhelmed. Do I have time think about this?"

"No."

Our man is faltering and looking a bit perplexed. I have to do something to make him recognize the uniqueness of this opportunity. It took me years to enlist both the Vatican and Don Orsini as partners. And now Gustavo's perfidy has put it all in his hands very quickly. You see, Don Orsini, who undoubtedly believes in insurance, has no doubt realized that the combination of E.C.'s takeover bid and Gustavo's pyramiding of the Somerset account could spell serious losses for him and his partner. He is a man of honor, to be sure, but the lie has put him in the position of hedging his bet. And his necessity translates into an immediate advantage for E.C. With Orsini and the Church as backers, the sky is the limit. It's actually an unbelievable combination. Finally, the transaction of my dreams! I'm trying to communicate with E.C. by whispering in his ear, but he's not receptive. And Bozo isn't here to help, either. Our man's gaze is wandering as Don Orsini becomes visibly impatient. It's fixed on the several hundred rosebuds in that large Dresden bowl. You know, it's a trick I haven't tried yet. But if I can make a chandelier tinkle and whip pages into the wind, I should be able to pop a simple rose open. There's a juicy, plump white bud with the pale green of its bracts slightly coloring its outer petals. I'm going to relax completely, and *will* myself temporarily into that flower. Just as E.C.'s giving it his most intent and glassy-eyed look, it bursts open. In an altogether magnificent way. Don Orsini is looking at our man, so he hasn't seen my bit of wizardry. But E.C. has. He's looking twice to make sure he's right. But there's no doubt. And he's taking it on cue as a perfect sign. He's putting his hand out to Don Orsini in a time-honored gesture and sealing it with some simple words: "In that event, Don Orsini, you have acquired a business partner and a friend."

Don Orsini is exchanging hairs from his mustache and our man's sideburn. E.C. is looking rather quizzically at him, but has the wisdom to go along with the custom.

Hallelujah. This couldn't have worked out better if I'd planned it myself. My old friend Orsini is now aware Gustavo is a total gutter rat. And from where I'm sitting, the money is riding on E. C. Douglas.

His Eminence is now approaching E.C. and the Don. He caught our man staring at the rose as it opened, and witnessed the spectacle. As a result, there was a loss of composure for the briefest of moments as he genuflected. Now approaching, he seeks eye contact with Don Orsini, who's giving him an approving nod.

"Mr. Douglas, I see you are getting along quite well with my old friend. He will not steer you in the wrong direction if your rudder is straight."

"Your Eminence, I have found Don Orsini to be the most engaging of new friends. I'm hopeful for a long relationship. And for, of course, a repeat invitation to your wonderful surroundings, which make me think I'm in another world. In fact, they make me feel twenty years younger."

"Yes, yes. This is excellent. And you are very kind. But we do not have to wait for heaven, since Miss Corsini has consented to sing for us. Please come . . . I know she will be disappointed if you are not present."

We're off to the music room, where Amalita is reclining against the very large German piano. The lights have been dimmed, and she's proceeding to fully demonstrate her abilities with a devilish piece by Donizetti. The group is wild. And not without reason. This is a most extraordinary voice. She's now singing an aria from *La Traviata*, and terminating with the Pochielli "Suicidio." Always a rather chilling piece.

As might have been expected, Amalita Corsini has eyes only for our man Douglas. And he is not rebuffing the stare. Miss Cleave is feeling a bit uncomfortable, and has dropped her handbag in an effort to gain his attention. But for him it's as if it never happened. He is totally mesmerized by the star. There are more rounds of applause, as Amalita curtsies to this very special audience. Those diamonds look like they might drip and drop right in between those most respectable promontories. For a moment there, as they heaved with the music, I had the impression one of her breasts might pop out of its cradle. But no such luck tonight.

Some of the guests are beginning to leave. Don Orsini has quietly disappeared with a knowing nod to the Cardinal and then to our man. E.C. and Cleave are taking the cue and preparing to depart as well.

"Good night, Your Eminence. As I said in so many other words, it's been a thrilling and very illuminating evening."

"I trust profitable as well."

"Yes. Without a doubt, and I'm sure thanks to your able assistance."

"My son, the business of being with the angels sometimes forces us to take up the sword. But we do know the meaning of the words 'friendship' and 'loyalty,' and we are hopeful our prayers will be most helpful to you. Miss Cleave, I do hope Mr. Douglas will bring you to see me again."

"I would very much look forward to it, Your Eminence. It's been a remarkable time. Good night."

With this, E.C. is now turning to La Corsini, who has quickly placed herself near the Cardinal to say *buona notte*.

"Miss Corsini, it's been a privilege being with you, seeing you, and hearing your unique and wonderful voice this evening."

"Ah, Mr. Douglas, you must call me Amalita the next time. All my friends do. Will you stay in Rome for a day or two?"

"I really don't know—we must be returning to the United States. But in any event, I would look forward to seeing you and hearing your beautiful music again."

"I am very sure our paths will cross. Good night, Mr. Douglas. Good night, Miss Cleave."

As E.C. and Cleave turn, they are unable to see the almost demonic look in Amalita Corsini's eyes. This woman is really a powerful and frightening creature. Old Tucci has caught this rather disquieting gaze, and is approaching the star with a stern look on his face.

"Amalita, my dear. There are so many men . . ."

"Yes, I guess so. But this is a very interesting one. So fresh. So naive. He would seem to have scruples."

"Then, my dear, as your confessor, I caution you."

"All I can say, Your Eminence, is: I have heard you, and I will try."

"*Cara*, that is precisely what I am afraid of."

Some of the other guests are saying good night. Amalita is taking her wrap, and majestically departing. It's time for me to catch up with E.C. and Susan. So I will reluctantly bid farewell to this brilliant atmosphere.

TWENTY-TWO

AMALITA CORSINI IS THE TYPE OF WOMAN WHO DOES NOT KNOW THE meaning of the word no. She arose this morning singing *La Forza del Destino* between her teeth. Sitting up in that enormous bed, against the peach-colored satin backdrop of her tufted headboard, those famous breasts are showing a tad of nipple. They're firm, hard, and taut. A man could bruise himself against them if he wasn't careful. A very stern-looking, tall, gray-haired maid, who quite apparently enjoys family status, has just entered with the breakfast tray. She is irreverently proceeding to open the curtains.

"Good morning, Amalita."

"Good morning, Sophia."

"Did you sleep well? You arrived very late. It must have been at least one in the morning. This is not good for your voice. I hope you did not drink too much."

"As a matter of fact, I had some champagne. And I also met a very, very attractive man."

"Amalita! No . . . I said no! This is your Nana telling you to behave yourself."

"But this man is very good-looking and quite different. And incidentally, not married."

"Was he alone?"

"Not exactly. He was actually with a very attractive woman. But I don't think she will pose much of a problem."

"Amalita, remember you have your music, and it must come first."

"But I can enjoy myself, as well. I sing best when there's a man around."

"Where did you put your diamonds?"

"I don't remember . . . oh, there they are on the other nightstand. I need a telephone."

"Be careful what you are going to do. Remember, old Nana knows what is best for you."

Amalita is paying no attention to her sage attendant and has proceeded to dial E.C.'s hotel. Luckily, Miss Cleave is picking up at the other end.

"Good morning. Would you be kind enough to communicate me with Mr. Douglas, please?"

"Good morning. May I know who is calling?"

"Tell him it is Amalita Corsini."

"Oh . . . Miss Corsini, this is Susan Cleave."

"Ah, yes, you were the lady with Mr. Douglas last night. How nice to speak with you again. . . . Is he in?"

"One moment, please, I'll see if he's here."

Miss Cleave has cradled the receiver on a nearby cushion. With a look bordering on anger she is telling E.C. of the black widow's phone call:

"Shall I tell her you're not here?"

"No. Don't do that. I'll take it."

As he reaches for the phone, he begins fidgeting and beads of sweat can be seen accumulating on his brow. Susan has immediately noticed these details. She is obviously disquieted by the entire scene.

"Mr. Douglas. Is it you?"

"Yes, Miss Corsini. To what do I owe the honor of your call?"

"Well, you see, I lost one of my earrings last night. And I thought you might remember whether I left wearing it or not. Could you help me with this very *leetle theeng*?"

"Actually, I don't recall. I was looking elsewhere . . . err, at other areas . . ."

"You are delightfully fresh, Mr. Douglas. Why don't you come to lunch today?"

"Well . . . er . . . yes. Thank you. But . . ."

"I understand completely, you cannot speak. I will send my address and directions to the concierge at your hotel. *Arrivedella.*"

"Goodbye."

As our man cradles the receiver, he has somewhat of a pleased look on his face. It's the middle-aged hunter look. The one with the stroked ego. Miss Cleave has reentered the room and is of course curious.

"What was that all about?"

"Oh, not very much. She lost an earring last night and wondered if we saw her wearing it when she left."

"Well, I hope you can see through that gimmick. Besides, if she had dropped one of those earrings, we would have felt the tremor as the building was structurally damaged."

"Now, now. Your fangs are showing, my dear."

"You be careful. I think Amalita Corsini is definitely bad news. Besides, I love you."

"I love you too. And I think we should do something about it right now."

"Try me!"

There are caresses and kisses. And suctions of various varieties. I'm embarrassed to watch. But not so much that I'm leaving. Now he's very gently unbuttoning her blouse and sucking like a complacent child on Miss Cleave's small but well-proportioned breasts. The room is darkened and she's pushed him against the bed. She's grabbed on to his zipper with her teeth and is proceeding to unzip his fly. It's taking them a bit of time to become completely naked, as each piece of clothing is removed with its own provocative gesture. This is uncommon. I used to rip my clothes off and jump in as quickly as I could. But not so with E.C. and Cleave. Also, she always knows how to say the right things.

"Oh . . . I do like big men . . . yes . . . if they don't do it too quickly."

To be sure, E.C. has a respectable cock. Big, but not so big you can't do anything with it. Besides, it's hard. And we all know a lot of those extra-large things never manage to become fully rigid. Susan meant it when she spoke. She does like large men. I should know. But it's also a masterful stroke. And womanly too. We all want to hear we're big. After all, show me a man who doesn't derive a substantial portion of his self-esteem from that thing flopping between his legs.

Mommy and Daddy tell you not to play with it. But they're awfully proud you have one. Then you go to high school or college, where boys shower together, and you take a good hard look at the next fellow's cock. It's a fact that most young men require reassurance as to the size of their members. And God forbid it should be too small, because then the other kids will joke and laugh and jeer at the guy with the peanut. Fellows who have one long enough to flop around in the shower are definitely the objects of respect, no matter how puny the rest of their physique. In my case, I must say, it flopped nicely. And when somewhat tumescent, it would actually slap against my thighs as I walked. E.C. has a good one too. It's one of those cocks that is fairly wide at the head and gently slopes a little to a slightly thinner base. Meaning that it stays put where he sinks it. It's straight, as well. Which is a good thing. Some of them turn to this side or that. Or worse yet, downward. But this is an aesthetically acceptable member.

Cleave is responding nicely. Although this meeting inspires a tad of jealousy in me, I'm also excited at being able to watch unnoticed. She's beneath him. And he's assumed a position of rigidity about six inches above her. With the head barely touching her receptive petals. Now he's plunging back and forth. In and out. Rather furiously. And just when he's got her fully scintillated, he's flipped on his back with her on top, and is now allowing Susan to do the work.

It's over. They're lying there, now pulling a sheet over themselves. It was a good scene, but I got the impression he was thinking about someone else. I think she did too. He has a guilty look on his face. It would seem he's still going to lunch at Amalita Corsini's. Now he's rising.

"What's happening? Where are you going?"

"I have to shower and go to a business meeting."

"Oh . . . I thought we were going to have lunch at Piazza Navonna."

"I had planned on it, Bernini fountains and all, but a business matter has interfered, so you'd best have lunch by yourself today."

"What about our return?"

"You can book takeoff time for late tonight."

"Okay. I'll take care of all the details while you're at lunch."

Our man is popping into the shower and quickly washing. He's actually out in a flash and into a light wool herringbone suit. I think it very proper for the damp Roman fall. That tie he's wearing not only reflects the gray from the suit, but adds a touch of burgundy, which is good, considering the look he's decided to assume. He's wearing brown wing-tip shoes. I've always liked brown with gray. It's soft, and casual, and in a way rather lordly.

Miss Cleave has noticed the care with which he's dressed, and would seem to be a bit curious. "Tell me something. You're not going to see that Amalita woman, are you?"

"No. But what if I were?"

"Well, I wouldn't approve. You have to decide for a playboy life, or for me. But they just don't go together."

He's faltering. Oh no, we can't have that. Come on, buster, be a good bucko and keep that lie up. She's going to love you anyway. That's right, regain your composure. Stiffen up a bit! Be aggressive! All great sportsmen go hunting. And if you're to be like me, you must follow through with the kill!

"Listen, Susan. You know, I really don't approve of these little jealous fits. You've never done this before."

"That's because I haven't previously had a tarantula like La Corsini at my door."

"Take it easy. Don't imagine things, I'll see you later."

With this gesture, E.C. turns around and is quickly gone. As he walks into the elevator, he seems to have become a bit inflated. This is typical of men on their way to a hot encounter. After all, as I mentioned earlier, that thing between our legs does provide a sense of comfort and self-esteem. Particularly when it's in demand. Now progressing through the lobby, he stops at the concierge's desk:

"Good morning, Enrico. By any chance do you have an envelope for me?"

"Ah yes, Mr. Douglas. It was delivered moments ago. Here it is."

"Thank you very much."

E.C. has peeled a large bill from the high-denomination Italian notes in his pocket and has adeptly slid it under the corner of the concierge's appointment book. As he turns, he's opening the oversize cream-colored envelope, which contains a very stiff card with the words "Amalita Corsini" rising in the middle of it, and crossed out with a black line of ink. The address is engraved, as well. And the word "noon" is boldly written in ink. He's proceeding into the waiting car, down the streets of Rome, to a charming apartment building in the more fashionable sector of town. E.C.'s out of the car into the midday sunlight. But something has troubled him. He's having second thoughts. I don't like this in a man. He should go up there and bang her silly. Perhaps I should provide a bit of reassurance. A pep talk of sorts. I know he can't hear me, but sometimes I have the impression I can almost influence him by act of will. He's walking down the street looking at the window of a small antique shop. As I whisper into his ear, he seems to become more resolute, and walks back to the entrance of the now-known location.

Inside the well-appointed apartment there is a scenario I have seen before. Amalita Corsini waits like the tarantula listening for the knock of her arduous lover. Every hair in place, and ready to list over all his sweetest parts. A luncheon is set out. And the scenario is prepared. With every deathly leg and spinneret in cocked position. She is the type of woman who rips a hole in men's hearts. To not so gently suck the life from them. A creature who visits quietly in the night with deathly tiptoes to strum all the silken threads of an affair. And drawing out each drop of blood, she does so with the very willing prey, who frequently will relinquish much in order to reign as part of her. There is a knock at the door. The aged retainer has opened it, and the opera star has walked into the foyer to greet E.C.

"How good to see you again, Mr. Douglas."

"Call me E.C. All my friends do."

"Perhaps I can call you Easy!"

"I wouldn't mind that either, Miss Corsini."

"Ah, no, no . . . but you are not playing by the rules. You have to call me Amalita."

"Well then, Amalita it is."

"Please come in."

She's showing him into the large drawing room, which sports a substantial piano in a Venetian finish, and is full of very colorful and pleasant matching furniture. This room is also littered with photographs of the star, as well as other famous singers and personalities. In the corner there is also a harp. The maid is bringing them little glasses of very dry, cold sherry. She didn't bother to ask, so E.C. didn't have much of a choice. But he's drinking the sherry. And to be sure, it's a respectable aperitif.

"I have a very light luncheon set out in the library. A little bit of white asparagus, fresh from Paris, and a bit of fish. I don't like to have anything too heavy at noon."

"You know, I would give anything to hear you sing again."

"This is something which can be arranged. . . ."

They're going into the library, where the luncheon has been impeccably presented in expectation of the duo. She didn't exaggerate. It's a rather light midday meal. Beautiful asparagus. Nice big white plump spears. And fillet of sole Véronique. This woman knows how to titillate a man. She's eating her asparagus in the European style, with the fingers. Which is, of course, fine when it's this firm. Americans sometimes take these things to extremes and attempt to eat limp vegetables with their hands. Always a disaster. In any event, these are white with that slightest tint of green at the tip, and robust, to say the least. She's taking one and dipping it in the hollandaise. Now bringing it up to her mouth as if it were an erotic object, and almost playing with it before ingestion. E.C. has picked up on this bit of toying and is becoming excited under his napkin.

"Do you like wine, Mr. Douglas?"

"Yes. This is a beautiful Montrachet, Marquise de la Guiche, no less."

"Ah, you *do* know. How refreshing to find an American who knows wine."

"Some of us know about many things, Amalita."

"But do you know about women? Do you know what makes a woman's soul sing . . . ? Speaking of singing, let us have our coffee in the sitting room, and I will sing for you."

They're rising from the table and are off to the adjoining area, where a tray of coffee with a rather baroque silver coffeepot is awaiting their reentry. To my surprise, the harp is not a prop. She's actually going to accompany herself on it as she sings. E.C. just can't keep his eyes off the woman. He continues to be in disbelief at the incredible resemblance. There is further electricity in the air as "Caro Nome" bursts forth in glorious vibration. Now that she's through with the aria, they're looking strongly at one another.

Just when I think he might pop one of her breasts out of its rather loosely fitting halter, he stiffens and makes an excuse, "This has been wonderful, but I must be going. I have an airplane to catch."

"Oh. But you cannot leave so soon, E.C. We are just beginning to know one another. When will I see you again?"

"Soon, I'm sure. Soon."

He's looking rather awkward now, and somewhat childlike. She walks up to him, and as she kisses him hard on the mouth, grabs his crotch insistently and squeezes with strength.

"Owww."

"Ah . . . so you do stir! We will have something to speak about the next time. Besides, I like substantial men. It would seem, as you say in America, *caro*, that you are all there."

He's giving her a rather reproachful look. But turning into the perfect gentleman, is now bowing to kiss her hand, as he smiles, looks her in the eye, and says:

"Amalita, please. There are reasons why we mustn't misbehave today."

"What reasons?"

"Well, its very personal, but you remind me strongly of someone, and I am a bit unnerved by it."

"Someone pleasant, I hope."

"Very. But enough. I must leave."

With this, he's out the door, but not straight to the hotel. For a while he seems to walk aimlessly. Then, with a visible change of mood, he directs himself to a familiar jeweler on Via Condotti. I know the place well. The scene of many lustful expenditures. Extremely sleek glass-and-bronze doors of this establishment tell you from the beginning there's nothing inexpensive within. An impeccably dressed and groomed middle-aged man with a touch of gray at the temples has greeted E.C. after the uniformed guard at the door allowed him admittance.

"*Buona sera.*"

"Good afternoon."

"Ah. You are from America. I am Antonio Ricordi, the manager of the shop. Would you like to look around, or is there anything special you had in mind?"

"Actually, I'm looking for some earrings. Long ones. And maybe also a shorter pair of the more tailored type."

"We have many. Please sit down and I will bring them. Would you like some coffee or refreshment?"

"An espresso would be very nice."

"*Bene*, I will return in a moment."

An attendant is very quickly evidencing himself with a bit of espresso in a tiny Ginori cup. Our man is sipping the brew as good old Ricordi returns with two leather boxes.

"Here we have several pairs of long evening earrings with various gemstones. These with the emeralds would be particularly attractive for a lady with dark hair. And of course, the diamonds are magnificent as well. Someone said these diamond-and-ruby earrings should be for a lady who dances. Look at the little links and the way the marquise diamonds would seem to cascade."

"I'll take the ruby ones. Now show me some shorter earrings."

The merchant is obviously overwhelmed in the presence of a man who has made so substantial a purchase in the twinkling of an eye. He has closed the first case and separated the ruby earrings. He's now rather nervously but expectantly opening the second leather case, which contains about a dozen or so pairs of ear clips, no less formidable because of their size.

"You see, sir, we have quite a collection."

"Yes, indeed. Tell me about these very large black pearls with the single diamonds above them."

"Ah, signore, these are one of a kind. They are South Sea pearls, and of course so large you are not likely to see another similar pair. The diamonds are also rather unusual in that they are not really square cuts. They are what we call a modified cushion, which in addition to being somewhat deeper is excellent for intense fancy yellow diamonds such as these. They would suit a woman of great distinction who wished to make a statement of quality. Mind you, if you are indecisive between the two pairs you've selected, the lady can always return the pair you select, if she is unhappy. Although no one would be displeased with either pair of these earrings."

"Actually, I'm taking both pairs. They are for two different ladies. So if you ever see one of them, the other pair should not be mentioned."

"Ah. We understand. Jewelers in Europe must be even more respectful of secrecy than priests. Mr. . . ."

"E. C. Douglas. I'll be giving you a check on my European bank. You may forward the earrings when the check has cleared."

"Yes, thank you. Allow me to excuse myself for a moment."

The manager of the store has now gone into the back room, where with a very quick telephone call he has a complete credit rating on E. C. Douglas. He's returning with the type of beatitudinous smile merchants acquire when they've gained jurisdiction over a new and very deep pocket.

"Mr. Douglas, here is *il bilanzio*, I mean, the statement. And, of course, your check is very good with us. There is no need to send the earrings—you may take them with the mere formality of showing me your passport."

"You are very kind. Here it is. . . ."

Mr. Ricordi is examining the passport photograph, and, well satisfied, is proceeding to register the client's address.

"Mr. Douglas, perhaps if you have a moment, I might show you the necklace which goes with these pearl earrings. It is only the second we have ever acquired, since these black pearls are extremely rare. You might wish to keep it in mind."

"Oh . . . yes, it's very special, and very heavy. I never really knew pearls were that heavy."

"Alas, the real ones are, Mr. Douglas. These are what we call Pinctada margaritifera. You need only call me if you become interested in them at any time. Here are your parcels."

"Ah . . . thank you much, Mr. Ricordi. I'm sure I'll be back."

"We very much hope so, Mr. Douglas. Bear in mind, if there is anything important you should require, I can come across the Atlantic and attend you in our New York shop."

"I'll remember that. Thank you again."

E.C. is now on his way back to the hotel. Once through the revolving door, he's making a beeline for the concierge's desk.

"Ah, Mr. Douglas. How may I help you?"

"I have a valuable parcel which should be delivered with my card to Miss Corsini. Do you have a bonded attendant who can make the delivery?"

"Yes, of course. You would not, I trust, be upset at offering me the pleasure of seeing the contents."

"No, not at all. Here you are."

With this gesture, E.C. is flipping open the parcel and opening the leather case containing the diamond-and-ruby chandelier earrings.

"Ah, yes, Mr. Douglas. Quite incredible. How do you wish them wrapped?"

"In brown paper. And with this card."

Douglas is now crossing his name out on his calling card and writing the following words: "Amalita . . . already you make me bleed." With this, he's putting the card in the sealed envelope, handing it to the concierge, and entering the small elevator.

Emerging on his floor, E.C. sports that facial expression children acquire when they've broken a vase or done something they shouldn't. After a pensive moment, the look vanishes and he proceeds to enter the suite. Miss Cleave is waiting expectantly with a predictably unhappy smirk on her face.

"Boss, I'm happy to see you. It's a bit late."

"Oh. Are we all set for this evening?"

"Actually, the best I could do was seven o'clock, so we should begin to get ready."

"Fine. Let me pack a few odds and ends I left out, and we can leave within the next hour or so. Oh, Susan, would you hold on to this parcel? It's something rather valuable, so don't lose it."

"Very well. I'll put it in my handbag."

Cleave has that knowing look women assume when they surmise their husband or lover has been playing around. It's a funny thing. We really don't want to believe the objects of our desire are delivering their goodies to anyone except us. We make excuses for behavior which is inexcusable, and at least at the beginning, are always willing to lend credibility to those stories about going shopping with the other ladies, or about late dinners with the boys. In point of fact, though, we all know in our hearts when we are being deceived in the game of love. We fight it, clinging desperately to any piece of information which would prove the contrary in our contortedly distressed lovers' minds. Susan Cleave is locked on the horns of just such a dilemma. She has the uneasy feeling E.C. has been up to no good this afternoon, and of course she's correct. On the other hand, she's looking for something which will justify his absence and somewhat aloof behavior. She doesn't know, but she's just put it in her handbag.

The farewells from the concierge and general manager at the hotel, complete with unsheathing of banknotes, and the ride to the airport are basically uneventful. Susan and E.C. are saying very little to one another. As they pull up to the waiting jet, the pleasant captain, copilot, and very serviceable little steward are smilingly awaiting their master. There isn't much of a delay, and before we know it, we're again up, up, and away.

At about thirty-eight thousand feet, E.C. has served Cleave a glass of champagne, but is himself hitting the Polish vodka. It would seem Susan's waited long enough and isn't about to contain herself further.

"You never told me what you did this afternoon."

"Ask me no questions . . ."

"You know, if I didn't know you better, I'd think you were out seeing that Corsini woman."

"Actually, after my meeting, I went shopping. I have a gift for you, but I can't give it to you."

"Why?"

"Because it's in your handbag already!"

"Oh . . . that's for me?"

"Yes, so you might as well look at it now."

Miss Cleave is opening her handbag and suspiciously retrieving the brown paper parcel. Once it is unwrapped, she fidgets a little with the case. When it is finally opened, she emits a delighted gasp.

"E.C., these are wonderful. You know I love colored diamonds.

And what pearls! Harriet Somerset would be very jealous if she saw these. They would go nicely with the necklace Henry gave her."

"Yes, that's right, Harriet Somerset does have black pearls. . . ."

"Wonderful ones. And I believe Henry got them in Rome, as well."

"Oh. . . ."

The crisis averted, and all suspicions momentarily allayed, the lovers are settling down for the long flight home. With some luck, they'll arrive in time to sleep the night in their beds. I, in turn, am looking forward to seeing Bozo again. After all, he is my most reliable link to this world. You know, while these guys sleep, I might as well blink myself back to Pyramid Hill and spend some time with the pooch.

TWENTY-THREE

I'VE NOW BEEN PLAYING WITH BOZO FOR THE BETTER PART OF AN HOUR. I find I'm able to move that blue foam ball he's been carrying around, and it's actually a lot of fun. At first, I could only displace it a little and really had some trouble making it go in the right direction. Then as I've become more and more adept, I've found I can propel it at speed against a wall, and even lift it into the air for a moment or two. Bozo, who I'm sure is now able to see me in my entirety, is receiving a real charge from the game. We're now both rather exhausted, and he's come near and is leaning. Certainly one of his best gestures.

When I went into his childlike canine mind, I was really taken by the beauty of it. You know, I've been thinking maybe we have it all wrong on the reincarnation bit. What if human beings are actually the least advanced of living things, and the progression toward the light takes us back into being creatures like dogs, and then maybe cows? And at the end, perhaps butterflies and beings which are almost pure energy. One of the people I knew used to say the whole trick had to do with giving things up. Especially traits of personality. I assume the first things you learn to relinquish are material things. I, of course, have never mastered this trick. Having found myself in this state of death, I've now figured out a way to enjoy my possessions through E.C. I'm wondering if this isn't very, very wrong. Perhaps there was a lesson to be learned and I've missed my cue. I'm constantly torn between intimations of a better state of being, with its concomitant healthier mental frame, and my desire to follow through with socking it to Harriet, Hooker, and Gustavo. Not to mention the government officials who undoubtedly colluded with them to cheat me out of the glory of my original deal.

Yes, the government's existence represents one of my pet peeves. As society is presently structured, there is no longer much room for the individual. In point of fact, the authorities hate individuals. That's why they have very cleverly realized that the best way to contain and control persons of all types is by dehumanizing and numbering them. An example is evident in this whole business of Social Security numeration. Originally the idea was a laudable one. Our government would create a fund designed to remedy the plight of those who had worked and were unable to maintain themselves in their declining years. It innocently gave each enrollee a number. When it realized these digits could be used to fully monitor the standard work force, this represented an epiphany second only to the invention of the wheel. Then, of course, as the tax system encroached and insinuated itself in crablike fashion into the lives of all citizens, it hatched the idea of identifying all taxpayers by these numbers. A little later it created laws and regulations designed to make it impossible to do anything without providing the blasted cipher. The result and application are no less gratifying than the digits tattooed on the arm of a German concentration camp inmate. Since you cannot open a bank account, obtain a telephone, or make any other significant transaction without providing your number, you have, in point of fact, been quantified and itemized. Put into a box and enslaved. And all of it in the name of convenience and public service. When you think about this, the government has pulled a very neat trick on us. By making it imperative that we use these numbers, it can also, with the vast, almost mind-boggling network of computers at its disposition, monitor our tastes, life-styles, preferences, and attachments. We can now be thoroughly quantified and treated as carbon units which fall into one category or another. If to this you add the thoroughly terrifying capacity which our sovereign has acquired for eavesdropping on its citizens, you have a *de facto* tyranny, cloaked under the thinnest presumptive veil of democracy.

The average unprotected citizen is unaware our government has created computers which can scan and process millions of pages per minute. The old adage that knowledge is power is first and foremost in its clever mind. For instance, it has acquired the capability of monitoring at the same time each and every electronic communication in the world. Its computers can thus theoretically earmark and select every conversation occurring at this moment in which the word "fandango" is used. Or, of course, any other word. The typical citizen thinks he's protected by the law in this respect. He's not. In fact, the authorities can entirely bypass due process of law and put a citizen away by just invoking "national security." The agencies that can do these things are not public, and function entirely beyond the law. Their budgets are not published, and they respond only to themselves and the absolutely highest spheres of government. The average citizen who becomes a target can't even fart in his bedroom without being overheard. Sure, perhaps the information can't be used as evidence in a court of law. But most federal judges will provide a warrant to eavesdrop secretly on almost anyone. And so what? Even if the snooping is illegal and can't be used directly, it provides a wealth of information on the antics and activities of real, potential, and imagined oppositors.

To these agencies of government, the end invariably justifies the means. So much, that the ways are not even contemplated. Of course, the whole gist of the matter has to do with seeming to conform. The sovereign is traditionally unsettled by those who look like they don't. Therefore, selectively earmarked infractors must be punished in varying measures. If you seriously encroach on national security, which is defined as whatever the government thinks is "national security" at a given point in time, then they can really rub you out. You can have a nasty accident, be sprayed with a particularly virulent germ, or, if you're in the military, become a *man overboard.*

The national economy is a close second in proximity to the heart of government. Those who tinker with the banking system or the stability of the currency are mercilessly slapped down. Government merely puts them in jail. And if that can't be achieved, it can use its bottomless budget for litigation and sue the poor buggers to death. On the other hand, you can do all of this while seeming to be a member of the club, and you'll only be slapped on the wrist. Even better, you can *be* government, or include it in the deal, and then you are impervious to punishment or opprobrium. Frankly, I always favored the partnership approach, rather than becoming a component of government. I could have never subscribed to being anything as frightful as a public servant.

The murderers, rapists, and numbers dealers are really quite low on the sovereign's priority list. The sovereign has figured out there will always be violent crime. But while the impression must be given to the populace that something is being done to provide protection, the truth is that such murders, rapes, and thefts merely become information equivalent to statistical computations. So as long as it doesn't get out of hand and encroach on something really important, the authorities are perfectly unflapped at having us maimed, robbed, and murdered.

This ultimately is no different from the art of war. Nations routinely spend the flowers of young maledom at an age when they're spunky enough to fight and dumb enough to want to do it. Wars have traditionally been fought for some of the stupidest reasons in creation. Like religion, for instance. Or then again, they can be fought for economic reasons. Like a recent war in Southeast Asia in which we engaged as a means of maintaining a productive economy. Our government was, of course, totally unconcerned about wantonly sending young persons to their deaths. After all, there were more important things involved. They've just never worried about individual life. You need only regard all these deals they've been making with extraterrestrials. Yes, I'm not kidding. The legitimate equivalent of *little green men*.

Such beings have been visiting our planet for millennia. With their transportation systems born of sophisticated knowledge of electromagnetic energy and antimatter. They've actually been arriving since long before the birth of history. The informed onlooker doesn't have to be a magician to make the necessary connections. The Aztecs described it as a flying serpent spewing fire. They called it Quetzalcoatl. Half bird, and half snake. A Chinese emperor told of having been taken into the sky to see the earth from a great height. Most sophisticated and primitive cultures alike possess a legend which is best equated with a visit from distant places. Even the Bible, in that most beautiful of books, Ezekiel, speaks with marvel regarding "the whirlwind from the north," and the prophet's "vision of four living creatures." The standard citizen suffers all variety of apprehension, vacillating between thinking our visitors nonexistent, benign, and menacing. The government prefers to have us believe that extraterrestrials are imagined. After all, such information could destabilize the population and make it aware of the existence of priorities before and beyond the ones distinctly related to the well being of the people.

You can therefore witness the presence of a hundred flying objects and you will be told it is a mirage. When government was less sophisticated, such stubborn witnesses were frequently put in asylums or lobotomized. But with the total control of global information systems, this is no longer necessary. Our citizens have become totally hooked on visual information. That is to say, the television. This being the case, they can be made to believe anything through effective control of that medium. In point of fact, the authorities have been in guardedly cordial contact with extraterrestrials for some time. There are deals which allow aliens to take human specimens for zoos, for research, and even for exercises in gourmet dining.

Bear in mind that of the intelligences which visit us, there are many different modalities. Some are peaceful. Others are warring. All are curious. For some, we represent an anthropological study. In certain instances, we are merely the prey in a typical hunting trip. For others, we are lunch. Because of my position in finance, I had access to bits and pieces of such things before I died. It became clear to me that the government was and is engaged in the study of dimensional intersection and travel, time journeys, and interstellar relations and communication. I am now, of course, fortified in my beliefs regarding parallel realities. But dead or alive, I continue to be offended by the frauds and hoaxes of officialdom.

Much to the chagrin of government, it still does not hold a candle to the biggest deception of all, which is to say religion. Here is yet another power which abhors nonconformity. All religions would like to re-create us in the image of their various texts and guidebooks. Such conversions render us manageable instruments of power. Mind you, these comments have nothing to do with my belief in God, which has always been there in time of need. But I'll wager I could even get a humble fellow to agree that if God had created religions, He would have done a better job.

Bozo has fallen asleep. He has a rather limited attention span. But this business of moving the rubber ball may actually become quite useful. There are wonderful rooms under this structure, and I want to introduce E.C. to their contents. There is also the matter of certain documents. With which very soon I intend to make a humdinger of a contribution to one of Gustavo's days. Yes indeed, I'll use that rubber ball to help me along with the next steps of my plan.

I became so engrossed in playing with the pooch I haven't noticed how very quickly time has passed. I must have fallen into one of those time warps in which hours seem like minutes. Very soon, E.C. and Susan should be arriving home from Rome. The servants have been advised, and seem to be scurrying around making things ready. Consuelo is finished with her duties in the kitchen and has just walked into the library with her arms full of roses. She's making two very large bouquets in the glass urns which are sitting on truncated wooden columns at each side of the entry doors. I don't mind following her around. You know, she's a lot of fun. A happy sort of person. Always smiling or singing as some of that fleshy mass palpitates to the rhythm. To be sure, there are other people here who arrange flowers, but I guess the woman just enjoys this respite from the usual. The dining-room table is in readiness for the lovers. More roses abound. They exude a wonderful fragrance. From the kitchen, the aroma of her flawless cuisine permeates the atmosphere. Smells of cinnamon and cloves. Into the main drawing rooms with a couple of other maids in tow. They're arranging an enormous spray of delphiniums flown in from Colombia. They definitely make a statement on the large round table in the foyer. Originally, I didn't have very much in this room. Considering my two statues of Sekhmet were designed to steal the show. But E.C. has softened things, and in a way, I approve. That table with its floral arrangement is beautiful and serene—a gentle touch in an otherwise very stern room. My lionesses like it as well. They have assumed that smug look of complaisance born of the expectation of a rich, tranquil evening.

The attendant at the gate has just notified the staff that E.C.'s cars are making their way toward the house. In a moment I hear the familiar sounds of automobiles outside. The great staircase is down, and through the doors come E.C. and Susan. I'm sort of thrilled to see them, even though I haven't been distant for very long. They're as I left them, of course. But with one exception: Susan is wearing those phenomenal clips E.C. gave her some hours ago. It's funny. You could almost say the earrings have added something to her demeanor. She seems more calm. More collected. And thoroughly composed. Extraordinary accouterments do this to women of style. Of course, if a person just doesn't have it, diamonds are a total waste, and pearls represent a parody. But when a woman has a great element of style implicit within her, a feather or a rhinestone, a jeweled compact or a fabulous bauble, just exponentially magnifies the *chic*. There's even a standard test for this type of situation. It's a simple one. A splendid creature can wear a good fake and everyone will think it's the real thing. But on someone who looks unsure of herself, even the genuine article will be suspect.

So Miss Cleave is looking smashing with yellow diamonds the size of peach pits afire on her ears. Complemented by stupendous pearls. After the usual greetings and questions, our man and Susan have retired upstairs to freshen up before dinner. When Bozo saw E.C., he curled that lip and came running so fast I thought he'd tear the carpet. The pooch was really delighted to see them. Something very nice has come across Bozo's countenance. He actually looks even more tranquil and confident now with E.C. back home. He's taking that rubber ball to him. But our man doesn't seem playful today. No wonder. Even though they were able to sleep on the flight, travel is always upsetting to the system. And now he has other cares. . . . E.C. and Susan have retired to separate bedrooms to shower and clean up. The superpooch has plopped himself down in the bathroom while E.C. is scrubbing.

I assume he'll be taking further steps tomorrow in the Siderurgica deal. If I'm to help him, I must now whip Bozo into shape. I think it's rubber-ball time again. My concentration has really improved regarding this type of thing. I can now move this toy so it does practically anything I wish. I'm making it look like Bozo is pushing the thing around. And E.C. is now out of the shower and has decided to participate in the game. I'm going to pull one of my extraordinary moves here and try to suspend the ball in midair after Bozo next drops it. That's it, good pooch. Now drop the thing so Uncle Henry can take it. Good! Good boy! I now have the little sphere firmly within my mind-grip, and I'm proceeding to raise it about two inches above the floor. E.C. is staring at it, and has totally paled. I don't want him to be frightened, so I'm going to quickly drop it and let Bozo grab it again. E.C. is gawking at Bozo and the ball as if he'd been struck by lightning. He's approaching the dog and seizing the little sphere with trepidation. Examining it very carefully. He's dropping it on the floor and allowing it to bounce. I'm now influencing the pooch to push the ball out of the bathroom, along the floor. Our man is definitely not about to let either dog or ball out of sight after his mind-boggling experience. So he's grabbing a silk robe and rushing after the two in bare feet. The Canine Supreme is now at the grand staircase, where with a little push, the sphere is merrily bouncing down the steps with dog fast behind. Through the great room, over the carpets, into the foyer. In order not to change directions too radically and scare E.C. out of his wits, I think I'll bounce this thing off the wall with billiardlike technique. There. It's going right through that little door down those granite stairs into the nether regions.

So here we are in the wine cellar once again. Bozo is standing in front of that stone mural. The fourth stone is again depressed, and the granite staircase pivots into sight. I'm having fun controlling the bounce down the thirty-three stairs to the room with the counting table and the red Bank of England chair. But today we're not stopping in front of the wall with the vault. Poochie and I are now squarely standing next to the far lateral wall. Bozo is following my directions expertly and pushing the ball against one of the baseboard stones. Again twice against another. Then once against this one, and once against the one in the corner. As a panel in the wall rises to reveal another great staircase, the entrance to this chamber we're in is sealed by the action of reciprocal force. Bozo knows the way, and is going first. Complete with rubber toy. As we now emerge into the great subterranean foyer, which contains doors to all of the various dependencies of my underground empire.

E.C. is dumbfounded by the height and size of the chamber. He's wandering down a passage to the generator rooms. A little farther, he's gasping at the perfectly preserved and sealed operating room. As the minutes turn into hours, he's wandering through vault after vault, where I have stores of almost everything you can imagine. There's the room full of freeze-dried food and nutritional aides. Including those very special iodine tablets which keep radiation from doing nasty things to you. And then, of course, there are the warehouses full of art objects. Not one of them inventoried as part of my estate, none of their whereabouts presently known. I bought them through European agents for cash and stealthily tucked them away over the years. There will be time to cue him in to the further treasures and secrets of this solitary domain. There is, however, one room I want him to learn about today.

Back in the great subterranean hall, I'm now having Bozo push the ball with confidence down the stairs at the end of the corridor. There are twelve filing rooms here chock-full of books, microfilms, microfiche, and information of all varieties, including cookbooks and mechanical manuals. The cabinets which contain documents all have the same combination. How will I now transmit this information to E.C.? I've got it. We'll bounce that ball again.

E.C. has caught on to the game and is intently looking at Bozo. "Hey, old man, now what do I do?"

First I'll get Bozo to select the correct cabinet. I must say, he's responding swimmingly today, as he walks over to the ninth cabinet against the wall and sits at attention.

E.C. is hot on his trail now. "Okay. So this is the cabinet. But how do I get in?"

I've got Bozo going for the ball again and throwing it into the air. The rest is easy as pie. I'll do three bounces first. One, two, three. Now Bozo can go for the ball again and throw it up once more. In this instance, I'll do nine bounces.

Our man is responding. "Hey, pooch, if this combination is three, nine, and something else, I think I'm going to church tomorrow. It's either that or the exorcist for you."

The ball is again airborne, and this time I'm outdoing myself.

After all, you've never seen a normal ball bounce seventeen times after a perfunctory throw. So here goes . . . one, two . . . fifteen, sixteen, seventeen.

Our man looks like he's getting ready to faint. He's sweating a bit. And now quickly approaching the cabinet. Just when I think he's going to put the disk into motion, he hesitates and says, "Right or left?" as he nervously looks at Bozo.

This is easy. I just command Bozo to move to the left side of the room. With this last gesture, we are turning that combination lock, which is clicking internally in joyous tandem to our little aura of communication. The lock turns into the final digits of its combination, providing the wonderful sensation such mechanisms impart when the tumbler stiffens as it moves perfectly into place.

The cabinet is now open, and our man is clucking and chuckling and patting Bozo on the head. Within, there is a file regarding Siderurgica which should very much open his eyes, and cause the implosion of at least a few comfortable existences. I'm exhausted. He's grabbing the portfolio and looking around, thinking he would rather not leave. But E.C. senses it's late, and wants to return to Susan. So dog and man are now up several flights of stairs, not without excitement. And back into that first little room with the necessary play of pivots and essential documents securely under arm. As he enters the grand foyer of the pyramid, my two lion goddesses are grinning broadly. So much that even E.C. has to look twice in order to ascertain his imagination is not playing rude tricks on him. Past my smug girls, up the stairs, and into the bedroom. The file is gently and expectantly placed on the night table. Where I'm certain it will soon become the object of further intense interest.

Our man has just realized he's been prancing around in a silk bathrobe and bare feet. Susan has knocked on the door, and is walking into the bedroom fully dressed and ready for dinner.

"My goodness, I'm tired too. But at least I had the stamina to dress. Is anything wrong?"

E.C. is toying with the idea of telling her about what he's just discovered downstairs. But I'm strongly suggesting to Bozo that he issue the tiniest of growls, which he promptly and accommodatingly proceeds to emit. Our man is now keenly tuned to my dog's responses.

"Actually, I am a bit tired," he says. "I must have dozed and forgotten all about dinner. Why don't you go downstairs and make sure the girls are ready for us. I'll meet you in the library for a drink in about fifteen minutes."

"Okay."

Now that Susan is gone, E.C. just can't contain himself and is quickly grabbing for the folder on the night table. Those powder-blue eyes are becoming crisper and clearer as they grasp the contents of this unique and most special of all archives. You see, these are the incriminating documents Von Richter surrendered prior to his rather timely demise. Here E.C. will find the scientific justification which renders the process both useless and dangerous. Glancing quickly at the underlined material, E.C. can't help noticing the red pencil under the following.

> After more than three months of continuous testing for metal fatigue, I have regretfully concluded that the spinning technology involved somehow weakens the molecular bond in a manner which is totally unsuspected, and defiant of testing until the thresholds referred to are reached, at which time the metal loses its elasticity, becomes brittle, and subject to fatigue and breakage (see graphs attached).

I do believe old Douglas is clucking under his breath there. He's looking up, as if to thank someone for this tasty shred of information. Well, kiddo, I'm right here! And you can thank me by thoroughly socking it to my reptilian friend Hooker, my prevaricating wife, and my treacherous nephew. Yes indeed, things are stepping up. E.C. is now putting that file in the dresser drawer, and proceeding to attire himself rather coyly for the evening. He's wearing a pair of baggy comfortable trousers with a velvet jacket and foulard. It's sort of a classy look, in spite of the fact I always thought ascots were a bit fussy. He's putting on a pair of needlepoint slippers which are old and charming. And bouncing down the steps with Bozo close at hand. Dog and man make an effervescent entrance into the library, where Cleave is neatly settled in front of the refreshment tray.

"No, no, Susan, I think I need a glass of champagne tonight.

Something rare and interesting, like perhaps a glass of vintage Dom Ruinart."

"Okay, boss. I'll have a bottle brought up from the cellar."

At the mention of the cellar, our man again looks like he's going to spill the beans, but restrains himself. This time without the benefit of Bozo's growl. She's back, and the champagne is on its way as well. Her look is quizzical. She's totally uncomprehending of E.C.'s joyous and buoyant mood.

"You know, if I didn't more or less know where you've been and what you've done for the last twenty-four hours, I'd think you'd hit the lottery or something."

"Actually, my dear, it's much better than that."

"Well, you don't seem like you're going to tell me about it, so at the risk of being unfeminine and indelicate, I'd like to say I'm hungry."

"Shall we bring the bubbly in with us?"

"Why not? I'm not in the mood for anything else tonight."

"Well, okay, champagne it is. And in point of fact, most appropriate."

"You continue to mystify me."

"That's all right. All will be revealed very soon. In the meantime, make a note that we have to place several very important calls tomorrow in this order: First, Don Orsini in Rome. Secondly, I must speak with Harry quite early tomorrow morning. Lastly, you need to make me an appointment with Harriet and Hooker for the day after tomorrow. Or better yet, make it for Thursday."

"Okay. As usual, your wish is my command. But aren't you going to give me a hint as to what's going on?"

"All I'll tell you is that I'm assuming control of your European stock portfolio tomorrow, my dear, in an effort to make you a few more pennies."

"Oh . . . Henry used to do that every once in a while as a special sort of gift. I never objected, and don't now. But what are you buying?"

"Just a few European steels."

"Oh."

As the couple walk down the hall toward that softly lit dining room, there is anticipation in the air. Tonight, the diners are confident, although a tad out of love. E.C. is full of energy, and thoroughly ready to go forward in every way. I, in turn, am tingling in every aspect of my being. No matter that somewhere there is a little gnawing pain. I must forget, and attempt to shed it, surrendering to the exhilaration of these moments.

Besides, in the distance it looks like a splendid dinner of baby flounder swimming in curry sauce. Not bad, if I do say so myself.

TWENTY-FOUR

IT'S ELEVEN O'CLOCK WEDNESDAY MORNING IN THE ETERNAL CITY. I'VE beamed myself over, in order to witness the European side of what I expect will be a memorable conversation. This is the day on which Don Orsini and Cardinal Tucci customarily have an early breakfast together. They've actually done this for years, but I had forgotten all about it. So I'm rather pleased and refreshed to find them together on Don Orsini's glassed-in veranda, with all of Rome beneath. I've also just realized that one of the more interesting aspects of my new existence is an understanding of foreign languages, very much as if they were my own.

"Ah, my friend, it is becoming a bit chilly now, isn't it?"

"Yes. Winter is ahead, but I must say it's a little warmer here than at the Vatican. Not quite so damp. Will you take a bit of an omelette this morning?"

"Yes, thank you. And do you have any of those little honey cakes you served me last time?"

"Ah, Tucci, always with that sweet tooth of yours. Talking about sweet teeth, were you able to keep our songbird in line?"

"I'm not sure, Orsini. You know, I tried very hard to keep her away from our American friend. But I fear her appetite has been whetted. Also, I sense some unusual form of attachment on his part which I do not understand."

"Would you like me to intervene?"

"No, no. You must contain yourself. After all, she is a national treasure."

"I must say, I reluctantly agree with you. Have you heard from our American friend?"

"No. But I'm confident he will be in touch. I have a strange feeling we have selected the correct candidate. A man of honor."

"Well, you and I have never had the same opinion of goodness . . . you think it's always an asset, and I think it can often constitute a liability. But we both agree honor is essential."

"What about the nephew?"

"As you know, we delivered the funds and took their entire portfolio as collateral. The matter is now basically in the hands of Mr. Douglas."

"Ah . . . if only Henry Somerset were here. Things would be different. You know, Orsini, he was a very vain man, with varied inner conflicts. A fellow often torn between different forms of pain, but nevertheless, special in many ways. I must say, I miss the wit, and the inventiveness . . . not to mention the humor."

"Do you think Douglas can fill the spot in our organization?"

"I don't know. It's a bit too early to tell. He has the attributes, and we've given him the backing. But how will he unravel this situation? After all, we're still committed to the other side to the tune of nine hundred million dollars."

"Yes. You know, this is the type of pickle in which someone like Henry would have known how to act and what to do. I can't help thinking of a line from Shakespeare. *Forces do I lack which Somerset did promise to supply.*"

"You with your Shakespeare. I always prefer Dante."

"Yes, I know."

A well-built middle-aged attendant who looks like he doubles on the bodyguard squad, and who's wearing a white waiter's jacket over his hardware, has just announced himself by gently tapping on the glass doors which separate the enclosed veranda from the palazzo. At Don Orsini's nod, he's entering and whispering something in his ear. The Don is nodding again, and the attendant is returning with the telephone and long trailing cord.

"It would seem, Tucci, that you are clairvoyant. No doubt, your connections with the world beyond . . ."

"You know I'm not allowed to speak about such things."

"It's a game we've been playing for years. You undoubtedly are aware we have our own intelligence. We know all about the children. And what's more, you frequently help us with your special knowledge."

"Yes. We know you have knowlege. But the time has never been really ripe for a full discussion. In spite of the fact that I highly value our friendship, and the frequent support of your organization."

"Well, Tucci, we both know there is a time for everything. In any event, I still contend you are using a sixth sense today."

"Why, what is it . . . ?"

"Somerset, I mean Douglas, is on the phone from the United States. I think we should attend him."

"Don't tell him I'm here, but convey my regards."

"Signor Douglas, good morning."

"Good morning, Don Orsini. Are you well?"

"Yes. Quite well, in spite of a bit of arthritis."

"Oh. I'm sorry. You know my grandmother used to take a mixture of vinegar and honey which she contended was very helpful . . . but I won't bore you with my kitchen medicine. How is the weather in Rome?"

"Actually, a bit chilly today, but crisp and clear. I am pleased to hear from you."

"Don Orsini, I must apologize for not calling sooner. I want you to listen very carefully to what I have to say. You recall those items the young man was buying, the ones he bought a bit too many of."

"Yes, yes. I follow you."

"Well, what I want you to do is to sell a similar amount for your own account."

Orsini's eyes are now wide open. "But you are talking about a very substantial sale which would affect the value of the situation."

"That's exactly what we're looking for. Establish the main position quietly and then sell a large amount so as to rip out the bottom. You will know when to cover."

With eyes now flat as slate, Orsini responds, "This can be arranged. What about our friends who might also have such items?"

"Get rid of them, and sell double beyond their holding. I unfortunately cannot directly do the same, but will see positive activity in the base company."

"This will precipitate a crisis with that young man if things go as you indicate."

E.C. is clearly containing his excitement. "You must have it all in place within the next forty-eight hours, before I proceed."

"Are you sure you can achieve this?"

"Yes, I'm now certain. By the way, our proxy seekers indicate certain nominee accounts have tendered their Siderurgica stock, for which I will be eternally grateful."

Now more relieved, the Don exclaims, "Ah. I'm so happy. These must be very good people to deal with. Incidentally, I saw my old friend the Cardinal the other day, and he told me to be sure to convey his regards."

"Yes, a very special gentleman. And with such interesting and beautiful guests at his dinner parties."

"I *do* know what you mean. But you must be careful, Mr. Douglas. Some of the most beautiful things in creation can sting or bite you very badly. Of course, I should not be providing advice."

"I am grateful. But do not be concerned. I am sturdy. I furthermore like the people I'm doing business with. I suggest you watch the newspapers. Incidentally, you don't intend to do anything earthshaking about that young man, do you?"

"No, no. Nothing terrible. Just a little reprimand. Remember, we in Italy always say, *He who is well born is grateful.*"

"You'll be amused to know I have a meeting day after tomorrow with the widow and her lawyer to press forward on the deal. I assume you will have your conversation with the young man sometime before that."

"Perhaps. Before, but not too far before. I must say, the other two will become, as we say, *like two scorpions in a bottle.* Good day to you, Signor Douglas, and thank you for the recipe!"

"You're very welcome, Don Orsini. Good day."

Click.

The old Cardinal is smiling in anticipation, waiting for a word from the Don, who has lapsed into a pensive moment after the phone call.

"So tell me, Orsini, what did he say?"

"It's rather unbelievable . . . he wants us to go short on steel stocks to the tune of the amount which Gustavo Somerset has bought, and even more."

"It's an enormous position, and there are great risks involved . . . can we trust this man regarding such a large amount?"

"You know we have always taken these risks together, your organization and mine. So the danger is somewhat diluted. We have decided to back Mr. Douglas. Furthermore, we have no alternative. Gustavo Somerset is a liar, a cheat, and a thief. He must be dealt with accordingly, but only after the matter is unraveled."

"So, Orsini, he wants us to go short . . . what else?"

"You will recall we had agreed that if something went wrong with the value of the Somerset account, we would ask Gustavo for the estate's Siderurgica stock in pledge. I assume from my conversation with Douglas there will be substantial news which will suppress the steel stocks within the next few days. Since the young Somerset is excessively leveraged, the value of the account will drop and we will be advised. I will call him and demand the additional collateral. He will have to go to the widow and the attorney to obtain it, or be totally discredited with us. I believe he will supply this. But all must be done very quickly, as Douglas meets with the widow late Thursday, and there will be news on the following Monday or Tuesday."

"Of course, Orsini, we defer to you in every way in matters of finance. Do with our interest what you may. Nevertheless, I would like you to keep me advised."

"Which I certainly will do. . . . Oh, one last thing. He did mention your nightingale."

"Ah, such a problem. She corrupts men."

"Well, perhaps we should just let it happen. We might as well know about his private and emotional stamina before he is fully admitted to the club."

"Orsini, perhaps you are right. But these are affairs on which I have some influence. So let me think further of what we might do. Ah . . . those little honey cakes, and hot as well."

I can't help chuckling to myself as the Cardinal puts forth his benign but grasping tendril to seize one of those deliciously hot little confections which have now found their way into his immediate presence. With a slight hesitation born of the smallest act of self-remonstration, he's grabbing for the butter spreader. Then, throwing all caution and guilt to the wind, he resolutely dips it into the butter. Which is being generously spread on the little morsel.

Don Orsini and Tucci spend a lot of time watching one another. But not as rivals are prone to do. It's more like a pair of musicians who've become accustomed to the bowings and fingerings. To the pianissimos, the rubatos, and the ad libitums. They watch one another with a kind of pleasure which is born of a very long association. Don Orsini anticipates the Cardinal's desire for that second honey cake, and the plate is under the Cardinal's hand a split second before the necessity makes itself fully evident.

"But tell me, Orsini, when do you intend to call Gustavo Somerset?"

"I thought I might do it now while you are present so you can hear the conversation. We shall wake him up, so to speak."

"You know, old friend, I need not be a witness to anything."

"No, no. I didn't mean it that way. I thought you might derive some pleasure out of hearing me make him squirm."

"You forget such things depress me."

"Ah, Tucci. Always the same. You the good one, and I the other."

"Well, I wouldn't exactly call you the other. I've always thought you have some very special qualities. Otherwise we would not have been friends for fifty years."

"And business partners, as well. I always wonder what others would think if they really knew the extent of our involvement."

"The people do not understand. Which is why His Holiness and we his servants must be the custodians of many secrets. After all is said and done, we must still keep those subterranean rooms full of secret documents which even occasionally refute some of our own dogma. Only the truly intelligent understand our importance through the ages as a civilizing force. It is true, much blood has been shed in our name. And to be sure, we are not proud of it. But neither are we ashamed. There are times when the sword must be taken up for what we believe to be a necessary cause. And the concept of necessity is of course measured by the state of the world and our capacity as an entity at any given historic moment. Now we are engaged in perilous times when mankind is losing contact with its more redeeming qualities. It is the function of the Church to attempt to reestablish man's contact with his divine inner self. And thus to put him a step closer to God."

"You really *do* believe, don't you, Tucci!"

"Of course I believe. Perhaps I do not believe He looks exactly as He's painted on the ceiling of the Sistine Chapel, but I believe. I am confident in goodness, and in the innate innocence of the spirit."

"You are fully aware I do not believe in that innocence."

"You would be surprised, old friend. I think the formidable Don Orsini is closer to God than he knows."

"We've had this discussion a thousand times, and we always end up in the same place."

"No. We always end up reaffirming once again that you are troubled. Of course, we are all disturbed, but by different things. You are disquieted because you have had to approach goodness from a rocky precipice. Whereas for me it has been easy—I've approached it from a field full of flowers. It does not escape me that perhaps yours is the more meritorious quest."

"You flatter me. Something you shouldn't do to people who know you well."

"No. I mean it. We are all sinners. Some with a purpose, some without a purpose. Some for almost justifiable reason, some for bad reason, and some for no reason."

"And Gustavo Somerset . . . what kind of a sinner is he?"

"I think he thinks he's a sinner for the reason of money, which would be a bad reason, but I personally feel he's a sinner for no reason."

"On this, Tucci, we agree. Let me call this sinner for no reason right now."

Don Orsini's gestures are almost feline in their restraint. One can tell this call represents an unpleasant activity. Yet, after an initial gesture best described as one of disgust, he's opening a little notebook, retrieving a number, and resolutely dialing it.

"Mr. Somerset . . . ?"

"Ah, yes."

"This is Orsini in Rome."

"Don Orsini, it's an honor to hear from you again."

"Thank you. I'm sorry to call you so early, but we have a bit of a problem."

"Oh . . . you must mean the slight drop in the steel stocks. There's nothing to worry about. I'm sure the market will correct itself."

"I am aware we are not yet at, shall we say, the threshold of pain . . . but should we reach the agreed value tomorrow or the next day, we will require additional collateral if we are not to liquidate the entire account."

"I don't know . . . you catch me quite by surprise. What do you have in mind?"

"The Somerset estate contains a large block of Siderurgica stock. Since this issue is known to us here in Italy, we would demand it be posted immediately upon reaching the danger zone. Of course, we would also accept cash."

"Cash is out of the question, and this isn't a decision I can make on my own. I would have to go to Mrs. Somerset and her attorney, Mr. Hooker."

"I am sure you do not wish to disappoint us, Mr. Somerset. I suggest you do this very quickly."

"I . . . don't know . . ."

"I must go now, Mr. Somerset. You may deliver the Siderurgica stock to our attorneys, who are well known to you. Good morning."

I'm really dying—I mean quite anxious—to see the boy's reaction to Don Orsini's tourniquet. So I'm going to leave these old friends and blink myself back to what is now the early morning at Gustavo's.

My nephew is sitting in his ultramodern apartment next to the telephone. In a cold sweat. He's wringing his hands the way he does when he becomes truly nervous. Now he's standing and pacing around in this cold apartment full of Barcelona chairs and tubular steel furniture. There's always something unpleasant about these very studied atmospheres where everything sits in its precise place. You get the impression that if you came home with an extra piece of bric-a-brac, you'd shatter the entire scheme. And therefore make the place less graceful and therefore ugly. Or uglier.

Gustavo is now looking blankly into the white marble Brancusi sculpture. After a while, he again walks over to the telephone and dials.

"Mrs. Somerset, please. . . . Aunt Harriet?"

"I'm worried, Gustavo. It's rather early and you only call me Aunt when you need something."

"That isn't true, but as a matter of fact I do need to speak with you quite urgently."

"Darling, can't it wait? I have appointments all day, and then this afternoon I'm due for a fitting. After that I'm off to dinner with Tom."

"It can't wait. And I really do have to see you, and it might as well be with Tom Hooker present."

"Gustavo, I don't like your tone. But if the matter is that urgent, you can have a drink with us at the office before we go to dinner."

"What time?"

"Say six-thirty."

"All right, I'll be there."

Well, good old Gustavo has really done it now. I've been wondering just how he's going to work himself out of this situation with Harriet and Hooker. I'm not sure I can wait until six-thirty for the fireworks. He's pacing around quite insistently accommodating his crotch. Nervously rearranging that thing between his legs which constitutes a pivot of his universe. Leave it to my nephew to give himself away at the least provocation.

The midafternoon is now upon us. While Gustavo fidgets, I think I'll look in on Harriet. When I tune in to someone, I never really know where I'll end up. It would seem I'm able to line up with the person's vibrations irrespective of the location. So here I am, at the couturier. In the fitting room at that! They're trying a rather slinky evening gown on Harriet which fits correctly in all the right places. Oh . . . seeing her like this does make me remember intruding into all those nooks and crannies. She's just asked the girl attending her for a telephone. It's been promptly brought. Those little fingers are dialing Hooker.

"Sweetie . . ."

"I always like it when you call me that, Harriet. Are we still getting together for dinner?"

"Yes, dear. But I think there may be some development. I received a call from Gustavo rather early this morning. I was in a rush to get to my appointments and the dressmaker, so I didn't call you then, but he was in a rather agitated state and insisted on seeing us today."

"Well, I wouldn't mind speaking with him as well, since there was some rather negative activity in the steel markets at the close of business today. You know, there are reasons for which we should watch this closely."

"Oh . . . of course you're right, but in any event, I told him to meet us at the office at six-thirty for a drink."

"Okay, I'll be waiting for you here. Bye-bye."

"Bye."

Click.

My very suspicious wife has acquired a particular look on her face which invariably takes hold when her rather acute feminine intuition smells a rat. Although right now it is not one of her most endearing aspects, I must say she always did have a very good instinct for bad business situations. She's experiencing that feeling now, and it's one which makes her feel uncomfortable. So she's cutting her fitting short once the evening gown has been fully attended to and leaving the suits for another day. The girl who's been pinning it here and there can't help providing her own observations.

"Oh, Mrs. Somerset, it looks so beautiful on you."

"Thank you, dear, it is rather nice, don't you think?"

"Oh yes, and I think it fits perfectly now. When will you be wearing it?"

"There's to be a special gala charity performance next week at the opera."

"And what will they be doing?"

"Well, I'm not much of an opera fan. My late husband used to adore it, though. But it seems it's going to be quite the event, since the soprano has taken ill and a rather famous singer has consented to make an unscheduled appearance."

"And who is that?"

"Oh, haven't you heard? It seems we are to be graced with the presence of the great Amalita Corsini!"

TWENTY-FIVE

I'VE REMAINED WITH HARRIET THROUGH THE END OF HER FITTING, AND the boring ride to Blackrock. When sitting in the rear of her car, she is especially cold and inscrutable. I'll bet that bit of negative intuition which intruded on her otherwise calm afternoon is gnawing and scratching at her insides. She is nevertheless seemingly calm. The only gesture giving her away is the nervous twirling of that wedding ring. When I see her in this mood I always remember the saying *May God deliver me from the still water, as I will save myself from all other.*

We've arrived. And she's walking through the lobby with the imperious demeanor of a grand duchess. Now into the executive office, where Hooker is sitting at the desk trying to make sense out of a financial statement. As she enters, he lifts his head and provides his usual reptilian smile.

"Well, you seem to be busy at work this afternoon."

"I was just going over the tax figures on the estate."

"That's a shame—that's work for bookkeepers and flunkies. You should be sharpening your pencil on the Siderurgica numbers. After all, you know we're supposed to meet with E. C. Douglas tomorrow to tender our stock and seal the bargain."

"Harriet, don't hector me this afternoon, please. It's been a rather rough day. I've been a little worried about the activity in the steel markets."

At this juncture, the conversation is interrupted by the intercom, indicating the arrival of Gustavo Somerset.

"Well, Gustavo's here. Did he give you any idea of what he wanted?"

"Actually not. But there was a sense of urgency in his voice which somewhat disquieted me."

"Well, we'll know soon enough."

Gustavo has unceremoniously entered the room. He looks terrible. Not his usual polished and well-coiffed self. There are dark circles under his eyes and he seems like he might be on the verge of tears. Furthermore, I'm sure he's been drinking.

"Hi, Aunt Harriet. Hi, Tom."

"It's good to see you, dear. I was meaning to call and ask for a report on our affairs. So when you rang me up a bit earlier, I was actually pleased."

"I have a great deal to say, and much of it isn't pleasant."

"Tom, maybe you'd better pour us a drink, if Gustavo is going to give us bad news. I'll have a vodka on the rocks, please. Is it about the portfolio, dear? Have you lost a few million dollars in today's drop?"

"Well, er . . . I don't know how to say this, so I'll just say it. When you dispatched me to Rome with the power of attorney to deal with the steel situation, I thought I might surprise you. So I bought some more steel stock and margined it as well. The result is that today's drop has put me in a situation where our entire account might be liquidated very shortly."

Harriet has blanched, as Tom Hooker takes control of the conversation.

"Gustavo, just how much additional stock did you buy?"

"It was about a billion and a half dollars' worth. I borrowed the extra nine hundred million from some people in Rome, and if we don't come up with either nine hundred million dollars in cash or some suitable collateral, they're going to liquidate us under the terms of the agreement."

Harriet is standing, and now fuming almost incoherently about what a thief and ingrate Gustavo is. Hooker is becoming cold, clammy, and beady-eyed, and prefers to ask questions before he jumps to conclusions.

"Tell me, Gustavo, when will we be in a position of being liquidated?"

"Tomorrow."

"And how much money do you need?"

"Nine hundred million dollars."

"Must it be cash?"

"Actually, that's a very good question, since the people who lent me the money are willing to take collateral well known to them in exchange for sustaining the position."

"What collateral?"

"They want the estate's Siderurgica stock pledged, in lieu of the cash."

"Well, Gustavo, I don't have to tell you Harriet is right. You are a liar, a cheat, and a thief. We're not swallowing your cock-and-bull story about wanting us all to be richer for one minute. You had it in mind to profit from this activity all by yourself, and now you're going to drag us farther into it."

Harriet is looking consternated and wide-eyed. After all, it's not every day she potentially sees nine hundred million dollars of her not-so-hard-earned money go down the drain. "Tell me, Gustavo, is there anything else we can do in this situation?"

"No. The loan carries my personal guarantee, as well as basically all of your ready cash. Not to mention repaying the indebtedness, which is such that it could cause some nasty problems."

Harriet and Hooker are looking at one another, trying to decide what to do. Hooker finally delivers his recommendation. "You know, Harriet, this is the worst of all possible situations. I don't want to become personal, because there will be a lot of time for that later, but I think it's essential we meet this obligation so the portfolio is not liquidated. I'm therefore going to recommend we allow Gustavo to pledge the Siderurgica stock temporarily until the market bounces back."

"But Tom, if we do this, and the market plunges further, we could lose our shirts."

"Harriet, I am very much aware of that, but it's unlikely the American steels will continue to drop."

"This is a terrible risk. Henry always told me never to risk my last cent on a gamble. It's something I really don't want to do."

"Harriet, I would like to personally bash in Gustavo's skull right now. And God knows I could use any one of these objects in sight, and do it with pleasure. But he has us by the nuts."

"He has *you* by the nuts. I don't have nuts, remember. And furthermore, I'm not so sure I wouldn't just rather lose the nine hundred million and call it quits."

This won't do at all. Harriet is actually exercising the prudent judgment which is the product of my many teachings. Not to mention that feminine intuition I spoke of earlier. I really do have to somehow draw her into the game or she's going to spoil it all. That's it, greed is her weakness. I'm going to do a heavy mind meld with Gustavo and get him to tell her what will happen if they win.

"But Aunt Harriet, look at it this way. Your downside potential is quite limited in terms of the historic pricing of these issues. You're not going to lose the Siderurgica stock. I just want to use it for collateral for a couple of weeks, or maybe less, until the steel stocks bounce back. When that happens, you're probably going to have an extra five hundred million dollars."

"I don't know, Gustavo . . . I have serious misgivings about this matter. Tom, what do you think now that you've heard my thoughts?"

"Look, Harriet, as I said, I'd rather not see this little bastard up here again. But right now, I don't think we have a great many choices."

"But what about E.C. Douglas? Here we've put together this very sweet deal, and now we're going to have to tell him it can't be done."

"We'll do nothing of the sort. When he comes tomorrow, you'll charm him with some of those feminine talents you always manage so well, and we'll delay until we can regain possession of the stock. That way, while I admit not without obstacles, we'll have our pie and our cake, and hopefully eat them as well."

"Even though I don't like this at all, I'm going to defer to your judgment on this one occasion, and agree to give him the Siderurgica stock."

Gustavo has been sitting motionless, sweating profusely like the lamb who mistakenly entered the Turkish restaurant. Now he's looking a bit relieved, and putting a finishing touch on the matter. "Actually, Aunt Harriet, I'm telling you that when the market bounces back, we're going to make hundreds of millions of dollars we had not thought of earning before."

"Gustavo, you're repeating yourself and furthermore, don't try to fool me. You never intended to give us a share of that money. We're only hearing about it because you need the pledge of the Siderurgica stock. I'm wiping you out as a signatory on the affairs of the estate. You should consider all your corporate privileges revoked pending further developments. Tom, when can you have the papers drawn so we can be through with this messy business?"

"First thing tomorrow morning."

"We also have to devise a strategy for tomorrow's meeting. Why don't we just say we've been held up by the Department of Treasury on the matter of estate taxes."

"That sounds good, Harriet, but how do you propose to delay him afterwards?"

"Leave that to me. I understand Mr. Douglas is a widower. And I just happen to be connected with a very socially correct opera gala occurring next week."

"In any event, Aunt Harriet, I'm very, very grateful for the support."

"Gustavo, you're not talking yourself back into my good graces. Tom and I both detest thieves. Get out of here, and don't let me see you around the house again."

My nephew is leaving with his tail between his legs. But nevertheless happy. The truly puny are never cowed by the pusillanimity of their actions when these weaknesses can be said to produce financial gain or relief. Such is the case with Gustavo, who, now out of the building, is actually looking relieved and happy. I can't say I feel a bit sorry for the other two.

Back at the office, Harriet and Hooker are sitting there in shock.

Staring at one another rather bitterly, and drinking vodka on the rocks.

"Harriet, I didn't mention it earlier, but I'm surprised to see you having straight vodka. You usually stick to lighter drinks. Besides, it's not good for your blood pressure."

"My blood pressure be damned! It's not every day I'm in danger of losing nine hundred million dollars. Besides, my blood pressure is rising anyway. I might as well enjoy the drink."

"It's not as if you worked for the money. Did you take your pills?"

"Sometimes you really irritate me. I'll have you know, I worked for every cent of that money. I put up with Henry's eccentricities, ill humor, and affairs. And furthermore, I put up with love, at least at the beginning. I've always thought it a thankless emotion. Something which I've confirmed in my relationship with you. And yes, thank you, I did take my pills."

"There's no need to become nasty."

"I'm not nasty, just truthful. I feel myself entitled to every red cent that's coming my way. And watch my words, if you don't protect me in this matter, I'll personally cut your balls off."

"You know, my dear, you're always so delightfully direct. But remember, this isn't a problem of my creation."

"It is now, so watch Gustavo very carefully."

"Sweetie, you know I'm going to do it."

"Don't sweetie me. And incidentally, I'm developing a headache and definitely don't want to go to dinner."

"How about a little something else?"

"What do you mean?"

"Well . . . I was sort of thinking of a little tumble in bed."

"Don't even dream about it until you return my money safely again. Back where it belongs. How could you possibly think I could be in the mood?"

"Okay, okay, I give in. But don't focus your anger on me."

"I'm not angry at you, I'm just worried, and ill."

With this comment, Tom Hooker gets to see Harriet's creditable ass moving away from him, and out the door.

I have to admit the woman is always somewhat unnerving to me.

So hermetic, so perfect. Totally paranoid. Which makes her dangerous. Whenever she thinks herself attacked, you can count on her for
a substantial reprisal. She also knows how to play sick. I've always
thought people are attracted to one another because of their weaknesses, as opposed to their strengths. I, of course, was also quite the
paranoiac. So it was logical that when I met Harriet, I would be very
taken with the mirroring of many of my own insecurities and doubts.
In that beginning, we were reciprocally congratulatory. Which is
what two self-respecting paranoiacs are likely to be. Also, since Harriet is quite intelligent, I enjoyed the mental sparring. But who was
to think the Ping-Pong game would never end, and one would eventually grow weary of having to constantly protect one's intellectual
positions.

As we grew to know one another's weaknesses and complexes,
we learned to play them as fine instrumentalists will play a violin or
a cello. At first it was fun to catch one another at the game. For
example, quite frequently I would surprise her doing something
which I thought was less than morally correct. Like, let us say, flat-
tering me. Upon my pointing it out, she would of course be forced
to make the admission. But her manner of acknowledging the trans-
gression was the clever part. She would take it to sort of an intense
reduction to the absurd, and say, "Oh yes, you're right, Harriet is
very evil indeed." The trick is coy, because it forces you to come back
and say, "Oh no, no—you're not very evil, just a bit naughty." In
doing so, of course, she just got you to partially disclaim your own
initial statement. We referred to this as "game two thousand four
hundred and thirty-one." As you can see, there were many others.

The most phenomenal game of all had to do with the withholding of sex. I've always been a horny bastard. Even now, disembodied
and all, my thoughts often turn to the realm of hanky-panky. Once
she realized how badly I needed this form of exercise, she held another trump card firmly in hand. By withholding sex, she could establish dominance. It was always unclear to me what the final goal of
this game was, since I often surmised she would have been unhappy
had the Pavlovian conditioning ever been complete. Of course, I have
to be careful. This last conclusion might represent a bit of wishful
thinking. I cannot entirely discount the truly devastating alternative.

She might in point of fact have desired a splendidly conditioned robot. The perfectly programmable husband and lover!

I have to say, though, beneath the beautifully groomed exterior, there is a very screwed-up little girl who occasionally lets go, and wants to have it unremittingly thrust up her ass. She enjoys every moment of it. And would afterward hate you enough to kill. I almost came to believe she had the type of personality that could snap at any instant. Toward the end of our relationship she started accusing me of the damnedest things. I'll never forget the morning she looked in the mirror and thought her hairline was receding. That time I was accused of putting something in her shampoo so her hair might fall out. My response was very simple: "Is that what you would do to me?" And of course, there was the usual silence after a riposte which had reached home. There's actually an old saying which fits the situation nicely. It is said that *the thief judges all things by his own condition*. I always thought a mentally ill person like Harriet could cause a lot of damage if painted into a corner.

I've beamed myself back to Pyramid Hill, where E.C. is having an evening by himself. The phone is ringing. It's Cleave. Something or other about having dinner with an old girlfriend, and then going home to bed. Our man is looking particularly handsome this evening with bare feet in exquisitely stitched black ostrich loafers. I picked the right guy here. Take these shoes. They're exactly like any regular cheap penny loafer. No change in detail or design to give away the luxury of the exercise. Ten feet away from the onlooker's gaze, they are as any similar shoe would be. But up close they're very special in every way. The skins are beautifully matched to show all of those places where the ostrich's feathers left their mark. The stitches are tiny and perfectly straight. As his bare foot releases one of them you can appreciate the extremely soft calf lining.

Something is troubling E.C., though. He's been reading a book. What is it he's absorbing tonight? Hah! Our man is reading Pascal. One of my favorite authors. Particularly the *Pensées*. He's reading that part which says *when our passion leads us to do something, we forget our duty*. I have a feeling he is sensing the imminence of his further involvement with Amalita. And he's wrestling with the possibilities. I can't help wondering why it is we're always attracted to people who really aren't very good for us, and to the evil things which can at times seem so divine. Harriet always contended people had made too much of the whole Garden of Eden scene. Her viewpoint was quite simple—she always said evil had been much maligned in the bargain. Since there was no evidence to assure us that Eve would not have tempted the serpent in the absence of his doing it first.

In any event, man and dog are quite introspective tonight. He's climbing the stairs, and making his way to the final level by means of the small elevator. This takes them up to the flat terrace at the top of my structure. From this parapet the moat and surrounding gardens are visible in the serenity of the night. He's looking into the sky. There's a bit of a moon tonight. And in this most transparent portion of the air, we're able to see an occasional shooting star. He's pacing now, and Bozo's following. I've got to understand the problem. Maybe I can help. He's looking the pooch straight in the eye. And saying only one word, but repeating it. The word is "why." Bozo tries to slurp him with a big, wet tongue. He's talking out loud to the pooch. I haven't heard him do this before. But it's quite interesting inasmuch as I don't usually have access to his waking thoughts.

"Hey, boy, I need your help. You know, I think we're all possessed by the spirit of Henry Somerset. And I don't know if I like that or not. I'm not sure I want to take the final steps and go through with Siderurgica. Yet there's a force within me that's pushing. And you seem to be a part of it. I'm confused. And the other thing is, I know Cleave would be good for me. But I want very badly to be with Amalita. This woman drives me crazy. Besides, it's almost as if my wife had reincarnated. It's the same look, the same body. I don't sense the same sweetness, though. But this too is attractive. The woman seems dangerous, and I like that. And then there are these creeps: Harriet Somerset, her attorney, and her nephew. Dangerous people with whom I must deal. Bozo, I want to be myself. Not someone else. I need a release. What to do, old bean? What to do?"

The pooch is taking one look at our man. And with empathy more remarkable than I might readily attribute to him, he's lifting his majestic head in the direction of the moon and emitting a series of phenomenally loud and blood-curdling howls. *AOwww. AOwwww.*

AOwwwww. Our man is smiling, and readily taking the cue. As he lifts his head, not quite as comfortably as Bozo, and also howls at the moon. I'm sitting here on the granite watching dog and man singing in tandem. Thinking perhaps I'm pushing things a bit too far. After all, look at him. I may not be doing any good with all of this. He's looking a bit unhinged. What if I'm really screwing things up every bit as effectively as I did while I was alive? But no, I can't think about this now. He'll be fine, I'm sure of it. And I shall have my revenge.

Talking about going crazy, and sitting here listening to them howl at the moon, I've been able to remember just a hair more about my last day of life. You'll recall that it eluded me completely when I first woke to the state of death. Now I've remembered something very important. I recall having overheard Harriet and Hooker speaking that day in the south conservatory, where the potted palms grow together with the other tropical exotica. They had repaired to the company of our botanical babies in the hope of somehow eluding my relentless surveillance. It didn't do them any good, though. I was immediately cued to their disappearance. The conversation is coming back as if in instant replay. Harriet was wearing that bright red suit with the short jacket. And Hooker was sweating profusely. No wonder. I now recall it perfectly, but why just now . . . ?

"There just isn't anything else to be said, Tom. I think he's been putting things in my food and cosmetics. It's either me or him. And I certainly have no intention of giving this life-style away."

"Be quiet, Harriet. Someone will hear you. Remember, you're the wife, and he loves you, so you can't go to jail as easily as I. Besides, if he gets wind of anything, he'll break us both."

"I'm telling you, Tom, it's going to be very, very easy."

"How's that?"

"Actually, you're going to love it. You see this little bush here."

"It's hardly little, Harriet. It must be fifteen feet tall."

"Well, being around Henry, one becomes a master at the art of understatement. In any event, look at these lovely large green leaves. You see how they have all these points."

"So what, Harriet? It's a plant. Have you gone completely daffy?"

"Not at all. You see, I've learned something about some of Henry's toys. This one, to use his own word, is a *humdinger*."

"Why?"

"You see, this plant is called *Ricinis communis*. But in spite of its name, there's nothing common about it. The little gray speckled seeds contained in those green pods where the new leaves are being formed are incredibly deadly. Six or seven of them will easily kill a grown man. In fact, Tom, in India when a woman wishes to kill her rival's cow, she dips her nails in the liquid which is squeezed from them and merely sinks her nails into the beast. I assure you, it promptly dies."

"Harriet, you're crazy. You're talking about *murder*."

"It's either him or us."

"I don't know . . ."

"Just leave it to me."

"How would you serve it?"

"That's the difficult part. It would have to be in something spicy, but cold, since I understand heat deactivates the poison."

"Would he die quickly?"

"No. That's the beauty of it. He'll contract a fever, and it'll last for several days. His body will excrete most of it. Then there will be complications and he'll kick the bucket. The masterful part is, by that time it will be practically undetectable."

"Harriet, you're incredible."

"Henry taught me a lot."

How could I have forgotten what I heard hiding behind the bamboo palms that afternoon? It's all coming back to me. And with it, waves of sadness and anger. I knew she had grown to hate and fear me, but one never really wishes to confront such feelings squarely. It's always terrible to face the realization that a loved one would murder you. I now recall, once they left that afternoon, I walked into the garden, sat by the goldfish pond, and wept. I cried so hard I thought I'd die. Then I went home to watch for the lethal blow. That's about as much as I can remember about that day right now. I know I need to retrieve more, but just can't at this moment. I guess Harriet and Hooker eventually *did me in*. And with my own beautiful castor-oil plant. I shouldn't be surprised, though. After all, it's always been said that *he who breeds buzzards shall eventually have his eyes picked out*. But why do I keep thinking there's more I must remember? I must put such thoughts aside. And I've got to stop this howling at the moon and place E.C. back on the right track. I must fire his imagination with something wonderful and unique. Something linked to the passions of men and the love of women. I know just how to do it, too. But first, I must motivate Bozo for a little more exercise in my suite of underground rooms.

I'm trying to insinuate myself into my dog's mental state by whispering into his ear. Now he's following me again. We're on our way back downstairs, with E.C. fast behind. Into the elevator, down to the first level, bounding over the gigantic carpets, past the statues of Sekhmet, now looking quite stern. Down into the nether regions. Past the pivots and through the walls, then to the end of the corridor, into a very tasteful little reading room done in Louis XVI style. It's really the type of room which shouldn't be here. But I've always liked these little incongruities. It has a center table with various rare books on it, and a chandelier above. Around the table in the various corners of the room are very comfortable chairs for reading. But I have a very special purpose in bringing him here tonight. Into this singular room which was built around my need for a special *prop*.

You see, dangling innocuously among the quartz teardrops of that lovely chandelier is the Moguk Diamond. I have to congratulate myself for the placement. Like many of my tricks, it requires knowledge and deciphering. Bozo is now sitting at attention with his ears erect waiting for my next command. By now, E.C. has learned to watch and listen when Bozo does his tricks. That's right, old boy. Jump up on the table. Stand up on your hind legs, and rip that one off. No, no, you've got it wrong. It's the one next to it . . . that one. Attaboy, attaboy. With some minor clatter, Bozo has fetched the teardrop from the chandelier and is now off the table depositing it, slobber and all, between the now seated E.C.'s legs. Actually, smack in his crotch. E.C. is too savvy to take anything for granted in this realm. He's grasping the drop. All one hundred and twenty-nine carats of it. Yessiree, it hasn't escaped him that this is one of the most phenomenal diamonds of all times. Complete with murky romantic history. You see, it's been said it was once the holy relic of an old, fearful Asian religion. Our man is becoming rather wild-eyed. I'm suggesting to him the various ways in which this bauble could radiate light under the heave and swell of Amalita's hard, ripe breasts. So, we have the woman, and we now have the diamond. It's just a matter of properly introducing them.

TWENTY-SIX

On a cool fall day, the wind whips through St. Peter's Square and the Vatican with the type of chill which presages a damp Roman winter. Cardinal Tucci has just arrived at his offices, where the usual panoply of affairs awaits him. That young priest with the curly hair, the one who fits so nicely in his habit, has just brought old Tucci his cup of fortifying espresso. As he sips and regards the wind lifting the leaves in the garden below, he is interrupted once again by the comely attendant. There's a whisper which elicits the response "Ah, Don Orsini." With this exhalation completed, he picks up the telephone receiver.

"Orsini? . . . *Bene*, good morning. How are you, my friend."

"I am concerned. Today is Thursday and the steel markets have continued to drop. Naturally we are protected by the guile of our American friend, who has so providently instructed us to remain short."

"So then what is the problem? Certainly we have no financial exposure."

"The difficulty is not financial, but personal."

"How can I help you?"

"Oh . . . I'm not the one you have to help. It is our American friend who will very soon require assistance, and I do not know quite how to deal with it. You see, Amalita is on her way to the United States to give an unscheduled benefit performance of *La Forza del Destino*. Need I say more?"

"This is very serious, and could also compromise our business situation. She could very well rip his emotions apart thread by thread, and then weave them again into the very material of self destruction. How could this information have escaped me?"

"I myself just heard a few moments ago. You know, Tucci, you are always so poetic. But I'm afraid what is required now is not poetry but action."

"No, no, Orsini. Please, not your type of action. I beg you to be prudent. We both know she can do a great deal of damage, but I will avert this crisis. I will fortify him personally."

"How do you propose to do that, considering you are in Rome, and she is at this very moment on her way to the United States?"

"We will use our resource. I will consult with . . . er . . . a higher . . . another . . . authority . . . and then if necessary I will travel. I promise you I will attempt to save the day. Incidentally, what happened with that transaction?"

"You will be very amused to hear the Somerset block of Siderurgica stock was posted with our attorneys in America as additional collateral earlier in the day. There was no further protest. In fact, if the market continues to slip, we may be in a position to require even further collateral."

"What do you have in mind?"

"Perhaps the guarantee of the estate."

"If that occurs, they will be ruined if the market continues to slip."

"Yes, I know."

"Well, Orsini, this matter must unfold as it may. As always, I leave it in your able and very calm hands. My people here will advise you as to my travel plans. In America, you may reach me as usual. God be with you."

"And with your spirit . . ."

Click.

Tucci is returning the receiver to its cradle with the delicacy of a demolitions expert setting a charge. He's staring blankly into the large portrait of Saint Lawrence suffering his martyrdom on a grid. After what seems an almost interminable instant of introspection but not repose, he rings the bell. Which again brings one of his secretaries into the inner office.

"Albani, bring me the Special Key."

"Yes, Your Eminence."

"And alert the guards I will be descending into the catacomb for a few moments."

"Your Eminence, if I may, you know such visits are often unsettling to you. . . ."

"But today I must. There are some things which I have need of understanding. So please call them."

With these words from the Cardinal, Monsignor Albani has unlocked the cabinet, and has handed a large and very heavy key to His Eminence, not without what I detect is a note of quiet resignation. After the Monsignor calls security, the two of them walk briskly through the halls and down a small staircase, which is taking them to a tiny foyer in which stand two armed guards. This is actually very interesting. I'm wondering what in the world could take so important a man into this setting in the basement of the Vatican when he's just getting ready to embark on an important trip. In any event, the guards have used a key on the elevator and the two men are now entering the cab. This is a very curious little lift. By the length of time it's taking, I can tell we are descending into the caves deep beneath the Holy City. Eventually the elevator stops. We have arrived at what appears to be a large subterranean hall.

It's not what I would have expected at all. It's well lighted, and there is a magnificent marble floor with a beautiful design. There's an eerie clicking as the two men walk across the surface for three or four hundred feet, until they reach a small door, which is also locked. Monsignor Albani uses a key on this door. Within, there is a small foyer guarded by two priests in dark cassocks. Strangely enough, they too are armed. I'm wondering what kind of treasure is being kept here deep in the recesses of the Vatican. And why it requires such extraordinary security. As the large key is inserted into the keyhole, I am dead behind the Cardinal. I want to follow, but some power is keeping me out of this room. As he steps aside to enter, to my great surprise, I see a delightful and well-lighted room, full of toys and children at play. Attended by aged nuns and a couple of old priests who seem to be blind. Near the entrance, a child almost squarely faces me and smiles. But to my great surprise, I notice this child has something very wrong with his eyes, which are entirely white. As the door closes, it dawns on me that these are the famous clairvoyant children. The ones the Vatican keeps in secrecy and would never make the object of an admission. As I wait for Tucci to emerge, I can't help noticing the wall above the doorway. It's full of crosses, icons, and sacred relics.

After what appears to be an awfully long time, but actually hasn't been, Tucci and Albani are leaving the room and carefully locking the door. The Cardinal looks worn and troubled. He's a degree or two paler than when they entered. As they return to the elevator, the Cardinal is again speaking:

"Albani, we must move with haste today."

"Your Eminence . . ."

"All appointments must be canceled for the next four days. Speak to the people in transportation and see if they can charter a supersonic for us as soon as possible."

"Where are we going?"

"To America. All must be done very quickly. Advise Archbishop Fromaggio of our arrival, with the usual notes of prudence, since this is not a state visit."

"And what reason should we give the American authorities for your presence?"

"You will tell them our visit is an unofficial one in furtherance of the Italian arts. Also, advise Fromaggio I will be using the Church's box at the opera while I am there. You will accompany me as well as Altieri, Pietro, and Salvatore. In addition, I now require very quickly the Holy Office's confidential file on Amalita Corsini."

"I will deal with everything."

"Thank you."

The Cardinal is again alone. This time looking less sprightly. As if he has suddenly begun feeling his age. It's almost as if the little whirlwinds down in the garden had recently penetrated his whole body and chilled him. For a moment, he looks very weary. Then he stares at the picture of the saint again, and becomes imbued with an almost otherworldly light, which stiffens him as it affirms his resolve. He repeats to himself: "Yes, I must travel, I must go."

I'm back in the United States. It is now late afternoon. And E. C. Douglas is again entering the now familiar ramparts of Blackrock. It's a rainy day, but Szilagyi has provisioned himself with one of E.C.'s excellent British umbrellas. This one has an ivory handle and a little gold plaque with "E.C.D." on it. He sees our man to the door and then returns to the waiting car. The entrance to Blackrock has become somewhat wet and dirty from the water being carried in on people's shoes. This time the elevator ride is relatively without incident. Our man is, however, chuckling as he remembers the urchin and the fat lady from his last ascent. Now he's into the eightieth-floor foyer in an equally uneventful manner. This time he's immediately escorted to the executive suite, where Harriet and Hooker are waiting, and looking unusually friendly. This is, of course, the look which the rock python assumed when it had the rabbit to dinner. Harriet is impeccably dressed today, wearing a little knit suit which quite appropriately mimics the black and brown spots of a leopard. Tom Hooker is looking slightly less confident, but is altogether and disgustingly affable. Our man has immediately sensed this new element, and has stiffened a little as if to protect himself from the imminence of great danger.

"Mr. Douglas, I'm so happy to see you again. I must say you are looking quite dashing in that light gray suit. Don't you think so, Tom?"

"Why yes, Harriet, I think we'll have to ask our friend to share the name of his tailor. You know, it's late in the afternoon. And considering all this business we're going to be doing we might as well have a little drink. How about it?"

"Actually, that would be very nice. Do you have a little vodka and ice?"

"Of course. Harriet, why don't you do the honors. You know, she isn't exactly domestic, but she is very decorative."

"Well, Mr. Hooker, I wouldn't know about the first item, but I can attest to the second. Getting down to a bit of business, my agents indicate you have not tendered your Siderurgica stock as we had agreed. Is there a problem?"

"Actually, we do have a slight difficulty which is causing a bit of delay, but it's nothing we won't be able to deal with. Allow me to explain. . . . As you know, the Somerset estate is a multibillion-dollar situation. The Siderurgica stock constitutes a substantial part of that inheritance. Since we assumed our affairs would move more quickly, we neglected to mention the stock had been pledged to the Treasury Department to guarantee death duties. We will very shortly be in the position of liquidating these taxes. We had of course hoped all this would happen sooner. But unfortunately, it hasn't yet, so we find ourselves in a very embarrassing position. We need another two weeks, perhaps three to be safe."

"Well, I thought we had a deal here. You are undoubtedly aware this will cause me substantial inconvenience. Not to mention the expense."

"What would you suggest we do, Mr. Douglas?"

"Why don't we complete the other half of the deal. I can sell you the rights to Von Richter's process and the American steels as well. This will provide me with some ready cash, which would be very convenient, given your delay."

"We understand, but . . . are you in a position to deliver the American steels without gaining control of Siderurgica?"

"I already have control of Siderurgica. We have acquired the European block as well."

The cat is now out of the bag. Harriet and Hooker look as if lightning has just struck them. Their advantage is now gone. The next thing they're expecting is for E.C. to request a reduction in price. But he's not going to do it, and of course I know why. The whole thing is taking a very clever turn. Hooker is jumping the gun and speaking first. "If you are, in fact, thinking of reneging on the deal, I really don't think that would be advisable. Since even with our delay, we will be in substantial compliance."

"No, Mr. Hooker, I haven't thought of that at all. But considering I'm behaving like a gentleman in the matter, I don't think you could object to a penalty clause in the event of nondelivery of the stock."

"Well . . . we had not thought about that, but I suppose it's something we might do."

"I'm thinking of twenty percent."

"That's a great deal of money."

"Those are my terms. I'm sure you can handle them."

Harriet has been quietly observing the volley, and is now stepping in to exercise her charms. "I guess you have us somewhat over a barrel, Mr. Douglas. I'm going to agree to some of your terms, but you must do me a little personal favor in exchange."

"And what is that?"

"Well, you see, I'm involved in a gala benefit at the opera. And I would ask you to take a box next to ours for the sake of the charity. The papers will be full of it tomorrow morning, since Amalita Corsini will be singing with an all-star cast."

E.C. is electrified at the revelation of Amalita's onslaught, and quickly responds. "Yes, of course. I agree to your very pleasant terms. Why don't you have your secretary call Miss Cleave at my office for a check at the first hour. Then it's all decided. We will both honor our bargains regarding the purchase and sale of the Siderurgica stock. I will grant you two weeks to make delivery, and you will on this Monday go through with the other half of the deal, and the sale of Von Richter's process. We'll attach a penalty of twenty percent for noncompliance. And lastly, I will enjoy the pleasure of your company at the opera. Good enough?"

"Well, from where I stand as a lady, twenty percent seems a bit harsh. Would you deny me the benefit of ten percent?"

"Fifteen."

"Done."

"Very good. Now I can enjoy this drink you served me. Tell me, Mrs. Somerset, have you been out a great deal since your husband's death?"

"Well . . . not really, but I would like to start showing myself again."

"I must be leaving, but I'm sure, with all respect, wherever you do that, you will cause a pleasant stir."

With this comment, E.C. has put his glass down, is shaking hands, and is now off into the outer corridors. Harriet and Hooker are left to their conversation. To which they affix themselves with zeal:

"You know, Harriet, sometimes I think you go a little too far. The way you crossed your legs and all. Why do you think he did it?"

"Well, I don't think it was because I crossed my legs, and I don't understand why he didn't make us reduce the price per share. You could have knocked me over when he told us he had acquired the European block. I don't understand, and I must admit, I'm very curious."

"I hope you know we'll be close to ruin if we're unable to go through with this deal."

"I am fully aware. It's a position which makes me feel incredibly uncomfortable. So much that it forces me to consider a fallback position."

"And what is that?"

"I may have to do something I haven't done since I was a young girl. I may, in fact, have to go big-game hunting again."

"Well, I'd be careful if I were you. He's not an idiot. And furthermore, remember you're the one wearing the spots today. Incidentally, did you notice the strange look on his face when you mentioned the opera? I thought that was rather curious."

"I did too. Do you think it was the opera or the singer?"

"I don't know, but perhaps you should investigate."

All this conversation about leopard spots and investigations is really rather amusing. And it has been said *a turbulent river inures to the benefit of fishermen*. But I think it's time to look in on E.C., who is now well on his way to Pyramid Hill. To be sure, knowing the two of them, they will continue bickering about what has just happened for the next forty minutes or so.

I've blinked myself back to the gardens surrounding the edifice. If I walk about half a mile down the hill, I can enter the maze of evergreen bushes which many think I created for the sheer pleasure of watching others get lost. Mazes are wonderful things. I don't rightly know who devised them originally, but I got the idea for this one in England. The trick here consists of having varied all the angles ever so slightly, so once you're deep into it, you never know where you really are. Sort of like life. When you reach the center, there are benches. Good cedar ones. The type you could sit on for the greater part of the day without really feeling uncomfortable. There's also a birdbath. So here I am in the late afternoon watching the water trickle through the hole drilled in the small boulder. Which sits in the middle of the fountain in the center of my maze. It's chilly here. But being disembodied as I am, I shouldn't feel the cold. I think what I'm perceiving is another type of "frost." It's the frigidity born of knowing something is awry. There are now three women in E.C.'s life. One of them wishes to possess his soul and enslave it. Wondrously capable creature that she is, there is more than a good chance she might achieve her goal. Harriet, who is the second, merely wishes to acquire his money, which is in many respects for her very much like enjoying the continuation of my money. And of course she's delighted in this luxury for a considerable period of time and is not about to give it up without a fight. The last is Miss Cleave. All she wishes is his affection. I'm wondering what I might do if I were faced with electing one of the three. I guess the child in me would try for having them all. But I don't think you can love someone if someone else owns your soul, and giving Harriet the money would also involve some serious compromises with the dark side. Not to mention an eventual loss of self-respect.

I remember the feeling quite well. As my marriage with her matured, and I realized there was a difference between marrying for love and acquiring a husband, I began to feel incredibly despondent. I recall our fifth anniversary. I had prepared a romantic evening. The bracelet I had ordered made was going to be delayed for a few days, because of some unavoidable catastrophe in the craftsman's life. Without a further thought I had a beautiful nosegay of my favorite flowers prepared for her with a touching card. I'll never forget when I arrived home and presented it, she icily exclaimed, "How nice," and proceeded to acquire a headache for the remainder of the evening. Obviously, she had expected a more valuable gift, and interiorized her anger with that migraine. In her own way, though, Harriet admired me. And it might even be said that in my absence life has been more difficult for her. After all, everyone wants a husband who comes home with diamond necklaces and provides the type of security chil-

dren expect from their daddies. But there is a great difference between wanting and needing this security, and being in love with the
man himself. Of course, Harriet is the type of woman who can propel
a husband to new heights through her Byzantine kniving and social
climbing. And in this sense, it may even be true such a woman can
be good for a man. But when money is the cheapest thing you have,
it really can't be said that acquiring more is of any benefit. And there's
absolutely nothing in it for the soul.

On the other hand, E.C. could also deliver himself to Amalita
Corsini, never to be recognized again. This would, in many respects,
be the least sensible but most understandable of mistakes. Sort of like
when a digger wasp approaches a spider, which after being neatly
examined and immobilized becomes the host for the wasp's progeny.
The sting only hurts for a moment, and doesn't kill the poor dumb
arachnid. It merely stuns it so the fatal egg can be laid within the
host, and later the digger wasp's baby can feed on its insides. Being
gorged on daily in a feast of lustful togetherness. Until, totally consumed, it gives birth to the spanking-new wasp. We can't really blame
the racy stinger. The creature is no more at fault than the spider is
for being very much itself. Sort of like putting white mice in with
snakes. The snakes are not bad and the mice are not good. It's merely
that the snakes are serpents, and the mice are gentle little rodents.
And the former invariably eat the latter. The question, of course, lies
in whether the melding of the pain and pleasure in the act of giving
yourself up to the sting of the digger wasp will in your own eyes
justify your own demise.

Lastly, there is the matter of Cleave. Young, but not too young.
And certainly wise beyond her years. A loving creature, but without
the titillation, excitement, and danger inherent in Amalita Corsini.
Or the fascination of true surgical social talent like Harriet's. When
it was my turn, I failed her. Thinking always that there would be time
to return, once the empires had been conquered, and the journeys of
the vagrant soul had been completed. To be sure, it's Susan Cleave
who'd be good for him. But I'm not certain it fits into my plans that
way. Nor, for that matter, do I think he's really interested in Harriet.
Although she looks a good fifteen years younger than her real age,
Harriet is just too cold and perfect for him. Besides, I think he sees

right through her. Alabaster skin and diminutive feet notwithstanding. I guess the selection has already been made by destiny. Judging from the resemblance between his deceased wife and Amalita, he goes for raven-haired continental types.

Our man has just arrived at Pyramid Hill. I sense his presence. So rather than be bored with prospective and speculative solutions, I'll blink myself out of this maze and deal with the genuine article. Back at the house, E.C. is up in the library taking a phone call. From the look of rapture on his face it can be from only one person. Yes, Signorina Corsini is finally in town.

"E.C.? This is Amalita."

"Amalita, how thrilling to hear your voice. Where are you?"

"I have just arrived, and of course could not help calling you immediately. You see, I am wearing your earrings, which remind me of the very tall, handsome man."

"You flatter me."

"You men are all the same. You complain about being flattered, but you nevertheless wish to hear it repeatedly from the women you love."

"Why the plural?"

"We are not children."

"I'd like to be one."

"This we can arrange."

"Incidentally, speaking of children, I have a special toy for you. One I think you will particularly appreciate."

"How marvelous. I love toys. Especially expensive ones."

"Amalita, you have no shame."

"Ah, you are correct. But I have other talents."

"I long to see you."

"Never before a performance. But to be sure, Monday night after the opera I will be waiting for you."

"I can't wait."

"But you shall. Men . . . I always wonder whether it's the pleasure or the pain you enjoy most."

"Probably both."

"An honest man. How very, very rare."

"And aren't you an honest woman?"

"Never. And you must not insult me by calling me one. I am a woman, no more, no less. Besides, I have always believed in the doubt a thousand times before the truth."

"I reluctantly understand."

"Not enough. But soon . . . Monday."

"Then it shall be Monday."

"*Arrivedella.*"

"Until then."

Click.

Our man seems to be throbbing a bit in the crotch after his telephonic encounter with the digger wasp. He's putting his hand in his coat pocket, from which he quietly extracts the Moguk Diamond. As he peers into its brilliant pristine depths, no doubt he sees mirrored, magnified, and reverberated all the future lusts and sins which might, and may, and can be committed for the love of such a woman. But the telephone is again ringing, interrupting the dreamlike quality of the moment.

"Mr. Douglas. This is Archbishop Fromaggio."

"Good evening, Archbishop. To what do I owe the honor of your call?"

"Actually, to an impending matter of importance which I am sure will greatly please you."

"Yes, what is it?"

"As it happens, His Eminence Cardinal Tucci will shortly be arriving in America for an unscheduled visit."

"Oh, how wonderful. I'm delighted to hear this. May I inquire as to the reason for his trip?"

"Yes, of course. As it happens, there is to be a benefit at the opera, at which Madame Corsini will be singing with other Italian singers of international renown. The Italian government is fostering several semiofficial activities in honor of our arts and artists. His Eminence had the time, and felt it would be appropriate to attend in order to lend the support of the Church. You undoubtedly know he is a great patron of the arts."

"Yes, of course. I am very happy to hear this. And I'm wondering if His Eminence will have any time to be my guest."

"This was precisely why I was calling. I have been asked by the Cardinal to arrange a meeting so he might pay his compliments to you. Among other things, on the completion of your Siderurgica takeover."

"Oh . . . of course, I'm very much honored. Do you think you might be able to arrange to have him visit me here at Pyramid Hill?"

"Yes. His Eminence had originally planned on a four-day visit, but will now be staying an extra two days. I believe such a meeting could occur late Sunday morning. We will confirm to you within the next two hours."

"Well, thank you, Archbishop. I also look forward to the pleasure of your company again."

"And I to seeing you."

"Thank you."

"You are very welcome. Goodbye."

Click.

This whole thing is becoming rather interesting. I wonder what old Tucci wants to discuss with E.C.? I suppose I'll just have to wait until Sunday, when I can become the proverbial fly on the wall.

As if there is to be no tranquillity here tonight, the phone is ringing yet another time. I must confess, this call is quite surprising, and somewhat unnerving. You see, Harriet is on the wire.

"Mr. Douglas."

"Yes."

"This is Harriet Weatherbee Somerset."

"Oh, Mrs. Somerset."

"Please call me Harriet."

"In that event, you must call me E.C."

"That will be fine with me."

"Then Harriet it'll be."

"Good. Now that we're through with that, I hope you won't consider me bold in calling you. You see, a lot of people think I'm very capable, and of course they discount the possible personal difficulties I might feel as a woman, by counting the size of my inheritance. But the truth is I've had somewhat of a frightening time getting back into the stream of things after the death of my dear husband."

"Yes, I can understand that. It's not easy to center oneself on track again after the loss of a loved one. But how might I help or be of assistance this evening?"

"Actually, although I might later need your help, or the help of someone like you, quite desperately, I'm calling on a social note."

"Oh."

"You see, I mentioned the matter of the opera to you, and to be sure you were very kind in sending your check for the box. I'm having a little reception after the performance at my country house. The principal singers from the cast will be present, as well as some friends. I've also invited dignitaries from the Italian government and the Church. I think we might enjoy sharing time in a nonbusiness atmosphere. And, in short, I'm calling to invite you and the guests in your party. A written invitation will find its way to you by messenger. But I didn't wish you to think that in reality I'm the cold businesswoman you have met at our offices, and wanted to be sure you'd come."

"Mrs. . . . er . . . Harriet, I'm very pleased to have the invitation, and confirm we will attend. I also appreciate the candor."

"I do hope we can become friends."

"Yes, certainly."

"Then I'll look forward to seeing you Monday evening."

"Yes. Thank you again for your very kind invitation."

"Good night."

"Good night."

Click.

While the previous look on E.C.'s face was one of lust and sexual anxiety, he is now achieving the transfigured countenance of a wry smile. As I might have expected, his index finger is up to his nose again in that characteristic gesture. I'm just about to caution him when it occurs to me I might do well to allow matters to take their own course. And then act opportunistically to further my ends. After all, I've always wanted to see Harriet hanged on her own chain. She must be desperate if she's playing the role of the candid temptress. And that "dear husband" business. I almost gagged on it! But this will make her vulnerable and subject to attack. Nevertheless, I must watch her closely. She's unflinchingly capable, and trained by the master himself, which is to say me. That means she is always very dangerous. Even when caught in the direst straits.

In a way, though, I have no one to blame but myself for having allowed her to do me in. It was I who taught her about the exotic plant with the lovely deep green eight-pointed leaves. It's always the same mistake. You end up teaching your lovers too much. And then, armed with less love, but with the resolve born of great ambition, they devour you. I'll never forget something my father told me in this connection when I was bemoaning the loss of a lover's affection, "Well, son, you have no one to blame but yourself. *You had a diamond in the rough, and if you had left it in the rough, you would have had a diamond in the rough forever.*" But right now I'd rather think of what he told me when my second mistress walked out: "Don't worry, son. *Once you learn how to drink Dom Pérignon, New York State champagne tastes terrible.*" And it is this principle which, in the ultimate involution of my love, I am hopeful of applying to Harriet.

TWENTY-SEVEN

THIS MORNING GUSTAVO SOMERSET HAS OPENED HIS EYES TO AN EX-
tremely unpleasant call. It seems his bankers in Geneva and Zurich
were wary and concerned after yesterday's additional drop in the
American steels. Furthermore, the lawyers for the entity which provided the additional nine hundred million for his project have now,
under instructions from Don Orsini and Cardinal Tucci, requested
the guarantee of the Somerset estate. For Gustavo, it was *like mentioning the rope in the house of the hanged*. I beamed myself over to his
room on a strong premonition, and have found him sitting here in
his briefs, unshaven and trying to decide what to do.

I enjoy seeing him in this state. By now all the consideration I
might have held for him as a nephew has been relegated to the arcana
of memory. The regard is gone, and now all I feel is the sheer pleasure of watching him stew. I must say, perhaps he's not quite as bad
as Harriet. After all, she gives the orders and he follows them. But I
shouldn't forget his bit of originality in bilking me out of what should

have been my reward in the original Siderurgica deal. I know what's going on in his mind, even though I cannot directly read it. He's mustering his nerve to speak with Harriet. This will take another two cigarettes and perhaps one more cup of very strong coffee.

The remnants of last night's sordid sexual escapade are to be seen everywhere in this bedroom. There are ashtrays full of cigarette butts accompanied by the rank smell of stagnant smoke. Empty champagne bottles and condom wrappers abound on the floor. Towels stand up mutely in their own dry erections, born of their previously sticky form. It's a depressing atmosphere in which things have been left in a state of abandon in tandem with the personality of their owner. The scene reminds me of something my psychiatrist once told me. He said, "Henry, when you go visit people, don't size them up by the cleanliness of their parlor. Go into the kitchen and look at the dog or cat's dishes, and examine them to see if they have clean water and fresh food. If it's all sitting there looking old and crusty, you shouldn't expect better treatment for yourself."

Now his courage is mounting, and he's calling Harriet:

"Good morning. Is Mrs. Somerset in?"

"No, she's not. May I take a message?"

"Who is this?"

"This is Rosy speaking. Is this Mr. Gustavo?"

"Yes. Where's my aunt?"

"I think she went to the office, sir. Should I tell her you called?"

"No. I'll just drop in on her there."

Click.

For a moment Gustavo is again looking somewhat consternated. And then, without benefit of shower, shave, or deodorant for that matter, he dashes on some cologne in the French manner and quickly dresses. I'm fast behind him as he grabs his car keys and is quickly out the door in a pair of tacky alligator loafers without socks.

If I were alive, I wouldn't be caught dead sitting in this car. It's filthy. Furthermore, Gustavo is driving like the perfect Latin prick that he is. Having lost all veneers of courtesy, he's proceeding to give the driver next to him the finger, as he is refused the possibility of cutting in to pass on the right. He's treating this car as if it were an angry extension of his body, which is something I've seen done in Latin countries, where men somehow feel an automobile has transfigured itself into a bigger and better penis. This is, of course, why they sometimes care for their cars with greater zeal than they do their wives and children. It is also why they must win the race.

Blackrock is on the horizon sooner than I might have expected. He's actually going to leave the car smack in front of the building in the no-parking zone. A rather amiable-looking dork of a traffic cop is approaching us as a result of the awkward placement of the vehicle.

"Hey, mister! I'm sorry, you can't park the car there. You're going to get a ticket, or it'll be towed."

"Listen, you two-bit cop. My aunt owns this building, this sidewalk, a sizable chunk of this town, and maybe half the country. If you just as much as touch this car with your dirty, grimy fingers, I'm personally going to have you fired out on your ass. And if you have kids, bear in mind that I'm a mean motherfucker, and I'll make sure you never get another job."

The rather round policeman has blanched completely at this uncalled-for and unexpected onslaught of fury. He's suffering the mental process which underdogs suffer when they're being pushed around. Frequently, as in a chess game, they yield because of their fear. And in this case, it appears he's going to allow Gustavo to have his way.

The cop is looking at one of the building employees, who is assuring him with a nod that Gustavo is the genuine article. The necessary mental process completed, the policeman is now attempting an accommodation.

"Listen, mister, you should be aware I could run you in. But I won't do that, because it looks like you're having a bad day. And maybe you can have me fired. But if you're as big as you say you are, why are you picking on a little guy like me?"

"Because I can. And don't you forget that for one minute."

With this, Gustavo is turning around and is on his way into the lobby and up the elevator. I have decided to remain for a moment, having caught a glimpse of the employee slipping the policeman a handful of something out of his coat pocket. Under closer scrutiny, the objects of the gratuitous transaction seem to be eight or nine little envelopes of sugar. Ohhhh . . . I see, they're going to find their way into the gas tank of Gustavo's shining Maserati. I guess about sixty or seventy miles down the road, my nephew will find his high-tech engine terminally gummed up with caramelized sugar. It's sort of like the Chinese cook who was abused and used to quietly piss in the soup. There's a lesson in it too. Never humiliate the little people. Each and every one of them may someday exercise his God-given ability to upset your fondest dreams and most neatly set plans. Like throwing the veritable wooden shoe into the machine. *There is no such thing as a small enemy.*

Petty sabotage accomplished, and not without a substantial level of amusement, I'm now blinking myself into Harriet's office, where she's just sitting there palely listening to Gustavo, with Tom Hooker standing behind her like a mute gargoyle.

"Now wait a minute, Gustavo. Are you telling me you didn't follow our instructions and protect the account by somehow hedging it?"

"Yes, that's what I'm saying, and I need immediate action, or there's going to be a catastrophe. I require the estate's guarantee to maintain the position until this ridiculous storm in the market subsides."

"Gustavo, do you know of any reason why these very good issues have been dropping so quickly?"

"No. I have all the information, and I don't understand it myself. Rumor has it someone has assumed a gigantic short position. But I hesitate to believe this, because when the market bounces back, a short of that magnitude will be caught with its pants down beneath its ankles."

"Well, Tom, you've heard it from my disgusting nephew. What shall we do now?"

"I'm sorry to say, Harriet, there isn't a middle position. We either expose ourselves to a three-billion-dollar loss, which could effectively put us on the road to ruin, or we stick with it. I can't recommend one position or the other."

"Tom, you always were a weasely little chickenshit when decisions had to be made. Just give him the guarantee, and get him the fuck out of my sight. And if you don't like my language, I think I'm entitled to a little profanity for three billion dollars."

"Gustavo, as you can see, your aunt is terribly upset. I am as well. Give us the necessary European instructions. The guarantee will be posted within the hour."

Without as much as a thank-you, Gustavo is leaving the executive office and stopping at Tom Hooker's secretary's desk to provide the needed information. The transaction completed, he's out of the building, looking even crazier than before. Although again sporting the shit-eating grin we've previously come to know. As he leaves the building, he smugly notes the Maserati is still there. And without the decoration of a ticket.

Back at Blackrock, Harriet and Hooker have been left in a state of total consternation by my nephew's visit. Harriet is ranting and raving about Gustavo's perfidy.

"I just can't believe it, Tom. Everything was so cozy. We had achieved practically all of what we'd wanted. Henry had the good grace to die, business was great, and now a member of my own family has blown the whole thing wide open."

"Honey, if I were you, I wouldn't get myself all bent out of shape about this. The day isn't entirely lost yet. We have a lot of assets in the estate, and I really feel quite secure the steel stocks will bounce back."

"That's not something we can know for sure."

"Well, of course not. But there is such a thing as a reasonable expectation."

"I do hope you're right. But let me tell you, if I lose my fortune on this deal, I'm taking you with me wherever I'm going."

"There's no need to threaten me, Harriet."

"Maybe this way you'll perform."

I'm a bit bored watching Harriet and Hooker slash one another apart. If ever he did have the hope of marrying, I think it's now permanently defunct. Now that I think of it, old Tucci must either have arrived or be due very soon. Strange, Don Orsini has remained behind. In the past, when necessary, he's traveled incognito, and with the full safe conduct of the relevant American security agencies. I have this feeling I should be looking in on that sector of world power and economy. So I'll blink myself across the Atlantic to the villa in the hills near Rome.

It's very late here. Yet the guards who quietly monitor the approach from almost a mile away are watchful as ever with their side arms and submachine guns. The house is reached by means of a long, winding gravel road which with its noisy pebbles announces the approach of any oncoming vehicle. Don Orsini always calls it his nightingale lane. The villa itself is constructed in the tradition of the great palaces of the Renaissance. There are no windows at the ground level. Just a heavily fortified door which leads through a series of foyers and entrance halls to similarly guarded passages. The actual living quarters are on the second and third floors. Tonight a light burns most insistently in the suite of rooms on the third floor, which has for many years been occupied by the Don himself. As I walk through the darkened chambers of the villa, I can't help noticing that all things here are opulent and expensive. It would seem the best of everything has found its way into these halls. It's a refined look, but much more evident in an almost indescribable way than the ages-old look of Tucci's apartments. The third-floor parlor, adjacent to Don Orsini's bedroom, is entirely upholstered in blood-red Venetian damask. In addition to the incandescent lights, there are candles here. Ah yes. It would seem Don Orsini is not fond of the darkness. He's sitting in a large, deep red chair, wearing a silk-and-cashmere bathrobe. And a pair of black velvet slippers. The half glasses he's been using to read the document before him have slipped down the bridge of his aquiline nose. By his side, and within reach, is a large engraved crystal tumbler, with two fingers of scotch from his own manor in Scotland.

The phone is ringing softly, and he's extending his manicured but wrinkled hand to grab the receiver.

"Ah, Tucci, I'm glad you called. How was the journey?"

"Excellent. You know, it's a magnificent airplane. I never cease to marvel . . ."

"And have you commenced your business?"

"Yes. Fromaggio has booked an appointment with E. C. Douglas on Sunday morning, and I am also hopeful of visiting with Amalita prior to the performance. There will in addition be a reception held by the Somerset widow after the opera, at which everyone will be present. But I am curious—has the guarantee been posted?"

"Yes, just hours ago. Now everything is complete. Mr. Douglas can proceed on Monday to unravel the riddle."

"And the other matter, the young man, the nephew?"

"I have been thinking tonight about what I will do."

"Orsini, I beg you . . . must you?"

"Old friend, why is it we always end up having the same discussion? You know who I am, and you know my code. And furthermore, it is not entirely dissimilar to yours."

"Ah, but we have other ways. Remember, deep in those rooms we never speak about, we preserve many of the ancient secrets of the heart and of the journey of the soul."

"Enough, Tucci. You have your mission, which is to save our friend from impending perils so he can be enlisted into the brotherhood. And I, unfortunately, have mine."

"I understand, but I am also very sad. I will pray for you."

"Thank you, old friend."

Click.

The conversation has left Don Orsini even more pensive than before. He's walking over to a little table that is laden with photographs. These are singular, in that they all have little black ribbons on them. They are the visages of departed wives and children. There's a knock at the door, and his faithful manservant is entering with a tray which holds a cup of steaming hot cocoa.

"Ah, the chocolate. Thank you very much. It's particularly welcome tonight. There's a chill in the air."

"You are up far too late again. And I know you've been looking at those photographs of the loved ones who have been lost to the various wars and causes."

"Yes, you know I do that. Always late at night."

"Will you promise me you'll go to bed after drinking your chocolate?"

"No, there's something I must do first."

"Then after that . . . ?"

"If I can sleep."

"I'll turn your bed down. But please, try to get some rest."

"I will. You know how I always labor over these ultimate decisions."

"People don't know that about you, but it's always been this way. I can attest to it."

"Perhaps it's better they don't know. I would seem weak to them if they understood the loneliness and sorrow inherent in sentencing."

"Then let us not speak of this, Don Orsini. Please go to sleep."

"Thank you, and good night."

No sooner does the attendant leave than Don Orsini reaches for the phone again.

"Ignazio, this is Orsini. Did I wake you?"

"Actually you did, Don Orsini, but I am, as always, at your disposal."

"You remember the matter we spoke of yesterday?"

"Yes, of course."

"You will inform your correspondents to proceed with it Monday."

"As discussed?"

"Yes. In every way."

"Good night."

"Good night."

Click.

Now Don Orsini is finishing his scotch and taking the cup of chocolate into the bedroom with him. He's bolting the thick chamber door, and has momentarily paused at the window to look at the night sky. Out of his bathrobe, this old man in pajamas seems fragile, and quite evidently very tired. He is now inserting himself between the sheets, to sleep fitfully, but nevertheless to rest.

This has been very revealing. And a tad chilling. I can't help zapping myself back to Pyramid Hill, which is bright with the illumination of the early evening. Inside, E.C. and Cleave are sitting in the library having an after-dinner drink. She's looking particularly beautiful in a loose red knit dress. Which by its very nature exhibits rather demurely her various curves and protuberances. He's sitting at the table going over a portfolio composed of many of the steel process documents he obtained from that cabinet in the room below. They're talking about the future.

"So now that you have the Siderurgica stock and have gained control of the company, what will happen?"

"On Monday morning, there will be a public announcement of my success in obtaining control of the company. At ten o'clock, we will be closing with the Somerset estate on the license of Von Richter's process and the sale of the American steels held by Siderurgica to the Somerset estate. At that point I will personally not own any American steels, and will also have avoided any related short position to eliminate the possibility of insider trading problems. At two o'clock, the confidential documents on the process will be leaked to the press. Doing it at that hour should create a furor and panic in the market. Tuesday morning should find our Siderurgica interest pyramiding in value, while the American steels should again plummet."

"And what about the Somerset estate?"

"For all I know, it could be facing bankruptcy."

"Why are you doing this? You're beginning to act exactly like my old boss."

"I don't know—perhaps I'm very much like him."

"I can't believe that. And I definitely don't want you to be as he was. Why not quit now and buy that island in the South Pacific? Or its equivalent. We could be happy."

"This is making me happy."

"But it's not making *me* happy. And incidentally, you've seemed distant in the last day or so. I hope it's just the strain of the Siderurgica deal."

"I don't know what you're talking about."

"You know, you're not a very good liar. I'll wager it's that woman. She must be in town already. I'll bet she's called you. Has she?"

"Actually yes, but it's only normal she would call."

"I don't believe you. I think you want her."

"Why are you doing this? I don't appreciate the unpleasantness."

"You're hedging the issue."

"No, I'm not. I just won't be pushed around by your suspicious emotions."

"You know I'm not the jealous type. But I see things happening. And I've recently realized there is an uncanny resemblance between her and the pictures of your wife I've seen. I just can't help noticing. I think we've both had enough of this for now. I'm going home tonight."

"I don't think I'll even respond. Have it your own way. But remember we have the opera on Monday. You're not going to stand me up, are you?"

"No, boss, I would never do that to you. At least not intentionally."

We've just witnessed a very interesting and characteristic scene. The male ego is always the same. Two-timing cheats like E.C. always give themselves away with some phrase or gesture. It's almost as if their subconscious is screaming out for recognition. As if they felt they should receive a prize for being big *macho* men and having a second love object on the hook. Sometimes they leave an address in their wallets where they know it will be found. Or they'll even tell their wives the second object is very attractive, or has paid some attention to them. But one way or another, they can never help revealing that in their intimacy they think themselves great studs.

Susan has a tear in her eye. But E.C. is so obsessed with the fulfillment of his proximate destiny he hasn't noticed it at all. He's looking distant. And smug. Bozo seems sad and tries to cozy up to E.C. as Cleave leaves the room and is on her way home. But this attempt is also rebuffed, as our man single-mindedly dials the telephone.

"Yes?"

"Amalita, it's E.C."

"I know."

"I've got to see you. I can think of nothing but you."

"Ah, men. You all say the same thing. Are you sure you haven't spent the day thinking about your billions and transactions?"

"No, Amalita. It's been you, you, and you."

"Such a flatterer."

"Can I come see you now?"

"Definitely not. I told you I will see you after the performance."

"I can't wait. Besides, there's something I want to give you."

"Yes, you told me, but it will still have to wait until after *La Forza*."

"Why do you torture me?"

"Because it gives me pleasure. Good night, *caro*."

Click.

Our man is upset and consternated. I'd actually rather see him run over there and nail the whore. But instead, he's going to sit around here moping. I'm not sure I appreciated the little scene Cleave just pulled. After all, women are always wanting to indelibly write their names on our cocks. I was offered true love. But I always thought I'd have enough time to enjoy the excitement of my affairs and then turn later to love. Very much like E.C., I was in demand. And, of course, being craved after is great fun, and wonderful for the ego. But the possibility of admitting someone to your most private feelings is also very special indeed. In that sense, I missed the boat with Cleave. Well, there's time to patch things up here. I'm sure he'll think of something to woo Susan back into the heat of matters. There's still time to repair this type of misunderstanding. One mustn't lose vision of the greater things that are within one's grasp.

There's excitement in the air. We're going to have a busy day on Sunday here at Pyramid Hill with Cardinal Tucci's visit and the preparations for Monday's financial turmoil. Then when Monday's daytime events are said and done, I can look forward to that very special evening at the opera.

TWENTY-EIGHT

THE SUPPOSED DAY OF REST HAS ARRIVED. AS E.C. SLEEPS, THE Sunday-morning light has found me ruminating in the gardens again. It's definitely cold today, and most of the deciduous trees have dropped their leaves. The bulbs are all snugly bedded in for their long winter's sleep. The fish ponds have been drained, and their new inhabitants placed in very large heated and aerated aquaria in the utility rooms of the pyramid. This is the time of year which has always fostered within me a feeling of heightened introspection. There is hardly a cloud in the sky today. So it's going to be one of those extremely hard brilliant late-fall days in which the air is clear and crisp and gemlike in the quality of its visual resolution. Along the periphery of the garden I spy the dried remains of a great sea of foxtail lilies. Reminding us that again next year they will come forth with renewed vigor in tall, dramatic yellow spikes.

I crept into E.C.'s dream world last night. I wanted to suggest things that might be useful during today's visit with Cardinal Tucci.

But instead I was waylaid by his mood. There's something I've re-discovered about dreams. We needn't be our own age in them. The dreamer can select whatever age he pleases, and therefore be a time traveler. Last night I was surprised to find E.C. as a wide-eyed teen-ager. He was confused, and felt his pain very acutely, in the singular fashion in which only the very young can suffer. His entire vision was totally adolescent. Granted, such grief is often tinged with melodrama and self-pity, and frequently lacks depth. But the young don't know this. In his reverie E.C. was naked, except for a bathing suit, and was sitting on the beach watching the waves come and go as he again assiduously counted grains of sand. I approached him, and he smiled a wan, childlike smile as he saw me and said, "Oh . . . Henry Somerset, it's you!" And then I asked him what he was doing and he informed me, very seriously, that he was counting the grains of sand. I humored him as he told me, "I mustn't miss any." He took a handful from one side, and he said, "These are Susan's grains." And then he took some rather sharp little seashells and looked me straight in the eye and then said, "These are Amalita's." From another side, he took yet another fistful of sand, and looked at me with wonder and a kind smile and said, "These are yours. I want to count them too." After a brief lapse, he again entered into a mood in which all he did was count. There was another pause then and we began chatting. At that point he said, "You know, I'm a bit confused. And there's so much to do. Wouldn't it be easier to buy a Pacific island that wouldn't have this interminable beach? I could be happy there." I must admit, I faltered a bit at that point. I wondered to myself if perhaps it wouldn't be the right solution. And couldn't help seeing a great deal of the youthful Henry in the young E.C. Yet, my own present self-interests in these matters prevailed, and I replied, "No, E.C., you'd be bored. You'd manage to count all the grains of sand. And then what would you do?" Again he replied, "I'd be happy. Isn't that enough?" And I quickly retorted, "But you'd miss the excitement." At that point, quite surprisingly, I began to feel ashamed and confused and left him unmolested to the remainder of his dream.

Back in the world of the living, I find myself drawn once more into my maze of evergreen. Down path after path, and on bifurcating lanes which bisect one another, I've made my way to the central court again. I'm just sitting, watching the water in the fountain trickle down. When I started this whole mess, I felt certain I was on the right path. Disembodied or not, a second chance to whack it to my enemies seemed like a very special opportunity indeed. Now I'm beginning to wonder about the human toll. What if my suggestions are making others unhappy? I mean people I love. After all, I couldn't care less about Gustavo, Harriet, and Hooker, but what if E.C. and Susan could be truly happy and I'm standing in the way? When I saw him in there last night, I mean in the dream, I thought I caught a glimpse of myself many years ago. At that juncture, full of ideals and the expectation of love, I might not have been willing to trade the real thing for a few dollars and the meaner pleasures of success. True, he was confused and even irrational in his reverie, but the child was beautiful and alive.

I once had a clever and handsome child inside me as well. No kidding. But I tied him up and gagged him so many times that he took to visiting less frequently. You know, there was something else last night. Something that touched me, and made me think. At one point in time I asked him why he was so alone. And he responded, "Oh, I put all this sand around me to make it a little more difficult and sporting for those who would find me here." And then he looked me in the eye and gave me a wry little smile and said, "You see, we all create little barriers around us. And spin petty threads of deception in order to make the ultimate find more rewarding and interesting. It's like a gift. If you just put it on the floor or on a table, it certainly might be good enough. But if you wrap it in a beautiful tissue and then place it in a box with a lovely ribbon, the framing of the present can imbue it with an almost magical quality. People are that way. We don't just want to be known incidentally or nakedly. We all wish to be resourcefully unfolded like the petals of a rose, or discovered as a hidden treasure. And so, we create those layers, one by one. It's like that maze you placed in the garden, Henry. It wasn't put there to keep people from finding the solution. On the contrary, you grew it in the hope that someone might reach the center."

So here I am on this bench wondering whether instead of being E.C.'s teacher, I have become his student. For the present, though, I have to exercise care with these thoughts. They're like charity, which try though you might to keep it at bay, will seep in through the roots, between the floorboards, under the doors, and through the keyholes. And right now, charity is a luxury I can ill afford.

Back at the house, activity abounds. The maids and menservants are wearing their best. The floors are sparkling with a jewellike quality. And everywhere there is the smell of fresh pastries baking. It would seem Cardinal Tucci is coming for a late-morning visit. So I assume it will be coffee and little cakes. And perhaps a stroll through my manicured gardens.

E.C. is up and around, and dressing in that very soft gray glen plaid cashmere suit. Within its design it harbors the faintest yellow thread. He's wearing a necktie which picks up the deep golden-yellow color. It's a combination I've always favored. And very appropriate. He's looking nervously at his watch. Down in the kitchen, they're putting the finishing touches on Bozo, now bathed, brushed, and combed. Everywhere he trails the fragrance of good almond shampoo and cream rinse. It's now eleven o'clock sharp. And as the clocks strike throughout the structure, the telephone from the gatehouse is ringing to advise our man that Cardinal Tucci's car and trailing security are approaching the first gate. The staff are being assembled in the front hall next to the two statues of our now stately lion goddesses. Looking proud and satisfied today. Serenely expectant. With the suspicion of a smile on those thirty-five-hundred-year-old lips. As Tucci's armored Mercedes approaches the gravel circle in front of the entrance of the pyramid, our man is pulling one of those dramatic touches so dear to my heart. What he's doing is fun. He's waited for the car to stop. And at that point, he's begun lowering the monumental entrance stairs. Tucci is still in the vehicle, as the granite block pivots and brings the gleaming stairs into view. He's smiling at this display of American ingenuity. The rather corpulent priests who were trailing in the car behind have now opened the doors to the limousine. And Tucci is emerging from the padded interior as our man descends those sparkling steps.

"Your Eminence, I'm so happy to see you again. Welcome to Pyramid Hill."

"Good morning, Mr. Douglas. I am also very pleased to be here. And I see it is indeed a real pyramid. Beautiful and most intriguing.

You know, I was invited when Mr. Somerset inaugurated it, but did not have the chance to attend the celebration. So now I will enjoy seeing it at your hand. I must say, though, as I approached, the gardens especially attracted my attention. Would we perhaps have a chance to see them later?"

"Why yes, of course. Whatever your pleasure might be. Even if it is a tad chilly, I'll be happy to give you a tour of my garden."

Tucci is looking radiant. And a bit younger than his eighty or so years. His eyes are sparkling today. As he slowly mounts the staircase and enters the great hall, his attention is gripped by the two statues. He emits a little gasp. Here, E.C. introduces the staff assembled to pay their respects. The Cardinal blesses them, and they disperse to perform their various tasks. But he can't help commenting on the surroundings.

"The statues are from Karnak, aren't they? Perhaps the temple of Mut?"

"Yes, I believe so."

"Of course, eighteenth dynasty. Magnificent! And I also couldn't help noticing the very fine obelisk as we approached the park. It reminded me favorably of our own, and also in a way of the very fine one at Caernarvon Castle. But I did not expect to find these two fabulous antiquities within. They are a treasure. The goddess Sekhmet, always serene, but fierce and strong. Yet also maternal . . . the deity of war, and also the protector of Ra. Very much in many respects like our Mother the Church."

"Yes . . . I had never quite thought of her that way. May I show you through some of the rooms and collections?"

"I would be delighted. You know very well that I'm a lover of beautiful things."

"I have seen many such things in your apartments . . . and beautiful people as well."

"Yes, I am aware . . . I know only too well."

A knowledgeable glance has been shared between the two as they placidly walk through the various halls and rooms. Looking now at this picture, or at that vase, or at a Rodin *Great Left Hand* sitting on a console. Finally, into the library, where coffee and little cakes are steaming with their warm welcome.

"May I offer you some espresso, Your Eminence?"

"Yes, thank you. Your home is beautiful. And almost magical. You know, it has a bewitched quality."

"Yes. So you've noticed as well?"

"Of course, I am a very old man, and I've seen many things. I would not be surprised if the spirit of Henry Somerset were alive and well within these walls."

"So you believe in such things."

"Well, not publicly, because our dogma prohibits such beliefs. But after almost eighty years of living in touch with the hearts and souls of men, and with the mysteries guarded by the Church, there is little to surprise me."

As Tucci helps himself to Pyramid Hill's own brand of delicious little cakes, E.C. pops the question:

"You know, I was surprised when they told me you might honor us with a visit."

"Why? I have become instantly fond of you."

"Well, to be rather frank, I don't receive the visit of the Vatican's Secretary of State every Sunday. And I assume when he visits, there may be a purpose."

"I expect there is no way in which we can be overheard here. Is that correct?"

"Yes, of course. You have my word of honor."

"And that for me is quite sufficient. . . . I don't know exactly where to begin, but I will try to explain. Throughout the centuries, there has been darkness and there has been light. I do not mean to be trite or simplistic. But in point of fact, since the dawn of mankind and civilization, there have always been two antithetical forces at play. Call them God and the devil if you like. Accordingly, there have always been men who have served either one force or the other, but ultimately, never both. Frequently, those of us serving on the side of light have had to do many things to preserve our position and further our goals. You see, Don Orsini, even though he comes to us with tactics usually associated with darkness, actually serves in favor of the light, particularly because he possesses a remorseful consciousness of evil. Quite often we must perform acts of which we are ashamed, in order to protect the precious and fragile light. At times we must sin in order to further our ends. And to be sure, we are never proud of it. But those of us enlisted to the cause are bound in a hermetic brotherhood for the furtherance of our belief in mankind and civilization as a God-inspired gift, and the maintenance of a clear and proper vision."

"But Cardinal, why are you telling me this?"

"When in our travels we come across someone who we feel might be enlisted into the service of light, we attempt to draw him close to us. You are such a person. And to be extremely blunt, we would wish to acquire you as a member of our very private club. Also, I am here to warn you."

"Regarding what?"

"Frequently we must consort with the darkness in order to maintain balance and understand what is happening. Sometimes we have the darkness even within our homes in the persons of guests. You met just such a being at my party. Beautiful, talented, and beguiling. Very much in the seminal vein in which evil has always appeared."

"You are referring to Amalita, aren't you?"

"Yes, but you must draw your own conclusions. And beware, I cannot protect you. You must guard yourself from harm."

"But the woman is fabulous. How can you say these things?"

"My son, we know many things. . . ."

"With all due respect, Your Eminence, I believe I can attend to my love life. But nevertheless, I'm grateful for the hint. I do have a very fine Madeira here which I think you might appreciate, even though it is a bit early."

"Yes indeed . . . but it is never early for a good Madeira. Afterward, will you show me the gardens?"

"Yes, certainly."

With this exchange, and after a few sips, the two men are rising and making their way through the halls and down the stairs into the gardens. Tucci is speaking now.

"Might I take your arm?"

"Of course, Cardinal, I'm honored."

"You know, growing old has certain disadvantages. But there are also positive aspects. The flesh is not so easily tempted. Incidentally, is that a maze down at the bottom of the hill?"

"Yes. Henry Somerset had the mature evergreens brought in and planted. So almost immediately, he had a grown maze."

"That is very much in keeping with his character. He was impatient. But nevertheless a special man. You know, I have always loved the English ones. Might we stroll in it?"

"Certainly."

As the late-morning sun is approaching the zenith, the dapper man in gray and the magnificent old Cardinal cut quite a picture walking arm in arm down to the entrance of this botanical puzzle. Someone has allowed Bozo to romp freely, and he's gamboling down to meet them. The old cleric is momentarily startled at the abrupt arrival of the behemoth, and the duo is momentarily detained.

"And who do we have here, Mr. Douglas?"

"Your Eminence, this is Bozo."

"Ah, Bozo. Quite a name. You know, Irish wolfhounds are dogs with great souls. Unfortunately, they do not live very long lives. A friend of mine in Ireland calls them the heartbreak breed. Bozo is beautiful, and large even for his variety. I think, Mr. Douglas, the way this dog is looking at me, there is something very special about him. I should tell you, I have a sixth sense for such things."

"The whole story regarding how he came to me is quite uncanny. You see, he was Henry Somerset's dog. And I found him at the cemetery by the Somerset tomb. When I tried to return him, the widow was totally uninterested. In fact, they just *gave* him to me. Ah, but here we are . . . at the beginning of our maze."

Dog and man and Cardinal are now strolling through the intertwining intersecting lanes. The ground underfoot is particularly interesting. You see, I had them cut out the turf and replace it with about a two-foot depth of compacted evergreen needles. The dry needles provide a cushionlike walk, which in addition to being soft and otherworldly, is also extremely quiet. It was frequently helpful for my little pranks. I customarily enjoyed sneaking up on people who were caught in the quiet detachment of this little world. They invariably heightened my pleasure by being quite startled.

They've reached the center of the maze now. And are sitting on one of the cedar benches. Bozo has most accommodatingly decided to lie at His Eminence's feet near the bright red slippers. Tucci has assumed a quizzical look on his face as he asks, "You know, there are times when through our experience, we sense we might be of assistance. My son, I have a feeling you carry a troubled soul. May I help?"

"As I was saying before we entered the maze, it all has something to do with this dog, with Bozo. You see, I was a fairly happy fellow, although not this wealthy. Then Bozo came into my life, and almost as a sequel, everything which had to do with Henry Somerset. Because of what I believe is his influence, I've magnified my fortune in a matter of days. But I've also suddenly become unhappy and full of lust for more. What am I to do?"

"Surely you exaggerate."

"No. The dog pushes puzzles of stone which open doors. And leads me to files, and helps me open combination cabinets with complex numerical sequences which were previously unknown to me. I'm also in love."

"With Miss Cleave, a fine woman."

"Yes, but no. You see, I have the instinct to be disloyal to her. And all of a sudden, I find myself disdaining what should be love in favor of lust, and wanting someone very badly."

"Ahhh, the beautiful Amalita."

"Yes, and the worst part is that I know she wouldn't be any good for me. But I'm nevertheless willing to throw myself down the precipice. There's something else I haven't told you. Amalita is the exact double of my deceased wife. How do you figure that one? I feel confused. . . . Your Eminence, what would signify the end of the world to you? I must confess to often thinking about ending things, and I never did that before."

"This, my son, would be a mortal sin. And furthermore, I should tell you we have in our own secret rooms evidence which irrefutably proves we can never escape by any means whatsoever from the unhappiness we create for ourselves or for others. You would be forced to return to witness it for as many times as were necessary to learn the lesson. But to answer your question about ending your existence, I will tell you. The end of the world is not a frightful precipice or an angry storm. It is not a great explosion, or a blue-black morn. It's not a tidal wave that tears the bottom off the ocean floor, nor an earthquake that cracks boulders like eggshells in a vise of stone. It's not a hurricane, typhoon, tornado, or monsoon. It's not when money leaves and ruin sets in. Or when the knock of justice calls. My son, it's not the water torture or the rack. Or even burning at the stake in holy zeal. It's not death's angel wasting all the flesh away with knowledge it's his own to so consume. There are, of course, the many who think those commonplace calamities spell out the end of all. But those who know the gnawing of the spirit are moved by fear and dread of only one demise. They know that only love's quiet, painful death can truly bring about the dying of the soul. Without which there can never be another ray of light, another world to see, another hand to hold, or another day to hope."

"Oh . . . yes . . . but I am still caught on the horns of a dilemma. Why is Henry Somerset here? And what must I do with regard to these continuing and uncanny happenings?"

"To answer the first question, I will tell you these spirits return after death to learn lessons which their stubbornness impeded during life. Frequently, they suffer great pain, and much of the loneliness which was endured while they lived. They come alone in their own individual dimensions, and proceed onward only when the lesson is soundly learned. If Henry Somerset is here, you must be careful not to allow yourself to become the pawn of his wishes and desires. They may not be in your best interest, and your yielding to them may not even be helpful to his troubled spirit. As for Amalita Corsini, I already know from a very private source that she is an exact look-alike of your dead wife. But do not be deceived. I am quite certain the similarity ceases at the level of the flesh. From what I have heard, your wife was a kind and spiritual person. Do not expect to find these attributes in Amalita. The best I can tell you is that she is talented and seized with all the irresistible charms of the darkness. She would not be good for you. . . . If in the thread of destiny it is written that you are to succumb to these charms, I must hope and pray for your emergence from them with the preservation of the integrity of your spirit. I am precluded by many, many reasons from saying more. You must make your own journey, my son. I am here to help, but you are the traveler. One thing . . . consider me a friend and a spiritual adviser. When you hold this, which is my gift to you in gratitude for a special morning, you will think of me, and of my words."

With these thoughts, the Cardinal has extracted from his pocket a beautifully wrought little gold-and-emerald cross, which he is pressing into E.C.'s hand. It's old, and from where I'm standing, seems uniquely wonderful.

"Cardinal, I can't accept. It's just too beautiful. It looks Byzantine."

"You are very right indeed. It is ancient, and very holy. And entirely mine to give to you. Whenever you hold it, you should think of yourself as having my blessing. . . . But it is late, and I must go. I will take your arm again, and we shall climb the hill together."

Walking up the incline now, again arm in arm, the two of them seem almost otherworldly. I just took a closer look at the beautiful little Byzantine cross. It sports five irregularly shaped emeralds. And very powerful emanations. They've reached the top of the promontory and Tucci is moving toward his car, but stops to make his brief farewells.

"Thank you again, Mr. Douglas. I have enjoyed being with you today. No doubt I will see you tomorrow at the opera and at Mrs. Somerset's reception."

"Yes, of course . . . and Your Eminence, thank you for everything."

The attendant has closed the limousine door, which has slammed shut with hermetic precision. Tucci is waving as his little entourage slowly makes its way over the gravel road, down to the main gate. Our man is still standing at the foot of the pyramid steps clasping the little cross tightly in his left hand. Bozo is leaning against him. Protectively. As if to ward off all evil.

After Tucci's car has long been lost in the distance, I can't help roaming back through the verdant corridors of my maze. Now again, in the center, I sit here thinking about the things the Cardinal said. And I'm drawn to consider his comments regarding this business of coming back to correct the unhappiness we've caused others and ourselves. It's an arresting topic. In any event, even if I were ultimately to change my viewpoint and agenda, it would seem there's still a bit of time to wring out that last little measure of pleasure. But now, in opposition to previous occasions, there's a part of me which is exercising caution and incorporating the element of doubt. Certainly, I'm enjoying many of the things in which I delighted before. Excitement, empire, high finance, and revenge. There's something about vengeance that just struck me a moment ago. Could it be we actually set people up to do us the harm for which later we will seek redress? Is it possible we need the revenge as a means of confirming our opinions as well as our most cherished weaknesses? And that in reverse order, we create the wrongs in order to avenge ourselves, thus protecting our beloved egos and tender psyches?

This business of fabricating things to protect our frail interiors has also alerted me to another important question. Why is it we always love the wrong people? Why do we customarily fall in love with the unworthy, unhealthy, or even dangerous? I've seen it a thousand times. Virtuous women besotted with scoundrels. And fine gentlemen falling in love with liars and cheats. Perhaps we fall in love with them because they help us to confirm our views about mankind, therefore preserving and protecting our own positive egotistical viewpoints about ourselves. That's one of the reasons E.C. is in love with Amalita. And that's why I loved a similar woman in my time. At the subconscious level, E.C. knows she's an evil person. He doesn't even have to be told. He's a man with the requisite level of spiritual advancement to discern, but in spite of this, Susan Cleave's bed will remain unused while the springs in Amalita's will strain under the burden of his desire. Why divorce the genteel and well-bred woman to marry the floozy who cuckolds you with a worthless adolescent? I guess we must think very little of ourselves to require bringing unworthies into our lives. Yet we do it again and again because we are unable to learn the lesson of placing value where it belongs.

I'll admit that a few hours ago I was anxious to see E.C. soundly stick it to the star. But now, I'm having second thoughts. The woman is no good for him, and would serve no purpose in his life. There's nothing she can teach him, except perhaps to beware of such spidery entanglements.

Back at the house, E.C. is on the phone to Harry the broker.

"E.C., for chrissake. It's Sunday. Can you spare me the aggravation on just one day?"

"You know something, Harry? You're a bandit. And you wouldn't be talking to me that way unless it was all done. Were you able to complete everything as I requested?"

"Of course, of course. Didn't you see the European confirmations? You are very, very long in the European steels. May God protect you if they should ever take a turn downward."

"Don't you know I lead a charmed life? Besides, I had a prince of the Church here today who gave me the type of good-luck charm you'd give your left nut to own."

"Well, you know I'm superstitious. But you don't have to believe in talismans to be nervous with a big position like yours. For goodness sake, E.C., why don't you sell some of it at tomorrow's opening?"

"Nothing doing. Besides, there's going to be news."

"When?"

"Tomorrow."

"Just be careful, E.C., that it's not the type of news that lands us in jail."

"Not to worry, Harry. We can't be blamed for science learned after the fact. Besides, it's anonymous, and anyway, we are long in Europe, not short in America."

"Very cryptic. I won't ask any more questions. Are you going to let me get back to what I was doing?"

"Okay, Harry, have a good afternoon."

"You too. Behave yourself."

Click.

E.C. is reaching for the phone again. Dialing Amalita. I'm concerned. Besides, I don't like to see a grown man moaning like a lovesick teenager. You'd think he'd discern between the ridiculous infatuation of uncontrolled adolescents and the true nature of the mature love experience. Why is it that lust turns us all into ridiculous creatures? He's finally reached her.

"Hallo . . ."

"Amalita, it is I."

"Who is I?"

"You know very well who this is."

"You must have a wrong number."

"Amalita, it's E.C."

"Ah, you again. You are turning into a bothersome child."

"Amalita, I really do have to see you."

"Is it a matter of life or death? In that case, let us wait and see. If it is a matter of death, it will resolve itself, and I need do nothing about you."

"Why do you behave this way with me?"

"I told you, *caro*, I like to see you suffer."

"Are you going to devour me after we make love, like the tarantula?"

"Only if you promise to enjoy it. You see, I host only willing victims."

"Amalita, all I can do is remember how very hard your nipples were when I last pressed against you."

"You are a very naughty boy to speak of such things over the telephone. People might overhear us."

"I don't care. Why can't I see you now?"

"*Caro*, never before the opera. I must sing a complete *Forza del Destino* tomorrow. I will see you after the performance."

Click.

E.C. is looking rather peeved, in spite of the fact Bozo is affectionately chomping on his slipper. The phone is ringing once more. And this time it's Susan Cleave.

"I had told myself I wouldn't speak with you until work tomorrow. But here I am like a foolish woman, breaking my own resolve and calling."

"What can I do for you?"

"I think we should talk."

"No. Not today. There's too much happening."

"E.C., I think we could have something worthwhile. And I wouldn't want to see it slip through our fingers without an effort."

"I don't know what you're talking about. Everything's okay. I've just been feeling out of sorts lately."

"I'm not convinced."

"Stop creating windmills in your mind. Everything will be fine."

"I care for you."

"I'm fond of you too."

"Fond of me isn't good enough."

"Well, you know what I mean."

"Tell me you adore me."

"It's not in my nature. Why do women always want us to adore them?"

"Because love provides security."

"As if you didn't have enough of that."

"But I don't. I desperately need you."

"I think you're overreacting. Why don't you have a hot cup of tea and two aspirins? I'll see you tomorrow morning."

"E.C., I definitely feel my replacement is being lined up."

"That's total nonsense. Do you have anything concrete to tell me regarding that stupid notion?"

"Well, no. It's a feeling."

"If I were you, I'd stop creating my own problems."

"Goodbye."

"Goodbye."

Click.

The scene I've just witnessed has brought many of my buried emotions to the surface. Some time ago I would have been cheering for E.C. But now I view such matters differently and think this is all very wrong. Susan is a magnificent woman. Perhaps she's latched on a bit too quickly, due to the reenactment of her relationship with me, but I can tell she genuinely loves him. You'd think a man seasoned in so many other ways would be able to opt for quality rather than enticement. But I guess the parks are full of virtuous women who've been divorced, and of fine men who've been abandoned.

E.C. looks like he's making ready to dial Amalita again. In fact, he's looking for the number in his daily diary. As if he didn't know it by heart! Maybe there's something I can do here, though. I know . . . I'll take that glass pitcher full of roses which is sitting next to his book and slide it right off the table. It's hitting the floor with an altogether satisfactory crash. He's accusingly looking for Bozo, but the pooch is at the other side of the room. Where he can't possibly be blamed. Our man knows he didn't touch it himself. So he's acquiring a funny look on his face. And quickly turning as if to catch me from behind. E.C. doesn't know I'm just here all the time. A rabbit's hair beyond his dimensional reach. Now he's speaking out loudly.

"Is it really you, Henry Somerset? Are you there?"

I don't think I'll respond. I can't possibly. It wouldn't be smart. I'd rather leave him in serious doubt. Having received no answer, our man is beginning to question his own sanity, as he murmurs to himself, "I must be going out of my mind." He's at that point where with the slightest provocation he might be willing to believe in my presence. Perhaps at some moment I'll present myself through some action designed to convince him. But for the present, why should I provide him with the certainty when I can preserve the perfect vehicle of creeping into his dreams and suggesting courses of action? All this while still retaining the mystique of the situation. And more important, his own concept of independence.

Speaking of dreams, I'm quite tempted to intrude upon a few tonight. Tomorrow is liable to be a rather spectacular day in the life of E. C. Douglas and others. And hopefully, no less spectacular in the death of H. W. Somerset. So I think I'll strategically find my way into a few dormant states. For instance, why not pop over to Harriet's and acquire real insight into her expectations for tomorrow?

Easy as pie, I'm back at the country house. As I walk through the halls of this splendid, rambling home now bedded down for the night, I can't help complementing good old Harriet on her excellent taste. Everywhere there are massive arrangements of lilies still in the bud, which by the time of tomorrow evening's party will be ablaze with open flowers. She's redone some of the rooms since we became estranged. A lot of heavier velvets and damasks have been replaced with bright silks and sharp, flowery chintzes. It's a more feminine touch, but, to be sure, quite pleasant. I must say, apart from the few details and some of the works of art, this is and has always been Harriet's house. She fell in love with it and bought it all by herself, albeit with my money.

Upstairs, my wife is asleep among the off-white tones of her slinky sheets. There's perfume in the air. You see, Harriet is squeaky-clean. One can almost perceive a Lady Macbeth complex at work here. She washes her hands twenty or thirty times a day. And then nicely wraps them, and her precious face, in creams and lotions for the night. She sleeps on her back. In the "royal" position with a silk mask over her eyes to completely avoid the possibility of admitting light.

She's receptive tonight. I can tell. So I shall smoothly intrude *like a soft caramel falling into an old lady's mouth.* Everything is rigid inside this mind. There are lots of rooms here, and many of them are securely locked, so not even her subconscious can penetrate into places which might deter her from her avowed ends. It's actually quite telling and interesting that Harriet's mind should have it all organized like a large interminable house. I'm walking past a room which is earmarked "love." This one has four locks and three chains on it. Yet I will stealthily slip through the keyhole and take a peek. Hah! Guess what she has locked up in here. There's a comely high school boy named Scott. Whose visage forever slumbers in the expectation of being awoken by Harriet's true love kiss. He's a chunky lad. And muscular. Big, strong, and extremely handsome. Slightly reddish hair, and green eyes. But there's a heartbroken look on his face. That's what Harriet did to him when she married me. I used to think people recuperated from broken hearts, but I've changed my mind. Some never really do. Surprise of surprises. I too am mirrored in this room. It seems at one point she really loved me. And then stopped. What is it about love with some people? How is it possible it can exist with such exuberance, effervescence, and strength, and then all of a sudden terminate to never surface again? I don't think I can take being here very long. So I'll leave through that keyhole as quietly as I entered. Alas, though, I've been caught. Harriet is roaming through these dream halls in her nightgown. Asleep or not, she can be counted upon for the same perspicacity. So now I've been apprehended and she's squarely face to face with me.

"Henry, what are you doing here? You don't frighten me . . . well, maybe just a little!"

"You know this is a dream, Harriet."

"Yes, Henry, but you're dead. And I'd much rather leave you that way. Furthermore, I saw you come through that keyhole. You've been skunking around in my memories. Is nothing sacred?"

"You should know better than to ask that question. Certainly, nothing is or has ever been sacrosanct to me. But I was surprised to see you loved me once. Can you explain? Why did it stop?"

"Oh, Henry, you can be so very tedious. But to answer you, I'm not sure it ever really stopped. Things just changed. Do you really want to know?"

"I wouldn't have asked the question if I didn't want the answer. Besides, you're safe. This is a dream. It's not as if I were actually asking you in real life, and you had to evade responding."

"You know, I've been wanting to get this off my chest for the longest time. . . ."

"And a beautiful chest it is."

"Oh, Henry, can't you ever stop thinking about sex? Besides,

I've already told you, you're dead. Getting back to what I was going to say . . . I'm going to admit I really did love you at one point, at least in my own way. Mind you, it wasn't at first. As you so indiscreetly saw a moment ago, I really was originally in love with Scott. But all of a sudden, there you were. You were dashing. And intelligent, and something told me you would be very, very rich. Then all of a sudden, as if by magic, you started sprouting oil wells like dandelions. I would have been mad to have married Scott at that point. I'll tell you, though, something funny happened shortly thereafter. You know those roses you used to bring me, and the fresh strawberries out of season? They really started affecting me. And all of your little considerations and kindnesses, and the way you learned to make love. I really found myself falling for you."

"So what happened?"

"Henry, as you became the person you are, I lost respect. And then when I started to suspect you were watching and monitoring my every move, I began to fear you. After all, I saw daily how you stopped at nothing to gain your ends. And how others were moved to ruin, and even suicide, because of your ambition. And the fear drove away the love. And then, as you became resentful with your knowledge of the change within me, and my infidelities, I began despising you. And then I began hating."

"Well, Harriet, at least hate is a quality emotion. I never felt you gave me half a chance."

"You didn't give yourself a chance. Anyway, why are you haunting my dreams?"

"Harriet, I'm here to tell you you're going to go broke. I mean bust. Like every cent. I've returned to take you apart piece by piece, and dollar by dollar."

"Don't be silly, Henry. You're dead and this is a dream. Besides, there's a new man in my life who's going to be just as rich as you were."

"Oh, so that's it. You're after E. C. Douglas now!"

"You can bet on it, Henry."

"You know, Harriet, I'll wager I can still terrify you. You think I don't know how afraid of poverty you really are. There's a room right down the hall here where you've bricked up the door so it can never be entered. But I've slipped in through the crevices in the mor-

tar. And I've seen the little girl with the fairly middle-class beginnings."

"No, Henry . . . I don't want to hear this. Go away. Leave me
alone."

"You must listen, Harriet. I'm really here. And before I'm
through with you, you'll be just like that again."

"Don't bet on it!"

Harriet is now screaming at me in her dream state. Telling me
to go away. She has all of a sudden opened her eyes in a full wakeful
state of unrest. As if by reciprocal force, I have been unpleasantly
evicted from the land of nod, and slapped against a wall with gale
force. It's worth it, though. I've learned a few tidbits I couldn't have
known before. And furthermore, I am now aware of her designs on
E.C. So I can protect him from this new predator in the game. I did,
however, miss something important. I should have discovered what
she did to me that last day of my life. I won't sweat it, though. Since
there will later be time for such inquiries.

I'm wondering if I might be able to slip into Amalita's dreams as well.
I'm projecting myself into her presence. Surely enough, here I am in
the opera star's tower suite. With lots of flowers as well. Beautiful
baskets for the prima donna. The large sitting room is now darkened.
In the small bedroom, Amalita's elderly attendant is fast asleep. This
is the same woman I've seen in her rooms before. The face is withered
and drawn. Not with the marks of gracious aging, but with the wrinkles and blemishes of anguish, sadness, and fear. Perhaps I should
penetrate this sleeping mind first. And thus gain additional insight
into the nature of the diva.

In I go . . . but this is definitely not a place I would care to visit
very often. It's sad here. Dark and dirty. With the dank smells of
desperate and stark Sicilian beginnings. There are sobs everywhere,
and the throbbing of unremitting pain. I now find this woman is
actually Amalita's aunt. In here, she witnesses nightly the tragic spectacle of Amalita's mother working herself to the bone to provide singing lessons for the spoiled, exigent, and ambitious child. I see a
mother dying of sadness and anguish, abandoned by her daughter.
Unable to be a part of her beloved's bright new life. I see the daughter
being unyielding to the mother, and denying her sustenance. It's a

horrible scene. Especially because of the coldness and crudeness with which it occurs. And now the knowing aunt has been turned into a servant to slowly wither and dry. She knows things too . . . she's seen the insecure child lusting after possessions, wealth, and fame. Clinging to men like a murderous, parasitic plant. Inserting each day a new tendril into their hearts, and enslaving their souls. I've got to get out of here. I don't wish to see any more.

I'll go sit in the parlor for a while and take hold of myself. After this preamble, I have second thoughts about intruding into Amalita's dreams. Mind you, I'm not weak of heart or stomach. But what I just witnessed was the spectacle of a human being who has forsaken all hope. It was a spirit so totally engulfed and demolished by the evil of another's nature that there wasn't even a ray of light to be found in that whole cold, dark place of night. But I'm curious. And since it can hardly kill the cat on this occasion, I'm going to compose myself and visit the great woman.

Through the doors, and into the sleeping chamber I go. There she is. Every hair in place. All is tended and cared for here. Yet there's something which makes me uneasy. On the night table lies the ransom in diamonds she was sporting earlier today. The nightgown she's wearing is of the finest ivory-colored silk with lace, no doubt handmade by a convent of nuns with hands like old dried branches. Beneath that tenuous garment, the legendary breast heaves in tune to the seeming complacency of her sleep.

As I enter her dream state, I note that all here is the deepest black, with occasional bursts of extremely bright red. Amalita is present, dressed in a crimson nightgown. She immediately sees me.

"Mr. Somerset, I recognize you from your pictures. What are you doing here?"

"Well, of course, Amalita, you should assume you've invented me for some purpose. Tell me, what are you doing in this dream?"

"You see all these precious little boxes. Well, I collect them. Within them I keep the souls of men."

"And how do you acquire them?"

"That is quite simple, *caro*. First I entice the poor creatures. Then I allow them to fall in love. Subsequently I enslave them, and later I destroy them."

"How very interesting! Shall we walk a bit down this dark lane here?"

"Yes, why not? You see all these men at one side and the other. They are drying, and decaying. And with the powder of their souls in my little boxes, I shall grow and become more powerful."

"I don't understand. Aren't you already famous, and rich?"

"But not beyond my wildest dreams, and besides, I enjoy seeing them suffer."

"And Cardinal Tucci?"

"I would like to enslave him, but he is beyond my power. Besides, he has secret weapons."

"What weapons?"

"The weapons of love, faith, and hope."

"But Amalita, there's a man here to my right who's looking at you with desperate, open eyes."

"He is my father. Pay no attention to this man."

"But I am very interested. There seems to be a play going on here."

"It occurs each night, but I am totally unmoved by it."

"Well, I wish to watch."

"In that case do so alone. I shall continue walking."

Amalita has imperiously moved forward into the darkness. I, however, wish to witness the nightly enactment of her dream. In it a very poor little girl is being taken down the street by her father. The child has beautiful shiny black hair, set in pigtails. Her father is a man of middle height. Coarse, and obviously unhappy with the burden of a female child. His dress is unkempt. Actually dirty. It's almost noon, and the bright Sicilian sun shines down on them unremittingly. The father is in a hurry, and he's pulling her along. The child is willful, and occasionally stops right in her tracks to look at one thing or another. On those occasions if she does not respond to his less-than-gentle tug, he slaps her. There is, however, something very singular about this tag-along child. She does not weep when she is struck. Obviously, at some point she did, but the feelings which would bring about such emotions have protectively buried themselves where they can no longer be reached by her victimizing parent.

The thing he's clenching tightly in his left hand is a bank note of undetermined denomination. He's obviously in a hurry to reach a particular place. All of a sudden, the child stops stubbornly. The face previously devoid of emotion is now trembling on its very surface with ecstasy and hope. She's looking at something in a store window. Particularly at the very pretty porcelain-headed figure within. In terms of doll manufacture, it really isn't very singular or special at all. But to the child, this is, without a doubt, the most beautiful one she's ever seen. *The finest doll in the world!* Her father pulls on her little hand. But with great spirit, she resists, motioning insistently to the little porcelain face in the window. The parent looks at the bank note, thinking to himself for a split second that he would have enough to indulge this childish whim. But then the instinct suffers a quick death and something deeper within him takes hold. The desire to fill his gut with cheap alcohol takes precedence over the incidental and solitary emotion which might have spurred him to purchase the mute companion. Amalita will not move. And is therefore repeatedly struck by her father until her face and arms are red with the marks of the abuser's blows. She's weeping now, and if there could be tears of blood, these would be they. He's now picking her up and carrying her into the bar, where the bank note is exchanged for a bottle. Amalita cries without anyone's notice. Yet soon, an organ grinder, complete with simian, enters the bar and proceeds to sing. The fellow likes children. She's stopped sobbing now, as the organ grinder finds it is no effort to dispense a perfunctory kindness to this scrawny and unhappy child. She's amused by the antics of the monkey. And also notices coins find their way into the singer's hat. Deep within her she resolves to never weep again. And then to sing.

The scene shifts to one which occurs years later. Now, a well-dressed young singer, beautiful and seductive, daily brings her father as many bottles of alcohol as he can drink. And here in the dream each night he again crumbles under the weight of his daughter's murderous offerings, until his body and spirit are totally consumed. While the nightingale laughs and sings, but never weeps.

I understand now why it is so terrifyingly dark in her dream world. And why in Amalita, sarcasm assumes the place of humor. Again, at some cost to my emotions, I've learned powerful secrets which will hopefully help me to protect E.C. from being collected into one of those *precious* little boxes. As I tiptoe out of her dream and into the parlor, I am struck with the reality of evil. You know, when we're children, they try to teach us that everything is good and evil does not exist. This is a terrible mistake. Because we actually grow up believing all of the goody-goody claptrap regarding the non-existence of darkness. But evil is very real indeed, and alive and well in people like Amalita who will stop at nothing to gain what they wish. The fact that it invariably comes from something twisted, like pain and suffering, does not justify its existence, or in any way mollify the harm it can do. And it is quite true that *by their fruits ye shall know them.* Certainly their words are often beautiful and beguiling. I now know with conviction that the good people must protect themselves against the reality of evil in our world. You know, this is the first time I've ever confronted the issue so squarely. Although I don't know why I'm so surprised to find myself on this side of the fence.

It's been a very long day. And so very much is going to be occurring tomorrow. Regular activities don't seem to cause a lot of wear and tear on my spiritual person. But these incursions into people's dreams, and into the secret rooms and quarters where they keep their most privately sequestered feelings and remembrances, totally exhaust me. I have realized quite recently that I too have such secret rooms. Sometimes I think love got buried in the avalanche. And so did I with all those special years which were released into a phantom who stands guard over despair in the empty rooms of my interminable night. It could be said he bounces off the walls and screams mute imprecations intertwining with those memories of fragrant hair, and all the little sounds she used to make. I could say, "There is no one there," and try to sleep. But it comes crawling through the keyhole. Clinging, like a suffocating beast. "Perhaps you do not love me anymore? And so, if then I must, I will stop loving and make peace that love is dead. But instead, and in your place, maybe I'll take another, and this time, it will be my own phantom of despair." So we shall wed, and *it* and I shall scream into the night with soulful zeal that none will hear. Except that once by chance someday you'll look into this frightful place. And also madden. So then, the two of us, and not just I, will choose to know where I have been and where I live. And how it's been each night.

This is all beginning to sound unhinged, even though it's coming from within me. Which definitely means it's time to try to rest in anticipation of further events. I now have mixed feelings about much of what I wish to do. But still, there is a resolve within. A compulsion which forces me to push forward with my plans. I have questions, though. Mainly about why I seem to be repeating the same actions, reactions, and situations. Could this constitute a terrible mistake? I'm not sure. But I shall think of this when I'm less tired, and there isn't as much to do.

TWENTY-NINE

MONDAY MORNING HAS NOT ARRIVED SOON ENOUGH. IT WAS A REMARK-
able night, made longer by the introspection born of witnessing the
emotions in those dreams at Harriet's and Amalita's. Toward the end
of the day, when I became totally fatigued, I found myself softening
a bit. But today, I intend to allow myself to succumb fully to the
charms of my overactive ego. Yessiree, I'll have a little revenge for
breakfast. And of course, I don't have to go over my little list. I know
it well enough by heart. Dying has provided me with one last opportunity to even the score with everyone. I don't care if this is my
last chance. I'm bouncing around playing word games with the concept. Once is certainly enough if it's the trigger of a gun, or the flutter
of a day-fly. And quite certainly if it's the slither of the serpent, or
the gila's fond caress. Once is totally enough if you are the husband
of the mantis or the queen bee's mate. And once is absolutely enough
if you are the playmate of the adder, or the mamba's pet. Once is
very much enough if it's the pallor of the nightshade, or the Amanita's

cap. And today, once will be sufficient regarding everything which I intend to do and wish to achieve.

I'm at Harriet's, where there is an incredible level of activity. She's up and fully dressed in a shocking-pink suit trimmed with black piping. Marching through the house, barking orders in her customary military style. Beneath the makeup there are signs of last night's little encounter with me and the remembrance of that bricked-up room. But you would have to look closely and know her very well indeed to detect them. It's nine o'clock and she's out the door and into the waiting car on her way to the office for the closing with E.C. She's less than her absolutely secure self today. Looking at her nails repeatedly, and occasionally twirling her wedding ring. Our arrival at Blackrock is rather quick today. Upstairs, Hooker is waiting with the stack of documents necessary for the purchase of the exclusive license to use Von Richter's process and for the sale of the American steels. Harriet briskly walks through the various outer offices and is now upon the lawyer, who has grown gopherlike under the weight of the impending transaction.

"Good morning, Harriet. I must say you are looking unusually smashing in that pink suit."

"Well, my dear, you know what Henry always said. *When an ill wind blows, put on a good face.*"

"In that case, you seem to be doing splendidly. Everything is ready, and I have the certified check being walked up from the bank at ten in the amount of four hundred and fifty million dollars, plus the larger one for the American steels."

"This had all better work. We're down to our last pennies after this transaction. All is committed to the steel stocks. Each time I think of it, I start feeling this inescapable urge to strangle Gustavo. You know, Thomas, there are times when I feel certain I could really do without relatives."

"Harriet, it just isn't worth torturing yourself. Pretty soon the steels will bounce back again, probably today. And you'll have hundreds of millions in your accounts again. Also, the acquisition of this process should very quickly generate phenomenal profits."

"Well, I don't know, Thomas, I have a very bad feeling. I think I might have preferred to fold rather than bet."

"Did you have an alternative?"

"No, no. Of course not. But let me ventilate a little. After all, it's my money."

"And my hard work. You fail to realize my entire firm and I will be ruined if all of this doesn't work."

"Well, at least I have a consolation."

"Don't be a bitch, Harriet."

"Stop it, Thomas. You know I dislike vulgarities in the mouths of others."

The intercom has just indicated the presence of E. C. Douglas and his attorneys. Harriet is ordering that they should be shown into the adjoining conference room. She's assuming her most beguiling demeanor, and Hooker is collecting the documents, which are in triplicate. They're now walking into the conference room, which is being entered at the opposing door by E.C.'s party.

"Good morning, Mrs. Somerset."

"Good morning, Mr. Douglas. But please, call me Harriet. I've told you already."

"Yes, you're right. It's my mistake. Mr. Hooker, how are we doing with the documents? This is my attorney, Mr. John Abernathy, whom I believe you've met."

"Yes, of course. Mr. Abernathy and I have met on several occasions. But of course it's nice to see you again. I've included all of the corrections you sent over yesterday. And you may, if you wish, read everything to make sure it all conforms."

"That won't be necessary. Do you agree, John?"

"Yes, E.C. I went over everything with Mr. Hooker yesterday. All we need to do is sign. I assume you have the check?"

"Yes. They just brought it up from the bank."

"In that event, why don't we proceed. Ladies first."

"Thank you very much. Actually, I'm grateful for the courtesy, because as you may know, I have a few guests tonight and much to do today. I *do* expect we'll be seeing you, Mr. Douglas."

"Oh, yes. I wouldn't miss it for the world."

Harriet is methodically signing and initialing the various documents. And then E.C. is doing the same. The checks are flipped into the hands of a bonded messenger, who will quickly make sure the funds are placed with Harry overnight. The whole thing occurs in a rather unremarkable amount of time. It's a proper transaction. The type of thing that happens under the purview of the finest attorneys. Mind you, I hate them. They're basically parasites. But the good ones are like skilled murderers and executioners who don't allow the unthinking host or prey to suffer unduly. Thus, these documents are in perfect shape and require no last-minute drafting or tiresome change.

So my wife has left still twirling that ring and looking at her watch. Her next stop is at the hair stylist, where she will enjoy a moment of respite and gossip. E.C. and the attorneys have received their copies, and the checks are on course to Harry. They're now leaving with the relaxed smiles endemic to the type of transaction where everyone feels he received something out of the deal.

E.C. and his little entourage are making their way down to the waiting cars. The attorney will return to the various duties of memorializing the transaction, and the messenger will deliver the funds. A third man, waiting at the curb, is now being handed a pack of substantial manila envelopes designed to anonymously find their way into certain mail slots. I'm taking a peek, and find them addressed to various financial news and reporting services. There's no "from" on them, though. E.C. is really doing it. He's blowing the whistle on Von Richter's process. I just can't wait to see and hear the fireworks. E.C. and I are now comfortably in the car, and on our way back to Pyramid Hill. Szilagyi has come forth with his usual conversation and is commenting on the more inane events of the day. But E.C. is unapproachable and intense. In his eyes, there is a cold, determined look. In point of fact, I can't help noticing something has happened to him. He's changed, and is genuinely enjoying the kill. Every once in a while, he puts his hand into his vest pocket. Aha! It's that diamond he's been carrying around. Touching it in anticipation of things to come. Why is it we frequently associate objects with the past or the future? Something will bring us memories, and a gift or token will be touched in expectation of the moment of giving, or at worst, the *quid pro quo*. In this case I assume it's both.

We're rounding the bend. The wall and silhouette of Pyramid Hill are now upon us. Through the gate and up the lane. The staircase is down in expectation of our arrival. E.C. is bounding up the steps, and paying little attention to the waiting pooch, who has patiently anticipated his arrival. We're now making our way into the library. And our man is quick to turn his television to the Financial

News Channel. There's nothing yet. I think he's assuming a reaction much too quickly. We're hearing the usual dumb claptrap about one issue or another being up a dollar. Or bonds being down "ten thirty-seconds" of a point. The phone is ringing. It's E.C.'s private line, and he's going for it with haste.

"E.C., this is me."

"Yes, Harry."

"You crazy son of a bitch, the steel market is in pandemonium, and trading has been halted in all the major issues after a phenomenal drop."

"Tell me, Harry, how much?"

"I'd say on the average, most issues are down a good fifty to sixty percent."

"That means there'll be lots of forced liquidations."

"You bet your sweet ass, baby, and here you just sold the American steels you held through your Siderurgica deal! Too bad you weren't short as well! I've got to say, it's brilliant, though. You're not going to be able to count the money you'll make with the European steels you held in Siderurgica."

"Oh, but I do want to count it. Every last little red cent of it."

"Hey, E.C., are you feeling all right? That's not like you at all. You're joking, aren't you?"

"No, Harry, I'm not joking. I think I'm beginning to like this money thing very much. I intend to milk it for all it's worth."

"You know, the European steels are going through the ceiling. There's going to be more money sitting in your accounts than even God can count."

"But I'm telling you I will count it if it takes forever!"

"Okay, okay, just thought I'd congratulate you. Aren't you just a little worried?"

"Thanks, Harry; and no, I'm not."

"Why? This whole thing could be a rumor. You know, they're saying the new process for steel isn't any good. What if it ends up not being true, and it blows up right in your face? What should I do with my other customers?"

"Harry, I have a hunch you should hold tight. Furthermore, if the issues aren't trading, it will probably cost you a great deal to cover if your clients are short. Better to watch it closely and wait until tomorrow morning. When all is said and done, and forced liquidations occur, you're going to be able to cover at a very advantageous price."

"You know, E.C., you're a clever bastard. You sold the American steels privately, and your European holdings are out of the reach of the American law. So you don't even have an insider-trading problem! Masterful, and incredible. To make all that money and not even be haunted by the ghost of the Texas Gulf Sulphur case. I just can't get over it."

There's a bulletin coming on the screen now, as our man raises the volume to catch every word. The financial reporter is actually looking a tad excited. He's a young man. One of those piss-and-vinegar television people who thrives on other people's misfortune. He meets all the standard requisites. He's got that good flat face which is so highly prized in good-looking men, and pedigreed Persian cats. Large eyes, lots of hair, angular Wasp features, and a good unfaltering voice.

"Well, ladies and gentlemen, there's panic in the steel stocks and markets today. After a phenomenal drop of over fifty percent in value, which occurred during a period of only fifteen minutes, trading has been halted in the four major steel stocks. The unusual drop is due to a shocking study which was anonymously released earlier today to the major financial reporting agencies.

"Our viewers will recall that a little over a year ago, there was a rise in certain steel issues which had decided to avail themselves of a unique manufacturing process invented by Karl Von Richter. Von Richter's process was quickly put into use by certain companies, under the auspices of Siderurgica Internazionale, thus creating a very substantial pricing edge in its favor.

"Today, a memorandum brought anonymously to light and prepared by the late Dr. Von Richter himself, discloses that without doubt the process eventually causes fatigue in the metals on which it is used. A scientific team was immediately called upon to evaluate Von Richter's data. The preliminary but unanimous consensus of the experts is that Von Richter is correct in his calculation that the steel manufactured by the process will fatigue and be subject to breakage within one or two years after its use. Apparently, because of the molecular relationships involved, it is a phenomenon which does not become evident until the decay is advanced. Substantial concern has surfaced in the markets, since the inability to use Von Richter's process will again make the European companies the leaders in the field of producing less expensive steel.

"The memorandum was apparently prepared for the late H. W. Somerset. If this can be irrefutably established, his estate may be facing some very substantial legal liabilities. Also of note: One of the experts we consulted before putting this important news on the air reminded us that the new government-owned Franklin Bridge was built almost entirely out of steel manufactured by means of the Von Richter process. More on this important news later."

E.C. is pouring himself a drink. It's that Polish vodka for which he's developed a taste. That old index finger is again up against his nose. And of course there is the quizzical little smile. But it's not the victor I want to see today. This reaction is predictable enough. It's Harriet, Hooker, and Gustavo that I really wish to scrutinize. I've zoomed over to my wife's now. I must say, the house is looking even more splendid that it did earlier today. Ah . . . I hear the car approaching on the gravel driveway. Enter the black widow. And with magnificent coiffure as well. Her hair is pulled back complete with tresses neatly set in the rear. I can tell she still doesn't know a thing. How wonderful! The phone is ringing. I don't have to be clairvoyant to know what this communication is going to be all about. The maid is picking up and handing the receiver to Harriet, who is looking sedate and dignified up to this point.

"My dear, it's Thomas."

"Yes, Thomas. You'd best be brief, because I have a hundred things to do here."

"Harriet, are you sitting down?"

"Don't be silly. What's happening?"

"Well, honey . . ."

"Thomas, don't honey me. Spit it out. Tell me what's happening."

"In three words, *we are broke.*"

"Stop it, Tom. This is a poor moment for a practical joke."

"The steel markets have tumbled. It's got something to do with a scandal about Von Richter's process, and I don't think the market is going to recuperate. Also, the value of the American steels which we pledged to the bank has dropped, so there will be foreclosures and other liabilities with which we can't possibly cope."

"Tom, are you crying over there? Stop blubbering. It can't be all that bad."

"It is, Harriet. It's a nightmare."

"Okay. Give me your worst-case scenario. How bad is it?"

"I'll tell you how bad it is. If a miracle doesn't happen, and I don't expect one, you are completely wiped out. As is Somerset Consolidated Industries."

"What about the Siderurgica stock? Can you retract the pledge?"

"No, we cannot. And furthermore, by the time we can act tomorrow, it will have been acquired in foreclosure to cover the drop in the European portfolio."

"What about the checks we delivered this morning? Can anything be done? Can we stop them?"

"No. Those checks were made good at about eleven-thirty, and the funds transferred to the E. C. Douglas accounts. Besides, you're forgetting we still owe almost a billion dollars in estate taxes. So if this situation doesn't bankrupt us, the government will."

"Is there nothing left that can't be touched?"

"In one word, *no.*"

"And who's responsible for all this? If Henry taught me anything, it was that *Humpty Dumpty was pushed.*"

"Well, it all seems to point to E. C. Douglas."

"Always E. C. Douglas. It's almost as if Henry had possessed him. First the pyramid, then the art, then Siderurgica, and now this. Tom, we just can't let him get away with it."

"Harriet, I don't know what to do except sit here having a nervous breakdown. My whole firm will go down the drain. So will I."

"Oh, shut up, you little weasel. Something has to be done, and I'll do it myself. You're forgetting we have the opera tonight, and I'm hosting a party."

"Harriet, I don't know how you can be thinking about the opera and a party at a time like this. Are you completely out of your fucking mind? You'll just have to cancel the party."

"Tom, I'll do nothing of the sort. I'm not going to sit over here weeping like a little girl over spilled milk. Besides, you're doing enough of that for both of us. I still expect you to be here at seven to attend the performance with me."

"Harriet, you're completely crazy."

"Thomas, our last chance to deal with these matters is at hand tonight."

"Sweetheart, I just don't think I can pick myself up and attend."

"Tom, I'm telling you, if I manage to save the day here, and you're not present in time for the opera, I'll personally destroy you anyway. And you know I mean it. I'm sending a car for you so you won't have to drive. Just be ready at your house in time."

Click.

Harriet has plopped herself down in that French bergère near the telephone. She's looking extremely red in the face. And deflated. It's the look that overcomes her when her blood pressure takes one of those unexpected turns and rises uncontrollably. She's taking deep breaths and twirling that wedding ring as if it were a merry-go-round. One of the maids has taken the cue that Madame is not feeling terribly well.

"Mrs. Somerset, you're looking like something terrible has happened. Is everything all right?"

"Well, something has happened. But I'll be fine. Just fetch my handbag from over there across the room, and bring me a glass of water."

"Yes, ma'am."

The maid has delivered the tiny red ostrich bag Harriet has been using today. She's fumbling with the little flaps that overlap a locking mechanism which makes this little handbag the leathersmith's equivalent of Fort Knox. From it she's extracting a beautiful gold-and-enamel pillbox, from which, in turn, appear the familiar tablets designed to regulate her blood pressure. The water is hastily delivered, and Harriet is now swallowing the medication. I have to hand it to her, she's a tough one. She's just been told her whole fortune has gone down the drain, and she's just sitting in that little chair twirling her wedding ring. If only for a moment I were able to penetrate this waking state, I would, no doubt, find that with each twirl of this simple gold-and-diamond channel-set wedding band, a thought is being honed as if on the most precise of lathes. It's not every day a bunch of billions slips through her hands like E.C.'s grains of sand. Yet Harriet, always hopeful and never defeated, is now calculating both her further downside and the possibilities of correcting this little slip of fate. To be sure, there'd always be a million or two available, so she wouldn't be reduced to holding a tin cup in front of the Museum of Art. But after you've become accustomed to unlimited funds, ten-million-dollar houses, airplanes, and classic cars, a couple of million won't take you very far. Harriet spends the income from that amount in one afternoon at the dressmaker's! Not to mention other essentials like jewelry, art, entertaining, and travel. Yessiree, she's up a tree now, and what's more, the old girl knows it.

I almost feel a bit of pity. She looks smaller. And more fragile. In a way it's as if that little body were making ready to give up and collapse. Blood pressure and all. So it's really only the will to go forward, the ego within, which, still imperious, refuses to concede. Yes, in many ways, Harriet is royalty. She will not bend her head to acquiesce to the executioner's ax. And in this respect, it's surprising to note I'm acquiring a certain admiration for the animal. Now she's picking herself up, little handbag and all, and taking a deep breath while walking through the house examining floral arrangements, and making sure everything is perfect before she goes upstairs to dress. Yes, Harriet has balls, which is more than I can say about the others.

Not wishing to watch her bathe, I've decided to pop over to Thomas Hooker's. Apparently he's advised his secretary he won't be taking calls. And he's just sitting there at his desk staring at the little black revolver sitting in the half-open drawer. No, no, Thomas, this is much too much of a *cliché*! You just can't blow your brains out at this strategic juncture! He's actually sitting there crying like a child. And to think I thought this guy was made out of the right stuff! He's thinking about money. And about tomorrow. Which is exactly what you want your enemies to do. Half the time if they were to center on today, or even on God, there'd be little you could do to harm them. But when you make them focus their thoughts on the insinuation of the danger which could evidence itself in the near future, you've really achieved something. And therefore are far ahead in the direction of enslaving their souls. Nothing torments men more than the fear of what could happen in the future. You can always keep a regular human being awake all night worrying about what might happen the next day. He is, of course, oblivious at that point to the fact that the lack of sleep will not improve his chances for tomorrow.

It's been some time since I've looked in on Gustavo. So I'll leave Tom Hooker and take my pre-opera peek at the nephew who wasn't. Yes, now I'm again here at this very distasteful modern apartment. As might be expected, he's already taken to the bottle, and is vacillating between tears, aggressive behavior, and fear. More than one of the scotch glasses has found itself smashed against the wall. He's sitting in his underbriefs, fondling himself, drinking, smoking, and stupidly wondering whether this is, in fact, the end of his world. Now he's entering the shower. Yes indeed, it looks like a penis, but smaller. And those tiny balls. There's not much you could do with them whether you were a girl or a boy. Now, actually shaving under the stream. Not without inflicting a bit of damage. He's acutely aware that time is running out, and he will soon have to leave for the opera. So he's out of the bathroom in a flash, and into white tie and patent-leather pumps. It looks so squeaky-clean under that starched shirt-front you could almost mistake it for a nice young man. Apparently, he's trying to make a decision. Ah, it has to do with the car keys. It didn't take him very long to decide to use the sports vehicle. I mean, the Maserati. From the look of things, it hasn't been used much since his recent abrupt exit from Somerset Consolidated Industries. So he still has a bit of a surprise coming.

I'm flashing back to E.C.'s, where he's putting the finishing touches on his attire for the evening. The doorbell is ringing. I hear it in the distance. And there are also soft forebodings on the staircase. It's Susan Cleave proceeding majestically, like an otherworldly goddess. She's dressed in a splendid white brocade gown which emphasizes all her curves. And yes, she's wearing my pink diamond. Well, they're ready, and chatting as they proceed.

"You know, you look wonderful tonight."

"Well, thank you, Mr. Douglas."

"Do I note a tad of pique here?"

"No, not really."

"That's good. It should be an exciting evening."

"Do those people know you've broken them yet?"

"Of course they do. They could hardly have missed it!"

"And there haven't been any cancellations?"

"Certainly not. I'd be terribly disappointed if there had been. It would mean we were not dealing with professionals."

"Oh . . . but tell me, why did you do it?"

"Listen, Susan, don't act as if I've intentionally broken the backs of these little sisters of charity. It's nothing personal. They had nothing to do with it."

"I'm not so sure . . . every day you are more like Henry. In fact, sometimes I think you're worse. Less humor. Colder."

"Well, you needn't worry about it. It's done."

"And you think Harriet will actually be there to host her party tonight?"

"Yes I do. It's going to be very interesting."

"Look at you. You've really turned into a Henry. Obsessive and compulsive, hard and vengeful."

"I don't pay you to criticize me."

"In that case, don't pay me. I've decided to quit anyway."

"But what about our situation?"

"You're the one who's quitting on that."

"I don't mean to."

"Yes you do. You've become just like Henry, a liar of the heart. It's probably because, like him, you don't really believe anyone can ever really love you. But look, I didn't come here to argue. I promised I would accompany you this evening, so let's go."

For a moment, E.C. is fondling the diamond in his vest pocket, and thinking about giving it to Susan Cleave. But very much like Amalita's father with the bank note, he will not. The opportunity of the moment lost, Susan and E.C. are now moving toward the car, and on their way to the opera.

THIRTY

IF WE WERE ACTUALLY ABLE TO RISE TO THE HEIGHT OF THE EAGLE'S flight, we would, at this seven-o'clock hour, when the last day's light is vanishing, witness a multiplicity of interesting movements.

A few moments ago, the bright and shining Mercedes limousine belonging to the office of the Papal Nuncio opened its doors to Cardinal Tucci, his two secretaries, and his dashing young assistant. The prelate sits sedately in the sparkling red vestments appurtenant to his rank as the vehicle hums forward through the evening traffic.

From yet another quarter, a famous, beautiful, and troubled woman, who will tonight, thanks to her art, be the object of all eyes, has entered her own automobile. Amalita is sitting brilliantly in black lace and diamonds, contemplating the various possible triumphs of the night. Her appetite has been especially whetted by the possibility of conquering and enslaving E.C.'s body and soul. She's kept him at bay almost beyond his limits. So she knows he will not welcome further delay. She sits complacently with every hair in place. Those digits are bright with the adornment of very long and well-tended fingernails. On them, rings bright with gemstones from the guts of the earth shine as if possessed by some magic incantation. Very much as brilliant colors in the animal world might be found on an especially dangerous animal or flower. Almost as if to serve as fair warning to a potential enemy or mate.

Harriet's car has departed as well. Hooker has been neatly fetched and sits propped up beside her. Almost bovinely, no doubt with the help of a tranquilizer or two. Harriet, in turn, all gussied up in that extremely becoming gown we last saw at the dressmaker's, is sedate, and actually nonostentatious. She's wearing my enormous black pearls. And those star rubies from Burma. But on her face there is a look of quiet determination. Which makes me wonder exactly how far she will go in her attempt to entrap E.C. and regain her fortune.

Within minutes of one another, the various vehicles are now arriving at the opera house. Which is bright with lights which would seem to announce the impending performance. There are posters, which in very large letters proclaim the name of Amalita Corsini, letter to letter with *La Forza del Destino*. It's a benefit performance, so anyone who is anyone, or who so thinks himself, is here to see and to be seen. Amalita makes her entrance at the stage door, where fans and aficionados known as the "claque" await to pelt her gently with fresh carnations and roses. As she sees them, she smiles with the satisfaction of a vampire supping on blood. But in this case, the feast is of energy and adulation. As she retires to her dressing room, the other guests will repair to the various pre-opera gatherings within the house.

A little later at the front entrance, Cardinal Tucci's entourage is arriving, complete with the benefit of police escort. It's not every night we enjoy the privilege of seeing a Vatican Secretary of State in full regalia. He's selected a particularly beautiful cross to wear as tonight's ornament. It's yellow gold, with eleven rubies the size of hazel nuts. An attendant from the opera has been waiting for his party, as his personal security guards usher him to the slightly off-center parterre box to which the Nuncio subscribes.

Harriet and Hooker have now made their way to parterre box twenty-five, which is practically at center. She's sitting up front, and he's sitting behind her. Gustavo has now arrived, and has made a crude attempt at kissing his unreceptive aunt. Farther to the right side, I now see E.C. and Cleave. There are actually eight seats in each of these boxes. So other guests of the individual parties are now making their way into them as well, and are now being greeted by their hosts and hostesses. As she chats with her guests, Harriet has taken her opera glasses in hand, and is presently assessing Susan Cleave with the precision of a Chicago butcher preparing to carve a side of beef. She's also carefully regarding our man and nodding with a smile as their glances meet. That's Harriet, all right! She's four or five billion dollars shy, but not a tremor to denounce her feelings. Hooker, in turn, is looking pale and uncomfortable. I suspect he will not survive the night without the aid of heavy drink, considerable medication, or both.

As the parties appraise one another, I can't help thinking *La Forza del Destino* is a most appropriate opera to complement the events of this day. And *the fatal urn of my destiny*. After all, it's an opera about love, hate, revenge, and the inescapable hand of providence itself. In which a man will be responsible for murdering his beloved's father and her older brother. As the thread unwinds, he will also be guilty of finishing off the remainder of the family. He will kill her younger brother, who will, in turn, stab her at the moment of his dying gasp. But Verdi pinked out on us. In the original Spanish play, the protagonist does the right thing and jumps off a cliff as his sweetheart dies. But in the opera, I guess they just thought there was a bit too much death. So the young man is at the end consoled by the Father Superior and the dying Leonora in that final trio, in which he is assured of God's pardon and being united with her at a later date in heaven. Pusillanimous ending or not, it's my type of story, and my type of music. And I'm thinking this not a moment too soon, since the house lights are being dimmed, and the Maestro is making his way to the podium. In a moment, the overture will be upon us with its six initial blasts and those groupings of four ineludible and compulsive musical notes.

It's been some time since I've been to the opera here. It's one of those exhilarations I had almost forgotten. Being in the Old House has reminded me once more of how very much certain things long ago became an unconscious part of me. It's the present-day equivalent of the Greek tragedy. And an evening with the right singers and music can constitute reentry and direct access to portions of the soul which had long been forgotten, or either intentionally or unconsciously put away.

Here the love of women, the passions of men, and the struggle between good and evil find their way before us. There can be humor as well, and contradiction. Convolution, and entangled plots. But it's the situations which force a hero into ultimate confrontations with himself and destiny that always leave me tingling and hyperactive.

Tonight is just such an evening. Although this is routinely an excellent orchestra with a very fine conductor, they all seem to be especially motivated by the brilliance of the occasion. To begin with, it's a benefit performance, and the public has dressed to suit the festive atmosphere. All the musicians are keyed into this, and have become participants in that feeling of shared excitement which comes from understanding themselves an integral part of a great event. You can tell, too. They're responding to every cue. The string players are bowing together with uniformity of tempo. They are neatly clipping along with a perfection of articulation and execution.

I caught Mrs. Inchabout nodding to Harriet when she entered her box. And I note with pleasure that tiny little Mrs. Jodes-Fandango has arrived in a black velvet gown, sporting three long chains of ten-carat diamonds which sway in tiers above and beneath her waist. It seems she's acquired a brand-new human work of art. This, of course, is the very ultimate pastime of the very, very rich. Look at him—he must be six feet three. And to judge from the enormous tootsie wedged into that patent-leather pump and the accompanying bulge in his trousers, he is more than capable of providing her with the necessary afternoon delight. The Fragonard twins, who are ladies of great taste and noted opera lovers, are also seated coyly in their grand tier box. Those boxes are a bit smaller, and only seat six. But many of them have over the years held occupants of great distinction. Such is the case here, as the ladies are of literary inclination. They write poetry, and hold soirées. They've never married. It's been rumored they are lovers between themselves. It really wouldn't surprise me. After all, if we were to judge by the number of times we all look at ourselves in the mirror, it might be rather delightful to have sex with yourself. Which is physically what a twin is. Except that they themselves perceive great psychological differences. Which must make it further interesting and kinky. These ladies always wear the same clothing as well. Which denotes a sense of humor in breaking the established rule that no well-to-do woman would be caught dead in the same gown as another. Looking about, I also note Colonel Reardon is here in his grand tier box with a couple of ladies, and three of his *"nephews."* The Colonel has long had a proclivity for beautiful boys and men. So he finds socially acceptable ones at the Athletic Club and coddles them with fine dinner parties, wine, evenings at the opera, and the insinuation of social and economic mobility. These young gay or bisexual lawyers or accountants starting out in big city firms are faced, so to speak, with the choice of dining at the corner deli or at the Colonel's. They inevitably bend. So he snaps them up. Perhaps for an evening, perhaps for a year. And at the end of the period, they go on to younger lovers, on whom they may spend what they have reaped as a reward. And more so, on whom they will apply the knowledge, taste, and wisdom they have acquired from the Colonel. In this sense, we could almost call him an educator. It's actually a story as old as time.

You might say the opera is like a beehive. Where the actors and singers are playing their parts, but where the public also constitutes a performance composed of many, many plots and subplots. All occurring at the same time.

As my attention returns to the proscenium, Amalita Corsini is onstage. There is a hush as she appears. The famous bosom is immediately put at heave. Evil though she may be, the sound which is pouring forth is unique and perfect. This, of course, is the quality of a great artist, or a great artistic work. Any good pianist can play the *Pathétique* Sonata. But only a consummate performer can interpret the music with coherence, nuance, and the injection of singular and special qualities usually identified with consummate virtuosi. Amalita is such a performer. The music pours forth effortlessly. And with great volume, which is of course rare in a modern-day soprano. This is what Tetrazzini must have sounded like, but here there is an undertone of desperate passion and true abandon. As the opera progresses, she will become entangled in the inevitable web which will ultimately bring about her character's demise.

I am again focusing my attention on E.C. and Cleave. I note that while cordial with their party, they are fraught with tension. He is intense with desire for the woman onstage, and she knows it. What is it about the lover's heart which makes it forever prescient about such things? A paramour may tell you she has a headache. You may be told the lack of interest in love or sex comes from a chemical imbalance, or a depression. The loving heart may even hear that "this is just the way it is." Or, "this is just the way I am, so you may not expect more." But the lover's intuition will eventually realize true affection has decided to abandon the nest. There's something within, which even without the frailest shred of evidence, creates the knowledge in one's heart that affection has fled, and there is another. These are the feelings which Susan Cleave is facing tonight. To be sure, she's doing her best to keep a dry eye and maintain her composure. But every once in a while, I notice her chest is slightly shaking. I'm drawn to her, and to the pain she feels. Something inside of this woman knows tonight she will be betrayed, and E.C. will find his way into Amalita's arms.

Harriet, on the other hand, is looking ivory-skinned and magnificent. It's almost as if she's taken the difficulty of the day and buried it in some place so remote it can never show through. Perhaps she's found a way of psychologically interiorizing it, with her fear of poverty, and her locked-up affairs. In her case, there is also anger. And tonight, behind the impassive countenance, I sense the presence of the superior strength which is born of those emotions. Yes, she's tightly wound, and I'm wondering when the spring will unleash itself. Hooker has become the equivalent of an expensive prop. He's almost inanimate in his consternation over today's events.

In the Nuncio's box, Cardinal Tucci is pensive and observant. The aquiline nose is appropriate for a man who sees so very much and registers his observations with such composed demeanor. Yes, he's been watching Harriet and Hooker very carefully. And I couldn't help noting the glimmer of sadness in his eyes as he nodded in acknowledgment at E.C. and Susan. Occasionally, he looks over to the black-haired angel at his side. There's admiration in that glance. And the remembrance of worldly passion. But I'm quite sure Tucci doesn't do anything about it these days. Sometimes it is enough to merely look. The other priests accompanying him, his secretaries, would also seem to be extraordinary men. Tight, and stiff, efficient, and precise. Just the type of assistants you would expect a prince of the Church to have. One can intuit a relationship as well. It's evident in the respectful way in which they look at their master. But Tucci is a man who has seen many things, and has yet many to witness. He is, in a sense, one of the *maggiordomos* of a repository of civilization. And tonight, without being able to help it, he is also playing his part. One can sense within him a knowledge of destiny and an understanding of many seeming vagaries of life. There are deep, dark secrets buried here as well. Some belonging to the cosmos, others to the world and the Church. And ultimately, some of his own as well. But Tucci is a man who is able to live with the burden of such knowledge. He's a person reconciled to the pain of conscious living, and one who has long ago learned the fine art of acceptance.

It seems we are now at intermission, and the house lights are again brightening. Most of the guests in the boxes are either on their way to the Club for a glass of champagne or visiting their friends in the adjoining enclosures. Harriet is aggressive tonight. She's breaking her custom, and leaving her box with Hooker and some of her guests. Aha . . . It would seem she is on her way to visit E.C. and Susan. In a moment, she, Hooker, Gustavo, and the Johnsons are making an entry.

"We thought we'd be friendly and come say hello."

"How wonderful to see you, Mrs. Somerset. Good evening, Tom."

"This is my nephew Gustavo Somerset. And our friends John and Cecilia Johnson. Oh, I'm sorry, this is Miss Cleave."

They're all chatting about the opera now, and trying to seem polite. Susan is looking a bit uncomfortable, and is actually astounded Harriet has exhibited the presence of mind to come salute the winner. Harriet is now grabbing E.C. by the arm, and in spite of Susan's stern glance, is attempting to take him for a walk in the corridor. She's succeeding. As they exit the little enclosure, E.C. decides to tackle the question.

"You know, Harriet, I'm beginning to think you are a very gracious woman. Either that, or extremely tough."

"I'm wondering what makes you say that."

"Well, perhaps we shouldn't talk about trifles, but I calculate you're down about four and a half billion as of late this afternoon. And there will be more to reckon with tomorrow."

"You have it about right. But I'm happy to report we are still going to be able to serve caviar later tonight. Tell me, E.C., why did you do it?"

"Oh, I don't know, maybe because I wanted to."

"Are you sure you haven't had a little help? You know, I'm not one to believe in hands grasping from the grave, but you have been acting very much like my late husband."

"Do you think so?"

"Yes, you definitely remind me of Henry. Now that you have everything else, I must, however, note there is one Somerset possession you have not yet claimed."

"And what is that, Harriet?"

"*Me!*"

"Oh . . . it had not popped into my mind. But I must say, you are a very beautiful woman."

"Well, I think you're a very interesting and attractive man. Perhaps we might do something about it."

"Oh, the house lights are flashing—we'd best be getting along. Let me escort you back to your box."

And with these words, E.C. is graciously giving Harriet the brush and entering the little foyer to my box in order to return my hungry wife to her seat. She's taken on a different look. It's like a glow, and I can't help thinking how beautiful she can be. E.C. has caught on as well. And I daresay he's also fantasized about being bitten by the bug. But not with any real conviction. One would have thought his male ego totally besotted at the presence of a third and very beautiful sexual object. But he has eyes only for Amalita. I must say, I'm most curious regarding the outcome. One thing bothers me, though. I would have really thought E.C. understood the difference between infatuation and love. It's the type of thing people usually face and learn about when they are teenagers. I had hardly expected to find a sophisticated man of his age throwing true love away for the mere infatuation born of a few overactive hormones.

It's funny, this whole thing has made me recall the occasion on which my little shit of a nephew, Gustavo, came asking for advice when he was fifteen years old. At that time, the portents of his nasty and valueless personality were beginning to show. His question was a simple one. He wanted to know whether a person could be in love with two different people at the same time. I think I responded wisely when I told him an individual could certainly love many people, but not be "truly in love" with more than one at the same time. He then proceeded to ask, "But what is it that I'm feeling?" So I responded with the word "infatuation." His next question had to do with asking me what the difference was between love and infatuation. I'll never forget, I gave him a very simple answer. I said, "Gustavo, when you're infatuated with a person, all you can think about is that next sexual encounter, and everything you're going to receive when it happens. But when you're in love, you spend a lot of time thinking about what you will do to make the other person happy, even if it's totally inconvenient or difficult." Gustavo, of course, has never learned the difference, and has arrested his development at the adolescent affective state of a fifteen-year-old. But I'm surprised and disappointed to find E.C. in the same boat tonight.

As we enter the final act, and Amalita bellows forth with "Pace, pace," the Cardinal's attention is completely drawn to her. He's staring at the opera star as if he were peeling away the layers and zeroing in on the contents of her soul. Occasionally, he clasps a very old little cross in his pocket. It's not unlike the one he gave E.C.—ancient, and quite beautiful in its opulent rusticity. He has continued staring at her until the very end of the performance, when the insistence of his gaze has been interrupted by the vigorous applause. Amalita is bowing and receiving bouquet after bouquet of roses. Say what one might, she is every inch a star. Accustomed to the adulation of the audience, and capable of fostering and reciprocating it as well. Yes, the famous breasts are still heaving as she takes the sixth curtain call. Old Tucci has now been derailed, and is looking insistently at Harriet, and then at Susan Cleave. No doubt he's figured out what is happening and is now speculating on the possible outcome of this evening's triple play. The audience is beginning to disperse. Tucci is being squired by his attendants, and is on his way to the waiting car below, as are also Harriet and many of the other more glittering guests. Amalita is back in her dressing room, where she is donning the black lace gown, and those famous diamonds which are her trademark. Her aunt, as usual, is omnipresent, and is now bringing forth an exuberant arrangement of orchids.

"And these, Nana, who are they from?"

"They are from the gentleman, you know which one. Mr. Douglas. Why not let this one go? There have been so many men. Too many broken hearts. You know, I almost developed a fondness for last year's industrialist, the one who jumped from the roof."

"Nana, you are always the same. Such a soft heart."

"And you have no heart. You are a *figlia del diavolo.*"

"Ha, ha, ha, Nana, you never change. You never vary a bit."

"But Amalita, this man is different. There is some goodness in him. I almost like him."

"You are growing old. You should know, there are no good men."

"Truly, you have become monstrous. There is not a drop of compassion in you."

"No, I have none. Not for men. And if you are not careful, I will put you out on the street tomorrow. So remember where your bread is coming from."

"Bread? You starve me as you starve them. But at least with them it is a quick death. With me, it is slow."

"Be quiet, and bring me the diamond necklace. Yes, and the earrings he gave me as well."

"As you wish."

I have witnessed further shameless comments from Amalita as the conversation comes to a close. I would like to muse over it all, but I am due at the reception. And I don't wish to miss anything. Not a beat.

By now Harriet has arrived at her country house, and is walking around with the authority of a brigadier general in heat. The house is quite perfect in every respect. The gardens are illuminated, and the flowers from the various greenhouses are to be seen everywhere. She's going up to her bedroom for a moment before the guests begin to arrive. I guess I'll follow. Yes, as she mounts the stairs, Harriet has that look of quiet determination which has allowed her to always attain everything she's ever wanted. Up to her chamber, where she's closing and locking the door. This really isn't very much like her.

She only locks the door to sleep. Now she's going into her closet. This is fun. She's going to the very rear and grabbing for a pair of red lizard shoes. I can't believe it. Such shoes would be extremely inappropriate tonight. Oh, but now I understand. My steely wife has no intention of wearing them. There's something in that shoe which she's looking for. I wonder what it is? Aha. It's a very tiny vial with a clear liquid in it. You know, I really think Harriet is making ready to poison someone. And I wouldn't be surprised if she's going to use one of my undetectable little substances from the vegetable kingdom. Well, as long as she's not going for E.C. or Cleave, I'm not stepping into the matter. Of course, if she tries to do something to one of them, I'll be forced to intervene and have her hide. The intercom is ringing, and she's being advised of the arrival of her first guests. A quick look in the mirror and the little vial finds itself placed in a little secret pocket of her gown. Harriet always has these included by the dressmaker for a hankie, or her blood-pressure medication. She looks completely serene and composed as she walks down the stairs, and is now ready to greet the hundred or so people who have been invited for the evening.

The small orchestra she's engaged is playing light music, and an occasional movement from a Mozart or Haydn quartet arranged for a larger ensemble. A number of guests have arrived and been greeted by her private secretary, and waiters are passing tulip glasses of champagne. The Cardinal's car has just made itself evident. And an attendant has whispered the information into her ear. She's going to the front door in person for this one. E.C. and Susan Cleave are not far behind old Tucci. As the Cardinal arrives with his three attendants, Harriet curtsies ever so softly and kisses his ring.

"I am delighted to have you visit my home, Your Eminence. You honor me with your presence."

"Thank you, my dear, I was looking forward to visiting with you. You know, we were very fond of your late husband."

"Why, yes . . . thank you. He was a unique man."

"Yes, I thought so as well."

"But allow me to show you in, and introduce you to some of my friends. No doubt you already know many of them."

Harriet is taking the Cardinal by the arm and presenting him to the various people present. E.C. and Susan Cleave have just arrived, and are sipping at their first glass of champagne as Harriet moves in to greet them a moment later, with the prelate in tow.

"E.C., allow me to introduce His Eminence Cardinal Tucci. And this is Miss Cleave."

"Oh, I already know Mr. Douglas and Miss Cleave. They have been my guests in Rome. How very good to see you again so soon. Tell me, how is it you are all so very well acquainted?"

"Well, it's a funny thing. First Mr. Douglas bought Henry's pyramid. Then the art, and now he's taken over Siderurgica. But after all, what is a little financial transaction here or there? To top it all off, Miss Cleave here was my late husband's assistant. Ah, I see the great lady herself is arriving. Excuse me while I go greet Miss Corsini."

Harriet is looking for a waiter, and finding him. She's grabbing for one of those fluted champagne glasses. No one has noticed, but she's just taken her finger out of that little pocket and ever so gingerly dipped it in the champagne.

"Signorina Corsini, I'm Harriet Somerset. Allow me to tell you how honored I am to have you at my party. The opera was magnificent, and we have secured a great deal of money for my charity. Welcome, welcome. Allow me to offer you a nice glass of champagne."

"Thank you, Mrs. Somerset. The opera is hard work. But I am happy I was able to come. And yes, I do love champagne."

Harriet is escorting Amalita Corsini as people make approving clinking noises with their champagne glasses. She has her eyes on E. C. Douglas, who is intensely staring at the star. And now walking directly over to her, leaving Cleave alone with Cardinal Tucci.

"Miss Cleave, you seem troubled."

"No . . . no . . ."

"You can tell me. Remember, I am a very old man, and I have heard many secrets."

"I shouldn't say this, but I'm in love with this man, and he's salivating over that woman."

"Ah . . . I see. Now I understand. Of course, I knew some of this already. But matters are frequently more clear when fully explained."

"What should I do about it?"

"Absolutely nothing, my dear. You see, the bare truth is that when something truly belongs to us, it cannot be stolen. And if it does not belong to us, then by definition, it cannot be taken away either."

"That's easier to understand intellectually."

"Ah yes, I know. I agree the heart has its own reasons. . . . But if I were you, I would control myself and refrain from all action."

"Perhaps you're right."

"Yes, believe me, this is really good advice."

E.C. has reached Amalita, and instead of speaking to her, is merely staring with his index finger placed against his nose. It's actually a little rude, particularly since this little quirk of his does not constitute acceptable behavior for such a congregation. But, of course, he is oblivious.

"E.C., why are you so intense? Speak to me."

"You are so beautiful, I have no words."

"Why is it men always say the same trite, stupid things?"

"I'm different from other men. I don't wish to be compared to others."

"Then, *caro*, I shall not compare you. But that in itself will not mean you are incomparable. This you must prove to me."

"When?"

"Tonight at my suite, at two in the morning."

"I shall be there."

The entire interaction among these characters is quite fascinating to me. Harriet is watching Amalita drink her champagne, and seems quite relieved to see it so neatly and totally ingested. Cleave is, in turn, watching Amalita as well, but mainly keeping her eye on E.C., who is on his way back to her. Hooker is sitting in a Restoration chair looking barefacedly drunk. Cardinal Tucci is watching them all with a benign but stern look. Come to think of it, though, there is one character I'm missing here. I don't see Gustavo anywhere. I'm sure he left the opera on time. I saw the valet drive the Maserati to the lower portal of the building with the zest which can only be mustered by parking lot attendants obtaining their dosage of semi-vicarious pleasure. I learned a long time ago to respect the joy that servants derive from their master's possessions. As long as it doesn't get out of hand, one just has to assume it's a fringe benefit of chauffeurs to enjoy their employers' fabulous cars. By the same token, one should never try to cheat the people who work and toil out of the pleasure of tasting the *pâté de fois* in the kitchen, or having a sip of the best wine. But I just noticed I'm missing someone here. Where is my nephew? I must tune in to him and find out what's happening.

There are times when one becomes ready to perform a simple task like blinking oneself into someone's presence and all of a sudden there is a premonition or apprehension of somehow coming into contact with the periphery of eternity. I just had that feeling when I willed myself into Gustavo's vicinity. All of a sudden, I'm on Ocean Drive, sitting next to him in his splendid little car. Instead of repairing directly to Harriet's for the party, my nephew has chosen to assuage his depressed and neurotic state by taking a long ride. As I watch him shift almost maniacally, I can't help wondering about where my nephew the child has gone. Surely I would hope that somewhere within this entirely corrupt and unpleasant young man there is a little boy gagged and bound, who once enjoyed the company of his Uncle Henry. He's taken to chain-smoking, and the car's otherwise delightful leathery aroma has been overpowered by the rancid smell of countless cigarette butts. It's a dark, moonless night. He's speeding around these curves a bit too quickly. But I feel sure he can negotiate them without dropping us from the cliff into the ocean below.

For some time now, I've been conscious of something my nephew has not yet noticed. It's a pair of headlights. Indicative of the fact a vehicle has steadfastly maintained the pace behind us. All of a sudden, we seem to be losing speed. Gustavo is becoming angry, and flooring it. This action is bringing about a strange burned smell. Almost like overcooked caramel. Oh, I get it. This is the revenge of the policeman who was so mistreated by Gustavo in front of Blackrock, just a few days ago. By now, the sugar has found itself into the farthest nooks and crannies of this powerful engine. So the equines are now chaffing at the bit in fits and starts, and finally giving up. I mean to say, the vehicle has come to a total standstill. Gustavo is out of control, and beating the steering wheel. As he also kicks at the floor of the car. In final desperation, he's opening the door, getting out, and slamming his foot against the side of the Maserati. This is really a most inhospitable place in which to be caught with a breakdown. It's so dark and overcast that no star is visible. The ocean is present, more by its sound breaking at the rocks below than by any visibility. Pines and evergreens, which have long been contorted by a century or more of exposure to the wind whipping around these cliffs, have taken on phantasmagoric proportions in the blackness of the night. I, who have nothing to fear from the living, am actually anxiously impressed by the bleakness of the setting. Yet Gustavo seems totally unafraid. And as usual is completely wrapped up in his own situation, without realizing the further precarious and dangerous possibilities.

The vehicle which was behind us has now approached and come to a stop in front of Gustavo's car. From it, two large and well-dressed men are emerging. They're wearing floppy raincoats, and don't look particularly friendly.

"Good evening. Are you having trouble with your car?"

"The damned thing just refuses to start. I think something has burned out in the motor."

"Hop in. We can drive you to the nearest gas station."

"That's great. Thanks a lot. Let me lock my car, and I'll be with you in a moment."

Oh . . . I don't have a very good feeling about this encounter. But why am I worried about Gustavo? After all, I've been wanting to see him squirm for a long time. In any event, they've put him in the front seat with the driver, and the other man is now sitting in the rear as they proceed. I've hopped in to see what this is all about. As we make the curve, which would otherwise take us into a less solitary area, the driver is unexpectedly turning up a narrow and dark road which has become overgrown with bushes. It would seem to lead deep into the adjoining forest. Gustavo is quick to take note of this, and question them.

"Hey, this isn't the way to the gas station. Where are you taking me? I'm warning you, I'm a very important man, and this can get you into some very serious trouble."

"Mr. Somerset, we know exactly who you are, and my associate is at this moment pointing a thirty-eight-caliber pistol at the rear of your neck. So I suggest you not attempt anything cute."

"If money is what you want, my aunt is a very rich woman, and she'll give you a great deal of it as long as I'm not harmed."

"Mr. Somerset, the time for conversation has passed."

All of a sudden, in one practiced gesture, the man behind pushes the pistol into the rear of Gustavo's neck as the fellow in front brings the car to a halt and proceeds to very quickly gag his victim. They've reached a small clearing, which looks like something my imagination would have conceived as the bleakest outpost of hell. It's quite damp here. And the wind is howling through the evergreens. The taller of the two men is now speaking to Gustavo, as the other has proceeded to beat him mercilessly.

"Mr. Somerset, money will not buy you out of this problem. We bring you a gift from Don Orsini. I think you'll appreciate it. No doubt you remember this little hair."

Gustavo has widely opened his eyes, and within them is a look of sheer terror. I don't know what to do. All of a sudden I've realized this isn't what I want anymore. Maybe there's some way I can avoid it. That's it, I'll move the bushes. But these men are not deterred. They're beating him again, and kicking his legs. It's too horrible. It pains me to watch it. Now they've loosened the gag. My nephew is pleading for his life. He's begging and groveling. But with a deft gesture, the smaller of the two men has loosened Gustavo's belt and pulled his pants down. And has now, in one fell swoop of his razor, disengaged the young man's testicles from his body. As the boy lies there bleeding to death, they're stuffing them down his throat. No, no. This is all wrong. This isn't the revenge I wanted. He was a stupid adolescent who went wrong. And for better or for worse, one of my charges. A child of mine.

The men are now leaving Gustavo in the clearing to die, and returning to their vehicle. One of them is extracting a bottle of alcohol from the glove compartment, and is meticulously washing his razor and hands as well. In a moment, they're within the car again, and gone. And I am here in the blackness of the night with my dying nephew. The blood is running out around him, uncontrollably. He's unconscious. This being the case, I think I'll be able to penetrate his mind as if he were asleep. There's no time to be lost. I'm again in the ugly realm of Gustavo's dreamworld. But of course, this nightmare is real. The interior walls of this phantasmagoric domain are flashing in iridescent white as if they were about to crumble and leave us on the brink of nothingness. In this unhinging of his parallel reality, the mature Gustavo also lies prostrate before me in the dream. But the six-year-old child, my nephew, is running disconcertedly through the dark corridors, grasped entirely by the terror of the occasion. I must reach him. I'll run after the boy, and catch him.

"Gustavo, Gustavo. Don't run. It's me, Uncle Henry."

"Oh, Uncle Henry, Uncle Henry. I'm afraid. I'm afraid of everything. I don't know what to do. I think I'm dying, and I'm terrified of death."

"Don't be afraid, Gustavo. You see, I'm here to make sure nothing bad happens to you."

"But I'm so frightened. It's very dark, and I hurt all over."

"No, sweetheart. You mustn't hurt. Come to me, and lay your head on my chest and try to fall asleep."

"Uncle Henry, I've been locked up and put away all this time, and I've missed you."

"I've missed you too, Gustavo."

"Will I wake up from this sleep?"

"Yes, of course, I promise you. But try to remember these happenings when you wake, and to be a good boy next time."

"I've been a wicked boy, haven't I?"

"Just a little."

"But it's because I've been so confused. I thought you didn't love me."

"Of course I loved you, Gustavo."

"Uncle Henry, I'm afraid again. I don't know what to do."

"Don't worry, I'm here. I'll protect you."

"You won't leave me the way my father did?"

"No, I won't, I promise."

"Uncle Henry, I love you."

"Yes, Gustavo, I love you too. Try to sleep."

If I were to look at myself from above, I would see the spectacle of an older man shattered by the uncertainty and incomprehension of his own feelings. Clasping a helpless child to his breast, and stroking his hair as if to comfort him. The child is slowly falling asleep. And I'm feeling a little better as it's happening, although still very much shaken by the experience. I'm being pushed out of Gustavo's dream state. Not bounced against the trees and rocks, as might happen had he truly slumbered and awoken. But rather, I am slowly and inexorably ejected like a long note dying on a string instrument. Now fully removed, I realize Gustavo is dead.

I'm sitting here weeping, trying to collect my mixed emotions. If this is vengeance, I want no part of it. I had thought it would be fun. I had visions of exhilaration and triumph. But what victory can there possibly be in a poor, terrified child weeping at my bosom? And to think all of this has happened because of money and ambition. And much of it because of what I've done in this afterlife. My head feels like it will burst. I now think I've ruined everything.

When I awoke to this new and perplexing state of death, it seemed only too easy to resume matters where I had left them. Alone with Bozo and my thoughts, and the temptations of E.C.'s very malleable and pliable state, it almost seemed right to go forward with a little revenge. I judged people from their surfaces, never remembering that they were and are the composite of everything they had ever been independently, as well as everything they had been with and to me. In Gustavo's case, I saw only the spoiled and irresponsible young adult turned into a cheat, thief, and liar. But I neglected to remember the boy within who longed so genuinely to embrace me and fall asleep on my chest. And I forgot I treasured that child. I'm legitimately ashamed. But that and a coin will buy me a ride to the madhouse.

I've never quite known such pain. In this sense, knowledge has brought me only further horror. But what else could I have done? How might I have avoided this? Is this whole thing one monumental test that I've flatly failed? To tell the truth, I'm so despondent and unhappy at this moment I would almost wish to return to the cemetery. But there are time imperatives involved, and at this very moment, Harriet has poisoned Amalita, and will probably not stop there.

I can't help Gustavo anymore, but I can certainly assist E.C. and Cleave, making sure they are able to go forward. Feel though I may for my little boy lying here all bloodstained in the clearing, I must return to my other responsibilities.

THIRTY-ONE

IT'S NOW ONE A.M. AND HARRIET'S PARTY IS IN FULL SWING. AT A MO-
ment when Amalita has been drawn into a conversation with Cardinal
Tucci, Harriet has decided to make her move on E.C.

"You know, in spite of today's happenings, I'm very pleased to
have you here tonight."

"Thank you, Harriet. You should know these business matters
are in no way personal. And while I've taken a sizable bite, I'm sure
the gracious lady will not lack for sustenance in the future."

"Yes. Of course. And thank you for the comments. You know,
it's becoming a bit close in here. I need a little space. Would you like
to see my greenhouses?"

"I should think we'll freeze to death walking down the hill. It's
rather chilly tonight."

"Not to worry. Remember, this is a Somerset household. We
are fully equipped with tunnel."

"Oh, in that case, I'd be delighted to see them."

"We'll go through the winter garden. There's a staircase there which leads to the passageway."

Harriet has seductively taken E.C.'s uncertain arm, and is now making her way down the steps into the broad and well-lighted tunnel which leads to her greenhouses. As they approach them, I can tell she is tightly wound and coiled. Fully ready to strike with the strength and purpose of a black mamba. Mambas, you know, are amongst the deadliest of the pit vipers. They are singular in that they pursue their prey with alacrity, and have been known to jump twenty feet in order to take a bite. My Harriet is, of course, much more attractive, but just as deadly. She has fully relied and capitalized on the support of his arm. As they approach the entrance to the main greenhouse, Harriet is pulling one of my old theatrical routines and flicking the master switch which now illuminates the giant ferns, the palms, and the various components of this very special and exotic realm. In this greenhouse she has all the warm-weather plants, including the tropical orchids.

"My goodness, Harriet, your phalaenopsids are beautiful, and so incredibly large."

"Yes, Henry helped me with these before he spawned his own greenhouses over at Pyramid Hill. Of course we have a colder greenhouse with the cymbidiums and paphiopedilums."

"Ah yes, the lady's slippers."

"Henry liked them because he contended they looked like sinister artificial flowers."

"Talking about lady's slippers, I can't help noticing you have the most beautiful little feet."

"I'm relieved you notice something about me. But you shouldn't limit yourself to just seeing. You *are* allowed to touch, you know."

"You are a most intriguing and attractive woman. If I had time and the inclination, we might do something about it, but alas, I don't. So I must apologize."

"Well, time can be made . . ."

"But I'm trying to be polite about the inclination. I'm sorry, I don't mean to be untactful. You are very beautiful. And it's true, I have acquired the dog, the pyramid, the assistant, the art, and the fortune. But something tells me I'm fated to leave you early tonight."

Harriet is becoming a little flushed. No wonder. Even the best of us are unhappy in the face of rejection. For her, however, it of course carries a deeper meaning. She will not regain her fortune. And true to her temperament, it would seem there is a contingency plan. She's pulling on a little lace tablecloth, which is covering a small table set against the outer wall. And has now revealed a champagne bucket and several glasses. The beautiful little hand is again in the secret pocket, where that most insouciant finger is being dipped in the substance of no return.

"Would you allow me to do the honors with the champagne?"

"I don't understand . . ."

"Well, I had hoped my attraction to men of power would be reciprocated by you. But in the absence of this, or its postponement, I wish to be sporting. So I had this little bucket of champagne stashed away here, in order to genuinely toast your victory and show you Harriet Somerset is not a poor loser. Let me pour you a drop."

For a moment, E.C. is looking somewhat unnerved. He had not expected such a sporting attitude from Harriet. And here she is offering him a glass of bubbly to celebrate his victory. He's thinking it's almost too good to be true. But is nevertheless swallowing the lie hook, line, and sinker. If I allow her to go any further, he will also drink the champagne, and become her second victim of the evening. What can I do, though? She's now handing him the glass, and I must act very quickly.

There is strength within me which had dwelt unsuspected. I now find I am able to levitate entire flower pots. I have raised a ten-inch pot by sheer act of will, and have placed it smack in front of Harriet's line of vision. Just when she was getting ready to hand him the innocuous-looking champagne glass with the angel on it! Neither she nor E.C. can quite believe their eyes as the pot, complete with blooming, pink phalaenopsids, hovers between them. Harriet is dropping the goblet. Which shatters into a hundred pieces on the black slate floor. Attempting to forget what she's just seen, and undeterred, she's actually going for a second glass! I have to hand it to her, she really has nerves of steel! Nevertheless, and in response, I have smashed the object against the greenhouse wall. She and E.C. are now fully impressed with the uniqueness of the occasion, and are huddling together, which is exactly what I don't want. So now, in a great act of will, I am moving ten or fifteen pots at a time through the air. And dashing them at their feet in order to separate the couple. It's effective. E.C. is in one corner, at present, and Harriet in the other. There are pieces of glass and terra-cotta pots everywhere. Harriet is beginning to shake, and is much redder in the face than I've ever seen her. She's holding her head with both hands, as if to ward off some great pain or evil. But this state of excitement is not of my doing. This is something that's coming from within her. All of a sudden, as she's grasping her temples, a rivulet of blood shows itself trickling down from one of her nostrils. Before E.C. can sustain her, she's falling on the floor over the broken potsherds. Our man is quick to attempt help. But Harriet is thoroughly unconscious. Realizing he can do nothing to aid her here, he's running down the corridor seeking assistance. Now the tunnel is alive with attendants and servants moving in their mistress's direction. They're picking her up and quickly taking her to the front entrance of the house. Soon a siren screams, causing further awkwardness among the guests, who have been asked to maintain their composure and not create a traffic jam before the ambulance leaves. Amalita, of course, has paid no attention, and departed summarily. Cardinal Tucci has given the last rites as a precautionary measure. Soon my wife is on a stretcher with oxygen and necessary medication. She will, no doubt, be taken to the wing of the hospital which bears my name.

I don't know why, but I'm strangely drawn to Harriet at this moment in time. Perhaps it's just that I wish to see what is ultimately happening to the wicked woman. After all, I created the disturbance which brought her blood pressure to an all-time high. Maybe there's something else too. But why think about that now? I'll hop into the rear of this ambulance with these two hunky male nurses and go along for the ride. They're talking as they monitor her:

"Hey, who is this woman?"

"You idiot, haven't you seen her in the society columns? This is Harriet Somerset, one of the most beautiful women in town, and one of the richest too."

"Well, she doesn't look all that great now."

"That's what you think. Feel those legs. This is a woman who hasn't had a bad day in her life. This is the type of rich bitch who gets a daily massage and rubs herself with hundred-dollar creams. Look at that skin."

"You'd better give her a little more of the juice. I'm running a really high blood-pressure reading. What do you think happened?"

"It looks like a cerebral hemorrhage. Did you feel her ass up?"

"Yeah. She's got cement buns, this one. A real humdinger."

"You know, this is the one who was married to the billionaire."

"What happened to him?"

"He died and left her all the money."

"Isn't it always the case. The guys work their asses off to provide for these rich women, and then they kick the bucket and leave it all to them."

"Well, I'll tell you this much, she doesn't look like she's traveling to the Riviera very soon."

As we approach Memorial Hospital, and the entrance of the Somerset Pavilion, an emergency team has been alerted and is waiting. She's being wheeled into the hospital rather quickly, and into a room where they're injecting her with dye. Dr. Stern has been called. I recognize him from meetings at the hospital. He's a brilliant neurosurgeon. And as the readings come through, he's indicating to his colleagues that emergency surgery must be performed immediately to eliminate a large blood clot in the brain.

Who would have thought her beautiful little head would have ended up under the surgeon's blade? Though I've hated her, I can't help feeling a slight pang of sadness. Harriet is a survivor. A mean and wicked one in every respect, but nevertheless, a fighter, and that's something I admire. It wouldn't make me happy to see her *swim so far, only to die at the edge of the water.* As far as I'm concerned, poverty would be enough of a reward for her.

She momentarily seems to be in stable condition. I suppose it will take several hours to prep her. And then they will take that *chic* little jigsaw and perform a full trepanation of the skull. In the meantime, I'm sure there's a great deal going on back in the realm of my other friends. I'm going to blink myself into E.C.'s presence.

I've done this just in the nick of time, too. He and Cleave are silently riding in the rear of the limo moving toward her apartment. A slight drizzle is falling, and all that can be heard is the rhythmic noise of the windshield wipers. They've reached her building, and she's now looking insistently at E.C.

"Would you come up for a nightcap?"

"No. I'm a bit tired. It's been a rather shaking evening for me."

"What if I really begged you to?"

"No, I'm afraid I can't do it."

"But I need you very badly now. Can't you see, I'm almost in tears. Doesn't it matter to you?"

"I told you, I'm sorry, it's not something I can do."

"It's that woman, isn't it? She's in the way."

"Don't be silly. She doesn't surpass you in any way."

"Yet she's the reason why you're not coming tonight."

"I'm telling you, don't be ridiculous. Furthermore, I'm just not going to respond to this type of question."

"Ah . . . I see, I see. I really do understand."

By this time, the tears are rolling down Susan's face. But this is the only indication of her emotions. E.C., on the other hand, is cold and distant in the style of people who have fallen out of love. I'm sitting here watching the whole scene, thinking it's a repetition of something I've seen many, many times before. It's the situation where two people have deeply loved one another and shared many of the aspects of their beings. They think it will last forever, and then something happens. Or should I say *someone* happens, and one of the two lovers ceases to have desire for the other. At first the guilty party will be confronted by his mate, and all will be denied. Frequently, the one will give a number of reasons for the behavior. It may be that the lover will say he or she is not feeling sexy about anyone. Or in some cases, a general decrease in libido will be protested, or it will be said, "That's just the way I am." But little by little, the coldness of the mate with the itch in his crotch will create a greater distance between the lovers with each passing day. The aggrieved partner will at first be uncomprehending. Questions will be asked, such as "Is it me?" At some point, there will be arguments. And the one being left will weep. But not even a Niagara of tears can deter the party who has fallen out of love, since infatuation is basically a hormonal imbalance caused by the segregation of chemical substances. Endorphins, which are the equivalent of addictive pleasure producers. When the eye of the roving mate finds its resting place on a new person, there is, therefore, not even the possibility of a semblance of competition. Virtuous, intelligent, talented, and even incredibly beautiful mates are cast aside ruthlessly and coldly, at the slightest whiff of the new and exciting penis or pudendum. At that point, the straying party will seem incredibly distant, and frequently complain of headache or other malaise. But to the experienced onlooker, there is only one illness. And it can be clearly seen in those eyes where one spark has died forever and been summarily replaced by another.

E.C.'s cruelty of tonight exactly fits the mold. Like a bull in a china shop, he will make a beeline for Amalita Corsini, without regard to the damage he is otherwise causing. I remember my own first mistress in tears because her mother had died, sitting on the stairs begging me to spend the night with her. But at my house rested one of the hottest physical commodities in town, so I merely said, "I'm sorry, I just can't do that." I'll never forget, she tried to commit suicide. After making sure she had not achieved her purpose, and therefore appropriately assuaging my guilt, I went straight for the other woman, leaving my grieving beloved in the hands of doctors and psychiatrists. Now that I see Susan suffering this way, I understand the other side of the coin. Her situation has created great anguish in me as an onlooker. I want to do something to help, but I'm powerless. I know she will cry her eyes out tonight. And I would like to provide some comfort. But I also wish to accompany E.C. and try to scuttle his affair with Amalita.

Our man is now by himself with the driver. Szilagyi has noticed the little exchange between E.C. and Cleave. I can tell he was a little upset to see her so mistreated. But for once, he had to be prudent and kept his mouth shut. After dropping Susan, E.C. has given the appropriate instructions and they're now on their way to the diva's apartment. At the curbside, a liveried attendant is opening the door and helping our man out of the car. The visitor has been announced, and is now on his way up to the flat. He's ringing the doorbell with great expectation and nervousness. After a few brief instants, Amalita's aunt is at the entrance motioning him inside. The scent of flowers here is almost overpowering. E.C. has been motioned into the parlor, and the aunt has now disappeared. A few moments later, the doors to the bedroom open, and out comes the signorina. In a black silk dress, which could almost double as a negligee.

"Ah, my beautiful Amalita, how are you?"

"A bit more tired than usual. I think I ate something at the party which disagreed with me."

"Well, it was a very stressful evening, considering the way it ended, with Mrs. Somerset becoming so ill."

"Ah, I am delighted. The woman had designs on you, and I hate any woman who looks at you."

"You mustn't say things like that. I don't think it's nice to be happy at the misfortune of others."

"*Caro*, I am Amalita. And I am happy when I am happy, and I am sad when I am sad. And in this case, I am happy that I have you all to myself. Come closer, *caro*. Touch me, hold me. I need you."

"You know, I've been thinking about you for days now."

"I want you to be my love slave."

"What does that mean?"

"It means Amalita wants to possess you entirely, body and soul. But let us not talk about it. . . ."

And with these words, the diva is dragging E.C. into the bedroom, and virtually undressing him at the outset. First she's pulling out his shirt and unbuttoning each of his buttons with the expectation of further revelations. As the shirt is discarded, she gasps approvingly at the muscles E.C. has cultivated. When the trousers are removed, Amalita pushes him into bed, where her very educated mouth finds its way to all his most special parts. They are both now naked, and the woman has become something akin to a lustful animal released from hell. As her red nails find their way to his back, they create bleeding scratches. She is rhythmically sucking on each of his fingers and is now moving downward. When she reaches the toes she mouthes them with great expertise. As her tongue finds its way into the area of his crotch, she gently toys with his testicles. Then somewhat playfully proceeds again to his hips, where she's licking and biting the protuberances near his hipbones. E.C. is mad with pleasure as she again approaches his nipples and pinches them hard. Now, she is biting on those little knobs, causing him to scream in a combination of pleasure and pain. While still holding on to them with her fingers, her mouth is again finding its way down to the area of his crotch. She's a very clever woman. Knowledgeable in taking him just so far. Now she's slapping the head of his member with her fingers. And deflating it a bit by inserting her nails. This will allow her to get him going again, this time in all the postures of insertion. The entire scene is much more sexual than any movie I've ever seen. The woman is incredible, and has quite obviously played him like a fine instrument of pleasure. The climax over, it is evident E.C. has never had a woman of this variety. He is totally besotted.

It's incredible! *They are doing it again.*

I have to admit, this woman is a genuine virtuosa of the flesh instrument. But there's something hard and frightening about this animalistic scene. Of course, I know that what I'm witnessing is not necessarily the act of making love. I've started feeling I must interrupt this production. It's just not right for him. All this guy can think of is a rude fuck. I will topple vases full of flowers. *There!* I'll take that one in the corner and smash it against the marble floor. Surely, I have interrupted everything here. Amalita has jumped and is looking unnerved. E.C. has also stopped dead in his tracks, and is now apprehensive of a repetition of my little routine with the flower pots.

"*Caro.* You didn't touch the vase, did you?"

"No, Amalita. Look, it was too far. I couldn't have broken it if I had wanted to."

"And then . . ."

"I'm beginning to think there is a poltergeist or spirit associated with me."

"This I do not like, *caro.* But if I must invoke the devil himself, to be rid of it, I will."

"We needn't go that far."

"Well, let us try to forget the vase. *Caro* . . . you said you had something for me."

"Yes, I have this trinket."

E.C. is now going for his trousers. And from them he's extracting the Moguk Diamond, which he is flatly placing in the palm of her hand. Amalita is lighting up, as if transfigured by a desire greater than the one she felt before.

"Oh . . . oh. It is very, very beautiful. I will wear it when I next sing, for luck."

"You know, no other woman except my deceased wife ever managed to interest me as you do. So this is for you. I want to see it right here, between your breasts."

"No, *caro*. They are your breasts."

All of a sudden, as they are measuring themselves for a repeat performance, Amalita doubles up in a paroxysm of pain. She is perspiring and has become pale.

"Amalita, what's wrong?"

"I don't know. All of the sudden I have this terrible cramp, and I think I am getting a fever. I feel hot."

"You are very pale. Shall I call a doctor?"

"No, no. I hate doctors. They always want to do things which can affect my voice. Nana knows how to take care of me. She will put me to bed with a cup of herb tea, and I will be fine tomorrow so you can come see me again."

"Then I must leave?"

"For tonight, yes, because Amalita is not well. But I promise you, tomorrow I shall make you feel tonight was merely a beginning."

These words have obviously exacerbated each and every lustful and hormonally inspired emotion in E.C. The endorphins are running amok, and he's flushed. Now suffering from the blissful disorientation of those who have recently fallen in love. Later he will attempt calling her, to say something stupid, like "I love you a lot" in his deepest and most gravelly voice. He'll make a total fool out of himself. But he won't care. I now realize men never do. But all will be for naught, since the diva is more than likely to be unavailable.

E.C. is back in his car and on his way to Pyramid Hill. I can tell from the look on his face that just for a fleeting moment he's thought about Susan. But instead of feeling the normal emotions of sadness and commiseration which might be expected from someone who has loved, he feels only anger. You see, as the party who has fallen out of love, E.C. now has eyes only for his new paramour. Anyone who is in the way will be the object of an angry reaction. Many such lovers subconsciously hope their ex-mates will take a long journey to Outer Mongolia, or conveniently kick the bucket. If in E.C.'s case he should, by his own standards, be lucky enough to have Susan commit suicide, to be sure there might be a bit of guilt. But also a great sense of relief to be rid of the very person whose existence would show him to be a cad, and constitute a perennial embarrassment. All of a sudden, I am seeing parts of E.C. which I genuinely dislike. This is not without a great deal of personal soul-searching, and the mirroring of self. I'm upset and think I'd like to leave his presence for a while. Besides, I've been thinking about Harriet, and wondering how she's doing.

The Somerset Pavilion at Memorial Hospital is a plush establishment dedicated to excellence in diagnostics and surgery. Like many such great facilities, it is associated with the local medical school. And therefore enjoys a brilliant contingent of physicians who also teach courses there. They have some very special suites within this wing which are designated for people of our particular financial standing. These chambers are decorated very much as if they were rooms in some affluent person's house. They each enjoy around-the-clock private nursing, as well as a menu which is not second to that of any first-rate restaurant. If indeed one must spend time in a hospital, this is definitely the most gracious way in which to suffer such a fate.

Harriet is lying in bed, still unconscious. The private duty nurse by her side is nervously looking at her wristwatch, and has now decided it's time to provide a bit of preoperative sedation, which she is proceeding to prepare. While all of this is occuring, I think I would very much like to visit. So I'm going to put myself into the meditative mode and attempt penetration into her present state. As I enter her internal reality, I find there is a new grimness, and an all-pervading sense of danger within the interminable rooms and corridors of Harriet's mental world. I've just caught a glimpse of her quickly walking down one of the halls. If I take a rapid detour, I'll manage to end up smack in front of her. As I turn the corner, she comes running into me, and stops in a fitful and startled state. Her hair is disheveled, and she's barefoot. She immediately begins banging her clenched fists on my chest. "Henry, Henry. You're here again! You know something? I hate you. This is all your fault. I know it was you flinging those flower pots around this evening. But I don't understand why I'm here asleep right now. This must be your fault as well."

"Calm down, Harriet. I'm not here to hurt you."

"You've done enough of that already."

"Well, perhaps, but that's my mistake, and I'll probably pay for it. If the truth be known, I think you've had a lot to do with getting yourself into this predicament."

"And just what is this *predicament* I'm in? Do you know?"

"Well, honey, I think your blood pressure has finally gotten the best of you, and you've had a cerebral hemorrhage."

All of a sudden, Harriet is stunned by the reality of the situation. Tears are quietly falling down her face as she attempts to seem composed.

"What's going to happen to me? Am I dying? Henry, I don't want to die, I don't want to die."

"No, Harriet, I don't think you're dying yet. Although I won't deceive you as to the distinct possibility. What they're going to do is operate on you very shortly, and try to solve the problem."

"Operate where?"

"Well . . . uh . . . the problem is in your head. It's a blood clot."

"No, no. You can't let them do that to me, Henry. No, no, sweetheart, protect me, protect me!"

"Why, Harriet, it's been years since you've called me sweetheart."

"And it's been years since you've called me honey, so we're even.

"But I'm asking you now, I'm pleading with you. You've got to help me."

"Sweetheart, I don't know if there's anything I can do. You don't seem to understand. I'm dead, I'm a spirit."

"What will happen to me?"

"I don't know, but if you want, as long as it happens, I can visit."

"Yes, please . . . don't leave me alone. Don't leave me alone. You know, Henry, I never stopped loving you. It was the fear and the distrust which made me recoil. But in my own way, I always missed you."

"Yes. That's why you murdered me."

"I won't lie to you, Henry, I thought about it. But I didn't kill you."

"And I'm supposed to believe you!"

"Don't you know the truth?"

"What do you mean? You fed me the juice of my own castor-oil plant. Just as you did to Amalita Corsini."

"I gave her something else. As powerful, but faster. I was desperate. Henry, you've got to believe me, I certainly didn't kill you. I'm really surprised you don't know the truth."

The nurse is now sticking a large injection into Harriet's IV tube, and everything is becoming incoherent and blurry in here. I guess that's what sedatives do. I'm vexed, but I'd best leave and return for my answers another time. Several other nurses and a male orderly have entered the room. And they're wheeling Harriet in the direction of the operating room. This woman has murdered me even though she denies it. She will probably be responsible for Amalita's death as well. And here I'm worried about her! I guess I should also have my head examined.

Within the operating room, Dr. Stern and his staff are now ready to use the tools of their trade. I can't help noticing there's a bit of loose conversation occurring, which is typical of the profession. One of Stern's assistants is commenting.

"Well, Doctor, I guess we have a really expensive baby here today."

"Yes, and it doesn't look terribly good. But of course, we must make the effort."

"Yeah, but think of the malpractice suit if we make a mistake on this one!"

"It's something that's occurred to me already. I assure you, we will not slip up. That also means there will be no heroic gestures today. Gentlemen, from now on, it's strictly by the book. And if there is any doubt, we will sew her up rather than run the risk."

With these encouraging words, they're taking Harriet's little head, which has now been fully shaved, and separating a flap of tissue preparatory to cutting through the bone. This is all too gruesome. Especially when I think it's happening to a woman I've loved. But here I am going back to my old obsessive patterns, and again thinking of Harriet as an object of affection. First I idealize her. And then I have all of these conflicting thoughts having to do with how she did away with my life. Perhaps I was wrong when I thought love died. Maybe the hormonal variety does find its demise. But for the first time, I think I've learned to separate them. To understand that castles do exist, with ramparts high, which still in sparkling harmony of love and patience await the sleepers' wakeful kiss. For true love is forever in the mode of vigil. Awaiting deep in the parapets of the soul, and then high up in towers of the mind, where swallows nest and banners fly, that moment when the heart, like any other nightingale or virtuoso of the art of flight, returns to roost. Where all the quiet fragments of the loving past await it still. With welcome's silent smile, and greeting's tender touch. No matter what the time, no matter which the life, always the gift the same.

It's almost seven in the morning now. And as I bounce around looking in on these people to whom I am strangely attracted, I find E.C. asleep complete with erection, and dreaming only of Amalita. Bozo is strangely restless, almost as if he possessed the intuition of things to come. Harriet is in the beginning stages of her surgery. And Susan Cleave has been unable to sleep all night. At Amalita's, though, I am witnessing a most unpleasant scene.

It would seem that after E.C. left her, and as I might have expected, the illness took a definite turn for the worse. She has refused to see a physician, and has remained sleepless, with an increasingly rising temperature. These symptoms, I am very much afraid, will intensify to the point where there will be a failure in several of her major systems. Her Nana is sitting beside her with the same gray and passive face which she has worn for the last thirty years. Crumpled on the night table are the famous diamonds. And in a nearby ashtray, the Moguk glitters with a light all its own. I fear it will never sit in that place between those promontories for which it was destined by E.C.

As time moves rather quickly this morning, I return to Susan Cleave. Around her are the remnants of a very bad night spent weeping. There are cups of coffee. And a couple of cards, and gifts she received from E.C. I see also some things having to do with me. It seems she's managed to find a few pictures. In one we are getting ready to take a helicopter ride over a portion of the West Coast. I'm looking dapper in a woodsy sort of outfit, with a bright plaid shirt. And she's next to me wearing a matching blouse and hat. Beside us is the helicopter pilot looking bright-eyed and bushy-tailed, as such people are prone to do. There's another picture of me all by myself. I had forgotten this one. It was taken in England. I'm standing smack in the middle of the nave at Salisbury Cathedral. She really captured the best of me in that snapshot. I'm looking a bit downward. Almost with modesty. Yes, it's a very nice likeness. She's been sitting here all night in a white baby-doll negligee going over these things. I guess in many respects the rejection she's now had from E.C. is similar to what I did to her. It was all because of that woman I was seeing. Of course, the *lady* is irrelevant. We needn't think about her. But the fact is that because of her I broke Susan's heart. And now it's being broken again. I guess each time it happens, we relive again and again all the previous occasions on which we've been damaged. She nervously looks at the phone. And I'm sure is making lots of mental excuses about why he hasn't called.

She's mustering all her courage, and grabs for the telephone. Now she's dialing the private number which rings by his bedside, but just prior to inserting the last digit, she relents. She does this on two more occasions, and then finally, as her courage mounts, completes the dialing process. Expectantly and anxiously awaiting his voice.

"Hello."

"E.C., it's me. I haven't been able to sleep."

"You know, it's awfully early. I didn't get that much sleep myself."

"E.C., what's happened between us? I thought we were a couple."

"Look, Susan, it's eight o'clock in the morning, and the last thing I need is a call from a jealous woman. I've basically decided I can't stick with a relationship like ours. It's suffocating me, and I need my liberty. It's time to move on. Besides, that's the way I am. It's sort of a take-it-or-leave-it. And your calling me this way doesn't make matters any better."

"But I hurt. . . ."

E.C. is now becoming more smug and angry. "Well, I'm sorry about that, but I'm not responsible for your emotions."

"Oh . . . I see . . . I think I understand fully."

"Well, I'm glad. You know, why don't you take a couple of days off and sort of pull yourself together?"

"You know, E.C., I thought you'd want to see me."

"No. I think it'll be better if you take two or three days off. Besides, the Siderurgica deal is complete, and I may be going to Europe on business."

"Without me?"

"Susan, you *don't* understand, *do* you?"

"Yes, I guess I do."

"Stop crying. I really don't need this. Why are you doing this to me?"

"Why am I doing this to you?"

"Yes, to me."

"I think, E.C., you should know better."

"Then, Susan, you must release me."

"Okay, okay, I understand. Listen, I'm just not feeling well. I don't want to speak anymore."

"Okay. I'll see you in a few days. Goodbye."

"Bye."

Click.

Now that I can witness the damage we can wreak on people who love us, I'm ashamed and mortified. If only I could do something to make her feel better. But what? For better or for worse, I'm still a disembodied spirit, stuck between one reality with which I thought I was familiar, and another of which I only have vague understandings, suspicions, and premonitions. I'll come up close to her and try to stroke her hair. But she doesn't feel anything. She doesn't know I'm here. As I cast my gaze around the room, I notice there are two dozen red roses in a vase. They have not yet opened. If I could only get her to look in that direction, I might open them very quickly and make her feel someone cares. There's a pencil on that table near the crystal vase with the roses. I shall again concentrate, and move it back and forth against the glass, making a gentle tinkling noise.

My idea has come none too soon. Susan is toying with a very sharp pair of scissors as if she were going to cut her wrists. She's actually trying them by gently drawing them across her flesh without yet cutting. No, no, this won't do. I'll admit I once thought suicide could be a justifiable phenomenon. But not anymore. No, my dear, your life is much too precious. And someone else will love you if E.C. has been fool enough to leave you for another. But the mental mention of the word "suicide" has triggered something unpleasant within me. The concept is, to say the least, distasteful.

She's praying now. And asking God for help, and for deliverance from the pain. Well, that's what I'm here for. And just as she's saying,

"There's no hope, there's no hope," I begin furiously tinkling against the vase with this rather dumb pencil. If I can make her look this way, I can repeat the party trick I did with the roses when E.C. met Don Orsini. After a few seconds, I've grasped her attention. And stopped moving the pencil just as her gaze finds its way to the flowers. I definitely don't wish to frighten her. Now, in a phenomenal expenditure of all the energy inherent in my spiritual existence, I am popping and bursting these buds open like a set of fireworks in the night sky. I'm doing it in rapid succession, one after the other. And she's just sitting there wide-eyed, almost transfigured by my little nonverbal message. I've got about six flowers left, which I'm holding for the last minute. She's smiling. And speaking.

"Henry, is that you? If it is, and you can do it, open two at one time."

To this little challenge I respond by popping two in tandem.

She's quick to reply. "Oh, Henry, I've missed you so. And I'm in such a predicament. I don't know what to do. But knowing you're around has made me feel better. I wish you'd help, I wish you'd help."

I'm going to pop the last four in one final gesture of hope. As I do it, she smiles broadly. She's now taken all of the roses out of the vase, and is lovingly clasping them to her breast with her eyes closed. I think moments like this are what love is really all about. Susan is more serene now, and has decided to shower and dress. This is good. I've been able to make someone happy without thinking of myself, or the consequences.

Now that I've achieved some measure of quiescence here, I had better look back on Amalita. The diva has definitely taken a turn for the worse. And is now suffering from a very substantial respiratory congestion. Harriet must have given her enough of the stuff to kill a horse, or a cow as the case may be. I think I would like to penetrate into her dream state. I know I will probably not be happy with what I see and hear. But who knows? Maybe I can help a bit here as well. Who would have thought I'd be doing this sort of thing? I must admit it's ironic.

I've blinked myself into Amalita's unconscious state. But very little seems to have changed. It's the same frightful, bleak place with dashes of alarming bright red everywhere. As in the prior dream, the star is walking without care through the miasma. As I approach her, she faces me directly.

"Ah, it is you again, Mr. Somerset. Why do you trouble me? Why don't you get out of my mind?"

"Actually, Amalita, I'm not here for myself this time. You see, you're in trouble. You're dying. Harriet has poisoned you. And I thought it might not be too late to help."

"I do not need your assistance. I do not require the help of any pig-of-a-man."

All of a sudden, as if magically, we're standing in front of the little shop with the doll in the window. It's the one the little girl desired so passionately.

"Amalita, look. There's the doll you wanted so badly. Why not enter the store and pick it out of the window for yourself?"

"Stupid man. I am not allowed in the shop. I have tried. And besides, even if I were able to enter, I have no money in this dream state."

"But Amalita, you have something better, you have art, and music. And you have yourself. You could have been generous with yourself and others, and there's still time. I beg you, time may run out sooner than you think."

"No. No. In any event, I tell you, I am not allowed in the shop."

"Well, maybe I am. Look, I'm grabbing the doorknob, as you can see, and the door is opening for me. And see . . . far from having to pay, a nice lady is handing me the doll of your dreams."

"I do not want it. I have better. I have diamonds, I have emeralds. I have men as slaves—"

"Amalita, take the doll."

"No."

"Amalita, just for an instant. Take it!"

"Well, maybe just for a moment."

All of a sudden, Amalita has, before my very eyes, become once more the bright-eyed girl with pigtails. Now tenaciously holding the object of her desire. She and her doll will remain here. No doubt until the end. When I hope some benign hand will completely release her from the evil she has perpetrated. As I leave, and again enter the bedroom, I find it full of physicians and attendants. And I also note from the clock on the mantel that unbeknownst to me, it is already night, and eight or nine hours have inexplicably passed.

Amalita is lying in bed inert. As her aunt passes her hand across the famous forehead in a resigned and loving gesture. But something is different. A look of kindness has come across the formidable woman. She is totally transfigured. And there is a smile. It's the expression of liberation from pain. The countenance of dreams accomplished. It is the face of a contented little girl.

I always marvel at how relative our conception of time can be. To me it seemed as if I was having a brief conversation with Amalita in her dream world. Yet, all of a sudden I find it's eight or nine hours later. And I really have no idea where the time actually went. I vaguely remember having read something on this topic when I was younger. Perhaps there is really no past and no future. Just one continuing present to which we might have access at various moments.

In any event, I'm concerned the hour is so late. I really do want to look in on my wife, and find out whether the operation was a success.

Harriet has just been wheeled back into her suite from the recovery room. It would seem hers was a very long and difficult surgery. Her beautiful little head is all bandaged. She is profoundly asleep. I'm trying to penetrate her dream state, but she is still heavily sedated. So my efforts are not bearing fruit.

Hooker has just entered, looking about ten years older than he did last night at the party. He has one of his partners with him, who doesn't look much better. John Goldfarb is a pragmatic and very candid lawyer. He and Tom Hooker have made a great deal of money together. Usually on the Somerset interests. But the bleakness and impossibility of their situation is initially patent from their faces, and further clarified by their conversation.

"Jesus Christ, John. She looks dead already. I'm not sure I can take seeing her like this."

"Did you have a chance to speak with her before she took ill?"

"No, no, it was all very sudden. And I certainly wasn't going to ruin the party by telling her the government has decided to pounce on Somerset Consolidated Industries for the inheritance tax."

"Well, she's going to have to know sooner or later if she ever snaps out of this. She's going to be a very poor woman."

"If that news doesn't kill her, she'll certainly drop dead when she hears about Gustavo."

"Yeah, that was really sort of frightening. I read it in this morning's newspaper. Can you imagine a good-looking guy like that having his nuts cut off and being forced to swallow them?"

"John, I know, I know. You don't have to remind me of the gruesome details. I was called at three a.m. with the terrible news. You know, between that and thinking about what's going to happen to us, I just haven't slept all night."

"It's very simple. We're ruined. We're broke. And by the time the various lawsuits against us start to fall into place, we'll be lucky if we can even obtain a discharge in bankruptcy."

"So what are we going to do?"

"You know, Tom, it always boils down to two solutions. We either fight or run. The irony of it is that if we fight, we'll probably invest the next ten or twelve years of our lives in the matter. And even if we win, we'll be old and gray. Of course, running is what cowards do. But remember the old saying—he who fights and runs away lives to fight another day."

"We could stall."

"There's something else we could do . . . but I don't know if you, Thomas Hooker, Esquire, have the guts."

"What's that? What are you thinking of?"

"Tom, as I recall, you are still trustee for substantial funds in the Somerset estate. And only your signature is required to use the money. I know the government has frozen the larger sums. But there must be twelve or fifteen million dollars in the ancillary accounts we use to service the interests."

"Are you suggesting I become a thief in addition to everything else?"

"Tom, don't play lily-white with me. We could cable the funds to Brazil, and never be heard of again."

"I don't know . . . I'm very confused right now."

"Well, this is something you'll have to decide quickly. You won't have a second opportunity to go for it."

"I'll tell you, John, I've never had great moral scruples. But as we stand here with Harriet looking so frail, I don't know if I could entirely run out on her. I've just realized I was sort of attached to the woman."

"Listen, I don't think she's going to recover. Furthermore, who do you love more, Harriet or her money? In any event, it may be moot. I heard the doctors speaking outside, and they said she would at best end up with almost no bodily movement. So if I were you, I'd make a rapid decision."

Thomas Hooker is now squarely on the horns of a dilemma. If he stays and fights, he will suffer. And his pain will entail poverty, ruin, and scandal. Not to mention the ever-present possibility of going to jail. Whenever you fall out of grace with the system for any reason whatsoever, including mistake or act of fate, the establishment responds by further destroying you in each and any way it can. *Everyone makes firewood out of the fallen tree.* This, in its own curious way, is a form of Darwinism. In which the weakened animal is preyed upon by the herd. If Hooker were a man of honor, he would stay and fight. He would buck circumstance, and revel in the shining honesty of his new tin cup. But he's now responding with exactly what his partner wishes to hear. It has been said that *the Lord makes them and they come together.* They are now, without even a silent, backward glance at Harriet, on their way to rape and pillage the remaining Somerset interests. To secure what they think will elsewhere constitute their happiness.

Back at Pyramid Hill it's now quite dark. Outside, it's a windy night, and the gusts are unrelentingly whipping around the angular granite facade. There are still some fall leaves left which were late to drop from the trees. And they form little whirlwinds in the dark, which might otherwise be mistaken for things and spirits of the night. Within the structure, E.C. is nervously pacing in his library. He's unshaven and wearing a pair of tan corduroy trousers, moccasins, and an off-white cashmere sweater. He's been drinking again. Apparently he's also frantically dialed Amalita Corsini's number, and received the same noncommittal response from the other end of the line. He's just poured another glass of vodka. And is again reaching for the telephone.

"Hello. Is this Signorina Corsini's suite?"

"Yes, it is."

"Who is this, please?"

"I am Signorina Corsini's aunt. May I help you?"

"Yes, look . . . please, this is E. C. Douglas. I've been trying all afternoon to reach Signorina Corsini, and I've just been receiving the same answer, to the effect that she's indisposed. Is something wrong? May I help? I really must speak with her."

"My niece is indisposed at present, and may not come to the telephone. Goodbye."

"No, no, please don't hang up on me. When may I call again?"

"Perhaps tomorrow. Goodbye."

Click.

E.C. is frantic. Through his mind are racing many ideas. Could it be Amalita is really ill? No. The woman is too robust. Then there is only one other alternative. She's deceived him, and is with another man. He's pacing back and forth like an angry lion. All of a sudden, he's taking the Sèvres statue of a beautiful maiden singing and suspiciously fondling it with both hands. He doesn't know what to do. Which is, of course, the conundrum of lovers who suspect their affection is not properly corresponded. Right now he's sure of only one thing. The object of his lustful affection is not present, and is probably intentionally making herself unavailable. He will not tolerate this for a greater length of time. All of a sudden, he flings the statue at the wall with force. As it shatters into countless pieces, he is up and out of the room as if possessed, and on his way to the bedroom. He's locked the door. And in a flash, he's into the bathroom, where he's taking the quickest of showers and shaving at the same time. Once out, and having only partially dried himself with a towel, he is again into a pair of winter trousers and brown lizard loafers. He's using his keys on one of the drawers in the dressing room. From it he's extracting a glimmering stainless-steel Smith & Wesson thirty-eight-caliber short-barrel pistol. He's stuffing it in his trousers at the waist, and donning a brown antelope sport coat to conceal the bulge. Now calling downstairs, and asking them to bring the red Ferrari around. For an instant, he again paces. This is a moment of truth. Will he throw all discretion to the winds and murder the bitch if he finds her in the arms of another? Perhaps, but he loves her too much. The gun is out of his trousers and is returned to the drawer. But then, with one sentence of blazing imprecation, he firmly returns it to its spot beneath his belt. "To the devil with it. If this is what God has to offer, I repudiate it. If the devil can give me what I want, I'll take it and promise to pay the price."

I'm standing here, incredulously hearing a man willingly deliver his soul to Satan in exchange for the love of a woman. To be honest, it's what I would have once done. But this is very, very wrong. Listen, E.C., you have true love. Susan adores you. She'll take you back. Forget about Amalita Corsini. She doesn't love you. But E.C. can't hear me, and he's now on his way to the landing at the head of the grand staircase. Where all of a sudden Bozo bounds up and begins to playfully romp. As if possessed, E.C. takes the back of his hand and slaps it hard against Bozo's head. The pooch cowers and yelps, as if taken completely aback by the brutality of the gesture. Then, in disappointment, he saunters quietly into a corner to sulk.

Our man is now down the stairs. Through the ground-floor rooms, and into the great hall. For a moment, he looks at the two statues of Sekhmet, which are now frowning displicently. In an angry and rather spoiled gesture, he gives them the finger. He's through the door like a bat out of hell, and into the car. I'm with him all the way, as the horses under the hood strain with his impatient handling of the vehicle. Sooner than I would have thought, we are at Amalita's. To the enormous surprise of the doorman, he's leaving the car at the curb, with open door. Inside, there's some protestation about announcing him to the persons in the apartment above. As if he hadn't heard it at all, he's stuffed a hundred-dollar bill into the attendant's pocket and pushed him aside as he takes command of the elevator. Once on Amalita's floor, he's now banging at the solid oak door. After a moment, the door is opened just a crack, as the ever-present aunt responds in a low hushed voice, "Please go away. We are not receiving."

"Listen, you can't send me away, you must open the door, I have to see Amalita. Is there someone else in there?"

"No. I am alone."

"Is Amalita in there?"

"Yes, but she may not receive you. But I have something for you. *This*, I believe, is yours."

Tata has opened the door a bit, and is handing the glistening

Moguk Diamond to E.C. At this gesture, E.C.'s rage has mounted, and he's pushing the door open, as he also steamrolls the surprised and disheveled aunt.

"I will not take this from you. She must return it to me herself."

"Signor Douglas, you do not understand. She cannot return it herself."

"Why? Why? Is there another man with her?"

"No. She will never be able to return it. You see, *my niece is dead.*"

At the revelation of this statement, E.C. is clasping his hands to his temples in disbelief, and pulling the hairs from the side of his head. As he now uncontrollably rushes into the bedroom where the pale dead Amalita lies under her beautiful embroidered sheets. All at once he is reliving the death of his wife. Step by step and blow by blow. He is thinking about everything which in his obsessive mind might have been. Of her body, and of the sex. He's screaming her name out, and kissing her dead hands and forehead. Almost under her voice, the aunt is muttering the word *sacrilegio*, and is now, in a gesture of renewed vigor, bodily forcing the weeping man out of the bedroom and apartment.

The grief-stricken and confused E.C., as if possessed, is now back in the elevator and rushing through the lobby to the waiting vehicle. He intermittently bursts into fits of anger and uncontrolled tears. And is now maniacally shifting gears, taking us to the vicinity of the dark and dangerous cliffs at Ocean Drive.

THIRTY-TWO

FOR REASONS WHICH I DO NOT ENTIRELY UNDERSTAND, MANY PEOPLE are drawn to the edge of the water when something goes terribly wrong in their lives. Particularly where love or disconsolate loss are concerned, men, women, and children alike are attracted to the eternal ebb of a lake, river, or ocean. Perhaps it has to do with the ancient evolution of mankind, and the birth of our predecessor species from the now more distant aqueous element. Whatever the reason, the liquid medium is like a magnet. Tonight is no exception to the rule. E.C.'s car is racing down the solitary clifftop road which borders the ocean. At this time of the year it is a hard, unyielding, and unsympathetic body of water. The waves crash into the boulders below, as if denoting and proclaiming the greatest possible anger, lack of care, and absence of empathy. The road widens a bit up front. In the spring and summer, it's a place usually frequented by lovers. But there are none tonight. A few hundred feet beyond, there is a little path which finds its way down to the stairs which have been carved out of the solid face of the precipice and lead to the beach below. The vehicle is now at a halt, and E.C. is just sitting here looking for a star in the overcast sky. Every so often, his thoughts are interrupted by a bout of uncontrollable weeping. He's thinking about Amalita. About everything he thinks could have been. He can never understand that for her, he was merely another slave-of-a-man. The rude fuck of the moment. Less, in fact, than her diamonds and emeralds. In the fantasy of the disconsolate lover, the dead or absent recipient is idealized beyond possible human proportions.

I feel terribly sorry for this fellow. He really has everything, but he's made all the wrong choices. He enjoys the benefits of wealth, intelligence, physical presence, and even sex appeal. Moreover, he possesses a woman who loves him. Completely and altruistically. But this obsessed man doesn't wish to be loved generously. He wishes only for the passionate embrace of Amalita Corsini. Having found his wife once, and lost her, and then having thought he discovered her once again in the person of her look-alike, he is taking this loss with particular difficulty and incomprehension. Somewhere in the lives of those who battle with destiny as opposed to flowing with it, a brittle moment overtakes them in which they must inevitably snap under the greater onslaught of uncontrolled, unwanted circumstances. E.C. is at just such a juncture.

The sensations involved are no less real merely because they are adolescent. How could I explain that Amalita has found her doll, and has no subsequent interest in E. C. Douglas? He would no doubt call me a liar.

He's turning the knob on his radio. Which brings forth the blaring of cheap popular music. Now, right on the hour, we're going to hear the evening bulletin.

The commentator is quickly going through the news. E.C. is just preparing to dismiss this interruption with action directed at the flick of a knob when the local commentary comes into evidence in an *arresting* way:

"Earlier today, federal marshals detained two local lawyers at International Airport who were apparently on their way out of the country in an effort to conceal a major embezzlement. The two attorneys, Thomas Hooker and John Goldfarb, were taken into custody as they were preparing to board an airliner for Rio de Janeiro. Federal

authorities had been tipped off to the possible fraud and embezzlement when a large wire transfer in the amount of fifteen million
dollars was ordered from the local Republic Bank. Upon making the
necessary inquiries, it was quickly ascertained these funds could not
legally have been transferred for personal use. The two have been
charged with misappropriation of funds and wire fraud. Bail has been
set in the amount of ten million dollars for each."

This bit of news has really stopped E.C. in his tracks. A wry little
smile has come across his face as he wipes some of the tears away.
He turns the volume up as the next interesting tidbit begins.

"In related news, local heiress Harriet Somerset was said to be
resting and in critical condition at Memorial Hospital after an emergency operation performed to correct paralysis caused by a cerebral
hemorrhage. The heiress, wife of the late H. W. Somerset, was at
one time said to be one of the richest women in America. Since Mrs.
Somerset is somewhat of a personage in our city, we will keep our
listeners posted on her condition."

E.C. looks as if something is troubling him. It would almost seem
he's having a pang of conscience over Harriet's difficulty. For a moment, though, he extracts the Moguk Diamond from his pocket, and
looks at it as if to request or obtain an answer to his dilemma. But
the stone shining with the compressed light of the ages is, as we might
expect, quite obdurate and mute. All of a sudden, the motor is humming again, and he's turning the car. We are apparently on our way
back to town.

I'm actually feeling a bit relieved. I had not seen him in such a
deep manic-depressive mood before, and would rather have him in
town, where my influence can be felt through Bozo and the surrounding objects. He's taking the fork in the road which would lead us to
the area of Memorial Hospital. I really think he's on his way to look
in on Harriet. This I find very interesting indeed. But there isn't a
great deal of time for me to perorate over the particular. Sooner than
I think, we are at the entrance of the facility, and the car is parked.
E.C. is now looking a bit more composed as he walks into the reception area and up to the information desk.

"Good evening, miss. Would you be kind enough to tell me what
room Harriet Somerset is in?"

"Are you a family member?"

"Why yes, I am related."

"She's in 666. You know, we've had a lot of calls and people coming by. So Dr. Stern has restricted access to family members."

"That's very understandable. I'm grateful. Thank you."

With this little bit of deception, E.C. is now into the elevator. And pressing the button for the sixth and last floor. Once on six, he is resolutely but quietly moving toward suite 666. As he approaches, he is confronted with the sight of Susan Cleave sitting on a chair in the corridor, facing Harriet's door.

"Susan, what are you doing here?"

"I could ask you the same thing. I'm not sure you'd be entirely welcome if Harriet were her old self. But to answer your question, the lawyers at the district attorney's office located me while I was briefly here looking in on Harriet's progress. After all, I *did* work for her husband for years. Anyway, they asked me to stay while they dispatched an associate with a sworn statement for me to sign regarding Hooker and Goldfarb. I'm afraid she's not doing very well."

"I feel a bit guilty. Even though I know I shouldn't. Do you have details?"

"The operation took an awfully long time, and was not a total success. Dr. Stern says she may be totally paralyzed as a result. But we won't know until tomorrow. What are you doing here?"

"I told you, I feel responsible. You know, I did put Harriet and her finances under a great deal of stress."

"I was also concerned. So I came by to visit. You know, she had been suffering from high blood pressure for years, and I guess it just eventually got the best of her. You probably knew all about Thomas and John Goldfarb."

"Yes, I heard it on the radio. But how were the banks tipped off so quickly?"

"A couple of associates at the firm thought the withdrawal from Harriet's trustee accounts was awfully large and called me. They figured that even though I no longer work for Somerset Consolidated Industries, I would probably be the person to consult. So I told them what I thought was happening, and presto, they caught two thieves!"

"What will happen to them?"

"Oh, I figure ten to twenty years. You know, it was pretty crass and rotten to do it while Harriet was under the surgeon's knife. I also heard about Amalita Corsini. I shouldn't have been, but I was very sorry to hear the news."

"Thank you, Susan. I'm having a tough time."

"I can help."

"No, I'm afraid I have to be alone."

"E.C., you know how I feel. Why don't we do something about it? I can forget what's happened. Come home with me tonight and we'll put it all behind us. And maybe buy that tropical island."

"No. I'm afraid I can't do that. I need to be alone. Thank you."

"Oh. . . . Then, be well."

She's touching his arm in a combination of a farewell gesture and a moment of tenderness. There are tears in her eyes. He initially seems totally oblivious to these feelings, but is now harboring a second thought. A moment of self-recrimination, which makes him briefly return to silently press the Cardinal's emerald cross into her hands. Then he quietly turns again. As he walks down the corridor, he begins thinking about Amalita. I shouldn't leave him alone for a very long time. But now that I'm here, I really do want to see Harriet.

I'm tiptoeing into this hospital room almost as if I could be heard. She looks sternly dazed. As I try to penetrate into her non-restful sleep, I again find her drug-induced state does not lend itself to a clear confrontation with the woman within. I must then return to E.C. and try to make amends for all this mess.

Our man and his very fast car are halfway to the house by the time I catch up with them. I find his style of driving very much changed. It's almost as if something within him has snapped, and he really doesn't care anymore. He missed a van a moment ago by what must have been at most an inch or two. It's almost as if he had given up all hope and placed himself on a dangerous type of automatic drive. As we approach Pyramid Hill, I find myself dreading the sight of the structure. All of a sudden, I find it pretentious and vulgar. All this money could have been used for something which might have made more people happy. Including me.

The electronic gates are opening, and E.C. is racing up the driveway. This is not at all the succession of events I would have wanted. He's out of the car and rushing up the steps into the great hall. For a moment there, as he walked through, I could have sworn the lionesses were weeping. But as I looked a second time, all I was able to catch from them was the blank serenity of the ages. He's up in the bedroom. And now behind a firmly bolted door. As he cries again, he's playing with the short-barreled revolver. As if toying with the idea of using it on himself. At the same time, he's pulled the Moguk Diamond out of his pocket. Weapon and diamond find themselves as dance partners. E.C. gently and resolutely toys with both. There's a scratching at the door. As it is unbolted and opened, the woolly behemoth bounds through with a canine gasp of relief. E.C. is happy to see him. Bozo slurps a big wet tongue across his face. For a moment E.C. smiles as Bozo curls his prodigious upper lip. But shortly thereafter, our man again collapses in a fit of weeping. After a while, he repairs to the music room, where sitting at the piano he plays that very plaintive twenty-fifth *Goldberg* variation again and again. Just when I think the music is going to drive me crazy, he interrupts his performance and sulks back to the bedroom. He removes his clothing and prepares for a night of restlessness. This is good. Because it will give me an opportunity to visit with him as he slumbers.

While E.C. attempts resting, I shall play with Bozo. He took one look at me and bounded into the bathroom. From which he's returned with one of those cute little rubber balls. As E.C. falls asleep, Bozo and I are as two children playing with a toy. But I am merely killing time. *I am deeply troubled.*

To be sure, the man was thoroughly exhausted when he arrived. So it's no wonder he's now breathing heavily, as if fully encompassed by the initial depth of sleep. I have great second thoughts about again invading his dream world. After all, this guy is in a very tender and fragile state. What if I do the wrong thing? On the other hand, I'm watching him make all these mistakes. Perhaps I can help him understand. And maybe provide the benefit of some of my experience. So I'll put myself into the meditative state, and proceed. As I enter a world now inhabited by palpitating bursts of purple and mauve, I can't help feeling the intense grief and sadness which have fully seized what used to be a fairly pleasant interior. It doesn't take me long to catch up with him. He's actually striking, and rather sexy, as he walks along the edge of a cliff, not unlike those near Ocean Drive. He's barefoot. But his handsome feet don't seem the worse for the rocks and stones beneath. He's naked, except for a pair of pink boxer shorts. Yes, the color of those boxer shorts has always been one of E.C.'s little jokes. Sort of a quiet and private act of rebellion by someone who can. I'm sorry to note that in this dream state he's not any different emotionally from what he was when he was awake. He continues to weep, as he walks aimlessly by the edge of the rock. As he catches a glimpse of me, I decide to come forward and speak. But all of a sudden, as I open my mouth, he is overcome by an additional wave of grief. So I instinctively embrace him and allow him to cry on my shoulder like just another child.

"I don't know what's happening to me. All I can do is weep."

"There, there, E.C. It can't be so bad."

"Oh, but it is, it is. I've made a terrible mess of things. And now Amalita is dead and I shall never be able to bring her back."

"Look, E.C., I don't want to hurt your feelings, but I've been with you all along, and I've seen the inner motivations of those around you. Amalita was a misguided and wicked woman who has now found her peace without you. E.C., I know as a fact she would have destroyed you."

"I don't believe it. But so what? Who cares? I loved her."

"You are an intelligent man, and you should understand intellectually that the woman was not good for you, and furthermore, didn't care a fig about you. You see, I was there when she died. And believe me, there was no word for you."

"Why are you telling me this? I don't want to hear it. You don't seem to understand. Anyone can love the good ones . . . but I thought she was wonderful, and I loved her in spite of her wickedness."

"And you would damage yourself for this. And hurt others around you, like Susan."

"Yes, I would go to hell and back if I could have Amalita."

"I tell you, you are making a terrible mistake. She never loved you. But Susan has always adored you. I think she loved you from the moment she first saw you. She's been patient, and she's forgiving. She's the one you really need. Don't you see what you're doing? Look at your mistake! If I were you, I'd opt for Susan in a moment. Besides, E.C., I feel very responsible. It was I who put you up to buying the pyramid and the art, and everything else. And it was wrong. You should have bought that Pacific island, and been happy."

"But I don't want to be happy with anyone except Amalita."

"Amalita's gone, and no one can bring her back."

"But I can follow her."

"What do you mean?"

"You know."

"No, you don't want to do that. Suicide is the worst of all possible solutions. Mainly because it's not a solution at all. You see, E.C., it doesn't resolve anything. I don't know why, but I'll bet people who kill themselves just end up returning again and again in order to face the music and make the right choices. With what I know today, I can tell you if you admire me at all, it's something I would never do myself."

"I do admire you. You had everything, and I wished to be as you."

"Well, that's where you're all wrong. Perhaps I had everything materially, but I was a very unhappy man. Whenever there was something I couldn't have, I tried to purchase it. And if that wasn't possible, I purchased something else in its place. You may be surprised to hear this, but I actually did love Harriet very much at one point in time. When I saw her drifting away from me, I tried to exercise control. And the more I tried, the farther away she went."

"I've screwed that up too. I think Harriet is probably dead now."

"You needn't feel any remorse. Harriet was a very misguided child. And it is she who was responsible for Amalita's death. But in this sense, she did you a favor, as Amalita would have destroyed you. E.C., we are all ultimately responsible for ourselves."

"That was my choice to make, not Harriet's."

"You're right, I agree. But I have a feeling Harriet will suffer her own private hell for those actions and for others."

"And you, why are you here? Haven't you done enough already?"

"I want to help. I want you to understand it was wrong. I attempted to live again in the reflected glory of your achievements. I've now realized it was a terrible mistake. I had no business trying to influence you to undertake the continuation of my life."

"Well, it seemed pretty good to me for a while."

"But were you happy?"

"Sure I was happy when I had Amalita."

"But you and I both know you had no business staking your happiness on the love of another. On an illusion."

"Hah. Take your enlightened concepts and stuff them! They certainly didn't do you any good when you were around. Or maybe they did, after all. *You* got everything you wanted."

"No, no. I'm telling you, you've missed the boat. I was a very unhappy man, and now I'm even less happy to see you this way."

"Look, Henry, just leave me alone with my grief, and get the hell out of my dream."

"You mustn't think about suicide. I'm telling you, it's not a solution."

"If death is peace, then that tranquillity will be mine. I can no longer take the pain."

"Don't you understand that my very presence here should indicate to you that there's no peace in death as you conceive it?"

"Listen, you're not fooling me. You're just another figment of my imagination. You're one of my own Judeo-Christian concoctions, designed by my subconscious to keep me from finding the peace I so very much desire."

"No, no, E.C., I'm real. Remember Bozo and the rubber ball?"

"Oh, fuck off, Henry! Get out of my dream. On second thought, just go to hell! Or back to hell, as the case may be."

E.C. is stirring now, and is all of a sudden fully awake. For a moment, he's disconcerted. In the style of dreamers who rouse and do not immediately know where they are. Once he's again oriented himself in his location, he begins shaking and crying. He's sitting on the edge of the bed in those defiant pink shorts. Bozo is leaning against him. Man and dog are now walking over to the small writing desk in his room. He's sitting down with pen in hand. And writing and writing and writing. An occasional tear drops on the stationery, where it is dried with a tissue. But this does not deter him. He's preparing instructions. And a holographic will. As he continues through the hours, I can't help feeling very helpless. Maybe as the first morning light arrives in an hour or so he'll feel a little better. If he falls asleep again, I might even have a second chance at convincing him. But the improbability of all these events is beginning to weigh heavily on me. As I too begin feeling exceedingly depressed and uncertain regarding the future.

I've been so wrapped up in E.C.'s situation I almost forgot to look in on Harriet. Our man doesn't look like he's about to move anywhere very quickly. He's just sitting there weeping. So I think it's pretty safe to blink myself back to the hospital.

Suite 666 is very quiet. It's now occupied only by Harriet and a very officious-looking private duty nurse. They've got her hooked up to all sorts of machines and monitors. I can't help feeling she looks extremely pale and helpless in her present state. The previous hardness of her features has relaxed just a bit, and she now seems to be sleeping more restfully.

That last conversation we had just before she succumbed to the influence of the tranquilizers has continued haunting me. I am concerned about what I don't seem to know or recall. Harriet has valuable information which might help me remember a little more about that last day of my life. I definitely recall having heard her and Hooker plotting to murder me with the seeds from the castor-oil plant. And I have certainly thought until recently that I was eliminated by my lovely and dangerous wife. Still, whenever I think about this topic, the relentlessly spinning wheel of that clock seems to come into my mind.

As I enter Harriet's thoughts, I notice there are two additions to the mansion of her psyche. The first is in the color. Everything is now flashing bright yellows, the ultimate tonality of fear and alarm. Also, even though the views through the windows continue to be beautiful and serene, it would seem that stiff iron bars have been added to each and every one. This doesn't really disturb me, since I'm here as an intruder with the certainty of being able to leave as I arrived. But within, I have found Harriet in an agitated state, nervously twirling her wedding ring as she speaks.

"Henry, Henry, I'm so happy to see you. I'm terribly frightened. I'm terrified of this place with all these bars . . . and I'm also afraid for what I've done. Henry, I've done terrible things. And they haunt me in this house of mine. Previously, I could wake up and leave it all behind. But now, I'm trapped. I can't seem to snap out of this at all. Henry, please help me, please help me."

"Well, Harriet, you are in sort of a pickle, I must admit. Do you remember what's happened to you in the outside world? I did advise you once before. . . ."

"No, no. Please tell me."

"Well, brace yourself. It seems your blood pressure has finally gotten the best of you and you've had a cerebral hemorrhage. I feel a bit guilty. Even though you did a terrible thing with Amalita, and were getting ready to do another with E.C. You see, I don't know if you remember, but it was I who made your blood pressure rise with the flower pots in the conservatory. Yesterday they operated on your head to remove a blood clot. Harriet, in spite of the past, I am deeply sorry about all this."

"My dear, I guess you did what you had to do. So we're even now. But tell me, will there be a terrible scar? Am I to be horrible? Was the operation successful? Will I recuperate?"

"Well, Harriet, the good news is you're not dying, or at least not at present. You will probably last a great many years. The bad news is you will be paralyzed, and unable to function as a normal human being."

"No, Henry, no. Tell me it isn't true. . . . Help me! You have powers. I know you do. You've always been able to overcome everything and anything."

"I can't do that now. I'm just a spirit, remember? But sweetheart, you must get a grip on yourself. Let me run my hand over your forehead and try to calm you."

"Oh, Henry, darling, I have missed you. I've missed your strength and your power. I've even missed fearing you as I did."

"Tell me, Harriet, is that why you poisoned me with my own castor oil seeds?"

Harriet is composing herself and regarding me in complete disbelief.

"You really don't know, do you?"

"You're repeating yourself, sweetheart, and I think protesting a bit too much. You were about to use this ploy before they sedated you for the operation."

"Oh, my poor Henry, Thomas and I had nothing to do with your death. The truth is, I had thought of it, and even discussed it that day with him in the conservatory. But in the end, as with everything, you beat us to the punch. I don't really know if I would have gone through with it. But by the time the next day came, you were dead as a doornail from an overdose of sleeping pills."

"No, Harriet. I can't believe that. This is some cock-and-bull story."

"Henry, you don't have to take my word for it. I'm sure if you try a little, you'll remember. You took about a hundred of those big fat red narcotic things you'd been hoarding for just such a purpose. We had a very difficult time hushing it up with the press."

"I can't believe that. I had everything. I enjoyed my wealth. I'm sure I couldn't have committed such an act."

"Henry, who are you trying to kid? Remember, this is me. I've loved you and despised you. But especially, I've known you very well. Toward the end, when you had achieved everything, you were in a constantly depressed state. And mind you, although I admit I must have added to your frustration, it was those accumulated tensions which constantly brought forth your anger, and the ultimate act of violence against yourself."

"Why should I take the word of a murderess regarding the way I died?"

"Yes, I am a murderess, Henry, and to tell the truth, I'm not sure I entirely regret it. But you don't know how very unhappy the whole thing has made me. In fact, I'd give anything to be back in the good old days before we discovered so much bitterness and pain. But as surely as the sun rose this morning, you committed suicide."

"I'm going to put this aside for a moment, Harriet. I'll think about it when I can. But there is one thing I do want to tell you. Everything is so uncertain, I just can't afford to waste the moment. You see, my dear, I thought I hated you. And throughout all this mess, I've realized I never stopped loving you in my very own way. And wicked though you may have become, that love has not perished within me. You know, Harriet, I don't think true love ever really dies. It's the infatuation and sex that grow stale. And all the reasonable facsimiles accompanying them. But the memory of the love is still here."

"Why, Henry, I believe you're weeping. You know, I've never seen you cry before."

"I did, Harriet, on many occasions. I just never made you aware."

"You might have. You know, I think I would have feared you

less, and loved you more. But Henry, what is going to become of me here?"

"I don't know. I think for the moment you're stuck walking these halls."

"But I'm terribly frightened, and all of a sudden I don't want to be alone."

"Think of it this way. Even though you are my very bad little girl, the knowledge that I have loved you and do love you might in some small measure sustain you through this loneliness until something better comes up. I must, however, leave. There are things I should do."

"What things?"

"I have to mend some deeds."

"Oh. . . . Will you come to see me again?"

"If I can. But if not in this exact mode, I have a suspicion the love will always find its way home in the end. Besides, Harriet, you have to enter many of the rooms in this house which you have locked, and squarely face your monsters of hatred and revenge, and all the dreams that might have been, but didn't come true. Goodbye, Harriet."

"Goodbye, Henry."

As I leave her to a now more restful sleep, I'm noticing the private duty nurse has called for one of the doctors. It seems our patient has regained only one movement. Harriet is now physically twirling an imaginary wedding ring on that beautiful, frail left hand. Just like a silkworm spitting forth a thread. And with it spinning a magical cocoon. But from this chrysalis she will not emerge, nor will she regain consciousness. Instead, I suspect she will forever, until the time of reckoning, spin that ring.

The whole conversation with her has left me in a totally disconcerted state of mind. I'm trying to remember that final day of my life, particularly the last few hours. And like a word long forgotten, and which I'm getting ready to flip off the tip of my tongue, it would now seem to be returning. It's the clock I remember. The one with the clinking wheel. And with it are surfacing other memories. But this is hardly the place for me to think about such things. I need serenity and tranquillity. So I'll return to my memorial at the cemetery.

As I blink back, I find myself in the twilight standing squarely beneath the Egyptial portal with the inscription. The steadfast columns mutely sustain the strength of this gateway. I'm slowly walking up the various paths. Winter is upon us. And though the morning sun is soon to shine, there's a terrible chill in the air. As I finally reach the area of my tomb, I can't help noticing E.C.'s marble edifice has now been completed, and his wife's remains have apparently been tranferred to the now sealed second vault. The building glistens serenely in the predawn light. I think perhaps I'll sit on one of his benches. To meditate a bit and try to remember. I'm tired and exhausted. It's all been too much for me. This isn't fair. I'm just overwhelmed by everything which has been happening, and what's more, there seem to be things totally beyond my understanding. I appear to be easing my way into that somnolent state between wakefulness and reverie. It's funny, I seem to be dreaming, but with a full consciousness of what is occurring.

All of a sudden, I'm back in the conservatory watching Harriet and Hooker plan my demise. They're leaving, and I'm remaining in the corner behind the potted palm. It's a large *Arenga*. I'm wearing a beautiful navy-blue suit. The one with the light blue stripe running through it. Complete with bow tie. I look pretty dapper. But in a moment, I'm sitting there weeping disconsolately. Why am I crying? Why does a man of my stature and ability weep? In the dream I'm speaking to myself, and I'm expressing my terminal sadness at the ways of people and the world. I, who have everything, am now fully disgusted with my life, and totally despondent about it all. There I am talking about love. I'm complaining to myself about how people fall out of love. I don't understand it. For me, it is a *forever* phenomenon. And I can't grasp why someone you have loved intensely can replace you with the flippancy of a schoolchild changing pencils. There's bitterness in me, and anger. Lots of it. I, who have seen everything, am totally uncomprehending regarding matters of the heart. Now I remember. That morning, Harriet blatantly told me she didn't love me anymore. In spite of the tantrums and my anger, I have to admit I was totally crushed. Rejection does that to people. It made me realize that in a way, I really did love her. And pushed my fragile psyche one step further. So then faced with the terrible fact that Harriet had substituted me for another, I started to blame myself. And I was very hard on Henry.

It has been said that *he who plants winds reaps tempests.* I now agree. How could anyone have loved me when I tried to control every person I was ever fond of? I made them fear me, not realizing that fear and love are totally incompatible. Which I guess is why most people will never know God. It's probably because they're afraid of him. They pray because they think a gigantic hand will come down and knock their heads off if they behave like bad little boys and girls. Now that I think of it, I guess love can never be felt for God or man if there is fear. As you can see, my mind wanders to thoughts of God and the universe. But then all of a sudden it once again focuses on the rejection, the sadness, the despondency, and the pain. On the helplessness and hopelessness of my situation, and on the turning wheel of that clock in my bedroom.

In the dream I'm picking myself up from the floor and proceeding resolutely into the great hall. I'm touching my two statues. They're weeping, with breasts full of apprehension. They seem to be pleading with me in their own quiet, dignified way. Telling me not to do it. But in spite of them, I'm walking upstairs, as Bozo follows presciently.

He's trying to cheer me up. Now curling that gigantic lip. But nothing helps. I'm into my bathroom, and now I've reached for a large jar of red capsules. The tears are rolling down my face as I draw a glass of water from the cooler. I'm also taking some motion-sickness pills. It would seem I really mean business, and do not wish to vomit what I am about to ingest. I'm sitting in my bedroom facing the clock with its unremitting brass wheel. Moving back and forth hypnotically. I've lined up the red capsules on the surface of my desk, and I'm playing with them in little handfuls. All of a sudden I'm crying again. For a moment, I want to grab the telephone and call someone, but instead, I start swallowing the pills, four by four, until they're gone. Now in my dream I quietly don my favorite pajamas. As I slip into bed, I cannot help feeling a great sense of peace and deliverance. I take one look at my clock. It's three thirty-three in the morning. The turning wheel is the last thing I see before I wearily close my eyes. Bozo has jumped up, and is lying next to me. He will later be retrieved by a member of the staff who will think I am dead asleep. That assumption will be unwittingly correct.

I recall vividly once again the great sense of peace I felt once on the way to my divorce from all the things of this world. Strange, that after seeking them with such alacrity, they should have been so definitely repudiated. . . .

I'm now beginning to wake from my semisomnolent state. I'm shaking. How could it be I forgot something as important as those last few hours of my life? And here I thought for all this time that Harriet and Hooker had murdered me. Perhaps if I had waited, something wonderful would have happened to shake my dour and depressed view of the universe. I could have found consolation in love. Or even in a greater belief in God. I might have secured peace and solace greater than the suicide's false tranquillity. I could have been less harsh with myself. I might have even learned to love Henry.

Sometimes I think I shall madden completely and lose all control. Then I think back to my present state and laugh a little at myself. One can certainly envision a human being going mad. But how wonderful and pathetic at the same time that a ghost or spirit might be able to do the same. Despair and loneliness can unhinge people. And rejection and sadness. . . . Yet with a minimal effort, we might accept what is available to us.

I need to project this message to E.C. I'll blink myself back to Pyramid Hill. Perhaps he'll fall asleep and I'll have a chance to chat a little and provide some help.

But as I enter his bedroom, I am displeased and concerned. It's just twenty or thirty minutes before dawn now. And he seems to have become much more anxious and irrational. There are stacks of sealed envelopes on the desk. And a little white box with a note and ribbon on it. Also there is a larger open parcel. It would seem E.C. has quietly purchased that string of black pearls we last saw in Rome. They are being sent to Miss Cleave as sort of a guilty consolation gift. He's also making an overseas call and unloading his miscellaneous portfolios in an orderly fashion to avoid any market tremors in the day to come.

I really don't like the look of this. He's dressing now. Not all that carefully. And the gun is again finding its way into that area near his waist. He's down the stairs in a flash. Bozo is right behind him, but is being told he must remain behind. When he insists, E.C. shouts at him, and that is enough to deter the sensitive heart of the dog-child.

The Ferrari is waiting, and is more than responsive to the now almost entranced shifting of the gears. Hah! We're going toward the cemetery again. I might have spared myself the trouble of returning. There once more is the famous gate. E.C. has stopped the car right in front of it. He's looking up at the inscription . . . and saying, "Ha, I hope so, but if not, let it all be damned." I don't like this. The gate's been opened by the attendants who arrive in the early morning, and who during the winter anticipate the dawn by a half an hour or more. The fellow at the entrance is obviously cowed by the vehicle, as well as by the driver's imperious attitude. All of a sudden, E.C. seems to have regained his composure, and he's slowly driving the car up Posy and past Brambletree as if it were a limo on a Sunday ride. He's out of the car and looking around. His eye is drawn to my memorial. And now he's walking straight toward it.

Once at the portal of my edifice, he's running his hands over the granite in an almost lustfully possessed fashion, and speaking in a soft voice.

"You know, Henry Somerset, I can't see you, but I know you've been here. I don't know why you selected me. Or maybe I picked you, but there were too many coincidences involved. I have to admit, I bit like a minnow going after a little piece of bait. I think I realized somewhere beneath my consciousness it really was you pushing me forward all along. But you know something? None of it has made me happy. In fact, I was a lot happier before you started trying to control everything. You see, manipulation doesn't get us anywhere. I would have thought a guy with your savvy would know this. But don't worry, I'm not blaming you. You may think you had something to do with these events. But I made things happen all by my little self."

He's crying again. I want to tell him it doesn't have to be this way. It's not too late. It's never too late. Someone will love him. Susan will. They can grow and age gracefully in the company of one another. I'm trying to whisper these things into his ears. But alas, he cannot hear me. He's pacing around now on the little plaza in front of my memorial. The activity is increasing, and I sense he is again anxious and feeling helpless. He's calling for God, but again, he's speaking to the god of wrath and fear. And this god will not respond, because he does not exist. It's funny, I now understand. If only E.C. were to look within himself, he would find the presence of a God of love, charity, beauty, and absolution. But E.C. is not in such a mood. Least of all, he is not in a forgiving mood about himself.

Something has taken hold of our man. He's stiffened. And even though the tears are rolling down his face, he isn't heaving or shaking anymore. The predawn light is beginning to shine more brightly. We must be in another time warp this morning, since it's taken so very long. I wish the day would come upon us quickly. But apparently, this is not to be, at least not as I wish it. He's back in the car again, and we're now anxiously racing down the little lanes. Past the sad trees, the hedges, and the tombstones. Down through the gate, and onto the road. He's now shifting again with unsettling determination. Looking only forward in the direction of Ocean Drive. As the vehicle enters the long and winding cliffside lane, he accelerates.

I've got to do something. I just can't allow E.C. to make my same mistake. I'm desperately opening the glove compartment and flooding the cabin with all the little papers and objects it contains. I'm slapping quarters and nickels against his face in an effort to deter him from this madness. But he just laughs dementedly and screams, "Stop it, Henry, it won't do any good."

He's whipping around the curves, each one with greater velocity. From eighty we go to ninety miles an hour. At a hundred and twenty I am totally terrified. As in one final gesture of acceleration and defiance, he looks straight ahead and says, "To hell with it." A split second later, the car is bouncing off the side of the road over the edge, and into the air. It turns upside down, again rights itself, and crashes into the rocks bordering the furious waters of the ocean below.

I'm standing here bewildered. Looking at the remnants of the smoking car and E.C.'s inert body. He's not dead, but certainly unconscious. Our man is badly hurt, and I sense he is dying. This is my chance. I will penetrate, one last time.

Everywhere within him there is the rawness of pain. I don't mean the physical anguish his poor body must be going through. There is something deeper. It's the suffering I remember just before I took the pills and "gave up." Everywhere the atmosphere around me palpitates. As if any touch would send it receding in the face of the horrible unhappiness caused by the ache and agony of his situation. When I walk a little farther, I again come to the beach. Where E.C. is sitting on a rock in woe, torment, and distress. As I approach, he looks me straight in the eye with an anguished and aggressive look.

"Haven't you done enough? Why, of all places, do you continue to torment me here? I think you should just leave. Let me be, and get out."

"Hey, E.C., take it easy. Give me a chance to explain."

"No, I don't think you deserve the privilege of an explanation. Just leave me alone."

"No, no. I can't do that. You're going to have to hear me out. And I think it's very important. You see, there are great parallels here."

"So why are you boring me with all of this?"

"Give me a chance to speak, please. You see, at the time I discovered I was dead, I still thought everything I had done was great. And I was proud of it as well. So I realized I could bounce back and forth between places, travel in time, and even communicate with people in their dreams and unconscious states. It wasn't that I set out to manipulate or control you. On the contrary, it was almost as if some silent hand had placed you in the way that day you encountered Bozo at the cemetery. I was there, and had found it quite impossible to leave the place."

"So why did you pick on me?"

"Well, I don't really think I picked on you. Strange though it may seem, it was almost as if the hand of destiny had manifested itself. I left with you and Bozo in the car that day. I was afraid Bozo would starve to death if I remained by my tomb. I didn't even think I would be allowed to pass beyond the gateway. And then things started to happen. I'll admit that after you started the ball rolling, I began enjoying the whole phenomenon. But it was also you who wanted to become more like me. And perhaps this responded to basic passions such as greed, lust, and the necessity of flexing your ego. Not to mention your own lack of love for yourself."

"Okay, okay, I'm willing to admit I had a great deal to do with everything, but are you telling me you didn't create the actual situations?"

"That's right. I didn't. Someone or something else has been doing that. And I'm not sure whether the scenario was kindled for your benefit or for mine."

"Oh, so I was merely the pawn, and all of this is for your spiritual enlightenment."

"No, no. I think you're again failing to see the point. I have a feeling there are lessons in this matter for all concerned. I think it's sort of a dynamic process. Something like congruent pieces in a multidimensional puzzle."

"So did you enjoy it?"

"Well, as I told you, at first it was a lark. And to be sure, I was full of revenge for people like Harriet, Hooker, and Gustavo. Not to mention women who screw up our lives, like Amalita."

"Leave her out of this."

"No, no. We can't do that. You really must understand before it's too late. As it all unfolded, I've realized what happened isn't really what I wanted. Now that I've lived again through your deeds, I've realized I did many frightful, terrible things. I've committed unspeakable acts. I've ruined people for sport. And worst of all, I've forsaken true love for plain old infatuation and lust."

"Well, from where I'm sitting, plain old lust still looks good enough."

"Stop it. Such feelings are adolescent, and you should already be aware of this. Are you convinced Amalita loved you?"

"Totally immaterial. I loved her, and that's enough."

"We let our hormones run away with us, and look where it's gotten us both. Do you really think true love would have brought you to this place of desperation?"

"Henry, I think you have a lot of gall coming here to my beach to preach morality in your underpants. You were a ruthless son of a bitch, and it didn't work out any better for you than it did for me."

"Exactly. I've seen a woman I loved badly hurt. I've watched another one become a living vegetable. I've been present at the murder of my nephew. And I've witnessed the tender sentiments and release of a very wicked woman. Now, I'm here at your death."

"Oh, am I really dying?"

"I'm afraid you are. You drove that Ferrari off the cliff at a hundred and twenty miles an hour. What did you expect? But there may be a little time. And if you'd only listen to me and realize I'm making sense, you might spare yourself further agony. Believe me, it hasn't been fun."

"First of all, if I'm dying, I'm glad. I was tired of everything, and I'm extremely angry."

"We could work that anger out."

"You can't bring Amalita back, can you?"

"No, I'm afraid I can't do that. But there is Susan. And she loves you."

"Susan be damned. Leave me alone."

"No, E.C., don't say that. You really must listen. I can't leave you here to count grains of sand this way. Not without telling you the truth."

"Believe it or not, it will have an end, and I shall count them."

"But if you listened to me, there might be a shortcut."

"I don't believe you. And furthermore, I'd rather find out for myself. Please go away."

E.C. is just sitting on the rock now, weeping. I'm beginning to feel the subconscious world around me showing signs of the disintegration which occurs when the body begins to die. I'm torn between leaving him here and trying one more time. I must again attempt to complete my mission. So I approach him a second time.

"Listen, E.C., I can't leave you here crying this way. In many respects, I feel like we're family. You know, connected. I would like to spare you the further pain of returning, and having to witness your mistakes. But perhaps this won't be possible. Don't you think, though, that you'd like to be rid of the anguish involved in loving someone like Amalita? Wouldn't it be better to grow old with the affection of a person who appreciates you fully?"

"Sure it would. But it's very difficult to change the basic feelings."

"Okay, but you'd try if you had a chance, wouldn't you?"

"Perhaps . . . yes."

"And if you could decide who to love, you'd pick the right one, wouldn't you? And you'd believe in true love after all?"

"Maybe."

"Then for what it's worth, I give you my solemn oath that Amalita was out to destroy you. She didn't care a fig about you."

"How do you know that?"

"Remember, I have powers. Not all the ones I'd like to have, but certainly enough to travel back in time and unveil her to you as she really was."

"I don't believe you. *Show me.*"

So now I'm exercising one of the abilities inherent to my state and interrupting destiny's little picture back in recent time. As we approach Amalita, she's engaged in torrid sex with a rather muscular young buck, and from the look of it enjoying every moment. E.C. is about to make a very predictable statement denying this is happening after he met her. I am prepared for this and silently motion to the ashtray, where the well-known pair of diamond-and-ruby earrings lie haphazardly. His face is contorted in a different type of agony as he realizes the scope of the picture. There are tears, but these are of rage. Unfortunately, though, he's still not fully convinced.

"I'm so torn up inside I just don't know what to say. But so what? You're telling me she went to bed with others. Who cares?"

"What if I conclusively showed you that she really had no feelings for you at all?"

"I can't believe that."

I'm mustering all of my powers, and deciding to return with him to a recent conversation between Amalita and her aunt which I witnessed.

"Nana, I just can't understand why you start feeling sorry for these stupid men."

"And I, Amalita, do not know why you must destroy them one after another.

"This Douglas man is very, very nice. He could make you happy. And he's mad with love for you. . . ."

"Do you think I could ever love such a stupid whining dog of a man?"

"Then what will you do with him?"

"I shall proceed as I always do. Having now captivated him, I will entertain myself for a while with my new toy, and then when he is my total slave, I will destroy him."

As I whisk him back to the present time, E.C. is looking almost unhinged in his displeasure and disbelief. There is further anger. And the feeling of having been taken for a fool. He's also snapping back to more reasonable, but still despondent, thoughts. "I guess I've made a serious mistake, and now it's too late."

"No, you're wrong. It's not ever too late!"

"But I should have stuck to loving Susan. She was the one . . . she was the one, and now I won't have the chance."

"You don't know that. Look at me. I thought as you do."

"So what do I do now?"

"Just try to remember what we've just discussed, no matter how long it takes. Would you promise me that?"

"Perhaps . . . I don't know . . . but why are you crying as well? You're not the one who's dying, you're already dead!"

"If anything, E.C., I'm just as afraid of change as you are. But it's growing late, and things are moving around us. . . . Give me a hug before I leave, and promise to remember you'll look for true love."

"Tell me again what you mean by true love."

"I mean love which occurs between people who love one another deeply. It's the love that gives, rather than takes. It fills you with happiness and confidence, rather than with jealousy and lust. I'm talking about the type of affection where the two of you would jump in the lake to save the other, even if both knew it would involve certain death. Do you really think Amalita would have endangered her safety to save you?"

"Of course not. But so what? I was crazy about her."

"And you really think that's enough? Come on, you know all the enticements of the body may momentarily overshadow true love. But ultimately, the two kinds of attachment are not to be compared. If you didn't have a penis, or the feeling of lust, would you love Amalita?"

"I don't know."

"See! You yourself would doubt it. In point of fact, people have made too much out of sex and attraction. They wane while the truly beautiful grows. And that's where your intellect and inner feelings must come before your infatuations. You must know what is good for you, and opt for it. Do you really think people who have been tenderly married for thirty or forty years still suffer from your Amalita syndrome?"

"There are some—"

"No, you're wrong. They might partially nurture themselves from the memory of the heat and passion of their original romance, but ultimately what sets in is a deep understanding. Like knowing where each hair, dimple, and freckle is located. And *that* in itself is beautiful, and enough. Relationships which prove themselves over time are not to be forsaken for temporary dalliance. They are like rich old wines, which in spite of sediment and occasional turbulence improve and become great experiences for the educated palate. I know it's very difficult for you to understand and apply these things with the present state of your emotions. But believe me, when all is said and done, true love is the only thing we really have to hold on to."

"But you did the same thing—you threw it all down the drain."

"Yes, but that's my problem, and I'm working it out. It's probably why I'm here, and why there are still lessons to be learned. So please promise me you'll try very hard to remember this conversation. If not word for word, at least in spirit."

"Okay, I promise, Henry. I promise. . . . One thing is for sure. I now know it should have been Susan all the way. Henry, I'm grateful."

As we stand there hugging one another in the twilight of E.C.'s life, I realize fully that I may not spare him intellectually what he must understand through experience. I think the embrace and conversation have somewhat dissipated the anger, and brought the truth to light. And I am hopeful he will remember his promise. . . . But as I sense him finally ready to experience the death of the body, I quickly slip out and again find myself facing the broken pieces of a red Ferrari, and a handsome man now making ready to undergo his transition. I wish there were something else I could do. His eyes are closed, and his breathing is very heavy. All of a sudden he coughs and gags a little, as he begins to bleed from the mouth. For a moment, his body shakes in a paroxysm of pain. Then he opens his eyes. Those very blue and beautiful eyes. And stares complacently into the morning light. As under his breath can be heard only two words: *true love.* I'll never know, now that he's gone, whether he was just mimicking my final conversation or really believed it. But I would like to think that for once I had some impact. And perhaps he will consider these matters in the times to come.

There are police sirens in the air. And soon this whole place will be in a state of great commotion. I'm feeling more depressed than ever. If only I could have been sure he absorbed the lesson. . . . But I guess this was not to be. Now with E.C. gone, I've begun feeling a great sense of emptiness and loneliness. I'm really no longer enjoying this business of being a disembodied spirit. If I were a child, I'd say I wanted my mommy. I must, however, control my feelings of unhappiness and apprehension. I would like to look in on Susan. I assume she will soon be told, and I'd like to be there and see if I can help in any way.

At Susan's very lovely and almost candidly decorated apartment, the morning light is beginning to pour through the blinds and sheer curtains. She's sitting in bed with her legs crossed. Almost in a meditative pose. I can tell it's been a difficult night. I know she understands that sooner or later she must stop crying, and release the object of her affection to whatever might come. Susan has of course told herself many times that she cannot and will not release E.C. But if this is, as I suspect, the genuine affection of our literary upbringings, she will soon, in spite of rejection, anger, and aggression, release him to the greater love of the universe.

The telephone is ringing. She's picking up.

"Good morning. Is this Mrs. Susan Cleave's residence?"

"*Miss* Cleave."

"Is this she?"

"Yes. To whom am I speaking?"

"Miss Cleave, my name is Sergeant Farley, and I would have come personally, as is our custom, but I'm afraid I have some bad news."

"Yes?"

"Well, your telephone was listed as the person to call in Mr. Douglas's wallet. There's been an accident."

"Oh, is he all right? He isn't hurt, is he?"

"I'm afraid Mr. Douglas has passed away."

"No, no. That can't be. . . . Pardon me, how did it happen?"

"He must have lost control of his car, and went off the cliff at Ocean Drive."

"Do you need me there?"

"Well, not here. But we'll need you to identify the body at the Forensic Medicine Institute. After that, they'll be taking him to a funeral home. It was all specified on the card in his wallet. Let me get its name. . . . There's a Mr. Onions there."

"You needn't give me the addresses. I know both places well. Might I have an hour or so to collect myself?"

"Yes, certainly. I'm sorry, Miss Cleave, I really am."

"Thank you."

Click.

The tears are rolling down Susan's face as she trembles gently. I wish I could be closer to her, but there isn't much I can do right now. She's pulling herself together and going into the bathroom to prepare for the grueling ordeal ahead. Just when I'm beginning to despair of her state, she stands up quite straight and stiffens. Hunk of a woman that she is! She looks at herself in the mirror, and resolutely says, "I will go forward, I shall make it through this day." I'm proud of her. She's dressing. And there's no place for me here. In fact, I feel very much like a person without a country now that all my people are gone. Perhaps it's best if I return to the cemetery.

Here I am at Posy Lane again, making my way to Camelia. Nothing has changed, with the exception of the winter and some activity nearby at E.C.'s tomb. It seems Mr. Onions has not wasted any time. And has sent his boys to shine the place up and make sure it will serve as the proper scene for a billionaire's farewell. As the day progresses, the winter sun is shining more brightly. Not having anything else which I wish to do, I'm witnessing the workmen who have arrived with a large canvas tent to be raised in front of E.C.'s memorial. I miss the guy, stubbornness and all. I'm trying not to think about everything that's happened, but the thoughts relentlessly return, and with them, waves of guilt and unhappiness. I'm depressed. More than I've been in a long time. And I've taken to weeping again. Not like spirits in the movies who moan and drag chains, but just quietly, feeling the tears roll down my nonexistent face.

Now past noon, I'm sitting here in the portal of this ludicrous and very expensive tomb. Nothing seems to give me comfort. I could blink myself back to Harriet. But I don't think there's a great deal left to say to her. This would now be a wasted effort. She's busy twirling that wedding ring, and working out the details of her own little private situation.

There are gardeners around E.C.'s tomb right now. I guess they're preparing everything. The boxwoods are being meticulously groomed for the impending occasion. I'm examining these attendants. Muscular young men in construction boots, blue jeans, and warm winter jackets. The taller and more attractive of the two nearest me has just plopped himself down on a bench and extracted a generous ham sandwich from a metal lunch pail. I always marvel at how oblivious such people can be to the more transcendental aspects of the universe. Yet occasionally a word of wisdom is heard from such mouths, and it humbles us. The fellow is chatting about how after work he'll go straight back to his wife without falling for the attractions of another woman who is after him.

I feel bitter. Susan deserved someone like him. All this depression and despondency is beginning to make me feel very weak. It's almost as if I have trouble moving around anymore. I'm just slowly sitting here watching the day go by.

It's past three now. And the gardeners are wrapping things up. The tent in front of E.C.'s memorial is looking almost festive in its magnificence. To be sure, they expect a rather large crowd. As the day has progressed, all my desire to roam through the necropolis has waned. I'm so unhappy that all I can seem to do is sit here in this immobile state, practically paralyzed. Some of the guys who were edging the now dry grass to make it look decent and culling out the ground cover were making jokes. In the old days, my sense of humor would have kicked in, and I would have laughed at them. But today, all I can do is think of what has happened, and how poorly I seem to have performed in this afterlife business. Perhaps I'm again being a bit hard on myself. But I don't think so. On the other hand, the truth is that no one gave me a script or handbook regarding the manner in which I was expected to behave. It would have been easier with instructions. Or some indication as to an expectation for my afterlife. Along with these thoughts, for the first time I'm feeling an almost crushing and devastating loneliness. This is frightening, as it very much reminds me of my desperation in life, of that accursed clock, and of my feelings on that last day.

I now recall that during the days preceding my actions, I had read a couple of books. One was a sort of unclever volume on the topic. Basically providing all the reasons why suicide is not a proper solution. Some of it true, mind you. But most of it claptrap designed for people who can reason. And how many people bent on killing themselves can really and honestly be viewed as reasonable? What I didn't like about the book was that it insulted my intelligence. With an attempt to frighten me, it basically indicated that if I cut my veins and survived, I might end up with ugly scars. And that car accidents and defenestrations could result, even if expertly handled, in living vegetables and situations where the suicide might lose control over his life.

The second book represented a more honest approach. It didn't try to deter the reader in any way. While it spoke of the seriousness of the act, it was obviously devoid of religious and moral positions. This little book told you just how to do it, and how to end the pain. A one-two-three manual for quietly wiping yourself out. In my very unbalanced state, I seized it with alacrity, and went to it with zeal. To be more exact, I started feeling the whole process of living just wasn't worthwhile anymore. My pain was so great that I felt a general loss of control over all the positive feelings in my life. With each new disillusion as the days went by, I just became weaker and more worn. So absolutely anything would have tipped me off the deep end. The irony in the whole thing is that in a way, Harriet actually did kill me. I was so unhappy and despondent that day I was hiding behind the potted palm in the conservatory that when I heard them talking about murdering me it finally established the necessary emotions for suicide. It didn't have to be that way, though. A kind word or something very positive might have granted me the balance to establish a new life. And today, strangely, I'm now again remembering vividly all the incidents of that last day. Well, I guess it's wishful thinking to torture myself over these things of the past. More time has elapsed, and the light hours of the day are soon to end.

I must say, though, a rather surprising thing has just happened. As I live and die, Susan Cleave is walking up Willow Lane, on her way to this place. She's wearing a very severe little navy-blue suit.

With a perfectly matched raincoat, which is open. She shouldn't do that. She could catch cold and become ill. And that wouldn't be a nice thing at all. She's stopping at E.C.'s tomb, now sitting on one of the benches. And staring. Though I lack energy and stamina, I must make the effort. I must go to her, and try to be of some comfort. But how? She doesn't know I'm here. So how can I possibly help? It's becoming a little darker now. A cemetery attendant is motioning that soon the gates will be closed. I must exert this last effort, and accompany her back home. Perhaps I shall then have my opportunity to converse, and lend some elements of affection, knowledge, resignation, and hope. I'm following. And we're quickly into her very comfortable red imported vehicle. She likes red. In fact, she's always loved bright colors.

Moving through the city traffic today seems devoid of the normal enticements. My humor being what it is, I have not taken much note of the things we're passing. At a corner, a newspaper boy is standing by a stack of the evening edition. Since we're stopped, Susan lowers the window, and buys a copy. The headline is clear enough: BILLIONAIRE DEAD IN CAR ACCIDENT. But the paper is folded, and placed on the seat beside her. Which I too am occupying. We've reached her apartment. And it would seem there are flowers waiting which were delivered sometime this morning. Together with the large parcel containing those pearls. I assume it's been a frightful day for the poor dear. First, that morning call. And then the visit to the Forensic Medicine Institute to identify the body. Not to mention her introspective walk through the cemetery. But we're home now, and an attendant is quietly following us with the large bouquet of rosebuds.

Once we're in the apartment, the flowers are placed on her desk. She's reaching for the card, and wipes a tear again as she reads the contents. The roses are, of course, from E.C. And the note says, "I'm sorry. Please forgive . . ." She's opening the box, and has now clasped the pearls to her chest with emotion. He must have left instructions to send them just before he took that final ride. She's also clutching the card to her breast, as the tears roll down her cheeks. I'm almost mad with grief myself. It's all been too much for me. And now witnessing this situation is just pushing me over the edge once more. Susan's lying down to rest. Perhaps she'll fall asleep, and I'll have an opportunity to be with her. I sense things happening within me.

Changes. And I'm not sure I will have many opportunities to do this again.

I'm wandering through these rooms as Susan tries to sleep. It really is the type of place which makes its owner known to you by its objects. One can immediately tell it's the habitation of a beautiful and loving person. There are photographs of friends and family. Some of them departed. And there's even a picture of me with her on a trip to the West Coast. Knickknacks and bibelots, cheap and valuable alike, are mixed without regard to monetary value. These are things which have been collected at meaningful times, or received as gifts. The place is feminine too. Lots of pretty fabrics and lacy coverings. On the table by her bed there are more objects. These are obviously her favorite things. As I look more closely, I'm rather surprised to find the beautiful little music box I once gave Harriet as a gift. I'll never forget the situation. I had learned to play a little piece of music by Beethoven entitled "Für Elise." It's the one all intermediate students play. Harriet, who was not the most musical person in my acquaintance, had once been impressed, quite strikingly, by my rendition. Infatuated as I was, and always seeking and seizing the romantic moment, I had the little gnomes in Switzerland make it up into a lovely music box. Which I presented at a birthday. I might have spared myself the trouble. During the week she received it, my detectives had determined she was involved in one of her more sordid affairs. She was first and foremost always a liar about such things. What I don't really understand is how that little token of love has ended up at Susan Cleave's.

She now seems to be soundly asleep. No wonder, after the exhausting day she's had. Tired though I also am, I'll put myself in the mood, and tiptoe into Susan's unconscious state. As I enter her mind, all my ideas and perceptions about this girl are pleasantly reaffirmed. It's a bright place. And cheerful as well. There's very little fear here, and not much remorse. But notwithstanding the crispness and forthrightness of the atmosphere, there is sadness. Susan is sitting in the midst of a great garden. With daffodils and jonquils everywhere. On a beautiful little cedar bench. She's patiently watching a bunch of children at play who are not too far away. As I approach, she smiles broadly. There are no remonstrations, just the same warm welcome.

"Oh, Henry, it really is you. You'll never know how I've needed you today."

"You weren't aware, but I've been here all along, always ready to help."

"E.C. is dead."

"Yes, I know. I'm sorry. In a strange way, he was also my friend."

"Oh, I actually sort of figured as much. . . . Henry, you know, the two of you were very much alike. I'm feeling devastated to have lost not one but two men I've loved."

"Susan, I hope you know I loved you too."

"But you also loved Harriet. I never understood it. She was a wicked woman."

"My dear, we don't necessarily select the people we love by their qualities. They're not made to order, you know. They are loved with their faults and weaknesses. And sometimes I think we're fated to love people who hurt us, because we're just working out things which have happened before. There are also many types of love. I never stopped adoring Harriet's body. And maybe that was a mistake. Because if I had realized she was merely using me and had stopped loving me in the ways I most needed, I might have been able to have found happiness instead of death."

"Henry, what really happened with Harriet?"

"First tell me how you ended up with the music box I gave her."

"Oh, don't you know?"

"No. I'm rather surprised to find it here."

"Well, just after you died, Harriet and I were speaking to one another. As you know, she occasionally had her endearing moments. So she asked me if there was anything in the house that I might like to have as a memento. I guess she expected me to select a work of art, or something really valuable. But I just asked her if I might have your lovely little music box. You see, when you gave it to her, I already felt for you. And I was secretly jealous. And besides, I had always hoped I would find a man who would do such things for me."

"But Susan, later, when I loved you, I gave you many far better things. What about that pink diamond?"

"Oh, Henry, you never really understood, did you? I've never had any great interest in money. And even objects don't entice me, unless they have some sentimental value attached. That music box was a true offering of love. And as such, quite beautiful. To me it seemed to embody your finest qualities. Sure, I could have spent my life thinking about your dark side. And how people who crossed the great Henry were summarily destroyed. But I also knew that within you there was a little boy, who once felt terribly rejected, and learned to respond to the pain of rejection with vehement acts of violence and aggression. So I said to myself, this little music box will keep the better of the Henrys close to me. And every so often I'd play it and remember you."

"Susan, I'm touched. I know it's a little late for providing satisfactions. But you were the only woman I should have loved. If it means anything to you, I shall always love you."

"And I you, Henry. Hug me, please. I need it."

"You know, Susan, even when we argued, I had unconsciously longed for this contact. You're probably not aware that at the end, when I was frequently crazed with anger and despair over Harriet and the world, I used to call your apartment just to hear your voice on the answering machine. By then you had decided that perhaps I was not the man for you, but I did in my own way love you very, very much."

"You became, in many respects, a frightfully obsessive lover. I think toward the end you were feeling extremely insecure, and that lack of composure took you to the unhealthy extremes of the crazed mate who can do nothing but think about the object of his desire. I resented it at first, but then I grew to understand, and almost interpreted it as a compliment. After all, how many women can say their lover wants to know what they do twenty-four hours a day?"

"I did it to Harriet too, but she didn't take it as well. When I was hot after her, all I could do was think about her beautiful pink skin. Then when she started having affairs, there was something in me that was almost subconsciously aware of it. The lover always knows deep down in his heart. When finally my confidence was shaken by one incident after another, I took the plunge and fed her to the detectives. Yessiree, they were professional eavesdroppers. But it didn't do me any good to hear Harriet sucking and copulating with her lovers. Eventually my ear became so finely tuned I could tell when this month's hunk was rubbing his stubbly beard over her hard nipple.

To be sure, it all drove me mad with rage and jealousy. And even now, I feel somewhat upset at the memory of that period. I didn't sleep, and I didn't eat. And privately, I'd given myself up to interminable bouts of depression and tears. Here I could write a check for a cool billion, and all I was worried about was what the woman was doing with her body."

"You know, you must have been rejected very badly at some point in your life, and felt it very deeply."

"How did you know that?"

"It makes sense. People don't respond so vehemently to every little rejection unless they've built their personalities in defiance of the concept. And you were a prime example, Henry. I could have said I was merely going to the beauty parlor, and you would have felt hurt and rebuffed. But I have to tell you, after a while, I grew accustomed. Even the presence of the detectives gave me comfort, since I knew I wasn't doing anything bad. Ultimately, it was like having bodyguards. And you, my dear, were like having a little boy who needed constant affection and reassurance due to his tremendous fear of refusal. You know, it's a basic thing in psychology books. When people are rejected, they become angry, and then aggressive, and that's when they say and do stupid things they don't really mean."

"My goodness, and you really *did* know all of that!"

"Sure. How do you think I could have put up with your tantrums, the jealousy, and some of the terrible things you'd say to me?"

"I really didn't deserve you."

"You're right. No, I'm just kidding. Of course you did. In most respects, you were a very giving, loving, and generous man, and I shall never forget you."

"Harriet was another thing, though."

"Well, sure she was. Harriet had a great deal to hide. Deep down inside she must not have liked herself very much. That's why she never gave anyone real access to the person within. And that's why she lied. Let's face it, Henry, it was much easier for her to use her beauty to entice a hunk and get screwed once a week than run the risks of being refused on other grounds. It was that terrible mother of hers. She felt rejected by the woman every day of her life. And that feeling made the little girl within unable to truly love. Capable only of infatuation. Men were used again and again, to confirm her mother was right. After all, the child always thinks she has been a very naughty little girl, and that's why Mommy doesn't love her. She will never think her mother was bad. This would be too terrible an admission. Instead, she'll find excuses to confirm her own wickedness, and therefore validate her parent's behavior. No wonder she spent her time lying to you about everything. Also, you were so possessive that she just had to beat you at the game in one way or another. By lying, she felt more intelligent, made a fool of you, and buttressed her own self esteem. Just as her mother did with her father. You know, people frequently repeat the errors of their parents in an effort to justify those parental actions they sorrowed over."

"Susan, you should have been a psychologist."

"Well, I think so too. Especially for children. I like children."

"We should have had a few."

"Oh, Henry, it would have been wonderful. Too bad we can't make it all happen now. But I can still fantasize. . . . You know, I do believe this dream is real. And there are things I want to ask you. Can you tell me anything about E.C.? Is he with you? Will he go to heaven?"

"Oh, these things aren't the way living beings think of them. But to answer your question, I just don't know. I don't see other dead people. I assume they must all be in their own little private dimensions. So in this respect, I really can't give you an answer. But I have a premonition you may not have heard the last of him. It's funny, I seem to be undergoing changes as well. Things seem to be happening to me today, and I don't even feel jealous anymore."

"Henry, hug me tightly again."

"Of course, sweetheart, anything you say. I wish I could stay here forever, but I have a feeling I must leave."

"You were going to tell me about Harriet."

"Ah yes. . . . Ultimately, as you would say, her fear of rejection and poverty transformed itself to anger and violence. You must also know Amalita is dead."

"I'm aware."

"Well, she was no winner, to be sure. But the truth is that Harriet poisoned her."

"Oh, how very terrible."

"And she was getting ready to do the same thing to E.C. in an effort to create a financial confusion with his death which would allow her to recoup some of her fortune in the market. You see, E.C.'s demise prior to his protective market actions of last night would have sent the steel markets into reverse turmoil, and then she would have had her chance to extricate herself with several hundred million still in her hands. When I realized this was her resolve, I decided to help him, and I ended up being successful. I used one of the parlor tricks of the dead and started lifting flower pots into the air in the conservatory. That's why her blood pressure rose, and she ended up suffering a stroke. I feel very guilty about this, because I did, in my own way, love her. What I mean is, there was a remnant of love. You know, something still there."

"Henry, in a way I think it was reciprocal. She feared and despised you because she knew you could destroy her, but she was also aware you understood her secrets better than any other man. And that at the same time titillated and unsettled her. You were actually the daddy she secretly desired. What will happen to her now?"

"Harriet is probably going to live for a long time. She's perfectly lucid in there, but the only thing she can do out in the real world is twirl her wedding ring. Because of her feelings and what she's done, even in her dreams she will grow old and ugly."

"That's a terrible fate. It's sort of like a life sentence in prison."

"Yes, but the good news is that Harriet is now learning things, and facing her fear of rejection. Perhaps when her real time to move ahead arrives, it won't be so terrible for her."

"You know, I never quite got over the loss of you. I'd take those little violets to the cemetery and remember our good times. In many respects, you were my shining prince. So gallant and so romantic. There were moments when I thought you were my Superman."

"In that respect, you made a serious mistake. There are no supermen, and none of us really have X-ray vision."

"I understand. Perhaps if I had looked at things in a different manner . . ."

"You mustn't think that way. After all, we're here, we're speaking, and there is still much affection between us. I think that's a great deal."

"Henry, I keep thinking of you as being alive, and I know you're really dead. What's it like?"

"Sweetheart, it's somewhat sad, and very lonely. And not exciting anymore."

"And what about God?"

"I have not yet met Him here."

"Do you suppose there's another phase? Like a trial, or an evaluation?"

"Perhaps, but it hasn't happened so far."

"What if they ask you about special things you've done which you'd like to present in heaven, as evidence of your worthiness?"

"I think you have it all wrong, sweetie. There hasn't been anyone here to ask me anything. And I don't know that there's anything else."

"But what if there should be? What if they should ask you? What would you say?"

"I would say that I have brought with me the love for my parents and sister. I would present before them my love for Harriet, and for you."

"What else?"

"I think I would say that I learned to play 'Für Elise' on the piano. And that out of love I had it made into a music box. Also, that I maintained fine friendships. And then I would mention a few things I've done in the last couple of days which have genuinely surprised me about myself."

"I guess they were good things."

"I think so."

"But you don't want to mention them to me?"

"No, there's no need to. And you, Susan? Are there any things you would take with you as evidence of your worthiness if your time came?"

"Yes, I would certainly tell them I had loved Henry. I would also mention I loved E.C. And if I ever have the chance, I should like to tell them I made lots of children happy."

"It's a good ambition."

"Hey, Henry, I don't know if you've noticed, but you seem to be losing some of your color. I actually think I can see through you."

"I'm feeling very weak, and I unfortunately think it's time for me to leave."

"Where are you going?"

"I think back to the cemetery."

"I'll visit."

"No, you have to liberate yourself from me, and let go. Besides, I have a funny feeling I might not be there for very long. No matter what happens, remember I still love you."

Just before I decide to blink myself away, we clasp one another in a final, beautifully serene embrace. There are tears for both of us. But also a wonderful feeling of releasing ourselves from something which was holding us back.

It's night now. And quite dark here at Sleepy Heights. I seem to be moving more slowly. It's almost as if I had taken a soporific and entered a semisomnolent state, or dimension of slow motion. The cemetery is both magnificent and imposing in the darkness. Since the quietus of winter is upon us, there are no noisy crickets or insects to make me feel accompanied. There's a chill in the air, but I'm not discomforted by the cold. I'm now tranquil. And feeling almost serene about everything. I didn't tell Susan about the headline on that newspaper she bought. But the second sentence read: "Magnate leaves entire fortune to secretary." So when Susan wakes in a minute or so, she'll find herself an instant billionairess, and the owner of everything. E.C. wrote a new will during that terrible night of weeping and anguish, and he left it all to her. Lock, stock, and barrel. At least in this sense, there was something to be said about love, and gratitude. In a moment, Susan will also find that as a parting gesture and final sign, I tripped the mechanism in that little music box. So as she wakes, it will be playing "Für Elise."

It's beginning to rain. It's one of those very cold, misty winter drizzles that fall in billions of cold tiny droplets, which almost seem like frozen, crisp fog. Quite beautiful, and almost phantasmagoric. I can't help remembering how terrified I was during my first night here. It seems like a million years since this all began. I guess there's nothing left to do but again go sit on those hard granite steps. Too bad E.C. isn't around. We could talk, and maybe joke. Like real buddies warding off the chill of this evening. But he's nowhere in sight. I will say this, though—I can almost see Bozo as I did that first evening when he scared the wits out of me.

Wait a minute! This thing coming toward me is no mirage. It really is my pooch again. He's gleefully jumping about and curling that wonderful upper lip in a smile. Now licking nonexistent me. And I am tremendously relieved by the wet shagginess of his presence. To be sure, he's not the kind of dog that would let a man down. So perhaps we'll sleep a while here. Together. Just Bozo and I.

I'm a little worried, though. I've been trying to make him rest, and he keeps running back and forth between E.C.'s memorial and my tomb. Just when I think I'm going to get him to calm down, he raises his head to the sky in a series of sad and mournful blood-curdling howls. It's cold. And he's very wet. Finally, in spite of my total lack of energy, I decide to put my foot down and retrieve him.

"Come on, boy, come on! You really can't behave this way. You've got to be a good pooch. This rain really isn't any good for you. After all, you're a house dog. Come . . . sit by me here, and in the morning we'll send you back home."

I think I must have slept more than I expected. Funny, I can't remember a thing about my dreams. But the mistiness of the early evening has now, many hours later, been superseded by the pristine clarity of the predawn sky. There were shooting stars a moment ago, and Venus is looming brilliantly on the horizon. Sometime during the middle of the night, I remember waking for a few moments. Bozo was breathing heavily, and coughing. I gave him solace, and brought him very close to my spiritual body. Where he again fell asleep, very much like a child in the arms of a parent. It's funny, I've learned we are comforted the most when we aid others we love. So it especially pleases me to run my hand over Bozo's dear, shaggy head, and help him.

He's breathing heavily again. And now I'm really worried. Perhaps I can find someone to take him home. I'll leave him here for just a second, and go looking for assistance in the rain. Maybe the cemetery attendants have already arrived. Surely I can in some way call their attention to my problem. But I'm roaming and rummaging all through this very still place. And there is no one in sight. I've lost almost everyone I've ever loved in this world, and I don't think I could bear to lose Bozo at this particular juncture. I'd best return to him and see what I can do. He looks so wonderful lying there in slumber. Sort of like the Sleeping Lion of Lucerne. I'll caress him a bit, and try to ward off the chill of the night. All of a sudden I'm realizing Bozo has become cold and very quiet. Try though I may to avoid this final reality, I am forced to squarely face the fact that Bozo has died. I guess the temperature and the rain were a bit too much for that great big childlike heart. I'm crying again. This time, I can hardly sustain myself through the fit of weeping despondency. It's been too much. It's all been more than I can take. I feel crazy. And yet, I can't be totally mad, since I can still relate to these facts, actions, and happenings.

As I experience the now unbearable anguish welling again, I hear a voice. This is again like the dream in which I saw my mother at the end of the corridor of light. As I turn and look behind, I'm immersed in the reverie, and Mother is calling me, with Father and Alicia right behind. Her voice has instantly made me feel calm. This is no illusion. For a moment, I think once more about the things of this life. As if I might once more be detained, but I conclude it's been enough. Besides, I'm weary of it all, and wish to be united with my parents and sister. Yes, it's time to leave everything here. I will turn around, and without glancing to my rear, walk down that corridor of light. Where I now have little doubt about everything which awaits me. Yes . . . I hear you. I'm coming. There is nothing worldly to make me further spin and turn. I am through.

THIRTY-THREE

"You know, Tucci, I was particularly impressed with the Madeira you served with the Parmigiano today."

"Well, I'm very pleased. I must say it's not every day I can get my friend Don Orsini to say he's been taken by something. It was the Terrantez Imperial Reserve."

"No wonder. Do you have a lot of it?"

"I think two hundred bottles. You may have some if you like."

"I will trade you for some old Port."

"Yes. I accept. The good thing about doing business with you is that I am never cheated in the bargain."

"Such business, such transactions. . . . We do so much real business that sometimes I wonder if we don't all belong to the same organization."

"Actually, Orsini, I've given it a lot of thought. To be sure, we are both involved in service. But I think there are still distinctions. And perhaps it was meant to be this way."

"Possibly. The gardens are really becoming quite alive and beautiful now. I see we've lost the crown imperials to the frost, but the giant alliums have really come up in force. And then there are the lilies. . . ."

"Ah, yes. You are undoubtedly aware, we sort of specialize in lilies."

"Yes, of course, but to only slightly change the subject, you know, Tucci, I can hardly believe five months have passed since all of the events having to do with E. C. Douglas and the Somerset family."

"Time sometimes moves inexorably toward strange ends. *Man proposes, and God disposes.* But do I note a special interest from the great stone-faced Don Orsini?"

"You know, old prelate, there are certain things we never speak about. But perhaps today, walking in this garden with the spring air and these wonderful lilies, I will confess my curiosity has been aroused."

"Well, I don't have to tell you about Gustavo Somerset. You were actually excessive in your response. We both know you should not have acted so vehemently."

"We have our ways, as you have yours. They are time-honored, and will not suffer derailment."

"Nevertheless, it was just money."

"No. There was a hair of my mustache involved. And the honor of the organization. But you should not scold me too bitterly, since we have served you well in this matter. Tell me, though, what do you know of the others?"

"Well, you have read the newspapers. And I was there the night Harriet Somerset suffered a stroke. It was terrible. You know, she later underwent a cranial operation."

"Yes, somewhat lamentable. . . ."

"After that, there was some momentary hope. But her condition worsened, and she is now a living vegetable. Impoverished. Able only to twirl her wedding ring. You also know that in a fit of obsessive pain over our wicked songbird, E. C. Douglas drove his car off a cliff and died almost instantly. This was truly a great loss for us. The lawyer was arrested. We have it on good authority he will be in jail for many, many years. Rumor has it he has become completely unhinged, and will never be the same. Also, a number of government officials are facing embarrassing situations due to the Von Richter steel, which is now deteriorating at an alarming rate. The Somerset estate collapsed summarily, and even as E.C. died, the Douglas fortune was proportionately augmented."

"Yes, so were the coffers of your organization and mine. He would have made a good member."

"Certainly. I agree, but the thread of destiny runs thinly sometimes."

"And the beautiful secretary. The virtuous woman. What has become of her?"

"Ah yes, the beguiling Miss Cleave. Well, apparently E. C. Douglas was awake all night before his suicide. He did many things. He left money to various charities. And he wrote instructions. But he performed two acts of special interest. You see, as you have probably been informed, he wrote a new will and left everything to Susan Cleave. Turning her instantly into one of the wealthiest women in the world. The other was a token of true love, but a tainted one. He left her, in a little box, a rather sullied but very large diamond."

"Does she wear it?"

"No. Our envoy has informed us it was sold at auction in Geneva. It seems she especially wanted these proceeds to be used for a very unusual purchase."

"And what was that?"

"Well, it's something very much in line with her personality and the ends of our organization. We were informed she funded an orphanage with the seven million dollars she received for the diamond."

"But she could have bought a hundred orphanages out of petty cash."

"Ah . . . one must understand this woman. Apparently, E. C. Douglas had previously gifted the diamond to Amalita. Miss Cleave knew this. And it was her way of neutralizing what she perceived as the evil inherent in that old eye of the idol."

"How do you know where it came from? A diamond is a diamond."

"Not one that big. Besides, we know."

"You undoubtedly have other information."

"Well, if you must know, the children told us."

"Ah, the children. The very special children. And today of all days, you are finally going to speak to me of them. You are aware we know all about you, as you know all about us. Certainly I have always held you in great affection. But I am particularly honored that today you are speaking to me about one of the great secrets of your organization. Incidentally, where do you keep them?"

"Well, they live in the catacombs, as if you didn't know. But we don't keep them, they almost maintain themselves. They are very special children born blind, but with the gift of second sight. We merely recognize these prescient beings, and bring them close to the Church. Then for a while they guide us. You see, they seem to have their feet in other dimensions, and in the afterlife."

"So then you know much more about this affair than you've been telling me. What do the children say?"

"The children were mad with anguish when I went to America for the opera and Mrs. Somerset's party. They perceived the presence of great evil, and predicted the possibility of many deaths. But of great and special interest was their perception of a player who had been unknown to you and me."

"And who was that?"

"The spirit of Henry Somerset. I don't have to tell you about spirits. You know when we die, we all enter into our own private hellish or purgatorial dimensions. For all, even the knowledgeable and prepared, it is a frightening and unsettling experience. The ultimate purpose is the growth and coming forth of the soul. But sometimes these beings are very disturbed. And often they can communicate with people and influence events. And such was the case here. The children indicate Henry Somerset attempted to relive a portion of his life through E. C. Douglas. In this sense, he fostered growth for himself, but caused some turmoil in other lives."

"And was not all of this predestined?"

"Well, I don't know. You see, it's not easy to understand everything they say. They live in a world and with a language all their own. It would seem according to them that there are selections to be made. And that the thread of destiny is a multidimensional, flexible one which can even correct and enrich itself by going back into time. In any event, they are at rest with what has happened."

"And how did Henry Somerset originally communicate?"

"There was a dog. A great and striking presence. I actually saw him once at the Somerset-Douglas estate. The animal had a very special physical attribute. He could curl his upper lip and almost smile. I actually had a presentiment that day. He was a prepossessing and very gentle creature. And, the children say, more enlightened than any of the humans involved. Curiously, we are told he was found dead near the tomb of his old master."

"And what of the spirit of Henry Somerset?"

"They inform me he has found peace, and has learned many lessons."

"And the others?"

"They will not speak about Harriet Somerset, her nephew Gustavo, or Amalita. In fact, they become fearful and distressed when pressed in any way on these topics. But something curious happened when the sun entered the constellation of Aries."

"And what was that?"

"We were informed two children were born almost simultaneously. Both were given up by their mothers for adoption, and both infants have now found their way into the great orphanage which is being run by Miss Cleave."

"And why is this singular?"

"Well, it would seem these children already exhibit special qualities, and particular traits."

"Like what?"

"I hesitate to tell you. But I have already gone this far, so I will. You see, one of them puts his finger up against his nose and smiles when he is pleased."

"And the other?"

"The other shows an almost genetically impossible propensity for being able to curl his upper lip."

"Oh . . . I see. Yes, how fitting they should both be with Miss Cleave. It will complete the circle of affections in another way. But are the children certain?"

"Yes, it's the one thing of which they have assured us."

"And what will happen?"

"They won't tell me, but I believe we may witness very good events. Wonderful things!"